SEP   2014

We Are Called to Rise

Laura McBride

Simon & Schuster

New York London Toronto Sydney New Delhi

90

Simon & Schuster
1230 Avenue of the Americas
New York, NY 10020

First Simon & Schuster hardcover edition June 2014

SIMON & SCHUSTER and colophon are registered trademarks of Simon & Schuster, Inc.

For information about special discounts for bulk purchases,
please contact Simon & Schuster Special Sales at
1-866-506-1949 or business@simonandschuster.com.

The Simon & Schuster Speakers Bureau can bring authors to your live event. For more information or to book an event, contact the Simon & Schuster Speakers Bureau at 1-866-248-3049 or visit our website at www.simonspeakers.com.

Interior design by Robert Ettlin
Jacket design by Christopher Lin
Jacket photographs: Blue sky © Bartosz Hadyniak/Getty Images; Mojave desert © Jaclyn Sollars/Getty Images; Ice cream truck © Hero Images/Corbis

Manufactured in the United States of America

10   9   8   7   6   5   4   3   2   1

Library of Congress Cataloging-in-Publication Data
McBride, Laura.
    We are called to rise / Laura McBride. — First Simon & Schuster hardcover edition.
    pages cm
1. Women immigrants—Fiction. 2. Mother and child—Fiction. 3. Immigrants—Crimes against—Fiction. 4. Murder—Fiction. 5. Las Vegas (Nev.)—Fiction. I. Title.
    PS3613.C284W4 2014
    813'.6—dc   232013034756

ISBN 978-1-4767-3896-3
ISBN 978-1-4767-3898-7 (ebook)

For Bill Yaffe

and for our children
Leah and Noah

and for our nephew
Stealth

We never know how high we are
Till we are called to rise;
And then, if we are true to plan,
Our statures touch the skies—

—Emily Dickinson

We Are
Called
to Rise

1

Avis

THERE WAS A YEAR of no desire. I don't know why. Margo said I was depressed; Jill thought it was "the change." That phrase made me laugh. I didn't think I was depressed. I still grinned when I saw the roadrunner waiting to join me on my morning walk. I still stopped to look at the sky when fat clouds piled up against the blue, or in the evenings when it streaked orange and purple in the west. Those moments did not feel like depression.

But I didn't desire my husband, and there was no certain reason for it, and as the months went by, the distance between us grew. I tried to talk myself out of this, but my body would not comply. Finally, I decided to rely on what in my case would be mother wisdom, or as Sharlene would say, "to fake it till you make it."

That night, I eased myself out of bed carefully, not wanting to fully wake Jim. I had grown up in Las Vegas, grown up seeing women prance around in sparkling underwear, learned how to do the same prancing in the same underwear when I was barely fifteen, but years of living in another Las Vegas, decades of being a suburban wife, a mother, a woman of a certain social standing, had left me uneasy with sequined bras and crotchless panties. My naughty-underwear drawer was still there—the long narrow one on the left side of my dresser—but I couldn't even remember the last time I had opened it. My heart skipped a little when I imagined slipping on a black lace corset and kneeling over Jim in bed. Well, I had made a decision, and I was going to do it. I would not give up on twenty-nine years of marriage without at least trying this.

So I padded quietly over to the dresser, and eased open the narrow drawer. I was expecting the bits of lace and satin, even sequins, but nestled among them, obscenely, was a gun. It made me gasp. How had a gun gotten in this drawer?

I recognized it, though. Jim had given it to me when Emily was a baby. He had insisted that I keep a gun. Because he traveled. Because someone might break in. I had tried to explain that I would never use it. I wouldn't aim a gun at someone any more than I would drown a kitten. There were decisions I had made about my life a long time ago; firing a gun was on that list. But there were things Jim could not hear me say, and in the end, it was easier just to accept the gun, just to let him hide it in one of those silly fake books on the third shelf of the closet, where, if I had thought about it—and I never did—I would have assumed it still was.

How long had the gun been in this drawer? Had Jim put it there? Was he sending a message? Had Jim wanted to make the point that I hadn't looked in this drawer for years? Hadn't worn red-sequined panties in years? Had Jim been thinking the same way I had, that maybe what we needed was a little romance, a little fun, a little hot sex in the middle of the kitchen, in order to start over?

I could hear Jim stirring behind me. He would be looking at me, naked in front of our sex drawer. Things weren't going exactly the way I had intended, but I shook my bottom a little, just to give him a hint at what I was doing.

He coughed.

I stopped then, not sure what that cough meant. I didn't even want to touch the gun, but I carefully eased the closest bit of satin out from under the barrel, still thinking that I would find a way to slip it on and maybe dance my way back to the bed.

"I'm in love with Darcy. We've been seeing each other for a while."

It was like the gun had gone off. There I was, naked, having just wagged my fifty-three-year-old ass, and there he was, somewhere behind me, knowing what I had been about to do, confessing to an affair with a woman in his office who was almost young enough to be our daughter.

Was he confessing to an affair? Had he just said he was in love with her? The room melted around me. Something—shock, humiliation, disbelief—perhaps just the sudden image of Darcy's young bottom juxtaposed against the image I had of my own bottom in the hall mirror—punched the air out of me.

"I wanted to tell you. I know I should have told you."

Surely, this was not happening. Jim? Jim was having an affair with Darcy? (Or had he said he was in love?) Like the fragment of an old song, my mother's voice played in my mind. "Always leave first, Avis. Get the hell out before they get the hell out on you." That was Sharlene's mantra: get the hell out first. She'd even said it to me on my wedding day. It wasn't the least surprising that she'd said it, but still, I had resented that comment for years. And, look, here she was: right. It took twenty-nine years. Two kids. A lot of pain. But Sharlene had been right.

It all came rushing in then. Emily. And Nate. And the years with Sharlene. The hard years. The good years. Why Jim had seemed so distant. The shock of Jim's words, as I stood there, still naked, still with my back to my husband, my ass burning with shame, brought it all rushing in. So many feelings I had been trying not to feel. It seemed suddenly that the way I had been trying to explain things to myself—the way I had pretended the coolness in my marriage was just a bad patch; the way I had kept rejecting the signs that something was wrong with Nate, that Nate had changed, that I was afraid for Nate (afraid *of* Nate?); the way that getting older bothered me, though I was trying not to care, trying not to notice that nobody noticed me, trying not to be anything like Sharlene—it seemed suddenly that all of that, all of those emotions and all of that pretending, just came rushing toward me, a torpedo of shame and failure and fear. Jim was in love with Darcy. My son had come back from Iraq a different man. My crazy mother had been right. And my whole life, how hard I had tried, had come to this. I could not bear for Jim to see what I was feeling.

How could I possibly turn around?

I AM NINE YEARS OLD, and inspecting the bathtub before getting in. I ignore the brown gunk caked around the spigot, and the yellow tear-shaped stain spreading out from the drain; I can't do much about those. No, I am looking for anything that moves, and the seriousness with which I undertake this task masks the sound of my mother entering, a good hour before I expect her home from work.

"Yep. You sure have got the Briggs girl ass. That'll come in handy some day."

She laughs, like she has said something funny. I am frustrated that my mother has walked in the bathroom without knocking, and I don't want to think about what she has just said. I step in the bathtub quick, bugs or not, and pull the plastic shower curtain closed.

"Should you be taking a bath? What if Rodney walked away?"

"He won't," I say, miffed that she is criticizing my babysitting skills. "He's watching *Gilligan's Island.*"

"Okay," she says, and I hear her move out of the bathroom and toward the kitchen. She is going to make a peanut butter and banana sandwich. Sharlene is twenty-seven years old, and she loves peanut butter and banana sandwiches.

"I'M SORRY, AVIS. I NEVER wanted to hurt you."

I was still standing naked at the drawer, my back to Jim, the red satin fabric in my hand. I didn't know what to say to that. I couldn't seem to think straight, I couldn't seem to keep my mind on what was happening right that moment. Did Jim just say he was in love with Darcy? Why had I opened this drawer?

And still I was racing toward Jim's apology, grateful for it, hopeful. One of the first things I ever knew about Jim was that he was willing to apologize.

I AM TWENTY-ONE YEARS OLD, and working at the front desk of the Golden Nugget casino. It's taken years to get where I am, years to extricate myself from Sharlene, years to create the quiet, orderly life that means so much to me. That day, Jim is just one more man flirting with the front desk clerk, one more moderately drunk tourist wanting to know if I am free that evening; I barely register that he has said he will be back for a real conversation at four. And, of course, he is not back. But at ten to five, he rushes up, carrying a bar of chocolate, and tickets to *Siegfried and Roy* at the Frontier. I hear his very first apology.

"I'm sorry. I know you thought I wasn't serious, but I was. I couldn't get here at four. I was hitting numbers at the craps table, and if I'd left, I would have caused a small riot. Please forgive me. You don't even have to go to the show with me. You can take a friend."

That's how he apologized. All straightforward and a bit flustered and as if he meant it, as if I were someone who deserved better from him.

I WAS WONDERING WHY THE gun was in the drawer. I was thinking that I would have to turn around. I was acutely aware of being naked. I didn't know which one of those problems to address first. Turning around. Being naked. Figuring out how the gun got in the drawer. And, of course, none of those were the real problem.

"I didn't mean to fall in love with her. It just happened. We've been spending a lot of time together at work. You've been so distant. I don't know. I didn't plan it."

He just kept talking. He seemed to think that I was listening. That he should talk. As if the fact that he didn't plan it could make it better. He said he was in love with her. Was that supposed to make me feel better? I wanted to get angry—I wanted to grab at the lifeboat of anger—but instead, my mind kept repeating—*cover your ass, where did the gun come from, always get the hell out first, did he say he was in love*—as if I were on some whirling psychotropic trip.

I AM SEVEN YEARS OLD, and Sharlene and Rodney and I have been living in and out of Steve's brown Thunderbird for a year. We fill the tank with gas whenever my mom can pick someone's pocket or Steve can sell some dope, and then get back on the road, driving until we are almost out of gas, until Sharlene sees a place where we can camp without the cops catching us, where there is a park bathroom we can use if we are careful not to be seen. We have criss-crossed the country, even driven into Canada. That was a mistake, because the border patrol might have stopped us. But they didn't.

The craziest thing about that year in Steve's car is that there are thousands of dollars crammed under the front seats. Steve has stolen the money, stolen it from a casino, and we are on the lam because he is afraid of getting killed, because he knows the owner of the casino will have him killed the instant he knows where he is, and Steve has decided the bills are marked, that the casino owner—some guy Steve calls Big Sandy—has written down the numbers on the bills and has banks looking for them. So he is afraid to spend any of it, not one dollar of it. Even when we are hungry, even when Rodney cries and cries because his ear hurts, Steve does not give in; he does not spend any of that cash, any of those bills. They sometimes waft up when the car's windows are open, and Rodney and I try to catch them, and Steve slams on the brakes and swerves the car and screams at us that not one bill can fly out the window.

"AVIS, I'VE BEEN TRYING TO figure out how to tell you. I didn't mean for it to be like this. I didn't mean . . ."

His voice trailed off. He didn't mean for me to be stark naked and totally exposed when he told me? Then why had he told me?

Oh, yeah, things were about to get awkward.

Awkward if you were in love with your girlfriend.

I lifted my hand to put the bit of satin back in the drawer, and I touched my fingers to the cold, hard metal of the gun barrel. I had never liked guns. I was afraid of them. Afraid of the people who had them.

IT TAKES SHARLENE A LONG time, all of the year I might have been in second grade, but finally she has had enough. She waits until Steve is passed out stoned, and then she grabs huge fistfuls of the cash under the seats, and she grabs us—I remember being grateful that she had grabbed us, that she had not left us with Steve—and we walk to an all-night diner. We hitch a ride with a truck driver, and after Sharlene and the truck driver are done in the bed in the back of the cab, we get a real hotel room, and a shower. Sharlene stays in that shower until the water goes cold, and each time that the water warms up, she showers some more, and after a night and a day and a night of her showering—with Rodney and me watching television sitting under the pebbled pink comforter, pretending it is a teepee, watching all through the day and the night, whatever shows come on—after that, on the second day, we take a bus, and we are back in Las Vegas.

"WHY IS THERE A GUN in this drawer?"

It was the first thing I had said since Jim started talking. I realized it must have sounded incongruous. It was the only thing I could make my mouth say.

"What?"

"The gun. Our gun. It's in this drawer."

I was still naked. My back was still to him.

"I don't know. The gun?"

He sounded shaken. He was wondering if I had heard him. He didn't know what I was talking about.

WE STAY IN A SHELTER when we first get back to Vegas, where I sleep on a cot near a man who burps rotgut whiskey and we line up for breakfast with a lady who screams that Betty Grable is trying to kill her. After a couple of nights, we move to a furnished motel where Sharlene can pay the rent weekly. That motel is not too far from the motel we lived in before Sharlene met Steve, though it is not the same one we lived in when Rodney was born, and it is not the same one we lived in when Sharlene first came to Vegas—when Sharlene came to Vegas with me, just a baby, and the boyfriend who owned the 1951 Henry J. The Henry J broke down in Colorado, and Sharlene and I and the boyfriend had to hitchhike the rest of the way to Vegas. That's what Sharlene told me anyway, that's what I know about how I got to Vegas—that, and that the Henry J was a red car without any way to get into the trunk.

But they were mostly the same, those furnished motels. They all had rats, which didn't even scurry when I stamped my small foot, and mattresses stained with urine and vomit and blood. In all of them, the neon lights of dilapidated downtown casinos blinked through the kinked slats of broken window blinds.

"THIS GUN USED TO BE in the closet. Did you put it in this drawer?"

I didn't know why I was asking these questions. I didn't care why the gun was in the drawer. I just had to say something, and nothing else that occurred to me to say was possible.

"I put it there. I forgot. I mean, I forgot until just now."

I waited. Still naked. Was he still looking?

"It was a long time ago. At least a year. I had it out. I was looking at it. And you came in the room. I just wanted to put it away before you saw it. I meant to go back and get it, but I forgot about it. Until just now."

I thought about this. The gun had been in the drawer for a year. Jim was looking at it. He didn't want me to see him looking at it.

"Is it loaded?"

I heard Jim move, quickly. I almost laughed. I didn't know why I had asked if it was loaded, but I had no intention of shooting it. And suddenly, it was not funny. Did my husband just imagine that I would aim the gun at him? That I was asking him if it was loaded so that I could hurt him?

What had happened to us?

WE DIDN'T STAY IN THAT furnished motel very long. Sharlene got the shakes. She said she couldn't be alone, not with Rodney and me anyway. So we went to live with a friend from the bar where Sharlene used to work. We lived there for four months, and while we were there, Sharlene smoked and talked and cried, night after night, with her friend. And then she stopped crying and she started laughing. And when Sharlene and her friend had collapsed on the floor, laughing about Steve and the bills and the wind from the windows, for the third time, I knew we would be leaving the friend's house, and we would be going somewhere else. Eventually there would be another man, and another apartment, and if I were lucky, another school. I would go back to school.

"IT'S NOT LOADED. AVIS, PLEASE. Turn around. Just look at me."

I didn't care that I was naked anymore, and I didn't care that Jim had apologized, and I wasn't even thinking about what he had said about Darcy. I had reached some sort of disembodied state, and what I was thinking about was whether the gun might be loaded after all, and why Jim had been looking at it a year ago, and if there was still any way to get my life back.

I picked up the gun, and it was heavy for something that looked like a toy. I remembered this from the one time Jim had showed me how to shoot it. It took me a second to open the chamber, to hold the gun so that the slide would move back properly. I felt oddly pleased at the automatic way that I had opened the bottom of the gun, released the magazine, checked it for bullets. As Jim had said: no bullets.

No bullets. What about all those stories? All those guns that weren't supposed to be loaded? All those toddlers killed, eyes shot out, lives broken? Bullets could hide.

.

I AM TWENTY-FIVE YEARS OLD, in the parking lot of the Boulevard Mall at an Opportunity Village fund-raiser. Emily is done walking, wants none of her stroller, sits perched on Jim's shoulders. Small grubby fingers cling to his hair, his ear, his nose, as she rocks there. Jim sees the truck, so I buy the ice cream, the simplest one I can find, but still a swirl of blue and yellow dye.

Emily is amazed at this experience. At the truck, at the kids clustered next to it, at the excited chortle of their voices choosing treats. And then the ice cream itself. Cold! Her tongue laps in and out.

"Jim, her eyes are like a lemur's. She can't believe she gets to eat that thing."

She kicks her small feet into his collarbone.

"Whoa there, pardner," he says.

"Oh, I'm afraid it's getting in your hair."

"I can feel it."

In fact, the ice cream drips along his ear and down his neck, and before she has eaten half of it, Emily has dropped the whole soggy thing on his head. And then she puts her hands in his hair, lays her cheek on the ice cream, and says, as clear and sweet as those ice-cream truck chimes, "Good daddy."

So what can he do? Except walk around in the heat with a cream-streaked child on his head, blue and yellow stripes dripping down his shirt, and me laughing.

And later, just weeks later, when Emily's fever hasn't responded to the Tylenol, when we have raced to the ER, when the nurse has plunged her in a tub of water, when the fever will not abate, when the doctor says it is meningitis, when he says it sometimes comes on fast like this, when thirty-seven hours and twenty-eight minutes and a hundred million infinite seconds pass, when Emily lies there, tiny in the ICU bed, her breathing labored, then faint, then fluttery (like a little bird), then gone, then a single heart-stopping gasp, and then, again, gone. And no gasp. Later, after all of it, I am so glad we bought that ice-cream treat.

"AVIS, I KNOW YOU ARE upset. I promise I will do right by you. We can figure this out."

"What about Nate?"

"Nate? I don't know. We'll have to tell him. Avis, I don't know. I haven't thought about this. I don't know what we're doing. What about Nate?"

"There's something wrong with Nate. He's different. You know he's different. Something happened to him. And he's not getting better. I know you've seen this."

"Avis. We're not talking about Nate right now."

"But we are. We are talking about Nate. What you are talking about is everything. Me, you, Nate, Emily, everything. We are talking about everything."

I had always known that I would never stop loving the man who left that little girl asleep on his head in the sun. But Jim must have held no equivalent debt to me. There was no image that kept him from falling out of love with me, no matter what happened, no matter how many times. No equivalent moment to a soggy ice-cream-stained child glued to his hopelessly knotted hair.

He stood up and moved behind me. I startled, and he breathed in. Jim was still thinking of the gun. He had said it was not loaded, but it bothered him anyway: the gun, and that I was holding it, and that I had not yet turned around. Then he pressed my bathrobe against my shoulders, offering it to me without quite touching me, his cheek very near my hair.

And I folded. I slipped to the ground with the bathrobe around me, and the tears began. I could not stop them. Awkwardly, Jim put his hand on my back, but I shrugged him away. He stood up and went out. Then I cried harder. Because I wanted Jim to hold me. Because how could I want Jim to hold me?

2

Roberta

I LIKE LAS VEGAS best early in the morning, when the valley stretches out peacefully below a blue sky, when the knife-edged hills that surround are pleated with the shadows of a sideways slicing sun, when a great quiet sits softly over the tiled roofs, the disheveled cottonwood, the miles of empty roads. It's not often that I drive the valley serenely. Usually I'm jolted to attention by the careening traffic, the cars pouring onto the freeways, the trucks filled with produce or gasoline or maybe chemical waste, the nineteen-year-old on a motorcycle weaving as if he is playing a video game, safe behind a console, the tourists sitting oddly upright in their rented Chevy Cobalts.

In the hush of dawn, it's possible to believe that all is right in the city I call home. I'm one of those rare Vegas locals. I was a teenager here in the early seventies, when the hippies dropped LSD at the Valley of Fire and painted their own hieroglyphics over the ones left so long ago. I went to the public schools, a standout Jewish kid in a small town filled with big dreamers. My dad was a gambler, forced my mom to pick up and move all of us when we were too small to remember, and he said he could run an electric company in Las Vegas just as easily as he could run one in New York. And that was true, because electricity was big in Vegas, and my dad had it all: a gambler's sense of the moment, a quick smile, an easy banter, good looks.

I loved being one of my dad's cherished daughters. I loved his hoarse, low-throated laugh, his purple silk shirts, the square gold cuff links, the fur coat and the diamond rings and the emerald necklace he brought home to our mother, the family vacations in hotel suites nearly as big as our home in the Scotch 80's, the ermine collar on my own seven-year-old's coat, the curling pool in the backyard where my friends and I would order Cokes from the swim-up bar that my dad had installed long before anyone imagined such a thing on the Strip.

Mine was a particular kind of Las Vegas childhood, neither common nor unique, but of course I remember other children; I remember the way other kids lived. Back then, there wasn't much space between the best parts of Vegas and the worst. People drifted in from every part of the country, all with their own stories, many without anything to back them up: not money, not education, not family, not wit. And their children tumbled along, left to survive or not as they could. I remember the kids who came to school hungry, the kids who came bruised, the girls whose eyes flickered with something I was too sheltered to understand. I noticed then, I remember now. It is all part of the life I live still.

MAYBE IT'S SURPRISING, BUT MOST Las Vegas children don't grow up quickly. They aren't fast like their coastal counterparts. In Vegas, children pass through their novel environment unconsciously, lacing up their cleats or humming to the radio while a parent maneuvers through the traffic on the Strip; while bare-chested men thrust pornographic magazines at open car windows, while women wearing a few feathers leer seductively from billboards, while millions of neon bulbs flash "Loosest Slots in Town" and "Babes Galore." And still the children don't notice. They've been taught not to notice, and it's only the transplanted ones—

the children who arrive from Boston when they are nine—who think to tell their friends back home about the naked billboards, the "Live Nude" signs, the doggy-sex flyers.

The families just off the Strip—the ones occupying mile after mile of nearly identical stucco houses—live conservative lives at home. Dad might be a dealer, mixing with high rollers at Caesars five nights a week, Mom might be a waitress, wearing a butt-skimming lamé skirt at forty-seven, but home is for another life. For first graders marching in the nearest high school's homecoming parade, for neighbors sharing abundant harvests of apricots, for peewee soccer tournaments and springtime fairs and little bags of treats left on door handles all through October. It can be cloying, it can be surprising, but after a while, it simply becomes the way it is. And the good in it, the old-fashioned neighborly niceness of it all, is one of the reasons people stay in Vegas, stay even if they can't explain quite why, even if they tell their friends they hate it, that the place is a dump, that off the Strip there is nothing to do, even if they worry about the schools and bemoan the lack of art and feel stranded in the stark vastness of the Mojave Desert.

And when the children are old enough, they move into the world their parents occupy. They grow up selling lemonade on the corner, and wind up, at seventeen or eighteen years old, parking cars at the Tropicana, or waiting tables in an Italian maid's costume at the Venetian. They make a lot of money, these insta-adults, and buy fast cars, diamond bracelets, designer clothes, Cristal. Fifty thousand earned in valet tips is a lot of money if you're young and single; less when you're middle-aged, when you have kids and a mortgage and an array of nonspecific health complaints: maybe it was the carbon monoxide.

If their parents came from somewhere else, if they were part of the rush of professionals who came to Vegas during the eighties and nineties, then the kids leave when they are old enough to go to college. They go off to Vanderbilt, the University of Michigan, SMU, and the other students call them "Vegas," and they miss being able to buy nail polish or paper clips or waffles at any time of the day or night, and before too long, their hometown becomes a myth to them as well, something larger and smaller than what it really is. They don't come back, those children, and when they try, the world they miss is not there; it existed only for their child-hoods, and now their friends are strange to them, caught up, as they are, in the world of late-night clubs, baccarat odds, celebrity parties.

And then there are the children who don't go to college and don't land on the Strip: the ones who go to war. In Las Vegas, armed forces recruiting centers dot the landscape like Starbucks shops, across from every high school, near every major intersection. Everyone knows some-one in the military. Thousands of people live on the base at Nellis; many thousands more owe their livelihoods to it. Schoolchildren thrill to the roar of Thunderbird air shows, commuters estimate their chances of making it to work on time when they see the four jets return to base in formation each morning.

We send our children off, knowing they will grow up, thinking the military will give them security, hoping they won't be hurt, praying they won't die, believing that ours is a patriotic choice. And our children come back with that war deep within them: a war fought with pow-erful weapons and homemade ones, a war fought by trained fighters and twelve-year-old boys, a war fought to preserve democracy, to extract revenge, to safeguard oil, to establish dominance, to change the world, to keep the world exactly the same. Yes, Vegas children fight America's wars. These most American, least American of children, these children of the nation's brightest hidden city: the city that is an embarrassing tic, a secret shame, a giddy relief, a knowing wink.

But, then, fighting a war, going to college, working at Caesars Pal-ace, these are choices for children who grow up. In my line of work, I worry most about the ones who might not.

3

Bashkim

EVERY DAY I WALK to school early and cross the street with Mr. Ernie. Mr. Ernie wears a vest and his fishing hat, and sometimes he puts his stop sign over his head like an umbrella. He does this to make us laugh, because it almost never rains when I am going to school. The rule is that nobody can step off the curb until Mr. Ernie is in the middle of the road and has called for us to come. Any kid that steps off before he calls us gets in trouble, even if Mr. Ernie doesn't like to get kids in trouble, because that is an important rule.

Another important rule is that kids have to stop reading their books when they cross the street. Even if they wait until the crossing guard says they can step off the curb, and even if they walk perfectly carefully, they can't be reading a book while they do it. I know that because last year I had library at the end of the day on Tuesday, and sometimes I would try to read my book while I was walking home the short way, but Mr. Hal would make me stop. And he would say, "Stop reading that book!" in a really loud voice, which made me almost drop the book the first time, but the second time, when I forgot about the rule, he said that if I didn't stop reading in the crosswalk, he would have to report me to the principal.

I can't be reported to the principal.

If you get reported to the principal, you get an RPC, which is a required parent conference, and you can't go to class until your parent comes in, and I don't think my baba would come in, and my baba might not let my nene come in, so I don't know what would happen then. Also, if my baba did come in, he might say, "*Budalla* Bashkim, I don't want to hear from the school!" Or he might say, "Bashkim, I have had enough of you reading books." Or he might flip the backs of his fingers against my nene, and say, "Arjeta, this is your fault. You are raising my boy to embarrass me." But in any case, whatever he did at school, he would definitely do something worse at home. That's why I go the long way and don't cross with Mr. Hal, because what if my foot just accidentally fell off the curb before he called to us, and what if he remembered about me reading the book twice last year? Then he might think I was the sort of kid who needed an RPC.

So I cross with Mr. Ernie, who doesn't have two strikes against me. Also, it's kind of nice to cross with Mr. Ernie, or even to hang around on his side of the street awhile and then cross, because Mr. Ernie has a lot of friends at my school, and he has a lot of people to talk to every morning. I like to listen.

Mr. Ernie has a high voice that sounds funny, which is probably because he is Italian. Mr. Ernie loves *Italia* and he loves soccer, and he always is saying things like "Did you see that story in the paper about Italia, Mrs. Bell?" or "How you feeling, big guy? You going to play in a game this Saturday?" Any kid who wears a soccer shirt hears from Ernie. "Hey, you play soccer? Are you a striker? Make any goals? What's the name of your team?" He likes it when the girls play soccer. He says girls don't play soccer in Italia, but in America, maybe the girls could beat the boys. "Whatcha think, Michael? You think Marissa could beat you? You better work hard, or she could beat you."

I don't play soccer. I don't play anything. Unless it is in PE. But I like to think about playing something. And having a uniform. I might do that some day.

Sometimes Mr. Ernie talks to me, even though I don't play soccer or anything. He says, "What you say, little man?" and "Did you get a good breakfast today? Why don't you hurry up and get some breakfast at the school?" He says that because I am skinny, but I don't eat breakfast at the school, because it costs a dollar, or you have to fill out papers. My baba doesn't fill out any papers except the ones that get me into school, and I can eat at home—good Albanian *buke* and *djath*—which is true, except sometimes there isn't that much to eat, and sometimes I know it would be better just to leave what is there so we can eat it at night.

My baba doesn't know, but sometimes my nene lets me eats the ice-cream cones in our truck. She doesn't let me eat the ice cream, because she says ice cream will make me sleepy in school, but an ice-cream cone is okay, and it just fills me up a little in the morning.

MY TEACHER IS MRS. MONAGHAN. There are five third-grades in my school, and none of my second-grade friends got put in Mrs. Monaghan's class with me. Alyssa Button did, which is sort of surprising, because Mrs. Monaghan is brand-new, and Alyssa Button always gets the teacher that everybody wants. Alyssa Button's mom helps at the school. She puts all the decorations on the bulletin board, and on Wednesday she reads in the hall with some kids who don't read fast. I don't read in the hall with Mrs. Button, because I am really quick at reading.

For a new teacher that nobody wanted, Mrs. Monaghan is pretty good. She has curly hair, and she waves her hands when she talks, and some days she wears red shoes. She is almost the nicest teacher in the school. She lets us do whatever we want during Earned Party Time, but she gets mad if we are loud other times. That's not too hard for me, because I am used to being quiet, but Levi Van Wyck can't be quiet. He has already gone to detention, and it is still the first month of school.

I really like red shoes. When I grow up, I am going to get red shoes for Tirana and my nene. Along with lots of other things. That's why I work hard at school. So I can take care of Nene, and Tirana too, if she doesn't have a husband or something. I have a list of things my nene wants, but red shoes aren't on it, because she probably doesn't even know how pretty red shoes are.

Mrs. Monaghan is from Australia, and she says things in an Australia way. I like the way Mr. Ernie talks, and I like the way Mrs. Monaghan talks, but I think it's funny how grown-ups speak with their accents at school. At home I speak Albanian, or sometimes American that sounds Albanian, but at school I just speak regular American. That's how all the kids do it. On the playground, Felicia and Santiago speak in Spanish, and with Mrs. Lopez, they speak American that sounds Spanish, but in class, they speak regular American. So I don't know why Mr. Ernie and Mrs. Monaghan always use their home voices. Mrs. Monaghan and Mr. Ernie have been here a long time, and in Australia, it is not even a different language.

AT MY SCHOOL, WE HAVE specials. A special is a class that you have just once a week. All of our specials are right before lunch. Mrs. Monaghan's class has art on Monday, music on Tuesday, PE on Wednesday, science on Thursday, and library on Friday. At 10:49, Mrs. Monaghan claps one time, and we all stand up and get in a single file line, real quiet. We have to have our lunches, and our notebooks, but we can't go until everyone is still and quiet. Sometimes even I get mad at Levi Van Wyck, because it is hard for him to be quiet, and when he finally does get quiet, he usually has forgotten his pencil, or he drops his notebook, or his shoelace is untied, and then we might be late for special. But it doesn't help to get mad at him or make any sound like Alyssa Button does, because then he just drops something else. Being late is a problem, because we have to walk down the hall at the right time, or the principal comes out and asks, "Mrs. Monaghan's class? Shouldn't you already be in your special by now?" The principal makes me really nervous, because I don't want an RPC, and I just look at the floor when she is there.

Mrs. Monaghan has us take turns being line leader. All of our names are on Popsicle sticks in a jar, and when she pulls out the Popsicle stick with my name on it, I am leader. Then she puts my stick in a different jar, so I won't get another chance for a long time. I gave her the Popsicle sticks. We have lots of them in our truck. I washed them before I gave them to her, but she still looked a little surprised when she saw them. I don't think she had ever seen that many Popsicle sticks. I was real careful to give her the best ones.

The leader gets to decide when the line is quiet enough to start walking and also how fast we walk down the hall. You can't walk too fast or too slow, or you never get to be leader again, but it is still nice to walk exactly the way I want to walk, and everybody else has to do it. At our school, we are supposed to walk with our first finger in front of our mouth. This reminds us to be quiet. It's hard in Mrs. Monaghan's class, since we have to have our lunches and everything when we go, so Mrs. Monaghan says that only the kids who have a hand free have to do it, because it's better not to drop your stuff than to put your finger in front of your mouth. But we still have to be quiet. The line leader has to stop if someone is not quiet, and wait, and not go again until it is silent.

At my school, everybody is proud of how quiet the kids are in the hall. We have 742 students here, and everybody going to specials and lunch and things all day long, but the halls are quiet. The principal and the teachers and the lunch monitors are all proud of us, but one time, when the principal was showing the school to visitors, I heard a lady say, "My, why is it so quiet here?" And I could tell that she didn't like it as much as the principal did. Well, I know what that visitor was thinking, because sometimes I have to be real quiet at home, and that's a scary quiet, but being quiet at school is not like that. Being quiet is just something Orson Hulet Elementary School kids do.

MY FAVORITE SPECIAL IS SCIENCE, because my school has a marine lab, and science class is in it. Some days I get to sit in the shark seat. That's the chair next to the tank where our sharks live. Sharks don't like to live in tanks, and they can't breathe if they can't keep swimming. That's why our shark tank is round, so the sharks can keep swimming around and around without bumping into a corner. When the sharks get too big—as big as her tibia, Mrs. Jimenez says—then we have to give them to the Mandalay Bay casino, because they can't live in our tank anymore. Anyway, our sharks always swim in the same direction, and they stare at whoever is sitting in the shark seat. Some kids don't like this, but all the boys do, and that includes me. I know one shark remembers me and waits for me to come each Thursday. I always say, "Hi, Shark," real quiet, when I first sit down. There are three sharks this year, but it is the biggest one that looks at me and stays even with my face when he swims around.

There are other things I like in the marine lab. When I am in fifth grade, I am going to be a tour guide, so I can show the little kids who visit our school how to hold an urchin, and where the hermit crabs like to hide, and how a sea star eats. The first thing that we always have to teach someone who visits our marine lab is not to say starfish. Mrs. Jimenez says that a sea star is not a fish, so why would we call it one? Fish have gills and fins, and sea stars don't have either.

Sometimes Mrs. Jimenez tells us to get out our notebooks and our pencils, and draw what is new in a tank. I like it when she does this. One time the lionfish had a big bite out of his prettiest fin, and another time we found babies in the nonaggressive tank. Mrs. Jimenez likes us to draw the coral tanks too, but I don't like to do this. It takes a long time for coral to change. Usually if there is anything new, it is some coral that has died, and that makes me feel sad.

THIS AFTERNOON MRS. MONAGHAN MADE an announcement. She has three kittens. If any of us wants one, we can ask our parents and then we can have one. They're too small, but Mrs. Monaghan doesn't have the mother, so she has to find homes for them right away. She can't take care of them when she is at school.

I guess her husband is taking care of the kittens today. He's a big guy, real tall, and one day he brought us popcorn. But he's still scary. Mrs. Monaghan is small. Why would she have such a big husband? I can't see that guy taking care of little tiny kittens. He might squish them and not even know it. I hope somebody asks his parents and takes those kittens home soon. I can't have one. I can't even ask my parents. My baba would go crazy if I asked for a kitten that would eat some of our food.

But I sure would like a kitten. It could sleep with me and Tirana. And if it cried, I would take it oh so carefully next to me, and I would say, "It's okay, kitty. I'm here. I will take care of you. Don't be afraid." And it would stop crying and snuggle up against me and fall asleep. And if my baba and nene were yelling, or if my baba pushed my nene, then the kitten would probably get scared, and I would have to keep it quiet, really quiet, but I would hold it so close to me, and so softly, and the kitten would not be afraid, and nobody would notice it but me. Also, I bet the kitten would like it when Tirana sings her baby silly songs, and when my nene hums while she is cooking, and the kitten could listen to my baba tell stories about his life not in America.

Kittens are funny, too. They leap really high, and they love strings, so if I had a kitten, it would probably make everybody laugh. And when Baba laughs, we are all happy. But I can't ask for a kitten. Just asking for it might make Baba mad. And that could hurt Nene.

I bet Alyssa Button gets one of those kittens. Which might be good for the kitten, because Alyssa lives in a really nice house. I went there for her birthday party when all the kids were invited last year. Also, I can't see Alyssa's mom yelling "Yiii, better I should be dead!" like Nene does sometimes. That would be really scary for a kitten. But I don't think Alyssa will love a kitten as much as me. I would love that kitten more than anything but Nene and Tirana.

Jasmine Jacob wants to know how come Mrs. Monaghan has kittens but no mama cat. Mrs. Monaghan says she can't talk about kittens all morning, but she tells us that the kittens showed up in the backyard, right next to her breakfast window, and she watched them for a whole day, but no mama ever came. The kittens were crying, and one of them finally came out from a bush, and Mrs. Monaghan realized they were going to get hurt if she didn't help them, because her neighbor has a dog, and he can get in her backyard even though there's a fence. She didn't want to be eating breakfast and see something bad happen right outside her window.

MRS. MONAGHAN SAYS "SOMETHING BAD," but I know she means slaughter. I know all about slaughters. My baba saw slaughters in Albania. That's why he hits my nene and makes bad noises at night. I don't know why it's my nene's fault, because she was just a girl when my baba saw those slaughters, but my nene says that Baba can't forget anything. I was born in Albania, but I don't remember it. Tirana was born here, so she is full American, but Baba and Nene and me, we are legal Americans. Nene says it's very important to be legal, and we are lucky. It's better to be legal Americans than born ones, I guess, because she never says Tirana is lucky.

My baba saw a slaughter right in the street in Albania, and he yelled at the policeman who did it, and he didn't run away fast enough, so he got put in prison. He was in prison a long time, and when he came out, he was skinny like he is now, and his left arm didn't work right anymore. Nene says he looked old. A lot older than plus-nineteen years in prison.

My baba met my nene when he got out of prison. She knew she was going to marry him right then, because their families had agreed, and also because Baba had lost a lot of time to have me and Tirana, and in Albania, every man has the right to a family. The women have to do it.

I wonder if they do it that way in Australia? Maybe that's why Mrs. Monaghan is married to Mr. Monaghan.

4

Avis

JIM AND I ARRANGE to go to the city council meeting together. Nate doesn't know anything about Darcy, or about Jim having moved into a room at the casino. Nate has been focused on doing well at the police academy, on passing the exam, and we agree that it is better to wait until all of that is over to tell him.

Not that a twenty-seven-year-old son will be upset about his parents' separation.

Jim stayed in the guest room the first couple of nights, but I finally told him he had to leave. I couldn't stop thinking about what he had said, couldn't stop imagining him and Darcy together, couldn't stop wondering if he was having his regular Tuesday dinner meeting or screwing his director of community affairs. I tried not to do this, I tried not to torture myself in this way. I told myself that the affair was the symptom, not the problem, but it didn't work. When push came to shove, this is where my mind stayed: on Jim's naked body or on Darcy's, on the image of Jim's eyes crinkling up at something Darcy had said, on the sound Darcy might make in an intimate moment.

Those first days, I couldn't get one single idea past these thoughts. I stumbled around our home, a place both our children had lived, and tried not to imagine my husband making love to another woman.

I USED TO RELISH THE light in this house on a fall morning. It would slant in, bright and clear and cool, and the shadows of leaves would form charcoal lace on the walls. For years, I came back in the house about nine, after walking Nate to elementary school. I would walk home alone, the last mom to leave the playground. I would watch the children line up on the blacktop, and then wait—not rush off but instead stand halfway back from the children, always a little awkward at being one of the moms who stayed, who perhaps didn't have any other life or loved this one more than she should. But I did love those five minutes before school started: when the children lined up, when the principal said good morning, when the loudspeakers crackled with instrumentation, and then, best of all, when seven hundred children, some wiggly, some tired, some born to perform, sang "This Land Is Your Land." Day after day after day, and it always pleased me. It never felt old. I used to love to hear those voices and think—*If ever I am too sick to do anything but lie in a bed motionless, I hope I remember this, I hope I hear these sounds, see these faces, smell this schoolyard smell, before I die.*

You see, it all mattered so much to me. Not even Jim realized how deeply I felt it. That was Emily, I suppose. To always know how quickly life could change, how quickly everything important could disappear, to always be trying to feel this unexpectedly beautiful life to its core.

JIM LOOKS GOOD WHEN HE comes to the door to get me. This is not exactly helpful, but I am ready for it. He's obviously in the better position here, and I learned enough from life with Sharlene not to convince myself that it might be otherwise. I am not pretending that he will miss me. Or that Darcy will have turned into a crone.

"Hi, Avis."

I nod hello, suddenly unsure of how my voice will come out.

"That dress looks really good on you."

I can't help it. I appreciate that he is trying, I am glad my dress looks good, even while I want to hit him, want to scream, want to do something to change the path we are on. But I don't reply. I pick up my bag and my sweater, and head for his car.

I WAS YOUNG WHEN EMILY died. And in the dead center of grief, I discovered I was pregnant. Barely pregnant. It was just a question in my head—*Is it possible?*—but, of course, it wasn't just a question. It was Nate, and before I knew it, before I could begin to let go of Emily, there was this new child, this little boy, this baby who gazed solemnly just as my brother Rodney had. And there I was again, right in the middle of life, whether I wanted to be or not.

I didn't want to be pregnant when I was pregnant with Nate, and then for years afterward, when I wanted another child—four more children, I wanted to drown in new children—I could not get pregnant at all. No reason for it. Nothing the doctors ever found. Just a woman meant for two children, one who lived and one who did not.

WE MEET LAUREN OUTSIDE THE council room, as we have planned, and make our way to the seats reserved for visitors. We can see Nate sitting on the left with the other officers who will be sworn in this evening: three men and one woman. Lauren seems uncharacteristically anxious: it might be that her fair skin looks wan under the fluorescent lighting, but I wonder if she has heard something about Jim moving out of the house, if she and Nate somehow already know what has happened, and my heart beats faster. I realize how unprepared I am to tell my son and his wife about Jim.

"Did you get to see Nate today?"

"No," she says without looking at me. "He already started training, and he came straight here from there."

"It's a big day," says Jim. "Nate did really well with this."

"Yes," says Lauren. I am beginning to wonder what is going on. If Lauren weren't so straightlaced, I would think she had taken something.

"Lauren, we really appreciate all the support you've given Nate. Avis and I know that it hasn't been easy. Since he came home this last time. Since he got out."

Lauren looks as if she might jump up and run, and normally I would catch Jim's eye, try to figure out what he is thinking, but of course, I don't catch Jim's eye tonight. We are only pretending to be here together.

"NATE, PLEASE. WHAT ARE YOU and Luke doing?"

"We're fighting, Mom. It's fun."

It sounds painful. It sounds angry. They lunge at each other like mad dogs every time they meet. My friend Cheryl tells me that I am lucky my son has a good friend.

But, oh, Nate was sweet too. Square faced, square jawed. He loved to hook his "beltseat" by himself, and to eat at "Boowga King," and to play "sowca" in the "pawk." If I had known how long he would carry around that dirty one-armed rabbit, I would have put more care into making it. Jim's dad taught Nate to kick rocks when he could barely walk, and for years, he kicked a rock "fo Bompa" everywhere he went.

SOMEONE ASKS US TO RISE for the pledge, and the city council meeting begins. The swearing in of the newest police officers is the third item on the agenda, after the approval of last week's minutes and someone's report about a parking lot. I am relieved that we will not have to wait through the seventeen-point agenda. I recognize two of the citizens in the area reserved for people who want to speak: they are always speaking on Channel 4, exercising their right to comment on city affairs. Seeing them makes me feel uneasy. I wonder where they live, wonder if either one knows my brother, Rodney, wonder if Rodney has ever sat here and commented with them. How could taking a stand on a traffic sign change or an equipment purchase possibly seem worthwhile to them? Are they here because the room is cool in the summer and warm in the winter? Does one hear voices, telling him to do this? Is this the only place where anyone ever pretends to listen?

I move over one seat from Jim so that I can get a better view of Nate. My son is tall and fair haired and well built. Every tour in Iraq left him a little more muscular, a little more tanned. Sitting in this public room, in his starched, new uniform, he looks like a movie version of a young police officer.

I smile. Nate needed those good looks when he was a kid. Needed something to offset the tipped-over chairs, the too-loud whisper, the overzealous romping, the forgotten homework. Oh, he was a boisterous child, a child given to moving too fast, hitting too hard, whirling around right when someone was passing by with a fragile school project. I always imagined people wondering where we had gotten him: I, who am dark and quiet, and Jim, who is dark and thoughtful. *Thoughtful*. Well, I am not sure that is the right word for him anymore.

EDNA NEAL ELEMENTARY opened the year Nate started kindergarten, and we were there for the first day of the first new school built in Las Vegas in a decade. It was exciting. I had just given up a job at Jim's hotel, just realized that I might not have another child and had better make the most of this experience before Nate got any older, and so I didn't really know the other mothers in the neighborhood. But we were all there, walking out our doors at eight thirty, headed to the school. Some of the women pushing strollers. New backpacks, new shoes, little girls with ponytails and red ribbons, little boys with scalped haircuts. I fell in next to Cheryl and Julie, who would become such dear friends, all of us kindergarten moms—Julie, like me, taking her first to school, and Cheryl taking her last.

I am not sure what we were expecting. Streamers and a band, I suppose. There were news trucks. I remember that. Seeing the news trucks, and saying to one another, "Oh, this is fun," and then walking around the back, to the kindergarten doors, and seeing hundreds of parents and their children. Fifty-seven five-year-olds waiting for one startled teacher to open up one brand-new classroom.

That was the beginning. The beginning of decades of that sort of madcap growth. They couldn't build schools fast enough, they couldn't hire teachers fast enough, for all those families moving to Las Vegas from all over the world. We complained about it, and laughed about it, and juggled zone changes and schedule swaps and double sessions and year-round calendars, for all the years our children were growing up. There were kids who changed schools nearly as often as Rodney and I had, yet they lived in the same house the whole time. This was part of having a child here, just like endless sunny days, and belly flops in backyard pools, and kids who didn't even notice when the women on the bill-boards were naked.

TO MY RIGHT, LAUREN FIDDLES with her bra strap, and I notice that she has a dark bruise on her shoulder. I see a bit of it when she pulls on the fabric of her blouse, and after I have seen it, I recognize the full mark under the light-colored cotton. It's a deep, fresh purple, no green. I try not to think the next thought, the one that wonders how she got it, the one that thinks of Nate, of how Nate has been these last months. I don't want to think this thought right now, at the very moment when Nate is about to achieve a dream he has had since he was eleven years old. I don't want to think this thought at all.

I have spent eight years with the constant fear that something will happen to Nate. Eight years trembling when the phone rang too late at night, eight years waiting for the one-line email, the five-minute phone call, the message that said my son was not hurt, he was still alive, he had survived another week in Iraq. I am deep-marrow tired of this fear. Is that fear why Jim is leaving me? Did I pay enough attention to us?

ON THAT FIRST DAY OF kindergarten, Mrs. Linfelter blew her whistle and addressed the "Edna Neal kindergartner class of nineteen ninety-four."

"Nineteen ninety-four?" we all whispered. "What's in nineteen ninety-four?" Someone figured it out, "Fifth-grade graduation." And we all smiled. Fifth graders!

"Edna Neal kindergartners, it is time to line up. Get in line right behind me, one by one, single file."

There was a confused rush toward the teacher. A few children held back. Julie's daughter Ella buried her head in Julie's thigh. Nate raced off, pushing to be the first in line.

Mrs. Linfelter ignored the scuffle of bodies banging into one another.

"One by one," she said very sweetly, like a cartoon caricature of a kindergarten teacher.

"No holding hands. Single file."

She kept at it, with her sweet voice, her clear instructions, nothing but business. And when all fifty-seven of them were ready, in a snaking line that filled up most of the dusty kindergarten play area, Mrs. Linfelter gave her first full-class instruction.

"Children," she said. "Stand up straight. Look at your moms and dads. And wave bye-bye. Good-bye, Moms and Dads!"

Then Mrs. Linfelter turned and walked in the room with fifty-seven five-year-olds in single step behind her.

Most of us were stunned. It was Cheryl who hooted. "Brilliant!" she said. "This Mrs. Linfelter is brilliant! Let's get some coffee."

THE MAYOR HAS ASKED THE cadets to stand, and he is reading off their names one by one.

"Staff Sergeant Nathan James Gisselberg."

He has used Nate's Army rank.

"Ladies and gentlemen, Cadet Gisselberg served three tours of duty in Iraq. He was awarded a bronze medal for service. We are particularly proud to welcome him to the Las Vegas Police Department today."

Nate stands still, like a soldier, and his face does not reveal what he is thinking. Jim and I and Lauren look at each other. Our shared pride is like a rod between us. I wonder if Lauren or Jim also feels the kind of melting gratitude that I feel. When you have sent a child to war, when you have seen what being in a war is like for that child, every single acknowledgment matters. Nate had so damn much courage. It matters to me that the mayor knows it, that he says it.

The cadets raise their right hands. The mayor asks them to repeat the words of the oath. He swears them in. And then, only then, does Nate smile. I know that smile so well. The smile of a little boy who has just caught the long fly in his mitt, who has just wobbled the bicycle down the street by himself, who has just asked a girl to a dance. When I see that smile, I think that everything is going to be all right. I look at Lauren, and I see it in her eyes too: we both believe that things will be okay.

MY SECOND LIFE STARTED ON that first day of kindergarten. Not when Jim asked me to marry him, not when we moved into a house where the master bedroom was larger than the apartments I had grown up in, not when Emily or Nate was born, but on the day that Edna Neal Elementary School opened, and Nate followed Mrs. Linfelter into kindergarten.

That's the day when my old life seemed to slip completely off me, when a group of women assumed I was one of them, a suburban mom with a sweet-faced child headed off to school. That was the first time I ever went to have a cup of coffee with women who had been to college, the first time nobody seemed to notice that my memories were not the same as theirs.

I suppose it was that Nate was so very much like their children, and my house so very much like their houses, and my husband so very much like their husbands. Just like that, Sharlene and the boyfriends and the weekly motels and the alcoholic brother melted into some other reality. In those years of Nate's elementary school, my days were punctuated by the hours I spent with other mothers. The cups of coffee, but also the soup at the deli, the gym classes, the midget football games, the walks to and from school, the hot scones left on a doorstep at six in the morning, the bottle of wine while the kids cannonballed in someone's backyard pool. Jim and I both loved the Friday-night barbecues then, when the children would "put on a show" for the adults. There would be banged-up heads, torn costumes, uncontrollable laughter, and half-eaten hamburgers all over the house. The dogs would rush in, thrilled to be let out of the side yard, and race to find all the dropped, abandoned food on the carpet.

There were good days, when Nate snuggled into a pillow and read *Where the Wild Things Are* all by himself, and bad days, when Emily's little feet kept jutting into my line of vision, reminding me and daring me. There were days when the contrast between my life and Sharlene's life threw me sideways, when I couldn't bear to hold in one heart the memory of what it had felt like to be Sharlene's child, and also the awareness of how young she had been, how little she had had, how alone she was.

JIM AND LAUREN AND I make our way out of the council meeting when the swearing-in is over. We wait for Nate outside, on Stewart. Somewhere behind us, the neon cowboy on the Pioneer Hotel lifts his left hand in permanent salute; beyond him, the blinking red and yellow letters of "Plaza" cast a strange orange glow. Lauren sees Nate first. She hurries toward him, and he grins as he wraps his arms around her. They look young and happy. I smile then too, and without thinking look to Jim, and for a second, we are there, eyes locked, just as we were when we were young. Of course, Darcy flits through my mind, but I don't let it take me, I don't go there, I just relish that Nate is happy, that he has a lovely wife, that he is not going back to Iraq, that Jim and I, no matter what, we did okay.

5

Bashkim

THE UNITED STATES IS in two wars, and some of the soldiers are from Las Vegas. That's because Nellis Air Force Base is here, right over by Sunrise Mountain. Mrs. Monaghan says that we should be supporting the people who fight for us, so our class is going to adopt some soldiers in Iraq. Adopt means that we are going to write them letters all year long. I have never written anybody a letter, even though I have family in Albania. I don't know why my family isn't the letter-writing type.

Tomorrow, or maybe the next day, Mrs. Monaghan is going to give us the names of our soldiers. We each get our own one person, and I am really excited about mine. Today we are going to learn how to write a letter, because these are soldiers, and we have to send our letters in a professional way.

Letter form takes up a lot of space. You have to write the date, and space. Then the name and the address, and space. Then Dear So-and-so, and space. I am almost at the bottom of the page, and I have not started writing anything. Mrs. Monaghan says we have to write a lot neater, and smaller, so that the letter will look right. I don't think I am going to like this part of writing letters.

Also today we are learning about Iraq and Afghanistan. It's pretty amazing, because Iraq looks like southern Nevada, and Afghanistan looks like northern Nevada. That's what Mrs. Monaghan says. She showed us pictures of Iraq, and if you don't look at how the people are dressed, and if you don't look for any big buildings, it does look like Las Vegas. Then Mrs. Monaghan showed us pictures of Afghanistan, and pictures of northern Nevada, and we had to guess which was which. And we couldn't. Because they both have snow, and mountains, and trees, and Mrs. Monaghan says they are both dry, and that's why they look alike. Even Carlo, who used to live in Reno and is the only kid in my class who has ever been to northern Nevada, got mixed up.

Isn't it weird that we are at war with two countries that look like Nevada? Even the people look like us. Mrs. Monaghan says we are not really mad at Afghanis (that's what she calls people who live in Afghanistan), but we are mad at people who are hiding in Afghanistan, and we have to find them. And we used to be mad at Iraqis, but we are not mad at them anymore. I don't know what we are still looking for there, but I might have forgotten to pay attention to everything Mrs. Monaghan said. I am looking forward to writing to a soldier, and I understand why we should adopt some of them, but I don't really like when Mrs. Monaghan talks about being at war. It makes my head hurt, like it does when Baba talks about Albania. There are a lot of bad people in the world, and I try not to think about them. Especially when I am at school.

Carlo was really excited about seeing the pictures of northern Nevada. His dad lives up there, and he liked living there better than here. He says Reno is just like Las Vegas, but bigger, with more lights. Which must be quite a lot, because where I live, it never gets really dark at night. I can always see the Strip glowing, usually kind of white but sometimes kind of pink. And there is a big light on top of a pyramid that points right at our apartment, like a laser. Tirana is afraid of that light, but I tell her that it's a spotlight shining at us so that we could never be lost. I suppose God doesn't really need a spotlight to know where Tirana and

I are, but I don't know that much about God, and I think it is good to have that backup light.

In Albania, the sky is black, and there are millions and millions of stars. My nene misses the stars in Albania, and I think my baba does too, because when she was talking about the stars and how she missed them, my baba put his head on Nene's cheek. Nene says that in Albania, there are so many stars, it feels like a sparkling blanket over your head, and she says that nobody ever gets tired of looking at them because they always find a star they never saw before. Plus, Nene has seen lots and lots of shooting stars. She says that in the summer in Albania, there are more shooting stars than I could count every night, and all the people go outside and find a place to lie down and just watch them. I have never seen a shooting star, but Nene says that some day we will drive out to the mountains, and I will see them then.

I am not sure why Las Vegas does not have as many stars as Albania or the mountains. Nene and Baba say that it is because of the lights on the Strip, but I can't figure out how that works. Mrs. Jimenez told us that stars are billions of miles away, and the light we see is actually thousands of years old. How could the lights on the Strip change that? Las Vegas is not very old at all.

Iraq and Afghanistan are old, older than even Albania, I think. And they are really hard places to be a soldier. In Afghanistan, the roads are bad, and the mountains are very high, and sometimes the trucks hit bumps on the road and fall off the mountains. Also, there are lots of places for enemies to hide, and shoot at our soldiers, and it is very hard for our guys from Nellis to find them. In Iraq, it is hot (just like it is here in the summer), and there is no shade or air-conditioning or swimming pools, and some people are so mad there that they make bombs and put them on their bodies and blow themselves up to try and kill some of our soldiers. When Mrs. Monaghan tells us this, I start to feel weird. I don't like to think about a person making a bomb and tying it on his body. It's so sad that I feel dizzy, like I do when Baba yells at Nene, or when Nene says that it would be better if she were dead.

I am getting kind of nervous now, but I am going to write very neatly to my soldier. I want him to know that I am sorry he has such a hard job.

WELL, TODAY WAS THE DAY. Mrs. Monaghan handed out our soldiers. My soldier's name is Specialist Luis Rodriguez-Reyes, which is going to be hard to fit on one line of my letter. I am a little worried about that, but otherwise I like his name. I think he is Mexican, like my friend Carlo, because Carlo has two last names too. Carlo's soldier is Chet Buckley, which doesn't sound Mexican at all. I don't think there are any soldiers with Albanian names. Maybe Albanians aren't soldiers. Or maybe they only fight in Albania.

All of us kids were so excited about getting our soldiers. There are even some girl soldiers, but Mrs. Monaghan didn't pay any attention to whether girls got girls or boys got boys, just like she didn't pay any attention to whether Carlo got a Mexican. I'm sort of glad I got a boy, but I don't say that, because that is the kind of thing Mrs. Monaghan does not like. Mrs. Monaghan says we don't always have to say what we like and what we don't like. We should just practice dealing with it.

Anyway, we were so excited about our soldiers that Mrs. Monaghan decided to cancel social studies and give us all that time to work on our letters. She is not really supposed to cancel social studies. She has a list of what we work on every day on the board, and the minutes we spend on each subject. Mrs. Monaghan does not like this list, but Nevada makes every teacher spend the same number of minutes on every subject for every student. And Mrs. Monaghan has to write down the minutes every week, and the principal has to be able to see the minutes written on the board if she comes in the class. Mrs. Monaghan says Americans are kind of crazy, and even though her husband is American, and she thinks we should support American soldiers, she does not like American subject minutes.

So anyway, I guess she doesn't think the principal will come in today, because she is letting us write our letters. I am a little nervous for her, since she is a new teacher at Orson Hulet, and she might not know how serious the rules are, so I put my social studies workbook on my desk, and I tell Carlo to put his on his desk too. Mrs. Monaghan thinks we are using our workbooks as writing pads, and she likes us to be self-sufficient about stuff like that. She doesn't know that I can put my workbook on top of my letter real fast if the principal catches her.

September 23, 2008

Specialist Luis Rodriguez-Reyes
A BTRY 2-57FA
FOB Kalsu
APO, AE 09312

Dear Specialist Luis Rodriguez-Reyes:

My name is Bashkim Ahmeti and I am in third grade at Orson Hulet School. I am eight years old, but I will be nine soon. My sister Tirana is three. My baba and nene have an ice-cream truck, and that's how we make money. My nene sometimes works at Kohl's too, during inventory, but when they don't have inventory, then she just works in the truck with Baba.

Most days, I go with my baba and nene after school. Lots of kids like to eat ice cream, so that is our busiest time. Tirana comes too, but she just plays.

I bet you don't know any other Bashkim Ahmeti. I am the only one I know, though there are probably some in Albania somewhere.

This is the longest letter I have ever written and I don't want to write anymore. Please write me and tell me about your life in Iraq. Have you had a hard time in the truck? Do you have to kill people? Does it make you feel funny? I have never killed anyone, but I feel funny when my baba kills our mice and things.

Your friend,
Bashkim Ahmeti

MRS. MONAGHAN LOOKED AT ME kind of funny when she read my letter, and later she told everyone that we should not ask our soldiers about their soldier work, which is going to be kind of hard for a whole year, but I think she sent my letter anyway. I don't think I could have redone it if she had asked me to, because my hand is still hurting from all that writing.

MRS. MONAGHAN SAYS OUR SOLDIERS' letters back to us have arrived. Every one of us got a letter back, though Mrs. Monaghan says this will not keep happening, and we cannot expect to get a letter every time we get a bag from Iraq.

The letters are in a camouflage bag. Isn't that cool? They were all bundled together, and sent on a special plane back to Las Vegas. Mrs. Monaghan says that won't happen anymore either, and maybe we are even going to start writing our letters during computer room time, so that we can send them without any stamps, but that might be a problem, because our computer room minutes are not just for writing letters, and she has to see if the principal will allow it.

I am pretty sure the principal will not, so I hope she has another plan. Also, I don't know how to type, so it might be really hard to keep writing letters if we can't even use pencils.

I can't stop looking at that bag of letters. I wonder what Specialist Luis Rodriguez-Reyes has written to me. I wish I had sent him a picture too, like some of the kids did, but it took me too long to write the letter part. I would really like a picture back from him. They probably don't have cameras or art supplies in Iraq, so maybe that wouldn't have worked anyway.

I am looking at that bag so much, and thinking about it so hard, that I almost can hear the soldiers reading their letters to us. It is like a whole bunch of people talking quietly at the same time. I am trying and trying to listen, but I cannot make out what they are saying, and I can't tell which one is Specialist Luis Rodriguez-Reyes.

"Bashkim, are you listening?"

"Yes, Mrs. Monaghan. I am listening very hard."

I am surprised that Mrs. Monaghan knew what I was doing. But when I look at her face, she looks surprised at me. I think she has been talking, and I see that some of the kids are standing up like they are going to go somewhere, but I am confused. In my head, I was thinking about soldiers.

"Bashkim, the blue reading group is going to sit in the hall today. Isn't that you?"

"Yes, Mrs. Monaghan." And I quickly get up and find my reading book, because sitting in the hall is a special privilege for students who will stay on task, and I don't want to miss it.

AFTER RECESS AND AFTER LUNCH—AT my school, we have recess before lunch, which the principal says makes us better students in the afternoon, but I am not sure, because I am always hungry in recess and always sleepy after lunch—anyway, after we get back to Mrs. Monaghan's room, she says it is time to hand out the letters. We have been waiting for this all day, so we all sit straight and get real quiet, even Levi Van Wyck, so that there won't be any delay.

Mrs. Monaghan says she will hand them out one by one, but that nobody can start reading until everybody has a letter, and she asks us if we agree to her terms, and we say we do, and she starts handing out the letters. My letter is in an envelope, and when I pull it out, I see right away that it is not very long. I try not to be disappointed, and just to read what Specialist Luis Rodriguez-Reyes has to say:

Dear Bashkim:

Yes, I have killed people here. I even killed a boy, not much older than you. He was carrying a bag, and around here that means bomb. It wasn't a bomb though. It was some charred wood that he was bringing home to burn again.

Everybody kills here. That's what soldiers do. You might as well start killing mice with your baba, or whatever you call your dad, because with a name like yours, someone is going to try to kill you some day.

Luis

I think my face must look sort of funny, because Mrs. Monaghan comes right over to me. She picks up my letter and reads it, and then she makes a throat sound, and everybody looks at us, and then I throw up. Right on Mrs. Monaghan's red shoes. I love those shoes. But I throw up again, because once I start throwing up, I really have to keep doing it. And even though I know my baba will hit me if he finds out, I start to cry, because I just can't help it. I am crying and throwing up, and Mrs. Monaghan is holding me and moving her feet and everybody is saying, "What's wrong with Bashkim? He's sick. Bashkim, why are you crying?" And then Mrs. Monaghan tells everyone that they should sit really quiet because she is going to take me to the office.

THIS IS THE WORST DAY of my life because I am having an RPC. It's not called an RPC, because I did not do anything wrong, but it's just the same as one, because Baba and Nene are here, and we are all going to meet with the principal, even Mrs. Monaghan.

The principal called Baba and Nene yesterday from school, and told them about the letter from Specialist Luis Rodriguez-Reyes, and my nene came and picked me up right then. Luckily, my baba was taking a nap with Tirana, because it would not have been good if he had come to get me.

The principal was waiting with me outside when Nene drove up. She seemed sort of surprised at our ice-cream truck, and I think she wanted to talk to Nene awhile in the parking lot, but Nene wouldn't talk. She was in a hurry to get me home, probably before Baba woke up. All the principal could get Nene to do was agree to come back to school this morning at seven thirty so we could talk about what happened. So I knew all night that I was having an RPC, which was even worse than Baba and Nene screaming and crying in our apartment.

Baba kept saying that he didn't want his son around any military, and who did the school think it was to make his son write to a soldier? And Nene kept trying to tell Baba that it was different in America, and that it was the soldier who was the problem, not the school, but Baba didn't agree. He got angrier and angrier, and usually Nene just shuts up and tries not to get hit, but she was yelling back, and Tirana was crying so loud that she was hiccupping and coughing, and until today's RPC, yesterday was the worst day of my life.

MRS. MONAGHAN IS NOT WEARING her red shoes, and she is not wearing regular school clothes either. She has on a blue suit, and her hair is not so curly, and she looks older. The principal always dresses like that. They are waiting for us at the office. When the principal tries to shake my baba's hand, he makes a noise at her and doesn't put his hand out, so I know it is going to be as bad as I thought. Nene shakes the principal's hand, and Mrs. Monaghan's, but Nene looks like she is going to fall down, so I don't think she'll be able to stop Baba this time.

Baba is upset, so his English isn't very good either.

"No right this school has! My son is my son. And he does not write soldiers. In America, you think soldier is hero. In Albania, soldier is snake. My son does not write soldier."

Mrs. Monaghan and the principal look surprised.

I don't know if they have ever met someone who thinks like my baba about soldiers. He thinks like that about policemen too. It's because of being in prison, but Mrs. Monaghan and the principal don't know that, and maybe they would not even care if they did.

"Mr. Ahmeti," says the principal. "We have not met before. I am Dr. Moore, and I am terribly sorry about what happened to your son yesterday."

"I not care if you're sorry," says Baba. He stands up. "Sorry mean nothing. You are stupid, and this teacher is stupid, and your stupid hurt my son."

Nene tries to get Baba to sit down. She says, "Sadik, please listen, please sit down" in Albanian, which I understand, but I don't think Mrs. Monaghan or the principal does, and Baba pretends like he does not hear her either.

"I want money!" yells Baba. "You pay me for hurt my son."

Mrs. Monaghan looks at me. I turn away, because I can't stand it here and because I knew that an RPC was the worst thing that could ever happen to me.

"Mr. Ahmeti!" says Dr. Moore, very loud. "This is not a shakedown. We are here to discuss what happened to your son, to apologize to you, and to find a solution. We are not going to pay you money for this."

She looks mad, especially when Baba slams his hand down on her desk.

"I am American," Baba says. "I have rights. I get lawyer."

Mrs. Monaghan has not said a word. She looks sick too.

Dr. Moore stands up and tells my baba to leave. She asks Nene to stay if she can, but she tells Baba he will have to wait outside. She doesn't know what a bad thing she did, telling Nene to stay when Baba has to go. Nene can't stay if Baba has to go.

Then Dr. Moore tells Mrs. Monaghan to take me out of the room and away from the office. That's a mistake too, because Mrs. Monaghan and I have to obey, but Baba does not believe that a principal can send his son somewhere when he is there.

I see that Baba is very angry, and I am afraid that he will hurt Dr. Moore. She is speaking to her radio now and asking someone to come to the office to escort a parent away.

That's when my nene says her worst thing. The thing she says when she is really upset.

"For love of Allah," Nene wails. "Just kill me and my children if this is how life will be."

Now Mrs. Monaghan and Dr. Moore really look shocked. Then Baba yells at Nene.

"Allah? Allah? You expect Allah to care, Arjeta? Stupid woman. Nobody cares."

Mrs. Monaghan has her hand on my shoulder, and when Dr. Moore looks at her, she leads me out of the office. I go, because Baba and Nene are too mad to notice, and I would rather be with Mrs. Monaghan. I see the security man walking toward the office as we go out, and I wonder what Baba will say when he sees his uniform. Baba doesn't know that the school has its own police officer. For a second, I am afraid that I will never be allowed to come to school again, but thinking that makes me almost throw up, and because I cannot throw up on Mrs. Monaghan again, I just make the thought go out of my head. I pretend that I am in a movie, and I walk toward Mrs. Monaghan's classroom with my movie face on.

6

Luis

FOR A MOMENT, I don't know that my eyes are closed. I think I have been blinded, or perhaps that I am dead, because all I see is white light. I can't make out anything but light, and I am straining to see, aching everywhere, wondering where I am. And then I start to orient. I am lying down, maybe in a bed. I hurt. I have never hurt this much in my life. The light is so bright, I am afraid to open my eyes. It's my head that hurts. My head feels as if it has been stretched from the inside, it feels three times its normal size, the pain is intense.

A black frame forms around the blinding light and grows inward. As the light shrinks, so does the pain. It is getting darker and now going black. The black is a relief.

THIS TIME, I REALIZE I am in a bed, unmoving, before I notice whether I can see or not. My eyes are still closed. If there is any light, it is gray. It is neither bright nor black. Everything feels muted. I don't know if I can open my eyes, but I choose not to. I sink into the gray.

"SPECIALIST RODRIGUEZ."

The voice is very distant, but there is something about those words—*specialist, rodriguez*—that means something to me. I struggle to piece it together—*specialist, rodriguez*—but the sense that they are meaningful, that they are words, starts to fade. Where am I? Who am I? Let me go away.

"I THOUGHT HE WAS GOING to wake up an hour ago. There was something in his face, like he might be listening."

"Has he opened his eyes?"

"No, I haven't seen him open his eyes."

SOMEONE IS NEAR ME. THERE is pressure on me, somewhere. I think someone is holding my hand, and then I think, *what is a hand? What is someone?* And I slip backward again.

THIS TIME, THERE IS DEFINITELY someone near me. Someone is moving me, lifting my arm, doing something to me.

"Specialist Rodriguez. Do you hear me? We are just going to change your position a little. We need to move you a little, so you will be more comfortable. Can you hear me, Specialist Rodriguez?"

Can I hear her?

I don't know. I want something to stop. I want that gray. There is something behind me. I can't quite figure it out. Where I am. What I want. What should stop. Something should stop.

"Specialist Rodriguez. Good. We hear you. Can you hear me?"

WHAT I HEAR IS THE deafening crack of an explosion, very close, on the left. "Sam!" I yell. "Sam!" Another explosion. This one farther off. Sam was to my left. Where is he? There's smoke and dirt everywhere, and I hear what I think must be Sam moaning, choking.

I stumble to the left, find Sam with my feet before my eyes, drop to the ground. He's hurt bad. I don't see his face. For a moment, I think his head has been twisted around, so that the back of his head is looking up at me from above his chest, but then I realize that the top of his face, part of his head, is gone. I am looking at his mouth, part of his nose.

Somehow I don't recoil. I drop my face next to that mouth, and I say, "Sam, Sam, man, I'm here. I'll get you out."

And I do. I get Sam out. I get his body out.

I am not even hurt.

SO WHERE AM I NOW? Why is someone moving me? Why can't I open my eyes? Are my eyes open?

SAM AND I ARE ASSIGNED duty on a Humvee. There is a driver, me, and a gunner, Sam. Sam says, "Are you even American, Rodriguez? Is the Army how you're getting your green card?"

"Fuck off," I say.

SAM AND I HAVE DONE ninety-one live runs. Nobody's done ninety-one. Nobody's done fifty. Sam and I have done ninety-one, and we are something like gods at Kalsu.

"Bring my friend, the spic, a beer!" yells Sam. "He just drove through a damn ambush, and we're the only two standing."

"Yeah, give my redneck motherfucker partner two beers. He's a heat-seeking laser," I say.

THIS DOESN'T MAKE SENSE. IS Sam talking? Am I? Where's his head? Where's his damn face? I didn't get hurt. I didn't get a scratch. So where am I? Who's touching me? Why can't I wake up?

"SPECIALIST RODRIGUEZ. I'M DR. GHOSH. I think you can hear me. If you can hear me, will you open your eyes?"

I can hear him, but I can't open my eyes.

"Specialist, I'd like to call you Luis. Is that okay?"

I don't feel my body. I don't know where I am. Is he a doctor?

"You're in the hospital, Luis. You were shot. Do you remember that?"

I can't remember that. Who shot me?

"I know this is hard, Luis, but I think you can hear me. And I think you can wake up. I want you to wake up."

Who shot me?

"SPECIALIST LUIS. IT'S DR. GHOSH again. I hope you can hear me. I would like to talk to you, Luis. Can you wake up?"

"LUIS, THIS IS DR. GHOSH. The nurse tells me you have been making a lot of noise. I think you can wake up, Luis. I am right here. You can wake up with me here."

"SPECIALIST LUIS. DR. GHOSH AGAIN. I am going to keep coming. Every day. Twice a day. I want you to wake up. I want to be here with you. I can help you, Luis."

If he can help me, why doesn't he wake me up? Am I asleep? I can hear other voices. I am in a hospital, I think, but I don't know where and I don't know why. I got Sam out. I wasn't hurt. Why am I in a hospital?

And that kid. Who's the kid? There's a kid somewhere.

There's something wrong about that kid. There's something wrong. I have to get out of here.

"SPECIALIST LUIS. THE NURSES CALLED me. What kid, Specialist Luis? What kid?"

PLEASE STOP TALKING ABOUT THE kid. There's something about that kid. I hurt the kid. I killed the kid. When did I kill a kid? I didn't kill a kid. The kid killed Sam. No, I killed the kid. Who killed Sam?

I got him out. Where was his face? Did he hear me?

"SPECIALIST LUIS. I THINK YOU can hear me. Please, open your eyes."

I can't hear you.

"SPECIALIST LUIS, THE BOY IS all right. The boy is okay. Luis, I want you to wake up."

And I do. I wake up.

I am in a room, with a lot of light. There's a lot more light than I was expecting. And there is a man, looking at me. I close my eyes.

"Specialist Luis, welcome back. Welcome back, Specialist Luis."

And I sleep.

HE IS THERE WHEN I wake up. Dr. Ghosh. The man. What kind of name is Ghosh? Sam would know. I look at him without moving. I wonder if my body can move. I wonder if I have a body. I should be worried about this, but I am not. For someone who is just waking up, I am really tired.

"Luis, I am Dr. Arjun Ghosh. You can call me Arjun if you like. I am very glad that you decided to wake up. We're all very glad that you're here."

That's nice. They're glad I'm here. Wherever here is. Whoever they are. I think I might have smiled, but I can't tell, because I still don't feel any connection to my body. It seems to me that Dr. Ghosh is seated next to me, and that he has a hand on my arm, but I don't actually feel this. I know this, but I can't feel my arm, and I am not sure if I have a body.

"Luis, I know you must feel very strange. You've been asleep for a while, and you are also on medication, but whatever you are feeling, I want you to know that there is going to be someone in the room with you. You are not going to be alone."

That's nice.

Why would there be someone in the room with me?

My head hurts. It really hurts.

THIS TIME, WHEN I WAKE up, I know that I am awake, and I know that I have been dreaming. It was a nightmare, and I am sweating, panicked, but I can't remember anything about it. Was it loud? Was there a kid?

My breathing is rapid, and someone puts a hand on my head.

"Specialist Rodriguez. It's okay. You're in a hospital. You've had a dream. You're okay."

She sounds nice, this hand. I close my eyes, and her touch grows heavy, and I feel myself slipping back to sleep.

IT IS LIGHT AGAIN. I have been lying here awake a long time, but I keep my eyes shut, because there is someone in the room, and I don't want to talk to whoever it is. I have started to remember. I know who shot me. I still can't remember the kid. There is a kid, though. There's something about a kid.

7

Roberta

A FAT SOUTHWEST AIRLINES jet lumbers impossibly close to the windshield of my car. McCarran Airport sits right in the middle of town, a few blocks from some of the largest casinos in the world, a mere roadway width from the parking lot at the new Town Square shopping mall, or from the office complexes on Sunset Road. It startles me that I could count the rivets on the wing of a commercial jet while driving down a road with the signs from a US Post Office, a Sonic Burger, and the Hy-Bar window company competing for my attention.

It's the light-blocking mass of a Boeing 737 balancing in the air above your head that startles, though the roar of the jets in your ears lasts longer. The sky is a living thing when one is a desert dweller, stretched out, vast and imposing, with its constant dance of cloud and color, the visual equivalent of a movie soundtrack to one's life. But, of course, in Vegas, the sky is not just a matter of wind and dust and water and light, but also of planes. The ponderous passenger kind, roaring in and out of town, nine hundred flights a day, forty million people a year, diving into the center of the beast and flashing back out again, but also military jets, whistling in, four high-flying, perfectly matched arrows, bullets set to a ballet score, speeding around the Sheep Range Mountains north of town.

For me, the belly of a jet blocking my long range view of the road makes me think of homeless kids—of Lester and Molly and Dawan, all kids I've worked with, all kids who spent a portion of their teenage years sleeping on the flat roofs of the Park 2000 office complex, conveniently located in the airport's flight path, shielded from the prying beams of police helicopters, which aren't allowed to fly there. Homeless teens feel safer on the low roofs, which they scramble onto easily enough but which pose a physical challenge to their older, less mentally stable comrades. It's the modern equivalent of a hilltop accessible from only one direction. Early in the morning, I used to park my car in a discreet spot, waiting for a kid to descend, to arise at the edge of a roof, slip off a corner tile, grab hold of the largest oleander branch, and dance down the bush to the ground, where I would be waiting, coffee and a McDonald's bacon-egg-and-cheese McMuffin in hand. The first sound out of the kid's mouth—*hello* or *hi Robbie, who are you* or *get out of here*—whatever it was, would blast forth, their hearing muffled by the roar of all those jets all night long.

Molly and Dawan and Lester. I wonder if any of them knew each other. I can't remember now how close in time they were. Molly shared her food with the feral cats that lived in the small courtyards off a few of the offices, and Lester kept his guitar stashed in an unlocked delivery box meant for pharmaceutical samples, which worked for quite a while, but then one day it was gone, and Lester never knew how or where. And Dawan. Well, Dawan is one of the kids I try not to think too much about.

I met him first in the wash, where Marty and I used to walk the dogs on weekend mornings. I don't usually meet kids on my own. I'm assigned a case as a CASA volunteer, or I take on a custody matter pro bono, or maybe I get involved with someone through the Las Vegas Homeless Youth project. But Dawan I met without any of these buffers;

Dawan I met because I noted the tramped-down area in front of the salt cedar bush he had turned into his home, because Rebel whined and sniffed and would not leave the area, and because I spotted the handle of a red metal cup deep within the brush.

"Hello," I called.

Marty stopped, already well ahead of me, and looked back quizzically.

"Hello, is someone there?"

Silence.

Of course, it could have been anyone. Any tramp. An adult passing through. I had no way to know it was a fourteen-year-old boy. But I had just gone to a seminar on homeless youth, and one of the speakers had talked about the wash, about how dangerous it would become for any teens living there as soon as a summer monsoon hit. Of course, floods in Las Vegas are always dangerous. When I was in middle school, someone's aunt washed away in her car. The water had come right over the road, and she had driven into it, not knowing there was a dip just there, not knowing that what looked like a slick of water across the surface was a powerful four-foot-deep rush. Those kinds of accidents aren't as common anymore, now that the county has spent twenty years building channels and walls and retention basins that sluice the water right through town. But all that effort has made the washes more dangerous: the water runs faster, and we are less accustomed to its power, so storm after storm, we lose a child who has the delightful inspiration to try to float in the sudden stream, or an unsuspecting nature lover, who perhaps hears nothing before he is swooshed away with the uprooted trees and the abandoned sofas.

That must have been what was in my mind when I called hello again, when I shook the branches near the tramped-down entrance, when I said that I had something to give him. I didn't have anything, of course, except a bottle of water and a rolled-up twenty in my pant cuff, but I wanted to see who was there, *if* someone was there.

It took a while. Marty gave up, whistled Rebel to his side, and said he'd meet me up top, near the train tracks, when I was ready. So I didn't have Marty or the dogs when the salt cedar started to shake, which was the first time it occurred to me that I should have asked Marty to stay, I should have kept Rebel with me. But when Dawan crawled out, slithering beneath what I had somehow thought was going to open like a door—a skinny, scratched, sunburned adolescent—my heart nearly stopped. His lips were dry and cracked, his eyes bloodshot. I could see a long, dirty cut high on his shoulder, near his neck.

"I got a knife," he said.

I should have been scared, but mostly I was shocked. He needed water, he needed a doctor. I couldn't believe how close I had come to walking past that bush.

I handed him the bottle of water, and his hands shook as he tried to pull the plastic off the lid. I motioned for him to give the bottle back to me so that I could help him, and the look in his eyes, just for an instant, when he thought I was going to take back the water, when something in him would have surrendered it, the politeness of a child to an adult, that look comes back to me at night, in the middle of night, in the middle of certain dreams.

"I'll open it for you. I've got more. I've got food."

He tensed up then, afraid, but he needed the water. He wasn't about to leave that water bottle.

As fast as I could, slower than I've ever known I could be, I opened the bottle, and he drank the water down. When it was gone, he looked at me, looked around me, looking for what I had promised: more water, food.

"My husband's got our pack. He's just up top. I'll call him."

He wanted to resist, I know he did, but he was too weak. I've thought about that since. The only time anyone was going to catch Dawan Jessup, the only chance anyone ever had to get him into some kind of system, was the day I found him, invisible but for the handle of a red cup in a salt cedar bush.

Marty didn't hear me calling, but Dawan waited there. I'll never know why, now that I know how hard he was to find, how impossible it was ever going to be to keep him. I raced to the top, to the tracks, and found Marty. The dogs beat us there, barking and leaping, happy to be sent back into the wash, and by the time Marty and I arrived, Dawan was standing, knife in hand, staring a startled Rebel down.

I whistled to Rebel, to Tank. They ran behind me, bumping into my legs, confused and frightened by Dawan.

"It's okay, son," said Marty. "We're not going to hurt you. The dogs won't hurt you."

Dawan did not relax. He stood, a scrawny savage, willing himself a foot taller than he was.

"Do you want a sandwich? I've got two here."

Marty handed Dawan the food, and the boy looked back, unsure whether to eat it right there or to take it into his now-discovered hideout.

"I'm Roberta. And this is Marty. What's your name?"

He looked at me.

Then he sat down on a large rock, washed there in some summer storm, and opened the sandwich Marty had given him.

We waited.

"Dawan."

And that was how it started. The four years of Dawan, the four years of trying and fighting and defending and hoping. Somehow Marty and I got him to an emergency room that day, and from there he went to Child Haven, and from there to a foster home, and then another, and then another. Somewhere in there he left, and I didn't hear from him for a while, but then one morning, Dawan was the teen dancing down the oleander bush, snatching up the McMuffin, calling out *Hi Robbie* in a too-loud voice.

I'll never forget the thrill of seeing Dawan that morning. Of finding out he was alive, of thinking that I had another chance.

I'll never forget that thrill, nor the call, three months later, from Child Protective Services: Roberta, we thought you'd want to know.

Some things, you don't want to know.

Some things, you always knew.

8

Avis

MY FIRST THOUGHT WAS that Jim and I should meet in some neutral place, that I didn't want him in our home. I was almost used to being there alone, and I didn't want him to come in, take a look at what was in the fridge, or see how many messages were blinking on the machine. But I kept playing out the possibilities in my mind, exactly why he thought "we should get together, make some decisions," and I realized that I did not want to be in a restaurant if certain things were going to be said. I had lived my entire life in Las Vegas. There was nowhere we could go without the risk of running into someone one of us knew.

"Jim, I think it might be better just to meet here. Maybe you could pick up something for us to eat."

I didn't want to serve him food.

"Okay. Sure. However you want to do it."

He sounds distracted. The hotel would be getting busier. Fall was busy, the holidays were busy. Even this year.

It's as if he is confirming a business appointment. I wonder if there will come a day when he leaves my calls to get picked up by Elizabeth.

"Yes, that's how I want to do it. Seven thirty."

My voice is abrupt, because I don't want him to hear how crushing his eight words were. I can't help myself. I am looking forward to seeing him. I miss my husband. I have lived with him my entire adult life, and if I just close my eyes and pretend I never heard what he said about Darcy, I miss him.

Cheryl says I had better stop closing my eyes. And I damn well better not forget about Darcy.

JIM AND I WENT TO Oregon once, for the wedding of Jim's college roommate. I felt uncomfortable around all those friends of Jim's, friends from a different life, who couldn't imagine how obscure their references were to someone like me.

Emily was a baby, not quite one, and she was fussy all weekend. Wouldn't let anyone hold her, didn't want to take a nap, screamed when the bride tried to take her photo.

After the wedding—it was in a beautiful park, with a red Japanese bridge arched over a sliver of water—Emily would not let me set her down. She kept clinging to my leg, literally trying to crawl up it, and her hand tugged the band of my skirt down obscenely. So I scooped her up, and held her, hoping she would not suddenly pull at my shirt and expose more of my flesh, and then suddenly, she was bent half over, reaching, trying to get back down. I resisted for a moment, frustrated with her, and then gave in and set her down.

Immediately, she dropped to her knees and lightning crawled toward a patch of rock and dirt surrounding a bamboo shrub.

"Look. You've got a desert baby. She likes rocks."

I stiffened, not sure if the woman, a girlfriend of another college friend, was being critical.

But it was true.

The patch of dirt was what Emily had wanted. She sat there, her pale pink dress smudged with brown, eyes bright, a rock in each hand, a telltale trail of dirt and pebbles disappearing between her lips. She gurgled happily.

"Wok. Dada. Wok."

I couldn't love Emily any more than I already did, but I remember the rush of warmth, knowing that she too felt out of her element, ill at ease in this wet, green world. And I remember looking at Jim, at his utterly unguarded face, as his daughter cooed *dada* below him.

Could anyone have imagined that I would have a life so sweet? A husband who loved me, a daughter we adored?

JIM ARRIVES RIGHT ON TIME, carrying food from the Japanese restaurant at the hotel. I pour some beer into frosty glasses I keep in the freezer, but when I start to set the table in the nook, I suddenly remember that this is where Emily took her first steps. It was tiled then, but she had gone from this edge of the nook wall to that cabinet, this exact place, with her wobbly, lurching, leaning steps.

We were so proud of her. We had her do it again and again. Walk between us. Lift her up. Laugh. Jim holding her in the air. And then, again. Walk between us. Walk to Mommy. Walk to Daddy. Look at our girl. Look at our big girl. A walker!

She lay in her crib crying the next morning, feet in the air, pink fingers holding her thighs. A little walking girl with muscles that ached. Poor thing. We didn't know whether to laugh or cry when we saw her.

It's too much to sit in that spot with Jim tonight, so I set the table in the dining room. I knew these kinds of thoughts would come up. I've steeled myself for them. I spent part of the day forcing myself to think about some of Sharlene's more memorable breakups. I figure if anybody has the core knowledge of what not to do at the end of a relationship, it should be me.

Jim takes the food out of the white boxes, and places it in six or seven different ceramic bowls. When he is done, it looks like we are about to have guests for dinner. I know that he is trying to be nice, just like I am trying not to think about whether he is still staying in a suite at the hotel, and whether or not Darcy stays there with him. Both efforts are worth something.

Still, he gets to the point quickly.

"I want to buy a house. These are the lowest prices we've seen in twenty years. And I want to sell this house. It needs work, and I think it would be better for you to have something newer, smaller. I'm willing to buy that for you."

I've been preparing for him to say something definitive all day, but still I am stunned. He's moved so much farther ahead of me—not *I won't be coming back* or *I want a divorce,* but *I want to buy a house,* and *I want to sell this house,* and *I will buy you something else.*

The divorce, the word I thought I was going to hear today, is already hindsight to him. So evident that he seems to have forgotten that we haven't actually discussed it.

My whole body reverberates with the shock.

FOR WEEKS NOW, I'VE BEEN dwelling on these questions that I some-how missed when everyone else was asking them. Maybe because I never went to college. I was never in a dorm room. You know: the meaning-of-life questions, the why-be-moral questions, the questions about scale.

Our eighty years is a fraction of a second in geologic time, and our planet less than an atom against the universe, and our individual lives puny against the seven billion people living right at the same moment we are. How could any of us think that our lives have meaning? And if they have no meaning, then why aren't I doing whatever I want? Why do I expect anyone to act in any certain way? What difference does it make if there is anarchy and mayhem and murder? Who does it hurt? And what does that matter?

I tried this argument out on Cheryl last week.

"Well, your human life might be trivial, Avis, but my fraction of a mite of an atom of an electron is fucking great. Do you think maybe you just need a drink?"

JIM LOOKS DOWN AT THE bowls of expensive Japanese food. He is realizing that he has handled this badly. That he should have gone slower.

Actually, he should have realized that it is none of his business if I stay in this house or not. Who the hell does he think he is? Planning my half of this new life?

I shiver with anger and hold on to the beautiful strength of this clean emotion.

"I'll make my own decisions about where I live, Jim."

"Of course. I didn't mean that, Avis. I mean, you could stay in this house. It's just . . . it needs a new roof. It's not well insulated. The power bills are too high. It would be a really expensive house to maintain . . ."

I am trying to stay angry. I am angry. But I know Jim so well. He is trying to plan this next phase for me. He has leapt way ahead, to a future in which I can't pay the power bill on this house, and I know already—because Jim is good at this kind of thing, because Jim would have thought out all the options—that he is probably right, that I am not only going to lose my husband, but I am going to lose my house too.

I TRIED TO MAKE CHERYL understand what I meant.

So what if three toddlers were drowned by their mother? So what if a sick old man rapes little boys? Even, so what if Emily died? I mean these are terrible things. We can all agree. And yet, to think they are terrible, aren't we elevating ourselves beyond what is rationally possible to support?

Is it terrible if an ant steps on the leg of the ant in front of it?

Is it terrible if a mussel dries out because a high tide cast it too far ashore?

Is it terrible if a cat burying its own dung scratches up a few blades of grass?

And in the length of time measured by infinity, and in the size of a world measured by countless universes, is it possible to believe that our lives are anything more than a few blades of grass?

"Cheryl, I don't just need a drink. I mean it. Why am I so mad at Jim? Why shouldn't he do whatever he wants?"

"Why are you so mad at Jim? Why aren't you *madder* at Jim? Jim is an ass, and what he did is wrong, and whether or not his life is meaningful has nothing to do with it. You shouldn't hurt the people you love, or the people you used to love, and it isn't any more complicated than that."

"Then to hell with Jim."

"To hell with Jim!"

And we laugh. Because we always end up laughing. Because if I could just keep laughing, I could get through this.

I HEAR THE CHIMES OF an ice-cream truck coming down the street. Jim hears it too, and we look at each other over the top of the uneaten Japanese food. I think of Emily's first ice cream, and then I think of Nate, a little boy, barreling full speed out the door. He always wanted to be first to get to the truck. First to get an ice cream. It's a crazy idea. Putting ice cream on a truck in the street. How many kids have hurled themselves in front of a car in a race to get to the ice-cream truck? You can hear the music for a mile. Kids are running into streets when the ice-cream truck is blocks away. My heart used to stop every time I heard that sound, imagining Nate running into traffic, knowing that he could, and that if he did, he would be going full speed and never know what had hit him.

"Do you remember how Nate used to go crashing out the door?"

He smiles.

"Yes. He wouldn't even stop so I could hand him a dollar. He'd yell, 'Dad, Dad, come quick! The ice-cream truck is here!'"

We look at each other for a moment. I try to keep it out of my eyes, everything I remember, everything I feel. I don't know how he does it.

I don't know how he remembers Nate at seven; how he suggests I leave our house, knowing that the same sound has brought the same darting child into both our minds.

ON BAD DAYS, MOSTLY IN the summer—when the thermometer hit 115 and it was too hot to go outside, too hot to run an errand, too hot to distract oneself with anything at all—I used to try to figure out if it would be better that I didn't have any other children. If Nate died, I would be childless. I wouldn't be a mother. Which was unimaginable. And yet, at least, I wouldn't be a mother. I wouldn't have to carry on. It was almost solace, that I would not have to live with Nate's death in the way I'd had to live with Emily's. I wanted more children, but at least if I didn't have any, I had that option.

I LOOK AT JIM ACROSS the table, and I see Nate in thirty years. They are more alike than I ever thought they would be: the way their eyes tip slightly at the corners, the flat plane of the cheek into the neck, the wide, square hands.

"I thought . . . I think . . . I don't know . . . Jim, could we try talking to someone? Could we go to a counselor or something?"

I hadn't meant to say this aloud. Not true. I have been trying to think how I could bring this into a conversation for weeks now. There just hasn't been any opening. Arguably, this isn't much of an opening now.

"Avis."

He stops. Looks down. I wait for a long time, but he doesn't go on. He doesn't reply.

I KEEP CIRCLING BACK TO these horrible ideas. If a man rapes a child, we are horrified. If a rapist murders a young woman, we are horrified. If a mother kills her baby, we are horrified. These are horrible experiences for the child, the young woman, the baby. They are horrible experiences for anyone who loved them, maybe anyone who knew them, maybe even anyone who heard that they happened. I get that.

What I can't get to is why it makes any difference that a mussel or a blade of grass or a human being feels horror.

There's a gun upstairs. I could kill myself. I could kill Jim. I could kill Darcy. I could kill a busload of children. Would it matter?

I CAN JUST IMAGINE MAKING that argument to Jill and Margo and Julie.

"Avis, do you hear yourself? These are not normal thoughts. These are not healthy thoughts. These are thoughts that say 'Get some Prozac.'"

"But I don't want a drug. I don't want to be drugged. I want to understand these things. I want to know the truth."

"Avis, you're not thinking about this right. It's like hormones. Your brain is not creating a chemical that you need. Like insulin for a diabetic."

"I don't see it that way. It's not that I don't believe you. But I think there's more to it. I'm not just a machine that needs oil or something."

"Give it up. Avis is not going to take a drug. We're going to have to use alcohol in her case. We're just going to have to drink our way through Avis's crisis."

"Right. Nothing drug-like about that."

And then, we would laugh.

I DON'T LET JIM OFF the hook. I let the silence stretch out, long. We have been married for three decades, and he is not willing to try one session with a counselor? How could he care so little for me? How could Darcy matter this much?

"I've made promises, Avis. To Darcy. I can't go back on those."

He can't go back on promises to Darcy.

"Then get out, Jim. Get out. You fucking asshole. Get out of this house."

I've spent most of my life making sure I could not be mistaken for my mother, and Jim looks physically repulsed when I say this, but I think that my language is perfectly appropriate and that I am not like Sharlene at all.

For one thing, I wasn't smart enough to leave first.

IF OUR LIVES REALLY DID mean something, would an Emily be dead? Would a child get raped? Would three toddlers drown slowly in a car rolled into the river by their mother?

How can both worlds exist? The one where a life is meaningful and the one where it means nothing? Does not the presence of one negate the other? Emily is dead. Children are raped. Mothers have killed.

Isn't it obvious that what is happening to me does not matter?

9

Bashkim

TODAY I AM DOING my writing project with Nene. Tirana is sleeping, and Baba is on the ice-cream truck by himself. Baba doesn't like to work on the truck without Nene, because he does not sell as much ice cream. That's because Baba scares some of the kids.

"What you want? I no got all day for you decide. Point at picture!"

There are pictures of all the ice creams we sell on the side of the truck. Well, not exactly all. There are some ice creams that we never have, even though we have pictures, because the pictures have been on the truck a long time, and our supplier doesn't make those ice creams anymore. Also, we have some ice creams with no pictures, because they are new, and we never got pictures to put on the truck for them. This is a problem, because nobody asks for those. So Baba always waves those ice creams around, and says, "Special deal. Two ice creams for twenty cents less." But that doesn't always work out, because Baba doesn't explain that you have to get two of those no-picture ice creams to get the twenty cents less, and then sometimes people get mad. Usually Baba gets mad too. Which isn't that good for the ice-cream business.

Nene sells the ice cream differently, and she can sell all the no-picture ones. When somebody points to a picture that we don't have the ice cream for, Nene says, "This is your lucky day. We have a brand-new kind of ice cream, and you are going to be the first one to get to try it." Which works almost every time. That's just how Nene and Baba are different. Baba worries about money a lot, but he can't make money as well as Nene can. Nene worries about money too, but between her good ice-cream selling skills and her job at Kohl's, she makes more money than Baba. I don't think Baba likes that.

Anyway, Baba agreed to be on the truck by himself because I have to do this project, and I need Nene's help. Baba doesn't want to have anything to do with my school anymore, even if this project is going to be about Albania. This year our school's theme is origins, and every student has to do an origins project. I got Albania.

The first part of my project is a questionnaire. I have to ask someone in my family some questions, and write down what they say. I read the questions to my nene.

"Question one: Where was your mother born?"

"I was born in Tirana, in a hospital, which was somewhat unusual for my family, because my older brother and sister were born at home. But my nene, your *gjyshe,* had a hard time delivering my brother, your *daja* Edon, and she was afraid to be home again. So she went to the hospital to have me. She didn't like being at the hospital, so she had your *daja* Burim, who is younger than me, at home again."

I write down: In Tirana, at a hospital.

"Question two: Where did your mother grow up?"

"I grew up on our family farm about fifty kilometers from Tirana. I loved the farm. My baba made me wooden skis, and in the winter, I would ski down the hill behind our house. Baba made a toboggan too, and all of us would get on that and go down the hill very fast. We had goats and sheep and chickens on our farm, and it was my job to collect the eggs each morning. You had to be fast to get the eggs out from our chickens, or they would peck your fingers, and it hurt. My nene would make *torta* from our eggs, and when Blerta and Edon and Burim and I got home from school, she would serve us a piece before we started our afternoon chores."

I write down: On a farm with goats near a hill.

"Question three: How did your mother get to Las Vegas?"

"When I married your baba, he had already applied for political asylum with the United States. This was a very hard process, because he had to prove that he was in prison for protesting an act of the government and not for being a criminal. It's hard to get a paper that says that in Albania. But my family and your baba's family had known each other for generations, and my *babagjysh* had gone to school with someone in the government. After we got married, my babagjysh knew that your baba would always be in danger in Albania, so he got the government to provide the right papers. Even then, it took a long time for the United States to say yes. That's why you were born in Albania. We didn't get to choose where we came in the United States. Catholic Charities in Las Vegas had space for three refugees, so we came here."

I think awhile. Then I write down: My grandfather liked the United States, and he told my parents to move here.

"Question four: What does your mother like best about living in America?"

"That is a hard question, because I miss my family and I miss how beautiful Albania is. I miss our mountains, and the ocean, and all the green fields. I miss the market, and I miss eating food fresh from our garden. In Albania, life is sometimes hard, and the government has a lot of problems, but the women are happier. In Albania, I would never spend a day without talking to my friends and my nene. In Las Vegas, there are no women for me to talk to at all. I miss my baba and my nene, and I wish that you and Tirana could have all your cousins to play with. I don't like living in America. It's lonely, and if we run out of money, I don't think anyone will help us."

My nene finally stops. Maybe she forgot she was talking to me. Though sometimes I am the only person she has to talk to.

"I'm sorry, *shpirt*. What is the question again?"

"It's okay, Nene. I have the answer."

I write down: My mother likes that the government is better in America, and that she can make money here.

I am getting tired of writing, and I can see that my nene is getting a little sad, so I decide to ask just one more question. I can put something in the other spaces later, because I pretty much know the answers.

"Question seven: How is your origin country similar to the United States?"

"People in America always ask what religion I am. I don't like to say Muslim, because Americans don't like Muslims. But I don't want to say I am not Muslim, because that is disrespectful to my baba. In America, people think that they are the only ones who have many religions together. But in Albania, half the people are Muslim and half the people are Christian. And nobody is worried about this. We don't care if someone Christian marries someone Muslim. I think people in America worry about that more."

I write down: Half the people in Albania are Christians. Albanians accept many religions, like Americans do.

Nene wants to read what I have written, but I tell her it is a surprise, and that Mrs. Monaghan is making a portfolio of our writing to give to our parents at the end of the year. That last part is sort of true, because the art teacher is making a portfolio of everything we are making in art, and some teachers do make portfolios of what their students write. In any case, Nene won't understand that my answers are good for her.

EVER SINCE THE RPC THAT wasn't an RPC, I have been getting headaches at school. It isn't that anything bad is happening. Mrs. Monaghan has been real nice, and the principal was nice too. She wanted me to come to her office, but instead of sending a note with another student, which would really have made me sick, she just mentioned that she wanted me to come with her one day when she was already visiting my class. We had most of our conversation just walking in the hallway, so by the time I got to her office, all she needed to do was give me some goldfish crackers (that's what they give at my school, since we have a marine lab), and she also showed me that she has her own aquarium in her office. She said I could come by any day and feed the fish for her. Which I might do.

It's not Mrs. Monaghan or the principal who are making me sick. It's just that I don't feel as comfortable anymore. Sometimes I think about what Specialist Luis Rodriguez-Reyes wrote to me—even though Mrs. Monaghan took the letter, and I never got to see it again—and it makes me feel like someone is going to hit me. Like I want to crawl under my desk table or put a sweater over my head or something. Mrs. Monaghan hasn't said very much about our letter-writing project. Some of the kids ask her, because everybody was so excited about adopting a soldier, but I think maybe my letter messed that project up. Nobody knows it's my fault, but they might be figuring it out, and that makes my stomach hurt too.

I think Specialist Luis Rodriguez-Reyes might be like my baba. Maybe he can't forget anything, and killing that boy is always in his mind, like prison is in Baba's mind. I feel sorry for the specialist and for Baba, and I feel sorry for the specialist's wife too. It's not very good when a man has a bad thing in his mind.

10

Luis

I SHOT ME.

I shot myself with a .22. A toy gun.

Didn't achieve the mission. Not dead. Three years in hell, three years of killing people, but somehow, I shot myself in the head, and I am still going to walk out of this hospital some day. Walk out. That's the goal.

I guess there was a lot of loose space in my head.

So now I'm here. Which isn't Iraq. It's DC. My *abuela* was always going to take a trip here.

I've messed myself up pretty good. My physical therapy goal is to walk five hundred feet unaided. My occupational therapy goal is to return to the military. That's what I said I wanted. It's not what I want. I don't want anything. So I might as well tell them what they want to hear. Especially since I'm stuck in their hospital, and they've got all the cards.

I suppose Dr. Ghosh is for the mental part. Sam said the Army didn't care a damn about us, but if you really fuck up and try to kill yourself, they care all over.

Must be in the paper.

So many of us grunts offing ourselves that they have to do something about it. It makes them look bad. How are they going to get more money for the war if their own soldiers are killing themselves?

That's my theory. That would have been Sam's theory. Maybe that's why I hold it.

DR. GHOSH IS NOT SO bad. He's persistent, anyway. He comes every damn day. It's not like I can do much about it. I can't even get out of this bed. And I sure as hell can't get agitated, because even though I didn't do enough damage to lose whatever they mean by "executive function," I did give myself a world-class headache. And it never goes away.

It's okay. I don't care if I have it forever. I don't know how I'll stand it, but it's not like I'm looking forward to something else. It's not like Sam wouldn't trade this headache for what happened to him.

Sam.

Damn fucking war.

"LUIS. GOOD AFTERNOON. HOW ARE you today?"

That's how Dr. Ghosh greets me every day. He says I can call him Arjun, but I prefer Dr. Ghosh. I don't care if he calls me Luis or not. I don't care what anyone calls me.

"Luis, it says in this report that you were talking in your sleep again last night. Talking about the kid. Have you remembered anything?"

Have I remembered anything?

I remember everything. But I'm not telling Dr. Ghosh about it. I'll take that day to my grave.

"No, Dr. Ghosh. I don't know why I talk about a kid in my sleep. Maybe I'm saying something else, and the nurses just hear *kid*."

"I don't think so, Luis."

"Well, maybe I'm thinking about someone back home. There's a lot of kids in my family."

This last isn't exactly true. I just thought he might buy it since I'm

Mexican-American, and everybody seems to think we have a lot of kids. I grew up an only child. My abuela raised me, and her children were all grown by then.

"Is that right, Luis? Do you want to tell me about your family?"

I like Dr. Ghosh. I like him because I like people who stick to things. That's a big thing for me. Reliability. And one thing about Dr. Ghosh, I can count on him being here every day. But I hate these shrink-stink questions he asks.

"Sure, Dr. Ghosh. My dad was a guy named Marco Rodriguez. But he died before I was born. He was probably a gang member. Or he died in a gang fight, anyway. My mom was Maricela Reyes. Real beautiful. So I must look like my dad."

"Are you close to your mom?"

"No. I am not close to her. And she's not real beautiful anymore. She's an addict. Has been for years. My grandma raised me. My mom left me at her house when I was a year old, and she didn't come back. I mean she came back a few times, to get money, or sleep on the couch. One time she came back so messed up, she thought I was my dad. I was about eight years old, and she thought I was her twenty-year-old Latin lover."

"Sounds tough."

I smile then. Because sometimes Dr. Ghosh is just funny. People think they know everything about me when they hear my dad was a gang member and my mom was a drug addict, but they don't. They don't know anything. Because my abuela is a saint, and she loved me, and the real true story is that I am just like any other pampered kid. My abuela had a home, and a good job, and she fed me well, and read stories with me every night. Her family came to America four generations ago. So she's American. She speaks Spanish, she likes Mexican food, but she's American. And she raised me nice. She raised my uncles and my mom that way too. It's just my mom got messed up real young. Probably because she was so beautiful. It's not that great for a girl, at least not for a Mexican-American girl. You end up with some asshole gang member like my dad.

"Do you want to talk about your mother, Luis?"

"No, Dr. Ghosh. My head's real bad. Could we just talk tomorrow?"

And I close my eyes. Because that's another thing I like about Dr. Ghosh. He's not too pushy.

THE NEXT DAY, I'M WAITING for him. Because it occurred to me last night that while I do not care a damn what Dr. Ghosh thinks about my family, I don't want some government report misrepresenting what my abuela did for me. What if I'm dead sometime, and this report that Dr. Ghosh is probably writing gets sent to her, and in it, she sees all this stuff about my mom and my dad and nothing about her. Imagining that makes me sick. I practically jumped out of my bed to tell the nurse to call Dr. Ghosh, but I knew they probably wouldn't make the call, and he probably wouldn't have appreciated it if they had.

"Good afternoon, Luis."

"Dr. Ghosh. I've been waiting for you."

"You have? Well, that's good. That's good news. What do you have to tell me?"

"It's about my abuela. My grandmother."

"Yes?"

"She raised me, you know. And she did a great job. Not that you can tell from seeing me here. I mean, what I did and all. But I had a really nice childhood. My mom was an addict, but she wasn't even important. My abuela loved me so much. I was really like a prince."

"What do you mean, 'what you did and all'?"

"What?"

"You said that I might not know you had a really good childhood because of 'what you did and all.' What did you mean?"

"Dr. Ghosh. It's not about what I did. I'm trying to tell you that my abuela gave me a very nice life. And I wasn't some screwed-up

Mexican kid who signed up for the Army to stay out of jail or something."

I almost said, "to get his green card or something," but that made me think of Sam, and I don't want to talk about Sam either.

"Okay. Okay. How do you feel about being Mexican-American, Luis?"

"What do you mean?"

"Well, you mention it a lot. You mention your Mexican heritage a lot, but then you talk about Mexicans trying to stay out of jail or your father's Mexican gang. I was just wondering how you feel about having Mexican heritage?"

Like I said, Dr. Ghosh has some really shrink-stink questions. I can't think of a response to this, so I keep quiet. I look away too, so it won't feel as uncomfortable. I really don't have anything to say to Dr. Ghosh about this.

"All right, Luis. Will you tell me about your abuela? She must be very special to you."

Dr. Ghosh has a slight Indian accent, and I've never heard anyone say *abuela* quite like he does. I want his report to say something good about her, so even though I am kind of irritated at Dr. Ghosh, I answer.

"She's a great lady, my abuela. She's got a good job. She went to college when I was a kid. Her husband, my abuelo, died in a car accident when my mom was about fourteen, which was really hard on the family. But he had insurance, so they were okay that way. My abuela had worked in his office part time, but then she went to work in the executive office of the Boyd Group, and now she has a job at the Mirage.

"I grew up in the house she bought after my mom and my uncles left. It's real nice. We have a pool. She sent me to Catholic school, but I didn't want to go after eighth grade. I had friends on my block and they were going to Valley, the public high school, and I wanted to go with them. So, you know, it's not like my childhood was really about who my mom was or my dad. I'm middle class. If my abuela hadn't taken me in, I would have been in trouble. But she did. She took me in. She did everything for me. She raised a whole second family. She didn't do anything wrong."

"Thank you, Luis. Your abuela sounds like someone I would like to know. I'm glad you had her."

"Yeah, well, I just don't want some report about me mixing up my story. Making her out to be someone she's not."

"Yes. My report. Luis, I have to leave now. I have somewhere else to be. We'll talk tomorrow."

"Sure. Thanks, Dr. Ghosh."

That's the first time I've used up all the time he had. Usually I quit talking, and he decides to go.

DR. GHOSH IS LATE THE next day, and for an hour or so, I am pretty pissed off. It would be just like the Army to stop paying for a shrink because I finally told him something. "Hey, we got you to talk. Not as tough as you think you are, are you? Yeah, we got you to talk. Now, suck it up and figure it out on your own."

I've built up a pretty good head of steam by the time Dr. Ghosh walks in. And even though he hasn't done anything, and apparently the Army hasn't either, I'm still mad.

"Good afternoon, Luis. How are you feeling today?"

I don't answer. I can't believe how angry I am. If my head wasn't busting open like it is, I'd knock Ghosh to the floor. Dr. Ghosh. What the hell sort of name is that? What are Indians anyway? Buddhist? Muslim? Something else. Dammit. Well, who the hell does Dr. I'm-so-important Ghosh think he is?

"Luis, you seem a little upset. Do you want to talk about it?"

Man, I hate those shrink-stink questions. I roll over, and then maybe I doze off, because the next thing I know, there's a nurse in the room, and no Dr. Ghosh, and she wants me to get to the chair so she can change my bedsheets. Change the sheets. Boy, I really did a number on myself this time.

THE NEXT WEEK, I START to let myself think of Sam a little. I want to remember that day, that mission. What happened just before. Why was Sam on the left? What was he doing?

I've thought about this day a lot, right after Sam got hit, just before I was hurt. And there's a blank there. Even though I didn't get a scratch, I can't remember that day clearly. Sergeant Reidy asked me to write it down. The Army always wants a detailed report when something like that happens, but I kept coming up blank. We were on the road, we were making our usual pass, and then there was the explosion. But why had we stopped the Humvee? Why had we gotten out? Why was I so far away from Sam?

I can't remember.

You don't survive ninety-one IEDs taking a random stroll. Sam and I never did anything randomly. We were lucky, sure, but we were smart too. And we never did something without thinking it out first. Not if we had the time to think.

And then I think about that other day.

The day I will never tell Dr. Ghosh about.

Or anyone else.

I am the only person still alive to remember that day, and I guess I tried to get rid of that evidence too.

We weren't on a run.

We were on a leave.

Off the base.

Sam wanted to get out. Have a conversation with someone not in Kalsu. Maybe a meal. But we were strung out. Three guys killed that week. Doing what we did. Could have been us. We pretended like it couldn't have been, like we would have seen something, sensed it, but when you've fucked with ninety-one IEDs, you value two things: care and luck.

Yeah, we were careful. Nobody was more careful than Sam and me.

But we were lucky too. And that's what we didn't talk about. Couldn't talk about. Because after ninety-one live ones, after enough guys die around you, you know that you don't own luck. You know that luck runs out.

So there we were. In this dust-bit dirty market that served as the center of the village. We were paying attention, of course. We knew they hated us. Roles reversed, we would have hated them.

But even though they hated us, they loved us too. Especially their kids. We had candy in our pockets, and Sam had this damn yo-yo. He was some kind of yo-yo champion back home. Ever heard of that? A yo-yo champion? Well, if you're from Wisconsin, it's possible. So he'd get this beat-up wooden Duncan going—really fast—and as soon as he knew he had some kids hooked, staring at him from doorways and tent flaps and things, he'd start doing tricks. Obvious stuff—around the arm, under the leg—and then stuff you've never seen a yo-yo do. Faster and faster—he had this extralong string—and all the time with this goofy spaced-out look on his face. Like he was in some other world. Like when he had that yo-yo going, he might have been in Wisconsin, or Nirvana, or God knows where. Sam usually looked stern, but when he messed around with a yo-yo, in the market, knowing the kids would be watching—hell, not just the kids, everyone—he blissed out.

I liked watching him too. But I hated that blissed-out stare. It didn't fit with the Sam I knew, the one I trusted. I was always on double alert when Sam was like that, because he didn't seem to be on alert at all, and I needed to keep it together for both of us.

So maybe it makes sense what happened.

A bad week. Me on double alert. In the market. None of our guys around.

There was a shout. Someone yelled something—I thought he said Allah, which scared the hell out of me—and then he came tearing at us, at everybody watching Sam. And something was on fire. He had a torch, or his shirt was on fire, I still don't know which. I don't know if he was attacking us or just trying to get some help because he somehow caught fire. People screamed, everyone was moving. I had my gun out, I was trying to see the man, trying to see what he was doing—fast, you got to think fast. And then I saw him.

The kid.

Ten, maybe eleven.

Looked like all the rest of them. Huge eyes. Thin.

And he was carrying something. A bag. Very gingerly. And I saw him look at the man, I saw that he knew him; he was so calm, he knew why the man was running. The kid had this bag, and he was headed straight for Sam. And I saw it. Everything had slowed down. My mind was crystal clear. I could see it all so perfectly.

The man was a decoy. The boy had a bomb. And he was headed for Sam.

"LUIS. ARE YOU AWAKE? IT'S Dr. Ghosh."

I'm awake. I roll over. I'm not mad anymore. I don't know why I was mad. But I am a little startled that he walked in right then. Just then. He can't read my thoughts, but sometimes it feels like he can. It feels like they might just beam out of my head and straight into his. And that makes me nervous.

"Hi, Dr. Ghosh."

"Luis, the nurse tells me your physical therapy is going well. You're working hard. I'm impressed."

"Yeah, well there's not that much else to do. Did you notice?"

"Yeah, I noticed." He smiles, as if I've said something funny. So it occurs to me that Dr. Ghosh's job probably isn't that much fun—talking to guys like me—and I give him credit for smiling when he gets the chance.

"Luis, I want to ask you about that kid again. The one you talked about when you were still unconscious. Have you remembered anything about him?"

Man, this guy does not give up.

That's what I mean about him reading my thoughts. I must have yelled about a lot of things when I was knocked out. How does he know to focus on that kid?

Well, Dr. Ghosh may think that he's smart, and maybe he even thinks I'm some dumb spic, but he isn't smart enough to get that out of me.

AFTER I SHOT, NOTHING HAPPENED like I thought it would. People started to scream, and Sam came out of his blissed-out yo-yo trance, and I yelled, "Get back! He's got a bomb!" Then the kid's mother ran right up to him, him and the bag, and collapsed over the top of him, and nothing blew. Nothing blew but my mind and that crowd and that mom.

And then some guy dropped down next to the two of them, holding the mom, trying to get to the kid. And he grabbed the bag. Held it up.

"This? This! Is a bomb?" He spoke English. He yelled right at me.

And he dumped the bag out.

And Sam, who hadn't even seemed to react to the guy on fire, just like that, he had his gun out, and he was pointing it, at the man, at everyone, and yelling, "This didn't happen! This didn't happen! This did not happen!"

And then he was grabbing me, and we were running, and we were back in the Humvee. We didn't go back to Kalsu, we didn't go back until the last possible minute of our leave. We drove all the way around to another village. Got out. Bought something. Sam did his yo-yo thing. Made eyes at some girl, enough so that some guy—her brother, maybe—came out and gave Sam a shove. Sam said, "Hey!"

And the whole time, I was shaking like a madman. I was shaking so hard that my teeth banged together and hurt for days. We didn't talk. We didn't say a damn word about what had just happened. There was a minute where Sam touched my arm. Just touched it and held his fingers there, and I think I stopped shaking. But then he let go, and the shaking started again.

Sam didn't react when the guy shoved him—the brother or uncle or whatever the hell he was. He didn't react, but he looked at the girl again. And the guy shoved him again. Then Sam was done.

It took me a while to figure out why Sam took those two shoves. I'd never seen him eye a girl wearing a *hijab,* and I'd never seen him take two shoves.

Sam and I were smart. And we were careful. And we didn't do anything without thinking about it first.

"LUIS. THERE'S ANOTHER BOY I want to talk to you about."

Boy. Dr. Ghosh had never used the word *boy* before. He used the word *kid,* which is the one I use, the one I must have used when I was unconscious. What does he know? What did I say?

"Yeah." I say it slowly, like I don't care, like I haven't noticed he used the word *boy.* Dr. Ghosh is smart. He knows he used *boy* for the first time.

"This is a boy who wrote you a letter. Do you remember that?"

Now I am confused, because I don't know anything about a boy and a letter. Dr. Ghosh must see this on my face, because he says, "You got the letter just before the accident. Just before you got hurt. Have you remembered anything about that day?"

I don't remember that day. I remember the fact. I remember that I shot myself. But that's it. Weird, huh? Like, why would I be sure I did that if I couldn't remember anything about doing it?

But I don't.

There was the time before I knew why I was in the hospital, when I was trying to figure out what Dr. Ghosh meant that someone had shot me, and then there was just the knowledge. I had shot myself. And I had done it with a .22. Which isn't even an Army issue.

And Dr. Ghosh and I talked about that too. When I told him that I had remembered, I told him that I remembered the information but not the event. He said that was pretty typical, and that I might never remember, or I might, and I should just talk to him about it if I wanted. I could bring it up whenever it came up, so to speak.

And he didn't seem to care about the gun. Where I got it. Why I used it. Dr. Ghosh didn't seem to think that was part of the story.

"Yes, Luis, you got a letter. From a young boy in Las Vegas. It was a school project in his third-grade class, I believe. To write to soldiers from Nevada."

I don't remember.

I don't remember anything about this letter. And I am wondering why Dr. Ghosh is bringing it up. What difference it makes. Last Christmas, we got boxes of stuff from people in Las Vegas. The Blue Ribbon Moms sent us stockings filled with coffee and licorice and socks.

"The thing is, Luis, you got a letter from this little boy. And you answered him. You wrote him a letter back, and you put it in the post. And then you shot yourself."

So that's why Dr. Ghosh is interested in that letter.

Because I wrote the boy back.

What did I write to him?

I can't remember anything about this. What would I have written?

Did I send a suicide note to an eight-year-old kid? The thought makes me queasy real fast, and my head just starts pounding. I can't stand it. I sort of gasp. And I look around for the button that calls the nurse. And then Dr. Ghosh is standing next to me, and he's holding my hand, and he says, "Luis, it's okay. It's okay, Luis. We're not going to talk about this right now. I am going to sit here, and you can rest. I'll have the nurse give you more for the pain."

And so I close my eyes. And my heart is beating. And my head feels like it has come off my body, it's the size of this room, but I keep my eyes closed, and I don't move, and I don't think about anything. Because I might be about to die, right here. No .22 needed. That's how much it hurts. That's how crazy my body is going.

11

Avis

I SWING BY NATE and Lauren's house about two. They need some glasses for a party they are having, and I have promised to leave them on their doorstep. Jim and Nate biked the Red Rock loop over the weekend and stopped to hike into Icebox Canyon. We used to love to take Nate and his friends on this hike, when they were big enough to manage the boulders and to follow the stream of water into the narrowing rock walls, until the sky was just a sliver of azure and the world the width of a hallway. If we hiked long enough, we came to a waterfall crashing over the mottled sandstone above and into a stone basin. Nate and his friends would splash there, and sitting at that clear pool of water in the desert on Sunday, Nate had gotten upset, angry that Jim wanted to sell the house.

I have to admit, hearing that made me feel good. On the night we told Nate about the separation, I thought he blamed me. He said something to Jim about giving me another chance, a comment that was still burning in me, so to hear that he had stood up for me yesterday pleased me. It's hard not to want Nate to be angry at Jim.

I AM SURPRISED TO SEE Nate's door standing open when I pull up. I get one of the boxes out of the trunk and call his name as I head up the walk. Nobody answers, but I hear a sound as if something has fallen.

Then I am in the doorway, shocked by the scene before me.

"Nate, what are you doing? Stop!"

Nate has Lauren in a vise grip. His hand is squeezed so tightly around her wrist that I wait to hear the snap. His other hand is in her hair, pulling her head sideways. She is oddly silent, intent on getting free, or on not antagonizing him further, or maybe even on not letting me know how much pain she is in.

"Stop it. Nate, stop it!"

My shouts make it worse. He begins to pull and squeeze harder, in rhythm to my voice.

I silence myself. Breathe deep.

"Let her go. I am calling 911."

I set down the box and hold up my phone. I am too far away for him to hang on to her and reach for my phone. I know what Nate is thinking. He will lose any chance at the police force if I make this call. I can almost see him making the calculation: *she will not make the call, she will not risk me losing my job—or will she?*

Lauren's hair is pulled tight across her temple, and her eyes are creased in pain. I shake the phone at him, my mouth tight. I feel a little like I did when he was three, refusing to climb down from the monkey gym, or eleven, threatening to walk out the door. Which doesn't make any sense. Because Nate grew up a long time ago.

Nate stares back at me. Something in his eyes makes me afraid. I am not sure he is going to let go. What is he thinking? Does he have control?

With a shake, he releases her. Lauren sinks to the couch, tears spurting out. Nate turns on me.

"Who the hell do you think you are, walking in our house without knocking? Don't walk in my house again!"

It is an absurd response to the situation. His door was standing wide open. Anyone could have heard what was going on in here.

WHEN NATE WAS FOUR YEARS old, Jim signed him up for a soccer team. I had never played soccer, and neither had Jim. The flyer said, "No special equipment. Wear tennis shoes and gym shorts. Shirt provided." The shirt was a navy blue uniform with a white 6 and the words "Las Vegas Parks and Recreation" on the back. I think we must have ten photos of him in that first uniform shirt.

But the team was a disaster. After the first game, Nate wouldn't kick the ball. He wouldn't even get near the kids kicking the ball. I offered him a dime for every time he kicked it, but Nate, who was a pretty tough little four-year-old, stayed away. Of course, the coach was very nice about it. He said that some boys aren't ready for team sports, may never be. Jim and I asked Nate why he didn't kick the ball, but all he said was "I don't want to." He used to suck his thumb on the way home from games, which was a habit I thought he had dropped.

And it wasn't that we hadn't noticed that every other child had on special soccer shoes and shin guards. We did notice. But this equipment was optional, and Nate didn't seem to like soccer, so we thought we were being moderate in not rushing out to buy professional equipment for a preschooler. And it wasn't until the end-of-the-season picnic, when the coach had the parents play the children, and one of those four-year-olds kicked me in the leg with a tiny cleat, that I figured it out. That's a true story. It never occurred to me that Nate needed those shin guards.

Nate never did tell us when he was hurt. Where did he get that idea? That he couldn't tell us if something hurt?

I STEP OVER THE BOX of glasses and make my way toward Lauren. Nate jerks forward, and for an instant, I think that he is going to grab me. Like that, I am a little girl—three? five?—and a man is holding my arm, digging his fingers into my skin, yanking my shoulder backward.

"Don't you ever touch my coat again, you little shit. I better not catch you near my things."

Then Sharlene is there, shrieking, and he is yelling at her. He lets me go, and I run, the opened pack of Life Savers from his coat pocket still in my hand.

Nate jerks, but he doesn't touch me. He passes by on my right, and as he heads out the door, he says, "Dad was right to leave you" in a voice so filled with hate it makes me feel weak.

I SEE NATE. SEVEN OR eight years old. A stocky child, wearing blue jeans and a brown football jersey. Bare feet. Jim is punting a football to him across a sun-filled park, and the ball sails up and up very fast, and Nate is at the other end of its arc, waiting to catch it, fairly dancing on those bare, fat toes, and trembling with delight and fear. Will he catch it? Will it hurt? And at first he doesn't catch it. He fails valiantly. Throwing himself to the ground beneath the ball, stretching his arms out far. But I know Nate, and I know he is deliberately coming up short. He is afraid that it will hurt.

And then he does it. He dives down, arms extended, no hesitation, and he catches the punt. And up he pops, like a marionette, and yells over and over, "I caught it! I caught it!" The delight in his voice, in his body, as he races all the way back across the park with the ball, to dance into Jim's chest, yelling, "I caught it, I caught it!" His arms lift the ball high, tugging his shirt up, exposing his belly. Everyone in the park can hear him. The absolute delight of a seven-year-old boy who has met his own hope.

"Mom, did you see it? Did you see me? I caught it! It went way in the air, and I had to fall to the ground, and I caught it!"

That's Nate. That thrilled child is my son. That little boy lifted in the air by his father and calling to his mother, for all the world to hear. *I did it! I did it! See how happy life makes me.*

I CROSS THE ROOM AND sink down next to Lauren on the couch. My heart is pounding, but as I pull her into my arms, I feel oddly angry. I want to go after Nate, I want to know what is wrong with my son, and I am feeling something like rage at Lauren. Why was she so silent? Why is she still just weeping in my arms?

What is wrong with her?

It is crazy to be angry at Lauren in this moment. I know that. But anger is what I am feeling. When Margo's husband told her that he sometimes had a one-night-stand when he was on a business trip, and that he thought talking about this might make their sex life hotter, she sat in my kitchen and sobbed for weeks. I wanted to shake her. I didn't care if she took the bait and had hot sex with her husband or threw him out on his ear, but that she would sit and cry about it, day after day, drove me crazy.

"MOMMY, WHY DO YOU LET him hit you? Why don't you hit him? Why don't you make him go away?"

"Shut up, Avis. I don't need your shit right now."

"Mommy, Rodney and I can help you. Mark has a gun. Rodney found it. You could use that gun."

"Avis, shut up. What are you doing going through Mark's things? Do you want to get us killed? Do you?"

I DON'T LET LAUREN KNOW I am angry. I sit and hold her. I stroke her hair, and I tell her I am sorry. I am good at comforting people, no matter what I am thinking. I could comfort Rodney, when he was such a little boy, and I could comfort Sharlene. I just take them in my arms, and I do not talk.

JIM AND I LET NATE get away with too much. I didn't have the slightest idea what a mother should do with a son. My basic idea was not to be Sharlene and not to have Nate turn out like Rodney. It wasn't much to go on. Compared to the other kids in the neighborhood, Nate did get in a lot of trouble. He got detention after school, had to run laps after practice, had to be grounded on the weekend. It all seemed mild to me. By the time it occurred to me that maybe Nate's small rebellions were more significant than I thought, things had already gone too far.

I HEAR NATE KICK SOMETHING in the side yard, and I hear the iron fence squeal open, and I hear the sound of his boot against the motorcycle stand. The motor chokes, then catches, and the bike roars onto the street.

"Mom?" Lauren says. "He was really upset today. He's been upset since he and Jim went biking on Sunday. And he's drinking. Just beer, but when he drinks, he . . ."

I can guess what she is going to say, but I wonder if she will be able to say it.

" . . . he scares me when he drinks."

Her voice catches. I stroke her hair. I think about Sharlene, holding clumps of hair in her hand, and crying, *he pulled out my hair, he pulled out my fucking hair.* I think that I would have killed Jim if he had ever pulled my hair, I think that Jim would never have pulled my hair, I think that Jim now loves Darcy.

IT MATTERED TO ME THAT Nate had so many friends in high school. I didn't have friends in high school. I started working at the Four Queens when I was fourteen. I carried sacks of change to the cashier and wrapped up keno tickets in rubber bands. I got tips from the regulars, and the tips were bigger at night, so by fifteen, I would usually work until one or two in the morning. It might have been Vegas, but nobody I knew in school worked in a casino. I suppose the ones that did dropped out pretty early. But I loved school. I just tried to keep my two lives separate: there was Sharlene and Rodney and the casino, the drunk men, the tips, my mother's affairs. And there was school. Where the PE teachers wanted me to try out for a team. And the US history teacher wrote me a college recommendation letter I hadn't even asked for. Where nobody knew.

Nate's high school years were different, of course. He and his friends scaled rock walls at Valley of Fire, skied off-run at Mount Charleston, played Fugitive along the train tracks, held midnight volleyball tournaments at the park down the road. When they went to a dance, they went in a big group, in a party bus, and someone's dad always figured out how to get them cheap prices for *Mystère* or *Blue Man Group*, and someone's mom always offered her basement for the party after. These things meant so much to me. I used to list Nate's activities in my head—all these normal high school things that my son did—like a nursery rhyme.

Of course, Nate was drinking at those parties. We never even talked about it. Beer seemed like a tame sort of rebellion to me. I had a son who was having an all-American childhood; I had won.

"HOW LONG HAS THIS BEEN happening, Lauren?"

She makes a sort of moan and pushes away from me. She doesn't look at me as she speaks.

"He's been different since he came back. Since last December."

December? This has been going on for a year?

Of course, I know what she means by different. I knew the instant I hugged him in the airport that time, that little course of energy through his body, that slight shiver. I knew the last deployment had been bad.

"Since December?"

"Well, not this. Not what happened today. This . . . this hasn't happened for very long."

I think about the bruise I saw on her shoulder the night Nate was sworn in. Why didn't I ask her then?

"I mean . . . he just, he's just nervous. A lot of times, he's really nervous. And I feel like I have to tiptoe around. I thought he was sad, but lately he gets angry. He gets angry so fast."

I look at Lauren's slight frame. I think about my son's fit body. It's frightening to me; what must it be like for her?

THE ACCIDENT HAPPENED THE SUNDAY night after one of those high school dances. The story was that there was some alcohol left. That might have been true. Or Nate and his friends might have been drinking every day by then. I wouldn't have been looking for any signs of this. Nate's world just seemed so safe to me.

Jeremy was driving. Speeding. Drunk. He wound up with seven months in juvenile detention. Paul was paralyzed. When it was all over, Paul could use his thumb and forefinger. I remember that. What a break it was that he had those two digits. Nate was in the backseat. Nothing but a concussion. Jim knew somebody, so it never came out that Nate provided the alcohol. It never came out that he had a guy who regularly bought alcohol for him and that Nate made a business out of reselling alcohol to teenage kids.

If it had, I wonder if they would have let him enlist. I know they wouldn't have let him join the police academy.

"HAVE YOU TOLD ANYONE?"

"No."

"There must be someone on the base. Someone through VA services?"

"Yeah, maybe."

"They won't put him on the force if they find out. He won't get through probation."

"I know."

What am I saying? Do I want my daughter-in-law to get professional help or not?

I don't know what I am saying. I am wondering if Jim knows someone, if Jim could persuade Nate to talk to someone. I am wondering if Jim can be persuaded to take time off from Darcy for this.

"I'll talk to Nate. And I'll talk to Jim. We'll figure this out. We'll figure it out, Lauren."

She curls back into my shoulder then. I keep stroking her hair, wondering what I am saying. Can we figure this out? Do we have time? Should I be calling the police?

AFTER THE CAR ACCIDENT, THE parties stopped, and the friends stopped hanging out in our family room. Paul's mother told me that Nate stopped by nearly every day after school, to see if Paul had done his therapy or if she needed help hoisting him into his exercise apparatus. I've always been grateful to Paul's mother for telling me that. She could have kept that to herself. She knew where the alcohol came from.

I STAY WITH LAUREN ANOTHER hour, until she decides that she will spend the night with her friend Ashley. Nate does not come home, and Jim does not respond to the text I send. I am not ready to call Nate, so I write him a note and leave it in an envelope on the table. I tell him to call me, that we have to talk, that changes have to be made. I tell him that his dad and I are ready to help him, and Lauren. I wonder if he will call. I wonder how a mother makes a grown son do anything.

NATE PLAYED BASEBALL FROM THE age of six. I must have sat on rickety metal stands—so hot for five months of the year that bare flesh burned on contact—and watched him play in a thousand innings. A little boy, squinting back tears after getting hit by the pitch. An eight-year-old, being chastised by the umpire for throwing his bat. A ten-year-old, stealing second, and then third, delighted. All those little boys, all those uniforms, all those games.

"Come on, Nate! Eye on the ball. Watch the ball."

"Nate, it's okay. Everybody has a tough game. You'll get the next one."

"Way to go Nate! That ball was a rope!"

"I knew you were going to catch it! I could just tell by the look on your face that you had that thing."

How could that little boy with the SeaDogs cap now be the man brutally twisting his wife's wrist, grabbing her hair, yanking back her head? How did those images go together?

12

Bashkim

TODAY IS WEDNESDAY, BUT it is the last day of school because tomorrow is Thanksgiving. And we are having an assembly. I love assemblies. At my school, we always have morning assembly for the little kids, and afternoon assembly for the older kids. That's because the multipurpose room is too small for 742 students plus teachers. The fire department has a sign on the door that says, "Maximum Capacity: 280 Persons." I think I am the only person that has ever read this sign, because even if we have two assemblies, we still have more than 280 persons in the room. I don't even have to figure out the problem, because I can do 300 plus 300 in my head, and that is only 600. Three hundred is more than 280, and six hundred is a lot less than 742 students, plus teachers, so I think that we should have three assemblies.

But I don't say that, because it is not the kind of thing Orson Hulet students say, and because I heard Mrs. Monaghan telling another teacher that I worry a lot. I don't want her to know that I am worried about this too. Mrs. Monaghan likes us to solve our own problems, so I solve this one by trading spots with my friend Carlo. That puts me close to the door, and if something happens, I have already figured out that I will yell to Carlo to follow me, and then I will head straight for that door. Even if it is black dark because of smoke, I know where the door is. It is about twenty-five steps behind me, plus two steps right. If I bump into something, I waited too long to step right, because there is a little wall right near the door. Also, I will keep yelling Carlo's name, so he hears which way to go. I think about whether I should leave Carlo close to the door, but he hasn't planned any escape, so he might just run in the wrong direction anyway. It is better if I know where we should both go.

THE REASON I LIKE ASSEMBLIES is because they are not all boring. First, every class sits in its own section. The teachers sit in chairs, and the kids sit on the floor. We are supposed to get in our sections quickly. The principal stands up front, and she holds two fingers in the air. As soon as she does that, we are all supposed to hold two fingers in the air and be real quiet. It's kind of funny, because somebody always forgets to look at the principal and keeps talking when everyone else is quiet. And it's kind of not funny, because I don't ever want to be the kid who keeps talking.

After we are all quiet, some fifth graders walk the flags to the front. There is an American flag, and a Nevada flag, and four flags with words on them: Effort, Respect, Honesty, Kindness. Those are important words at Orson Hulet. And then we sing a song. Usually we sing "America the Beautiful," but today some kindergartners come in, and they sing a song about Thanksgiving. Which is pretty good for little kids, but I think my class sang it better when we were in kindergarten.

The best part about today's assembly is that Mr. Loomis, the music teacher, is going to do some magic for us. Mr. Loomis is a real-life magician. He has a show on the Strip, at the Hard Rock casino. Alyssa says we can't go to it because you have to be eighteen years old to get in. She knows, because she asked her mom to take her. I don't know why Mr. Loomis teaches us music if he has a magic show at a casino, but he does. In music class, Mr. Loomis is a little bit cross, but at an assembly, he is so funny.

Today Mr. Loomis has a bowling ball. He throws it up in the air and catches it. It is very heavy. Then he tries to spin it on his finger, but it doesn't work, and it falls on the ground. *Boom.* Everyone jumps. Mr. Loomis puts his toe on the ball, and he just looks at it. Then he puts his finger on his eyebrow, and makes a face at the ball. All the kids are laughing because we know Mr. Loomis is going to do something funny.

He takes off his hat. Then he sets the hat on the floor, sideways, and rolls the ball into it, very slowly. When he lifts up his hat, the bowling ball looks like it is going to drop right out the bottom. Then Mr. Loomis looks at us, and he makes another face. He looks at the hat. He looks at us. He looks worried. And then, bam, quick, he slams the hat on his head with the bowling ball still in it. The ball is so heavy, it makes Mr. Loomis's knees buckle, and he says, "Ouch!"

We are all laughing.

Later Mr. Loomis gets out a big sketchpad and a black marker. He asks us kids what he should draw, and we all yell out, "A dog!" "An elephant!" "The Eiffel Tower!" and stuff like that. And Mr. Loomis draws what we yell out. Then he has some kids from the front come up and reach into his pockets. And they pull out the things he has already drawn on the sketchpad!

How does he do that? It is so cool, and we are all laughing, and I am wondering if Mr. Loomis will ever call me up to the front, and then Mr. Loomis gets a funny look on his face. He puts his finger to his eyebrow again. And he walks all over, like he's looking for something. We are all wondering what he is looking for. We ask him, but he doesn't answer us.

He just takes out the sketchpad and draws a bowling ball. So, of course, we start yelling, "It's in your hat! Look in your hat!" Mr. Loomis keeps walking around, pretending he can't hear us. So we are all going crazy, and some of the teachers stand up to remind us that we cannot get too wild. So we keep yelling, but quieter, and Mr. Loomis just can't figure it out. He keeps looking and looking.

And then he takes out his sketchpad again, and he points at the bowling ball. And we yell, "Your hat!" And he keeps pretending he doesn't hear us, and then finally, when we are about to go insane with trying to get him to look in his hat, he mouths, "My hat?" And we say, "Yes, your hat!" And Mr. Loomis—this is so funny—he draws a hat next to the bowling ball. "Oh no," we are all thinking. And then Mr. Loomis—this is why I like assemblies so much—Mr. Loomis takes the sketchpad, and he shakes it real hard. *Boom!* The bowling ball drops right out of the sketchpad and onto the floor. We go crazy. Mr. Loomis stops the bowling ball from rolling with his toe again, and then he takes off his hat to show us that it is empty. And bows.

It is the coolest thing I have ever seen. Nene isn't even going to believe me when I tell her. I wish I could be a magician. I wonder if a magician makes enough money to buy a house. I am going to buy a house for Nene. If I were the Hard Rock casino, I would pay Mr. Loomis a lot of money.

AFTER THE ASSEMBLY, WE ONLY have an hour until the end of the day, so Mrs. Monaghan says we might as well have a talent show. Mrs. Monaghan says that anybody who has a talent and wants to share it may do so. When Carrie asks if she can practice first, Mrs. Monaghan says no, this is a spontaneous talent show, which none of us has ever heard of before. Mrs. Monaghan says she will go first.

I wonder what Mrs. Monaghan's talent is. It turns out, she can dance a jig. She says she learned this in summer camp in Australia. "When is summer in Australia?" Mrs. Monaghan asks. "In the winter!" we yell back, because this is one of her favorite questions to ask us about Australia. Then she dances her jig, which looks just like Albanian dancing, but I don't tell her this.

Some of the girls can also dance jigs, or something like them, so they all get up and do this for us. Mrs. Monaghan has an iPod player in her room, so she lets the girls pick a song called "Hot N Cold," and they all dance, and since it's a spontaneous talent show, it looks a little bit like everybody just doing what they want. Listening to "Hot N Cold" makes some of the other girls want to sing "So What," and Mrs. Monaghan has this on her iPod, so they do that too. Carlo says it is time for a boy to show a talent, so he demonstrates his jumping ability. He jumps straight up a bunch of times, and then Mrs. Monaghan lets him move the table in the front, so he can jump out too. Carlo is a very good jumper. Then Danny says he is a good drummer, so Mrs. Monaghan lets him show off his drumming on the desks. He doesn't have drumsticks or anything, but it is still pretty good.

I think this is the best day I have ever had at school, and I wish that it wasn't going to be Thanksgiving so soon. Mrs. Monaghan asks me if I want to say something in Albanian, for my talent, but I say no. She doesn't mind, and then Araceli and Ricky say that they want to speak in Spanish, so we listen to their talent. When Dr. Moore comes in to tell Mrs. Monaghan that we earned a party next month for getting the most "Good job" stickers from all the specials teachers, we say, "Can we have a talent show party again?" Mrs. Monaghan says yes, we can have a talent show party. And Dr. Moore says that she will supply the pizza and cupcakes, so we all leave for Thanksgiving break happy.

THANKSGIVING IS NOT AN ALBANIAN holiday, so we don't have turkey dinner at my house. Before Tirana was born, we used to go to Thanksgiving at Catholic Charities Refugee Center, and I still remember what stuffing and cranberries taste like. I don't know why we don't go there anymore, except one year the mayor came, and Baba doesn't like mayors. Baba also doesn't like holidays if it means there is no business for the ice-cream truck, but he likes Thanksgiving because there is a big soccer tournament on the other side of town, and Nene got us a permit so we can sell ice cream there. We don't actually have to sell anything on Thursday, but we spend that day cleaning up the truck and filling it extra full with ice-cream treats.

You might think that people don't want ice cream at Thanksgiving, but Las Vegas is hot, and especially if you are playing soccer. There aren't very many places to eat by those soccer fields, so we sell a lot of ice cream to people who wish we would sell hot dogs or something. We can't sell hot dogs because that takes a different kind of license, and Baba doesn't like licenses. Sometimes Nene says that we should get a lunch truck, but Baba says that she should not trust America so much.

Anyway, we will be really busy all weekend. I don't think kids mind having ice-cream treats for lunch, not as much as grown-ups. We all have to be there, even Tirana, who is kind of a lot of work, but there is no one to watch her at home, and Baba and Nene need my help.

This year, our truck is facing Field D, so we can watch the games a little bit. I have never played soccer, though I have a soccer ball, and Baba sometimes kicks it to me in the park. He says he is an old man, and can't play *futbolli* anymore, but he is really quick. He can kick it with either foot, and he switches his feet so fast, I can't find the ball when I am trying to get it. Baba loves soccer. He keeps yelling at the players on Field D.

"Hey, you, number three! Go up the left! Use your left foot. Go up the left!"

He yells so loud that it surprises the people coming to buy something at the ice-cream truck, but I don't think the boys on the field can hear it. I hope not, because they look about my age, and I don't want it to be someone I know from school. Lots of kids at Orson Hulet play soccer.

If I were on a soccer team, I would like to be a striker. That's the person who shoots the goals, and everybody always likes the striker. Even if the striker misses, everyone just yells for him to try again. I wouldn't want to be a back, because everybody gets mad at those guys. They can block ten shots, but if they miss one, everyone is upset. I would hate to be a back or a goalie, because it would just make me feel sick.

"Hey, what are you doing selling ice cream? Why aren't you playing soccer?"

The man's badge says Coach, and he seems nice, so I think he says this because maybe he is a big soccer fan like Baba. But my baba thinks he is being critical.

"He cannot play futbolli with these rich kids," my baba says. "He has job. For his family."

My baba does not realize that I do not want him to explain these things to the coach. The coach looks uncomfortable too, and he puts an extra dollar on the counter. My baba thinks that this is a good way to make more money, so all afternoon, he keeps talking about me.

"This boy, he could be a great futbolli player. But he is working for his family. He has too many responsibilities to play futbolli like rich kids."

We do seem to get more tips when Baba says these things, so there is no possibility that he will stop, but I am having a bad day. People keep looking at me, which I hate, and then they look like they feel sorry for me, which I hate even more, and I am just waiting, all day, to go home.

Nene knows that I am having a hard time, but there isn't much she can do. The truck is really small, and if she says something to Baba about my feelings, he might yell at her. And we all know that when Baba yells at Nene in the truck, we don't sell any ice cream.

So I stay away from the window as far as I can, and I make sure that the freezer drawers have all the different treats in them, and I play with Tirana, so she will not get too bored or cranky. My nene does one amazing thing. She slips me a dollar, which someone must have given to her when Baba was not looking, and I put it in my shoe. It doesn't really make me feel better, but I know she wants it to. That's the part that makes me feel a little better.

13

Luis

DR. GHOSH SAYS THAT human beings under stress are capable of extraordinary things: some good and some bad. There are people who have lifted cars in the air to save someone being crushed after an accident, and people who have survived days treading water after a shipwreck. There are also people who have drowned their own children or set themselves afire because they just couldn't bear what Dr. Ghosh calls the "physical, emotional, psychological, and spiritual" stress of certain experiences.

I memorized that list: physical, emotional, psychological, and spiritual. Because that's true. What happened to me was all those things, all at once. I don't even know which was most important. You're physically wrecked when you're downrange. It's hot, it's dusty. Man, the dust in Kalsu is unbelievable. It gets everywhere: in your mouth, in your ears, in the skin of your neck. It's in your equipment and in your food and in your bed. Nothing you eat tastes like anything you've ever eaten before anyway. Your CHU is like a tin closet, and it echoes. And you're constantly going from complete inactivity to chaos. You're either bored out of your mind or waiting to lose your mind to some homemade explosive.

And the spiritual piece. That's tricky. A lot of guys pray. We even got a Muslim in my unit, and he prays five times a day. At first the guys didn't like it. They said we were in this country because of the Muslims. But it's different now. You spend all that time together, you get close. These guys would die for me, and I would die for them. What does it matter what name someone uses for God? At first I felt a little weird about the evangelicals praying to Jesus, like Jesus was different from God. I'm Catholic, so we're careful about stuff like that. But then there's this guy named Eric, who's Jewish, and he told me it made him feel weird that Catholics talk about God like he has a human body.

Some guys get religious in a war, but other guys start being against religion. That's kind of how Sam and I were. I prayed a lot, but Sam could hardly stand anyone praying. We didn't talk about this. I didn't pray in front of him, or at least not so he could tell, and he didn't say too much stuff about religion in front of me. When you're in a combat zone with someone, you stop focusing on how you're different. The only way anyone is going to survive is with help from each other. That's the real religion.

Dr. Ghosh says it will help if I can start to recognize the signs of stress in my life. I guess I'm pretty violent in my sleep, and some nights they tie my arms so that I don't rip out my tubes or damage the equipment or something. I know that I am having nightmares at night, but I don't remember them. Dr. Ghosh says that I should try to remember, when I first wake up, and he says the nightmares might be really bad, but it will still help if I remember them and talk about them.

It's strange. I like Dr. Ghosh. But a lot of what he thinks I should do is the exact opposite of everything I needed to do to survive. I would have been dead months ago if I started thinking about my nightmares. If I thought about anything other than what the mission was, how to survive it, what were all the ways I could die that day. If you're not thinking like that, if you're not ready to do whatever you need to do to live, you aren't going to make it downrange. You're just not. That's what folks back home don't get. When you're there, you're living every single second with the possibility of an IED shooting nails and barbed wire through your head, with the chance that some maniac is going to use his vehicle as a weapon, with the reality that it could be a woman, an old man, a little kid. You don't know what's going to come at you, 24/7.

And when you're in that situation, it's bad. It's really bad. But parts of it are weirdly good too. Like, you always know what the priorities are. Survival. Being there for your squad. There's a bunch of little shit, like who prays to who or who eats what, that guys might talk about—they might jaw about just to release some stress—but nobody cares about it. When you're in a combat zone, you know what's important and what's not. And the most important thing is what you will do for the guys around you and what they will do for you. That, and that you never let up, you never relax.

Which is the one thing I never figured out about Sam and that yo-yo. Because if there's any guy over here who never let up, who never forgot what could happen, it was Sam. But when he got that yo-yo out, he did let up. And he did it on purpose. Maybe he knew he was still on, somewhere. Maybe he just had to let it go sometime, and he figured he'd rather die doing that than anything else available to do over there.

You gotta be able to react—no hesitation—if you want to live. If you want to have a good shot at living. Otherwise, it's just dumb luck. And luck always runs out. This is what Sam and I figured out about each other on a mission. We both could make a decision fast and stick to it. Hesitation kills.

So Dr. Ghosh says now I should start thinking about my nightmares. Noticing what gets me upset during the day. What the triggers are. I don't know. That's going to be hard to do. He says the nightmares and the yelling and whatever else I do at night is not crazy. Even the way I get really angry during the day, sometimes over stupid stuff, I know it's stupid, but I just can't help it. There are noises these nurses make that kill me, I cannot stand this cart thing they have. Dr. Ghosh says all of that is the opposite of crazy. It's a normal response to how I have been living. But it is isn't going to work when I get out of this hospital, and I came damn close to killing myself—as close as you can get without doing it—and so I need to figure out what the triggers are before I try something like that again.

It's nice when Dr. Ghosh says stuff like that. Like it matters to him. What I do. What happens to me. It feels nice and then it feels bad. Maybe that's a trigger too. Someone acting half decent.

Dr. Ghosh worries about me trying suicide again. I can't imagine it. It's not like you can pop a soda can twice. It pops the first time, and then whether or not you pulled it open, the explosion has happened. That's me. I popped. And now, what's left in me is really bad, and maybe it will even build up again, but it's not about to pop. That's not what I feel like: someone about to pop. Maybe I feel like someone who *is* popped. But how would Dr. Ghosh know that?

DR. GHOSH SAYS I WROTE a letter to an eight-year-old kid in Nevada. Damn. That's a young kid. I was still sleeping next to my abuela's bed in third grade. I would go to sleep in my bed, but in the middle of the night, I would go into my abuela's room, and curl up on the floor with a blanket and pillow. I did that for years. I know I was still doing it in third grade. She should have stopped me. I was too old for that. Even though I never even remembered walking in there. I just always woke up on the floor. My abuela didn't talk about it at all. She just woke me up when it was time for school, and I carried my blanket and pillow back to my room.

Thinking about waking up, on the floor there, it's making me feel really strange. I wish I could wake up there right now. I wish I were eight years old, and my abuela was waking me up, and all I had to do was take my blanket and my Superman pillow back to my room. I wish my abuela were downstairs, humming her bad music, making me some huevos. I wish I were eight. I wish I'd never grown up. I wish I could do it over again. Do this last year over again. I want to take it back. I don't want to be a man who killed a kid. I don't want to be the man who didn't get killed, when Sam did. I don't know how I can live with that. I don't know what I'm supposed to do with it. I don't know how to get out of this body, this life. My abuela would never believe what I've done. I could never tell her. I'm never going to tell anyone. But what do I do with it? Why can't I take it back?

How could an instant change everything? One thought. One instinctive reaction. I can't take it back. I'd give anything to take it back. It doesn't seem possible that I tried so hard to do the right thing, to do my job, to do it well, to be a good soldier. I wanted to be a good soldier. I was a good soldier. And then one split-second fraction of an instant, and everything is different. And I can't fix it. I can't change it. I can't get that kid back. I can't help that mother. I hear her crying at the back of my mind all the time. I can hear her wailing. How much she hurts. How much she is always going to hurt. There can't be a worse sound in the world. She has lost everything that mattered to her. How could I tell my abuela this? How could I tell my abuela that I'm the man who did this?

Sam knew how crazy it was making me. And he covered for me. For the way I couldn't concentrate, the drinking, what an ass I was making of myself. So is that what happened to Sam? Did I make a mistake? Did I let go for an instant? Long enough for him to get killed? I think that's what I can't remember, why I can't remember, because it's my fault. Because I fucked up, and Sam got killed. It's the logical answer. You can't let up, you can't relax, you can't get distracted. And I had that kid, and that mother crying, in my head all the time. All day, all night. I know I'm the reason Sam is dead. I just can't remember exactly what I did.

Buddy fucker. How am I supposed to live with that?

WHEN YOU'RE A SOLDIER, THE most important thing you can do is take care of your buddy. Because you have to know that your buddy is going to be there for you. Everything is built around that. Starting in basic training. Esprit de corps. Or whatever bullshit French word they want to use for it. And in basic, there are days when you think you will never care a damn what happens to your commanding officer, and then you get to Afghanistan or Iraq, and you care. Man, you care. Sam and I probably never would have even spoken to each other stateside. He really did hate spics. But there, man, that is the closest relationship I have ever had in my life.

And gringos are right about one thing: Mexicans do care about kids. When you're Mexican, children are really important. That's not just for the women. That's for everybody. My parents aren't the best example of that, but my abuela is, and that is how Mexicans are.

So I'm the Mexican who killed an innocent kid, and I'm the soldier who got his buddy fucked. I wish I had killed myself. I wish I hadn't used a .22. I wish I hadn't jerked, or missed, or whatever the hell I did. I wish I felt like I could pop again. Because I don't think I have what it takes to try that again. But I don't know how I am going to live with what I did. I don't see how Dr. Ghosh can make that any better.

And I don't deserve to have it be better.

But how am I supposed to live?

How do I go back to my abuela and Las Vegas now?

And if I do pop again, if I do find a way to get out of this, how is my abuela supposed to live?

14

Avis

LAUREN SAYS NATE READ the note I left, but he never called me, and he didn't answer when I called him. Lauren and I have spoken each day, and from her I know that Nate is back home, that they are "doing better," that Lauren has not yet talked to him about seeing a counselor but "is going to do it." I am uneasy. Nate and Lauren are twenty-seven years old. They're married. What really is my role here?

Is Lauren in danger?

I don't get to Rodney's house until almost ten. I've been wondering if Nate will show up, but as soon as I arrive, I see that the two of them are hard at work already. Boxes litter the square patch of dirt that serves as Rodney's front yard, and Nate's arms are piled high with pieces of Santa's sleigh. Rodney sits at the front door, patiently testing a big mound of light strings in the outdoor socket.

"Nato, what do you think of putting a rocket launcher in Santa's hands this year? Think I'd make the six o'clock if I did that?"

Nate laughs. Rodney has been trying to get featured on the six o'clock news for years. He says he's sick of the uptight folks on Hondo

Court getting all that free press each year. What's wrong with the lights down on West Adams?

And Rodney has big plans for this Christmas. Nate wasn't around to help him with the lights much over the last few years, but now that Nate is back at home permanently, working at the police department no less—which Rodney figures is going to save him a lot of money in driving tickets—my brother is going all out.

There hasn't been any room in the garage for his van in years, and as far as I can tell, he's spent most of this fall's Social Security checks ordering more decorations off the Internet. Rodney won't throw anything out, so the plastic sheet of Disney characters will still cover his garage door, the hundreds of mothy old stuffed animals will still be perched along the edge of the lawn, Nate will still hang the three white-light angels over his front window, the slightly crooked fat snowman will still welcome children coming from the elementary school down the street, and, of course, Santa, his sleigh, and all eight reindeer will still take center stage across the lawn. Most people might think that there really isn't any place to put more decorations, but most people aren't Rodney, and I can tell from the stack of boxes that have never been opened that there is going to be a lot more to look at this year.

NATE HAS BEEN HELPING RODNEY decorate this house since he was four years old. That's the year Rodney and Sharlene moved in, and the year they decided that the tasteful display of white lights at our house was "just too pansy ass" for their boy. Jim stayed out of all that. He helped them get the mortgage on the house, and ten years later, when things were going well, he paid off what was left and gave the deed to Sharlene. Jim did this sort of thing quietly; he didn't, for example, wrap up the deed and present it as a gift. He just mailed it to Sharlene in an envelope, with a note that said she should probably get someone to look at the air-conditioning unit. I found the note when I was helping

Rodney go through our mother's things after she died. I wonder what Sharlene thought of that note, much less the gift. She never mentioned it to me. I only found out because I asked Jim why our tax returns looked different that year.

"You didn't have to do that, Jim. Sharlene and Rodney can take care of themselves."

"It was twenty-two thousand dollars, Avis. It doesn't make sense for them to be paying interest on a mortgage."

"Well, thank you," I said awkwardly.

"Avis, don't thank me. It feels weird for you to thank me."

That's kind of how Jim was with my family. He had this idea about what a man should do, how he should use his money, and he did that. He didn't even think much about it. On the other hand, he didn't really pay attention to what Sharlene or Rodney were doing or how they lived. He didn't seem to worry about their influence on Nate, like I did. He didn't worry about whether they were drinking around Nate or what they talked about with him. If they wanted to put up some really tacky Christmas display for Nate, and if Nate liked it, that was fine with Jim. When Nate was little, Jim would go down to the house on West Adams and examine the lights, the sleigh, the stuffed animals, with him. Once Nate got older, I doubt that Jim even knew whether they were still putting up the lights or not.

RODNEY MAY NOT HAVE WORKED in the last two decades, but he is a professional when it comes to Christmas lights. It takes him and whoever is helping him three days to take the display down in January. Every light set is meticulously returned to its original box and organized in the garage according to the order in which it will be rehung the next year. If I know Rodney, he already has calculated to the last inch where the new decorations will fit in and has a detailed plan for rewiring the whole affair. It's the big event of his year, the thing that everyone knows him for, and as much as I hate the idea of Santa holding a rocket launcher, I have always been glad that Rodney has this.

I LEAVE MY CAR ON the street, where it won't block the garage door, and make my way to the front entrance. I kiss Rodney on the cheek and walk into the yard to give Nate a hug. We embrace awkwardly, given what happened, and I say, "Nate, we have to talk about what happened. I've invited your dad over next weekend, so the four of us can talk."

"Okay. Okay. Mom, I know. I'll call."

"What's the secret?" Rodney yells out. "You making big plans for my Christmas present?"

Rodney is feeling fine. He doesn't look too good—his skin is a pale sort of gray-yellow, and there are deep pouches below his eyes—but he's feeling fine. No doubt there's a flask tucked in the side pocket of his chair.

Rodney switched to a motorized wheelchair about three years ago, and he's aged a lot since. He has a long list of medical problems, partly because he's been in the chair since he was nineteen years old, and partly because he drinks, but also just because he's never really done much. He was a good athlete as a little kid, like I was, but things went downhill quickly for him.

Sharlene let Rodney come home to live after his accident because they were friends. Not just mother and son, but friends. When he was twelve years old, Rodney would sit at the kitchen table with Sharlene, smoking and sharing her whiskey and talking about the shit at the Four Queens just like one of Mom's bar hostess friends. I was sixteen and pretending to be tough and starting to see how life was different for other people—starting to imagine that even I might live another way. I used to yell and tell her that Rodney shouldn't smoke, that he shouldn't drink, that he was just a kid, a skinny kid, who needed his brain cells, but they both laughed at me, and if I kept it up too long, Sharlene got mean. She would ask me if sleeping around was better than drinking and smoking. She knew I had made a mistake, and she knew how much I regretted it. Sharlene could always take care of herself; if it meant cutting her daughter to the quick, she didn't think twice about it.

IN THE END, MAYBE IT worked out that Sharlene and Rodney lived together. She gave up the boyfriends; he made a life for himself on this street, in this house. It wasn't what I wanted for him. If I let myself remember Rodney as he was—a little boy, so sweet, so much sweeter than I was—and then think about how his life turned out, I feel ill, but if I let all those images go, if I forget about all those times that I promised him things would get better, that I would take care of him, that I would not let anyone hurt him, then I think that he is happy enough with his life—as happy as anyone else I know.

Nate has begun to set the largest displays where they will be anchored, and I go in search of the box with the plastic garage door panorama. When Nate was a small boy, the panorama featured Donald Duck stringing Christmas lights around Pluto instead of a Christmas tree. Nate loved that. He laughed every time he looked at it, and he would chatter on about it at dinner. *Do you think Pluto wagged his tail when Donald Duck wrapped the string around it, Mommy? Do you think Pluto eats the lights?* Just thinking about the image would make him laugh.

Rodney let the colors get really faded on that one, since Nate loved it so much, but for quite a few years now, the panorama has featured Mickey and Minnie and Goofy opening a big pile of presents. I find the box, and as is true every year, realize that it is a lot heavier than I am expecting. I tug it toward the garage door and then stop to check that the hooks that hold it are still in place.

Just then, there is the loud sound of lights exploding. Nate yells, and before I even know he has moved, he is throwing me to the ground and pushing his arm against my back.

"Stay down. Stay down," he hisses. Then he gets up, running in a half crouch toward Rodney, who is holding a hissing string of exploded lights in his hand.

"You going to shoot me, Nato?" Rodney asks, in a long, slow drawl. "You think I'm one of those Taliban guys?"

Rodney is grinning, but my heart is pounding. What will Nate do? Rodney is delicate. Nate can't just throw him to the ground. I struggle to get up quickly, thinking that somehow I can stop what is about to happen.

But it doesn't happen.

Nate stops. Looks around. At me, trying to get up, and at Rodney, sitting cool as a cucumber with his lights.

I freeze.

But then Nate starts to laugh. He laughs so hard, I think he might also be crying. And Rodney laughs too. Rodney laughs, and he says to Nate, "Man, them Ahabs really got you going. You just as bad as some of those winos on Fremont Street. You just plain old nuts, Nato."

And for some reason, this makes Nate laugh even harder. He is laughing so hard, he has to sit down on the grass. And I am laughing too, because I can't remember when I last saw Nate laugh, because I am so grateful to Rodney, grateful because Nate loves him so much, and I am also crying, because something is not right with Nate; something is really wrong.

NATE WAS ALWAYS HOTHEADED. HE was always a risk taker. There was a period of time—after the car accident his junior year of high school, after basic training, after that first incredible growing up that happens to a boy who joins the Army—there was a period of time when Nate seemed to have wrestled his demons, when it seemed that Nate was becoming the best man he could be.

Jim and I were close then. I still remember talking with Jim that first year or so that Nate was in the Army.

"Jim, the military has been good for him. He made the right choice. We were so worried, and yet he made the right choice."

"It's amazing, really, how much he has changed. He was telling me last night that he set up a savings account with an automatic paycheck deduction."

"Yeah, I know. When I walked in yesterday, he was polishing the wood floors, on his knees, and he said, 'Mom, I just wanted to do something for you.' I had to walk away, because it hit me so hard. His being nice. It's like we have our old Nate back."

"A lot of boys have trouble in high school, Avis."

"I know. But I was so afraid. So afraid that he would be angry forever, that it was my fault, that we had let him get away with too much."

"Yeah. I never felt like we were too easy on him, Avis. He was a tough teenager. We could have done it differently, but I've never been sure there was a better way."

NATE JOINED THE ARMY RIGHT before 9/11. He got out of basic training three weeks after. That was scary. Because, of course, we had told ourselves that the Army would toughen him up, that it was a good time to join the military, that the world was relatively at peace. Do you remember that? How just before 9/11, it seemed like the world was more peaceful?

And then it changed. And we knew it would just be a matter of time before Nate was deployed somewhere awful. Boys were joining the military in record numbers then, but Nate got in just ahead of them. Just in time to be first out of the gate.

And still it took a while. More than a year before he went to Iraq. Back and forth. Three tours.

And in between, when he was home on leave, he made plans. Each time, he seemed older and surer. He started talking about coming back home when he was done. Joining the police force. Coming home was because of Lauren, of course. Somehow, Nate had gotten back in touch with his middle school sweetheart, and they were in love.

When Nate told us that he was dating Lauren, that they had gotten back in touch, that he was planning on getting out of the military and coming back home, I thought, for a while, that everything was working out. Working out better than I had dared hope.

Jim and I were doing well, Nate was doing well, everything seemed right. I thought it meant that we had done it right after all.

And then Jim and I started to run out of things to talk about. He worked a lot. I couldn't seem to figure out what I wanted, what I was supposed to be doing with my life. Last January, just weeks after Nate got out for good, he totaled his car in an accident that didn't quite add up. He wasn't hurt. Wasn't drinking. (That's what I thought, of course, that he had been drinking.) But his blood alcohol test was fine. He said he had just looked down at the radio, had somehow veered, looked up too late to miss the wall altogether. Just got slowed down enough not to get hurt.

It could have happened that way. Jim believed him.

"Jim, do you think that is all that happened? That he looked at the radio?"

"Avis, stop it. I can't go there with you. I can't do this with you anymore. Of course he just looked down."

But I was right. Whatever happened with the car, I was right about Nate.

His bachelor party was so out of control that he arrived at the rehearsal dinner with fresh red bruises all over his face. They were blackish at the wedding, yellow in the honeymoon pictures.

He got suspended from his job at the Luxor for a day. Never told us why. We would never have known except that I stopped by to give them a table from Nate's old room. Lauren blurted out that Nate had been suspended. The suspension was one thing, but it was the way that Nate looked at Lauren when she told me that surprised me.

I READ THE ARTICLES, OF course. I know about post-traumatic stress, and the possibility of minuscule brain bleeds from powerful explosions.

I've read the scenarios about hundreds of thousands of soldiers with "shaken" brains from IEDs.

My question is, what am I supposed to do about that? What is Nate supposed to do? My son came back from a war alive. But who came back? Who's the man who just pushed me to the ground, who nearly attacked his disabled uncle?

A WEEK LATER, THE FOUR of us sit down to talk about what happened between Nate and Lauren the day I dropped by. They come to my house. Our house.

I make a meal, and Nate and Jim and Lauren and I sit there for the first time in months. It is only the second time Jim has been home since he left. We sit down awkwardly, in the same chairs we have always sat in, feeling oddly formal.

But by the time we are done with dinner—by the time Jim has told a story about an eighty-six-year-old man who has been eating twice a day at the buffet since 1993, and whose Keno numbers finally came up; by the time Lauren has told us about the new program she is trying out with her seventh-grade special ed students; by the time Nate has given up refilling his plate and is just standing at the stove, eating the last of the curry out of the pot—we are a family again. I have to pinch myself to remember that this is not real, that Jim doesn't live here anymore, that we are not going to have many meals like this one.

And all of that mutes the shock of what I saw Nate do to Lauren and the fear I felt in Rodney's yard. It seems simple, really. Nate is having a hard time adjusting to civilian life. He's having anger issues. Well, of course. You can't pick up a newspaper or turn on the news without reading about this.

There are services offered at the base. It's important to be discreet, not to jeopardize Nate's new job with the LVPD. It's true. I actually convince myself that this is just a new normal; nothing that a modern family can't manage.

And maybe there's a hint of how wrong I am in Lauren's face. In the time it takes before she answers Jim's question.

"Lauren, has anything else happened? Are you feeling okay?"

She pauses. A long, quiet pause.

"Nate and I have talked a lot. I know Nate loves me."

If you think about it, this doesn't answer Jim's question.

"Have you and Nate talked to a counselor yet? Have you contacted someone at the base?"

Nate takes over.

"Dad, Lauren and I have worked this out. I know the services that are available to me. I know you and Mom are worried, but I'm not a kid anymore, right? Lauren and I are fine. I love Lauren. I would never hurt her. You'll have to trust me."

Of course, we want to trust him.

We look to Lauren, and she smiles. She smiles at Nate.

And right then, when we have just been so happy together, when life has been so normal, it makes sense. They are deeply in love. Nate would never hurt Lauren.

15

Roberta

ONE THING ABOUT A desert: it accentuates certain distinctions. If you live in one of the master-planned communities shoved up against the red rock hills or set down in a natural basin with an artificial lake at the center, then you might spend the ordinary moments of your life with palm trees fringing your view of the sky, with green grass abutting tended walking paths, with flower beds that are unearthed and replaced monthly, with artfully lighted pools that appear to magically slip into the horizon. Such resort-like luxuries are everywhere in a town that has an abundance both of cheap labor and of people who know how fantasies are created.

But the desert is unforgiving to the indigent. It offers no relief from the harsh landscape of unplanted, dusty yards, of blowing trash, of peeling, sunburned wood siding, of cheap tilt-up concrete walls, of wires sagging between rough-hewn wooden poles, of potholes and graffiti and men curled in the foot-wide shadows cast by faded, abandoned campaign signs. Without water, there are no leaves, no trees, no bushes, no meadows, no fields, no loamy dirt rich with life to soften the barren ugliness of Las Vegas's poorest communities.

The neighborhoods crouching along Washington and Carey, between Martin Luther King and D, are low and flat and desolate. Tiny dirt yards, occasionally pitted with curly dock or oxalis, are enclosed by battered-looking chain-link fences; a wide-shouldered pit bull might strain at the rope tied to a stake in the ground, or a scrawny mutt sidle head down, waiting to be kicked, along a broken curb. Plastic chairs line up near the front doors of multiresident complexes, every building identical to the one beside it: all one story, all the same gray-white shade of untended stucco, all rising starkly from the dusty earth, not a green shoot in sight. In some chairs, people sit, aimlessly watching what little goes on, or calling to a neighbor about the sounds heard in the middle of the night, or offering advice to the single mom fired from her job the day before. Twelve-year-old boys slide by, the laces of their enormous athletic shoes dragging on the sidewalk, and a younger boy plays soccer with a basketball against the side of a building.

A lot of people I know have never been to this part of Vegas, close as it is to town, and even more of them wouldn't dream of stopping here. Too bad, because the Seven Seas has the best fried catfish in town, and Marty and I laughed our way through a lot of Saturday nights there, back when the electric slide was the dance we did, back when everybody had a crack about my flat ass or Marty's ham-footed moves, back when somehow those cracks were proof that we were welcome anyway.

Today I'm meeting Teddi-Ann Mapes at the Seven Seas. I haven't been here in a while, and although it's a dilapidated-looking structure set on a desolate corner, and the thought crosses my mind that my car might be gone when I come out, I'm still looking forward to lunch. Teddi-Ann's son, Emmitt, is in preschool at the Baptist church nearby. We can talk for an hour, and then I'll walk over with her to pick him up before naptime starts. Emmitt doesn't like naptime.

She's there when I walk in.

"Robbie, hi. Is this table okay? Or do you like to sit in the bar?"

"No, this is great. "

We're in a small room next to the take-out counter and the kitchen. It's not as smokey as the main room.

"Teddi, you look good. Your hair's long again."

"Yeah, it's easy at work because I can just clip it up, and it's cheaper than getting it cut."

"You doing all right?"

"Oh yeah. I make great tips. I just can't stop buying stuff for Emmitt. He's so cute, Robbie. He doesn't look like anyone in my family, and he doesn't look like George, so I guess I just got lucky."

George was Teddi-Ann's boyfriend for years. If you could call a drug addict that pimped a fifteen-year-old girl a boyfriend. I suppose Teddi-Ann would say that George was a step up from her father, a fanatic who believed in harsh discipline and the right of a sire to mount his own daughters.

Teddi-Ann was one of the first kids I ever worked with as a volunteer advocate. She was yanked out of her house when she was ten, after a school nurse reported a venereal disease, but all Teddi could think about was getting back home because she had a seven-year-old sister there. I'll never forget the way her determination to go home rocked my world. We were all rushing in, trying to protect her, and she fought like a hellion for the right to save her sister.

Well, some lessons you never forget. Some people you never forget. Even if they're only ten years old. In the end, the system I was part of, as a volunteer CASA advocate, as a lawyer, as a concerned citizen, didn't do much for Teddi-Ann at all. We never got her permanently removed from her father. He did whatever a judge ordered him to do. Took classes, attended meetings, signed pledges, and got to the courtroom, wearing a tie, on time. He got those girls back. And then Teddi-Ann met George, and we lost her for a while, until she showed up, pregnant and alone, at the Shade Tree. But if Teddi-Ann inherited one thing from her father, it was his ability to figure out a system, and when she was finally old enough, she used that skill to set herself free.

She was chosen for a long-term transitional shelter program and left four months before her contract ran out, because she'd already made it. Teddi had a good job, day care for her baby; she was ready to manage her own life.

"How's Emmitt doing?"

"He got into Agassi Prep! I got the letter last week. That's why I moved here, Robbie. That's why I'm living here, so he would have a chance to get in, and he did."

Her grin's a mile wide, and I can't help it: my eyes water. A lot of times, I see that people don't get what they deserve, one way or the other, and then sometimes someone does.

"Come on, Robbie. Are you crying?"

"No. I'm happy for you, Teddi. I'm happy for Emmitt. It just makes me happy."

"Well, I mean I really thought he would get in. It's a lottery, but you have a better chance if you're in the neighborhood, and we meet the income preference too, but then I was waiting, and I just got so scared. When you called last week, I didn't even want to tell you what I was waiting for. But it worked out. Everything works out, Robbie. It really does."

"Well, it's wonderful news. It's going to be great. Is he excited about Christmas?"

The question was out of my mouth before I remembered about Teddi-Ann's odd upbringing.

"Oh, yes. We have a tree up. I put lights on our patio too, and I even helped them make popcorn garlands at his school. It's a Baptist school, so Emmitt sings 'Jesus Loves Me' every night. I took him to church on Christmas Eve last year, and I'm going to do it again."

"I like Christmas too."

"But you're Jewish."

"Yeah. But I like Christmas."

WHEN I WAS TEN, A girl I knew from Hebrew school came over to my house. She'd been to my house other times, but I guess she'd never been there in December.

"What's that?" she asked, as if she'd never seen a Christmas tree.

"It's our tree. You don't put one up in your house?"

"No. We're Jewish. I thought you were." Her voice dripped. I hadn't known she'd care. Maybe I hadn't even noticed that our Jewish friends didn't put up a tree. Which sounds funny, but it was no big deal in our house. We went to Hebrew school, we belonged to Beth Shalom, and we put up a tree.

My dad loved Christmas. He'd stay up with my mom, smoking a cigar while she wrapped all our gifts in foil paper with red grosgrain ribbon. He didn't wrap himself. He had fat fingers, and no patience for measuring or tape, but they'd stay up after we went to bed Christmas Eve. I could hear them laughing in their room, and I would imagine them pulling out gift after gift, my mom meticulously wrapping, my dad puffing away. The next morning, I could smell my dad's cigar in the paper, in the ribbons. I'd put the gifts to my nose and sniff before opening them.

A few days after my friend's comment about the tree, I got up the courage to talk to my dad.

"Dad, why do we put up a tree? Is it okay?"

"Okay? Of course it's okay. It's not big enough for you this year? You think we should have it bigger next year?"

"No, Daddy. I just, I don't know, we're Jewish."

"Popkin, we're Jewish. So we can't have a tree? Is that some Talmud law? Jewish kids can't have a tree? Where's it say that in the Torah? Hmm?"

"Well . . ."

It was hard for me to get out, because I didn't want to make my dad mad, and I didn't want to hurt his feelings. But I'd been thinking about it, and I was a little scared.

"It says no false idols. It says a Jew who has false idols is a non-Jew."

My voice came out small, and for a while, my dad didn't say anything. And then I heard his big laugh, and his arm slipped around my shoulders.

"So, Popkin, you're trying to tell me you been praying to that tree?" His eyes sparkled.

"No, Daddy."

"Popkin, this is why we live in Vegas. When we came to Vegas, I said no more people looking at us, no more having to live one way and not another. No more being the Jew, not being the Jew, are you being a Jew. We're Jewish. We couldn't get away from that if we wanted to. Ask your friend Jackie if she wants to come over on Christmas Day. Tell her we have a present for her. See what she says."

TEDDI-ANN LOOKS AT ME QUIZZICALLY.

"I'm sorry, Teddi. I was thinking about Christmas. When I was a kid."

She smiles. I wonder if she has any memories of Christmas as a child. It's not something her dad would have gotten right. But she's smiling anyway.

"Emmitt loves the lights in people's yards. There's a house down on West Adams that's incredible, and I told him we could drive by it every single night. I mean, he just loves all the reindeer."

And that's how it is with Teddi-Ann Mapes, who had some of the toughest breaks I've ever known a kid to get. She's barely old enough to drink a beer in a bar, but she makes me feel like the world's going to work out; like everything anyone ever does—no matter how small, no matter how inept—is worth it. Because one of these days, the person you help is Teddi.

16

Luis

I KNEW SHE WAS there before she spoke. It's how she smells. Which I can't describe because I don't know the word for her smell. But my abuela's skin has its own odor, and one of my earliest memories is of that smell, and how it meant that no matter what had been happening, everything would be okay now.

I lie there, as still as I can, and try to breathe her in without letting her know that I am awake. I want just to take a deep breath in, but I don't want her to say anything, I don't want to open my eyes, I don't know what to say to her, so I lie there, still, and let just the hint of that odor in.

She is sitting in Dr. Ghosh's chair. I hear her shift position once or twice. My abuela is short, with a round apple body, and I can almost see her perched on the edge of the chair so her feet will touch, and then shifting on the seat to rest her back, and her toes lifting off the ground. I smile slightly at this, and she notices immediately, because, of course, her attention has never wavered.

"*Mi amor*. Luis. I am here."

I've been dreading this moment. Because of course I've been waiting for her, I need her, and I can't bear for her to see me like this—to know what I have done, even if nobody has told her the whole story yet. Tears start to leak out of the sides of my closed eyes, which is exactly what I don't want, and I keep lying there, perfectly still, concentrating on thinking about nothing, and feeling these hot tears sliding down my temples and pooling near my ears.

"Luis. Luis, Luis, Luis."

She says my name over and over like it is a prayer, almost sung. This makes the tears come faster. I can't help myself. I take a sort of ragged breath in, and then I stiffen, because it was hard enough to face Dr. Ghosh with everything I feel, and to face my abuela is impossible.

You can't get away from anything in a hospital. You're lying on a bed, and you can't even get up to go to the bathroom by yourself, and if someone comes in and just foists something on you—some experience, some memory—you cannot get away. You are just there. Abuela is not going to go away, so my heart starts racing. I really can't deal with this.

"Luis. You don't have to talk. You don't have to say one word. Later, maybe you can open your eyes, just for a moment, so I can see you. But you don't even have to do that."

I open my eyes.

Everything is blurry, because of the tears, but there she is, exactly the same. Everything that has happened to me, the way being in her home feels like someone else's life, hasn't changed her. She is the same.

She doesn't lean in too close, and she doesn't touch me. My abuela always knew that some pain requires space. When I was a little boy, she would wait until I crawled in her lap or reached up for a kiss. She didn't lean in to me or pull me toward her. I still remember how safe that felt, and how much I hated that my mother, the few times she saw me, would rush in for a hug, pull on a curl, and say, "What, Luis, you aren't going to give your mama a hug?" I should hug her, though I never knew that she was coming, though she never said good-bye. My mother would kiss me, my body taut, then set me down, and say, "Mama, he's kind of uptight. Are you too hard on him? You know that doesn't work. Look at me, right?" And laugh, her stretched laugh, as if we were supposed to believe she found this funny, when anyone could hear that she had lost the ability to find anything funny a long time ago.

"Thank you, Luis."

That's all Abuela says. And I close my eyes.

WHEN I WAKE UP, SHE'S still there. Not in the chair, though. She's by the window, and she's fiddling with the string that controls the slats. Those blinds have been hanging at a slant, because the one string is pulled tighter than the other, for as long as I've been here. Of course, she's fixing it.

"Abuela?"

My voice is stronger than I expect it to be. For some reason, I don't feel as upset as I did. I feel rested, and I feel like she's not going to make me tell her anything.

"Luis, you're awake. Are you hungry?"

I smile. If I don't have to tell her anything, then having her makes everything better.

"No. They feed me a lot here. It's part of my therapy. Using a fork. So I don't ever get hungry."

"How about some water? I just put ice in that pitcher."

"Yes. I'll have a drink. But let me do it."

She watches me as I struggle to pull the tray over my bed and then to sip from the bent straw in the glass. When I was a kid, I liked the straws that bent, and that little strip of accordion pleating that allowed one to create just the right angle. Abuela didn't buy straws, and if I'd asked for them, she would have bought the cheaper ones, made of paper, without any pleating.

There's not enough water in the glass for me to get any, and I can't manage the pitcher, so I sit back a little, and my abuela pauses, to see what I will do, and then pours me some water. I wonder if this is how all families are, if this is how it will be for me some day with a wife: that words are not necessary, that not using words is a kind of caress.

But I won't have a wife. Why did that thought come in? All that's gone for me. It's impossible to imagine this future. And I shouldn't have it.

Abuela adjusts the blankets near my feet and pulls the chair a little nearer my bed. She has found a pillow for the back, and I see that she can sit in it now with her feet on the ground. I wonder if a nurse brought her the pillow or if she simply went and found one. My abuela wouldn't have bothered anyone with something she could do herself.

"I'm staying at Fisher House. It's for the family of patients. They're very nice."

I want to nod, but these are the gestures I can't always do when I think of them, so I'm not sure if my head moves or not.

"We were always going to go to DC, Luis. Now we are here."

I smile.

"Abuela, you should go to the Smithsonian. You should see the monuments. I'm fine here. And you could tell me about them."

"Hmmmm. Maybe."

We sit for a while, and then she sees it in my eyes, and she leans forward and rests her cheek on mine. We just stay like that for a long time, and it must hurt her back to lean in so long. But for me, I just concentrate on taking it all in: the soft orb of her cheek and the smell of her skin and her strong hand pressing into my shoulder.

DR. GHOSH AND MY ABUELA meet in my room. They must have spoken to each other on the phone, because Dr. Ghosh greets her when he comes in.

"Mrs. Reyes, you're here. Welcome. I am Dr. Ghosh. How was your trip?"

"Dr. Ghosh. I am pleased to meet you. My trip was fine, and thank you for telling me about Fisher House. They're very kind."

"So how's our patient? Luis, how are you today?"

I'm not sure what to think about having Dr. Ghosh and my abuela in the room at the same time. I'm not going to talk to Dr. Ghosh in front of her, and I wonder if he thinks I will. I nod my head—I think I'm nodding my head—warily.

"I just have a minute, but I knew your grandmother was coming in, and I wanted to say hello."

Dr. Ghosh says this so that I'll know he understands what I'm worried about. I should have known that. Dr. Ghosh and my abuela are actually sort of alike, if you think about it.

"I am going to visit the Lincoln monument," says my abuela. "When do you plan to come in to talk to Luis?"

"I'll be back tomorrow. About two."

"I'll go then," says my abuela.

And it is done. My abuela isn't going to make me speak of things while she's here. That's Dr. Ghosh's job. It's such a relief: to have her here but not to have to tell her why I'm here. She knows of course. If she didn't know, she would ask. I wonder how much she knows. Does she know about Sam? About that day in the market? About the boy in Las Vegas?

Because the fact that I shot myself would be enough for her to know. I don't know how she is bearing that, how much it took for her to bear that, so I hope that Dr. Ghosh hasn't told her anything else. But he might have. Or he might still. And I can't think about that. I let it go. Who knows what was said. At least as far as Abuela goes.

THAT NIGHT, AFTER ABUELA LEAVES, I think about the letter I wrote to that third grader. It's kind of a mystery how Dr. Ghosh could have read a letter I sent to some kid in Nevada. I mean, the kid got it, so how did Dr. Ghosh see it? I'm guessing it must have been a hell of a letter, and the kid's parents probably complained about it. The Army hates stuff like that. Could I be court-martialed? It's okay if I am. Because I ought to be sent to Leavenworth for something.

Dr. Ghosh said he would show me the letter, but when I asked him last week, he changed the conversation. Maybe there's something in his books about not showing a guy his own suicide note. I mean, that must be what I wrote that kid. I shot myself right after. Poor kid. Damn. I can't believe I sent something like that to a kid.

I don't remember wanting to kill myself. I don't remember having that thought once. I was sick about the boy in the market, really loco, but it was nothing like how I felt after Sam got hit. I can't even explain that to you. I wanted to be dead. That's true. I wanted to be the one that was dead and not the one that had screwed up. I was afraid, too. I couldn't get Sam's half-blown face out of my mind. It was always there; sometimes I could actually see it. Not like in a nightmare, but while I was just sitting around, eating something, or checking my equipment, or trying to actually do my job. I could see Sam's head. Like I can see my hand right now.

And it scared the shit out of me.

I mean, all the stuff I'd been through. All the explosions. Guys down. And what scares me shitless is this floating head that I know perfectly well is in my imagination, but which seemed totally real. I'd leaned down and held that face. I'd even put my lips to that mouth and tried to resuscitate him. I mean, I couldn't comprehend it, I couldn't figure out what had happened; I was just trying to remember everything I needed to do in an emergency. Every way that I could give Sam a chance.

Even when I brought him back. Even when the sergeant said, "Luis, get out of here. You can't help him now." Even then, I couldn't believe it. I kept going back over the day. We were in the Humvee, we were talking shit, and then, nothing, a big blank, and I'm leaning over Sam's half a face. Why were we out of the Humvee? Why was I on the other side from Sam? What did I do? What was the mistake?

MY ABUELA LEAVES AT ONE thirty for the Lincoln Memorial. I'm feeling relaxed, so I let my guard down and think about Sam, and that day. I try again to remember what happened just before the explosion. I have to go a little deeper; try to remember.

"Luis, you look troubled. Do you want to talk?"

I didn't hear Dr. Ghosh come in.

I don't answer for a bit, because it's hard to get my brain to shift away from Sam, out of Iraq, and back into this hospital room.

"Were you thinking about Sam?"

I don't want to talk about Sam, so I don't say yes.

"I was thinking about the letter I wrote, and the kid. I'd really like to see it."

"I brought it with me. I thought today might be a good day to talk about it."

And then he pulls out the letter. Or a copy of it, actually. So that was easy. I thought I was going to have to fight to see the letter. I wonder why Dr. Ghosh thinks it's okay to show me the letter now.

Dr. Ghosh says that the kid's principal contacted the Army, and by the time they had sent the letter through all the different commands and gotten it to my sergeant, I was already in DC. Sergeant Reidy sent the letter to Dr. Ghosh. Sergeant said he wasn't sure what the Army would do about it, but it might be a moot point if I didn't get better. So that's how Dr. Ghosh got it.

Now that I'm going to see the letter, I'm not so keen about it. My whole body starts trembling.

"There's information in it that is startling to the Army, Luis. There may be consequences for it. I don't know. But I think today is just about you and me and this letter, Luis. It's not about anything else. Not today."

Now I'm really shaking, but Dr. Ghosh gives it to me anyway. And it's my handwriting. My signature. I don't read so well yet, so I hold the page, and Dr. Ghosh reads the words to me.

Dear Bashkim:

Yes, I have killed people here. I even killed a boy, not much older than you. He was carrying a bag, and around here that means bomb. It wasn't a bomb though. It was some charred wood that he was bringing home to burn again.

Everybody kills here. That's what soldiers do. You might as well start killing mice with your baba, or whatever you call your dad, because with a name like yours, someone is going to try to kill you some day.

Luis

I hear these words, and the bed spins. It spins fast enough that I think I'm going to be thrown off of it, and I actually grasp the rails so I can hang on, like a damn roller coaster or something. I hear my breath chugging out of me. Dr. Ghosh just sits there, not saying a word. I look down at my legs, and I will the bed to stop spinning. It slows, hiccups, spins a bit faster, and then finally stops. I am sitting with my back raised off the bed, which is not that easy for me, and my fingers are purple around the bed rails, and I'm panting like a dog after a rabbit. I'm one fucked-up soldier. Dr. Ghosh has set the letter on the tray next to my bed, but I don't want to touch it.

I don't remember anything about that letter.

I don't recognize the kid's name. I don't know what I was talking about with his name. I can't believe I wrote down what happened in the market. I must have already known I was going to kill myself. I must have thought I was going to be dead. And what? I wanted to be sure my abuela knew the truth about me? I wanted to confess to some eight-year-old kid who probably still sleeps on the floor next to his mom's bed?

I didn't think things could get any worse, but the wave of repulsion that comes over me is more than I can bear. I hate everything I have ever done or ever thought. I hate that I exist. I hate that I have failed everyone who ever cared a damn about me. All I have ever done in my life is hurt people.

"Luis?"

I can't talk to Dr. Ghosh. I can't breathe. Now I want to die.

"Luis. I know you're upset. I know you feel bad."

He doesn't know. Dr. Ghosh really does not know.

"Luis. This is what I was talking about. About war and stress. Luis, things happen to us that are more than we can take. And we break. We break for a moment, for a while. But that break is not who we are. It's not the sum total of who we are."

His words are just washing around me. I want to grab hold of them, hang on, but I don't want to be saved again. I don't want to keep coming back and then have to fall again. I can't listen to him.

"Luis. We've been talking together almost every day for weeks now. If there was ever a man who did not want to kill a child, it is you, Luis. I know this is not what you wanted to do. I know that it was a break. I know what you have been carrying."

I can't hang on any longer. I cry then. I cry and cry, and I don't think I will ever stop, and Dr. Ghosh gets right on the bed and holds me.

WHEN MY ABUELA COMES BACK after dinner, I see her register that something has happened. She can see it in me, but she says nothing. And I don't say anything that night, because I don't know what she is thinking, and I wouldn't know how to bring up the letter I wrote to that kid if I did want to talk.

But having her there helps me think about it. In my mind, I pretend that my abuela does know about the letter and what I wrote, and that we're talking about it. I think about what she would want me to do. I think about that kid the way my abuela would think about a little boy.

It changes everything. If I think like my abuela. If I think of myself like my abuela thinks of me.

A FEW DAYS LATER, AFTER Abuela has gone home, I get a chance to talk about the kid with Dr. Ghosh. The boy in Nevada. The one who got the letter.

"Do you know anything about him? Did he read the letter?"

"I know he read it. Everybody regrets that. Somebody should have read the letters first before they handed them out to the children, but nobody thought of it."

"Yeah. Do you know anything else?"

"Not much. The principal was pretty upset. And the parents, of course. That's about it."

"I need to do something about it. I need to do something for that boy."

"Hmmm. Yes, I see. It might not be easy. Nobody is going to want to put you back in touch with him."

"But I have to, Dr. Ghosh. I have to do something. I can't leave it. That letter. It was so cruel. I can't do anything about everything else. About Sam. About . . . about everything. But that's a kid from Vegas. I just can't leave it like that. Please. Please, help me do this."

Dr. Ghosh starts to say something, but then he stops.

"Okay. Luis, I'll see what I can do. Maybe there's a way to contact the school principal. Maybe. I'll try."

And that's the first time that I want something. The first time I have wanted anything since I woke up in this hospital. There has to be something I can do for that kid. And that's the only thing I want. If my abuela never believes in me again, if I spend my life in Leavenworth, if I die in Iraq, I just want to do something for that kid. I want to do something right.

Maybe it's my Mexican roots. Maybe it's because of what my abuela did for me. Maybe it's just that he's another boy. A boy who is alive. Maybe it's what I said about the kid's name. I don't know. But ever since I thought of the kid and realized that he was out there, that maybe I could change one thing, it's all I can think about. Doing something for that kid.

I don't want to scare him, of course. His parents are already mad at me. But I just can't leave that letter like that. He shouldn't grow up thinking a man sent him a letter like that and never fixed it.

THE THING IS, I CAN'T actually write a letter by myself. I can't hold the pen, and I can't write. I can read characters, and sometimes words, but it is hard for me to see a set of words. I haven't read a sentence yet; I can only see part of a line. I am working on reading with my occupational therapist, so I decide to tell her that I want to write a letter and see if she will help me. I trust Alison.

ALISON AGREES TO HELP ME, but since I'm in therapy, it comes with a set of conditions. When I can read three lines without help, she'll write the letter. I remember to tell her that she'll have to print, because the letter is going to a child. I think about what she might imagine from that detail, and it's so far from reality that I feel a bit discouraged. Still, when I have the letter, I'm going to ask Dr. Ghosh to mail it to the principal. I'm going to do something about what I did to that boy.

17

Bashkim

MRS. MONAGHAN SAYS THAT the principal wants to meet with me today. I am going to go there right after lunch. I must be getting more mature, as Mrs. Monaghan says, because I am not too upset about this. I have been to the principal's office a couple of times on my own before school. She likes me to feed her fish. Dr. Moore is not so bad, and she keeps food in her office. She needs kids to eat it, because some people donate it to the school, and she does not want them to think that she wastes it. I have a lunch, though, so I won't be able to eat any of that food today. Maybe just a cookie or something.

I go straight from the lunchroom to the office. I am not tall enough to see over the counter, so it is a little while before Mrs. Hartley, the aide, realizes that I am there.

"Hi, Bashkim," she says. "Are you here to see Dr. Moore? She is waiting for you."

I wait for Mrs. Hartley to unhook the gate into the office, and then I walk back to the principal's room myself. Like I said, I have done this before.

"Bashkim, it's nice to see you. Thank you for feeding my fish. Would you like something to eat?"

"No, thank you. I just had lunch."

"Good. Well, Bashkim, I have something interesting to talk to you about today."

I really am getting more mature, because I am not worried that she is going to say anything terrible. She does seem a little worried, though.

"Bashkim, I have received a letter from the soldier who wrote to you. He wants to write to you again."

I am worried when she says this. I don't like to think about Specialist Luis Rodriguez-Reyes, and whenever anyone asks if I want to talk about him, I say no.

"Bashkim, I don't think your parents would want you to communicate with this soldier. And I respect your parents' wishes. But I also think that Specialist Rodriguez is very sorry about what happened, and he wants to make up for hurting you, and I think that reading his letter would be helpful."

I am confused. I really don't want to read that letter, and I don't understand why Dr. Moore is saying that she respects my baba and nene but that she wants me to read the letter. She knows how Baba feels about soldiers. If I read the letter, I couldn't tell my baba. Does Dr. Moore want me to lie to him?

I say nothing.

"Bashkim. This is an unusual situation. I don't want to get you in trouble with your parents. But I also want you to know that there are lots of good people in the world, and that sometimes an adult can make a mistake and still be a good person."

"I know that."

"That's good, Bashkim. I'm glad you know that.

"Bashkim, now you know I have the letter and I have read it and I think it would be nice for you to read it. Why don't you take some time to decide if you want to read it, and if you want to tell your parents about it, or if you would like me to tell them about it. And whatever you want to do, that's what we will do."

I am getting a headache sitting here, and I don't even want a cookie anymore. So I tell Dr. Moore that I will think about it, and I go back to class.

I THOUGHT ABOUT SPECIALIST LUIS Rodriguez-Reyes's letter all weekend. I asked my nene if she thought the soldier who wrote me was a bad person.

"Oh, Bashkim. Are you thinking about that letter? He might be a bad person, but he also might be a good person. I don't know."

My nene stops sweeping, and she looks out the window for a long time. I am not sure if we are still talking, but I don't leave the kitchen, just in case.

"Writing that letter doesn't mean that he is bad, Bashkim, because war is very hard on a man."

I listen carefully, because maybe she is talking about Specialist Rodriguez, and maybe she is talking about Baba.

"Maybe the war that soldier is in is too much for him. Maybe he is a good man, and he was never supposed to be in a war."

I don't ask my nene any more questions, because I am not ready to tell her about the letter, but I listen. Is Baba a good man? Is prison the same as a war, if you never did anything wrong to get there?

ON MONDAY I STOP AT the principal's office to feed her fish. She is not there, but I tell Mrs. Hartley that I want to talk with Dr. Moore. About nine o'clock, Dr. Moore comes to get me in Mrs. Monaghan's room. We walk to her office together.

"Do you want to see the letter, Bashkim?"

I do, so she lets me have it when we are in her office. She says she is going to stay right there doing her work, and I can talk to her whenever I want. I see right off that Specialist Luis Rodriguez-Reyes knows letter form too.

November 24, 2008

Mr. Bashkim Ahmeti
C/O Dr. Martina Moore
Orson Hulet Elementary School
2201 Navarre Drive
Las Vegas, NV 89120

Dear Bashkim:

Thank you for reading this. I know it must be scary for you to read a letter from me. I am so sorry about what I wrote before. I feel terrible about it, and I lie awake at night thinking about how you must have felt when you read it.

I don't know how to explain myself. I don't even remember writing the letter to you. I was very sad about something that happened to a friend of mine, and I think I went a little bit crazy. I am not making an excuse, but that is what happened.

I am very sorry for saying something about your name. People used to make fun of my name. They would ask why I had two last names, and why I didn't know how to say Luis, when they were the ones who did not know how to say it. I know I must have been crazy the day I wrote you, because I can't imagine writing something like that to anyone.

If you would like to write to me again, I would be happy to keep writing to you. Again, I am very sorry.

Luis

I see something funny about the letter. His name doesn't look the same as the rest. Luis writes his name shaky, like Baba does. I wonder if Luis is as old as Baba. Can old people be soldiers? I didn't notice that he had a shaky name before.

I don't know what to say to Dr. Moore after I finish reading the letter. Did Luis shoot the boy because he went crazy? I don't want him to talk about that boy again, but I don't want him to pretend there is no boy.

I feel sorry for Specialist Rodriguez too. This letter is nice. He doesn't even sound like someone who would kill a boy. Maybe my nene is right that wars can be too hard. Maybe Specialist Rodriguez wasn't supposed to be in a war. What if I had to be in a war?

I sit in the chair awhile, looking at the letter, and then I don't want to sit there anymore. I help myself to some goldfish crackers that Dr. Moore has.

"So, Bashkim. Do you want to talk about what Specialist Rodriguez wrote?"

I don't really, right that minute, but I do say, "My nene says that war can be too hard for a soldier. She said that Specialist Rodriguez might be a good man or a bad man, and we couldn't tell from that one letter."

"I think your nene is wise, Bashkim. I am glad that you have talked to her about Specialist Rodriguez."

I decide not to tell Dr. Moore that I have not really talked to my nene about him. Instead, I say:

"My baba was not in a war, but he was in prison. He went to prison for seeing a police officer do something bad. That happens in Albania. And it makes my baba kind of . . . mad . . . too."

I wish I hadn't said that last thing about Baba. I don't want to tell the principal about how my baba gets mad, or how he hurts my nene. That could really cause a lot of problems. I start to get up, because I don't want Dr. Moore to ask me any questions.

"Bashkim. Thank you for telling me about your baba."

"Yes, Dr. Moore." I am standing up now, because I really want to leave.

"If you ever want to talk about what happened to your baba, you can come here anytime."

I nod my head, and then I walk back to my classroom fast. I almost forgot not to talk about some things.

December 12, 2008

Specialist Luis Rodriguez-Reyes
A BTRY 2-57FA
FOB Kalsu
APO, AE 09312

Dear Specialist Rodriguez-Reyes:

Dr. Moore gave me your letter. I understand about soldiers feeling bad in war. My baba is sometimes crazy from being in prison in Albania. He did not do anything wrong, but he was in prison anyway, and that is what makes him get mad at people.

I hope you are having a better time in Iraq now.

Your friend,
Bashkim Ahmeti

December 19, 2008

Mr. Bashkim Ahmeti
C/O Dr. Martina Moore
Orson Hulet Elementary School
2201 Navarre Drive
Las Vegas, NV 89120

Dear Bashkim:

Thank you for your letter. I really appreciate it.

I am not in Iraq anymore. I am in Washington DC, in a hospital. You call your father Baba, and I call my grandmother Abuela. My abuela raised me. I never had a baba, or at least one that I knew.

I grew up in Las Vegas too. Have you ever ridden a dirt bike in the dry lake bed? I used to love to do that. I broke my arm once, but it was worth it.

Do you play any sports? I played basketball, and I ran track a couple of years in high school. In Iraq, some of us would sometimes get a pickup game started, but I guess that stopped after a while.

I hope school is going well for you. Hello to your baba—

Luis

December 30, 2008

Specialist Luis Rodriguez-Reyes
A BTRY 2-57FA
FOB Kalsu
APO, AE 09312

Dear Specialist Rodriguez:

Do you want to stop using letter form? If you do, that's okay with me.

I play soccer for the Las Vegas Storm. We have orange uniforms, with blue letters, and every kid has his own bag. I am number 4, and my bag has my number on it too. That way, everyone knows it is mine.

My baba was a soccer player in Albania. He was almost like a professional, until he had to go to prison. He shows me how to play, when I am not in practice with my coach.

Why are you in a hospital?

Sincerely,
Bashkim

January 9, 2009

Dear Bashkim—

I hate letter form.

   That's cool that you play soccer. I played on a team for a few years when I was younger, but then I started liking basketball more. What position do you play? How is your team doing? Are you playing now?

   My abuela is a big soccer fan. She loves México, and Brazilia. She loves Brazil just because they used to have a great player named Pelé. Have you heard of him? A lot of my friends played soccer or baseball. But I liked basketball best. My abuela let me choose, since she had never played any sport and could not help me herself.

   It sounds like you have a great baba. I didn't have a dad growing up. I am glad you do.

Best wishes,
Luis

p.s. I got hurt in Iraq, and they flew me to this hospital in DC for rehabilitation. I'm fine though.

January 18, 2009

Dear Luis—

Las Vegas Storm won a big soccer tournament last Thanksgiving, even though there were teams from other states. I am a striker, and I scored two goals in the championship game. My baba was so happy, and my nene too.

   My friend Carlo is Mexican, and he has two last names too. They are Garcia-Lopez. I figured you were Mexican as soon as I saw your name. Carlo has four brothers and sisters. That's why he can't play soccer. Because there are too many of them to all get uniforms and bags and things.

I am going to be a magician when I grow up. Our music teacher at school is a magician, and he is really good. ~~Are you glad you are a soldier?~~ Have you ever seen a magician?

Sincerely,
Bashkim

p.s. I'm sorry you got hurt in Iraq.

February 3, 2009

Dear Bashkim—

My uncle Timo likes magic tricks. When I was a kid, he used to pull quarters out of my ear, and he knew so many card tricks. It takes a long time to become a good magician, so it's good to get started now.

My abuela does not like magic acts. She went to Siegfried and Roy once—that was a big magic act on the Strip before you were born—and she says the tricks made her think that the magicians knew the devil. They must have been pretty good magicians, huh? My abuela would never let me go to a show, but maybe I will go see your teacher when I get home.

I bet the weather is nice where you are. I am starting to think about going home a lot.

Take care,
Luis

February 15, 2009

Dear Luis—

Happy Valentine's Day, late.

My teacher Mrs. Monaghan had a big party for us yesterday. Some of the kids brought food. My nene let me bring ice-cream treats, which I never did before. The kids liked them even better than Alyssa's cupcakes.

We had a talent show for entertainment. Mrs. Monaghan believes in spontaneous talent shows. That means we don't practice. But we all knew we would have one, so Carlo and I did a talent. I sat on his knee, because he is bigger than me, and we pretended that I was a puppet and he was a venterwilkist. Everybody laughed, because Carlo is funny.

I hope you had a good Valentine's Day too. It was one of the best days I have ever had.

Bashkim

February 21, 2009

Dear Bashkim:

There's a group of volunteers at this hospital, and they had a Valentine's Party for the patients. We didn't have a talent show, but I ate a lot of heart-shaped cookies. I thought of you too, because I figured you would have a party or something at your school.

I'm going to be in this hospital for a while, but when I get out, they are going to send me back home, at least for a while. Maybe we can go to a park or something. I don't know if I am going to be too good at soccer anymore, but we could kick a ball around. I'd like to meet your baba too.

Have fun at school,
Luis

18

Luis

THE FIRST TIME I heard his voice, I was strung up in the walking machine. It's kind of like a conveyer belt with a harness hanging above it. The therapist hooks me into the harness—which holds me like a swing—and then my legs dangle until they lower me enough that my feet touch the moving belt. I can't move my feet, but the doctors say that I don't have any nerve damage, I will be able to move them, and walk. I just have to get my brain to remember that my feet are there.

Like I said, I am one fucked-up soldier.

The walking machine is a lot of work, not just for me but for the two people that are moving my feet too. There's one person holding my left ankle and another holding my right. I can't feel them holding me, but I can look down and see that they are. And they just move my foot and my ankle and my knee as if I were walking, and I sort of stumble-walk in my harness hanging above them. They have to keep a rhythm, so Terence, who has my left foot, says, "Left, left, left," in a really steady way, which reminds me of the movies I used to watch when I was a kid about being in the Army. It doesn't remind me of being in the Army, though. That's kind of funny.

I try to amuse myself when I am in this contraption, because as stupid as it looks, it's a hell of a lot of work. I'm sweating and panting and, man, I just want them to quit, I'm just waiting for them to say it's been long enough. Every day, I have to do it for a few more minutes. The first day, we counted the number of steps I took, but now Terence times me for a certain number of minutes, and then I get a two-minute break, and then we go back to it. Over and over. I want a smoke.

But I still noticed his voice. I was on the machine, sweating and pushing and trying to feel my feet, and I noticed this voice asking for directions. I heard it clearly. For some reason, it stuck in my head a moment. But then, I was concentrating on walking, and I forgot to think about that voice.

The doctors say my brain doesn't know that my feet are there, but that's not quite right. I know my feet are there. I can almost feel them, I know they're moving, they're being moved, and I can almost imagine moving them myself, but they just don't feel like my feet. They feel like an idea of feet.

Weird, huh?

If it weren't me, this whole brain thing would be pretty interesting.

WHEN I GO BACK TO my room, the nurse mentions that someone has asked about me. She says he didn't leave his name, but he looked like a soldier.

That makes me nervous. I suppose someone is doing an investigation. And I'm cool with that. I'm okay with being punished for what I did. I mean, I think I am. I still feel scared. And I can't even stand to think about how my abuela will feel if it gets in the paper or something. If her friends know about it. I always sort of thought I made up for what my mother had done, for the way my abuela didn't have any nice stories to tell about her daughter.

Yeah, that's over.

I asked the nurse if he left a message, but she said, no, he didn't leave anything.

I've got an hour free before I have occupational therapy, so I look out the window and I think about whether I'll be able to see the sky if I get sent to jail. I figure I should look out the window a lot, try to memorize everything, what I see, what I hear. Which is mostly birds, and cars way down below, and a lot of wind. I keep my windows open no matter how cold it gets, because I like to hear something outside of this hospital, and it helps me relax: the wind, a bird chirp, a squawk, a horn, the low chug of a truck engine waiting at a light. It's been raining a lot, day after day, so everything looks slick and shiny out the window. I wish I could hear the rain. I don't know how tall this hospital is, but the fourth floor is not the top, and I can't hear the rain.

It doesn't rain much in Nevada, but when it does, it comes down like someone dumped a bucket. When I was a kid, I could never quite imagine a raindrop. Rain in Las Vegas is a sheet, it's a deluge, and then it stops. It wasn't until I went to basic training that I felt drops of water from the sky, you know, before the rain really starts or as it stops. I suppose it must be possible to feel that in Nevada, but I never felt it; it's not how I thought of rain.

HE COMES IN WHILE I am thinking these thoughts.

Quiet. But I hear him breathing. I'm pretty sensitive that way. And I'm starting to be more on alert here.

The thing is, I don't move easily, not even to turn my head, and when I do move, there's nothing subtle about it.

"Luis Rodriguez?"

I knock a pillow off the side of my bed trying to shift position and look toward him. My arms and legs jerk like that sometimes when I'm just trying to move my head. That's the brain thing.

"Yes."

He doesn't say anything. He just stares at me. Really stares.

I'm thinking: wow, this is some funky investigation. Is he waiting for me to crack, start yelling that I shot a kid or something? Because he's really not making me that nervous. He better ask me straight up if he wants me to tell him something.

"You look like him."

Like who? This dude is weird.

"I thought you would. I mean, I remember that. But, shit, you really look like him."

There's something about his voice. I realize it's the voice I heard in the gym, on the machine. Of course, he's Mexican. That's part of it. He sounds like a lot of guys I know.

I decide not to speak. Not to ask him who I look like. I really don't care. I wish he would just do what he's going to do, get his information, read me my rights, whatever, and get out. I can't imagine the Army wants someone as fucked up as me in Leavenworth. They'll want me after I can walk again. When I can really miss my freedom.

That's a joke. Sort of.

"Do you remember me?"

What the hell? Do I remember him? I've never seen him in my life. He's too old to have been downrange with me. Unless he was an officer or something. And he doesn't look like an officer. He looks like a grunt.

"I'm your Uncle Mike. Miguel. Your dad's brother."

Fuck me. I didn't even know my dad had a brother.

"You don't remember me."

That's for sure.

"You didn't even know I existed, did you?"

He looks upset.

I still don't talk. Because my life is really getting crazy. Who is this guy? My dad died before I was born. I never met anyone in his family.

The only things I know about my dad are things I heard my mother and my abuela fighting about, when Abuela would spit out the word *gang*, or when my mother would be so fucked up on the couch, she'd call me Marco.

"Your dad was my little brother. I loved him."

That's what he says. That is all he fucking says.

And then he just walks away.

"Hey! Hey!"

I yell, so he sort of turns and says, "Later, man. I shouldn't have come. But you sure look like him."

It takes a lot of effort, because I've just been on that damn walking machine, but I push myself up in bed, I kind of shove my chest out, and I flail my arms. I guess I'm trying to get him to think I'm going to follow him. He stops. Watches me thrash around there.

Then he digs in his pocket, and he pulls out a rosary. I know what it is, of course. He looks at that string of beads—they're kind of chocolate brown in color, like they might be seeds or something, not glass, not plastic or anything—and he looks at those beads for quite a while.

I don't say a word. I try not even to breathe, because I can tell the man is struggling.

He lifts the beads to his face, and he kisses the cross, just barely. "Adios, *Papi*," he says.

Then he lays the beads on my lap.

"These belonged to your abuelo. My dad. He made a lot of trips around these beads, once every day for me and once every day for your dad. Once every day for you too."

We look at each other, eye to eye, but for some reason, I don't speak. I'm kind of in shock or something. And then he walks out of the room.

And that's it. I'm stuck in the bed, right? It's not like I can chase the guy down. It's not like I can do anything. I don't even know where he lives. Mike Rodriguez? That should be simple. Not too many of those out there.

How the hell did he find me? How the hell does he know who I am? Why did he think I'd recognize him? Why did his voice stick in my mind when I heard it in the gym?

Do I know him? Did I meet him? When I was a kid?

Did I meet my grandfather?

I don't remember ever knowing anything about my dad's family. I wouldn't have forgotten that my dad had a brother. I used to wonder about my dad all the time. I would remember that.

So who's Miguel Rodriguez? And how did he know who I was? How long has he known who I was?

WHEN I WAS STILL AT St. Anne's, in eighth grade, Sister Antonella told us all a story about a cloistered nun. This nun had taken a vow of silence. She spent her whole life praying. But she wrote a diary—I don't know if nuns are really supposed to do that—and she left it behind when she died, and somehow Sister Antonella got to see it. Maybe they were related, Sister Antonella and the cloistered nun. I can't remember. But in the diary, the nun wrote that she had stopped believing in God, that she couldn't do anything about it, that she wanted to have faith, but that she didn't. And still she kept praying. She kept her vow of silence. Sister Antonella said this nun accepted God's will in not granting her the gift of faith.

It sounds weird, but I never forgot that story. I never forgot about that nun who kept praying, who lived behind fucking walls, even though she didn't believe in God. How could she accept God's will if she didn't even think there was a God? How did she keep from talking to anyone? How did she keep praying?

But that's what she did.

I prayed a lot when I was in Iraq. I probably prayed every day, every single time I felt fucking scared. It was automatic. I didn't let anyone know I was praying, certainly not Sam, but I couldn't really stop it. I was just always talking to God, always just hoping that maybe someone was listening.

But you know, I never thought it made any difference to God whether I prayed or not. I mean, I didn't think God was going to save me because I prayed, or not save me because I didn't pray. I just never bought that idea. I mean, if he's God, he already knows everything anyone is thinking. How could it possibly matter if one person said some words and another person didn't?

That's one thing I think. But the other thing I think is that my abuelo said the rosary for me every day, and maybe that's why I'm alive.

WHEN DR. GHOSH COMES IN the next day, I tell him about Mike's visit. He's interested, I mean, it's a pretty interesting thing, but he doesn't know anything about him. The hospital has security, but there are a lot of people coming in and out all the time. And the rehab floor, where I am, has outpatients. So it's really easy to get in here.

"Have you called your grandmother? Did you ask her about him?"

"No."

I thought about calling her. I thought about it all night. And suddenly, I don't feel like talking to Dr. Ghosh about this. About how I thought about calling Abuela, and how I imagined the conversation, and how I imagined me getting angry at her for not telling me whatever it is she knows. How ridiculous would that be? For me to be angry at Abuela, given what I've done, given how badly I've messed everything up.

"Do you want to talk to your grandmother about this? Do you want to see this uncle again?"

"I don't know. Maybe."

Dr. Ghosh waits.

"I mean, the thing is, I don't know what I am supposed to do with any of this. With all of it. What am I supposed to do, Dr. Ghosh? About Sam? About that fucking kid? About Bashkim? What do you want from me? What am I fucking supposed to do?"

By the time I get to this last question, I am practically screaming. I wasn't expecting this. I wasn't feeling worked up at all, and then, all of a sudden, I'm going loco on Dr. Ghosh. The thing is, it's just impossible, living with this, thinking about Sam, having this Mike come in my room, looking at that rosary, writing letters to that kid Bashkim. I can't do it. I don't know what to do with all of this.

I stop talking, and I lie there, sort of shaking. I am trying not to cry.

"I think you are just supposed to feel it, Luis. I think your job right now is to feel it all."

This is about the stupidest thing I've ever heard Dr. Ghosh say. It makes me mad, which helps the shaking, and it lets me get back to the issue of my so-called uncle. Dr. Ghosh and I look at each other for a while.

"I just don't want to talk to this Mike right now. I don't want to think about something else right now. I've kind of got everything I can stand. Right now, I mean."

"I think that's fair, Luis. I think it's fair to say that this is not the time when you can think about your dad or his brother. If he is your dad's brother, he'll be out there. You can find him, you can find him when you're ready."

"Yeah?"

"Yes. Definitely. You learned something yesterday. And it might even be important. But it's not what is most important right now. Not unless you want it to be."

It's weird how I was all worked up a second ago, and now I feel calm again. That happens to me a lot here. But I do feel calm, calm enough to tell Dr. Ghosh what really surprised me about Mike Rodriguez's visit.

"The thing is, he said he loved my dad. He misses him."

Dr. Ghosh says nothing.

"I never thought about someone loving my dad before. I never thought of him as someone somebody loved."

Then he looks at me. Sometimes I can tell I surprise him. Maybe he thought spics weren't that interesting before he met me. Maybe he just can't figure me out.

I SPEND THE NEXT FEW days doing my rehab, which keeps me pretty busy, actually, and thinking about my Uncle Mike's visit. I think about Dr. Ghosh's stupid idea too, that my job is to feel it all. I mean, that's all I'm doing isn't it?

But on Thursday night, I try it. I just try feeling some of it. I think of Sam, and for just a second, I think how much he wanted to live. I think about Sam having a little brother, how he didn't want his little brother to enlist, and I think about the way Sam looked when he got an email from his girlfriend saying she "had to move on." I think about the way Sam used to step in front of me, put me a little behind (unless I was quick enough to stop him); I think all of these things, and the tears start rolling. I mean, I really start crying.

No one's around. I cry because I miss Sam and because he wanted to live and because he should have lived. I cry because the war doesn't make sense, and because there are so many of us over there, and because the people in Iraq are so fucking poor. When I am done crying, nobody sees me, I still feel sad, and sort of limp, but I hear this little girl in the hall—she's saying good night to her dad or her uncle or somebody—and she's telling the person she's with that she likes her dress, and she likes her hair, and she likes her shoes. And right then, right while I am feeling all that sadness about Sam, I also feel something that is sort of like joy about that little girl, about the fact that she's alive; about the fact that she's got a dress she likes.

And I realize this is something new: to feel everything that has happened, but to also feel something that is happening now. It's like trying it Dr. Ghosh's way, trying to feel it rather than trying not to feel it, has swelled me up from the inside. I don't feel buried by the feeling. I feel bigger, big enough to have two different feelings at once.

Maybe this is all it is ever going to be.

Maybe it never does go away.

But maybe sometime, I'll be able to feel it all. Everything that hurts, and everything that is right in front of me, at the same time.

19

Avis

IT'S BEEN FIVE MONTHS since Jim dropped his bombshell about Darcy, and here I am, packing up our house on a Saturday morning. The movers are coming on Thursday. Five months is a long time if you are a prisoner of war. It's a long time for a newborn or a butterfly. But for me, who has lived in the same place—slept in the same room—for more than half my life, it feels like I've been thrown down a chute. I'm careening forward, trying not to get too banged up, utterly out of control of my descent, and somewhere in the dark, there's a hole waiting for me to fall through it.

I SHOULD HAVE ASKED SOMEBODY to do this with me today. I am not sure why I thought I could do it myself. The house seemed so empty after Jim left, after he asked if he could take the leather couch, after he took the guest room furniture, the photo from a Gisselberg family reunion, the bookshelves, the desk from his study.

"It's half done," I chirped to Jill. "Jim took the heaviest stuff months ago."

Who was I kidding? Twenty-nine years in a four-bedroom house? Two moving vans could not hold all the stuff in this house.

But I wanted to be alone today. I wanted to go through my house by myself, decide what needed to be tossed or given away, what I would keep, what I would use again, by myself. I cringed at the thought of explaining anything to anyone.

"Avis. Really? You are going to wear this green dress again? You wore it to Jim's fiftieth birthday party, and that was years ago. If you haven't worn it in a year, you never will."

"Did you save all of Nate's school projects? How many of these boxes do you have?"

No, I didn't want to have these kinds of conversations. I wanted to go through things slowly. I wanted all these memories, this chance to put my life in some kind of mental order. I thought it would sanctify something.

WE DID MAKE IT THROUGH Christmas, this new family order and me.

Nate and Lauren stayed at the house the night before, Jim came by for a few hours in the afternoon to exchange gifts, we all kept up a sort of polite neutral patter. I was nervous before Nate and Lauren arrived. My thoughts kept slipping to that gun, still in my naughty-underwear drawer. Should I lock it up somewhere? Should I make sure the bullets were still in the closet, where they had always been?

I don't know if I was afraid of Nate finding the gun or of somehow needing to use it myself. My mind kept darting away from the thought before the question could be formed. Of course, Nate has his own guns. A gun in my dresser drawer would not increase or decrease any risk. Would it? Why was I thinking about risk at all? Again, I couldn't finish the thought.

I didn't open the drawer. I didn't check the closet.

Rodney wasn't with us for Christmas. He was in the hospital with pneumonia again, and maybe that is what kept us all so quiet: the realization that Rodney, the most innocent of all, wasn't holding court for the neighborhood kids in the middle of his lights but lying in a hospital bed, struggling to breathe. We went to see him that evening, Lauren and Nate and I, but he was too weak to talk. He blinked his blue-gray eyes, and he tried to say something to Nate, but could not.

I OPEN ANOTHER CUPBOARD, PULL out another box.

Every centimeter of this house is familiar. I've painted every room, washed every baseboard, dusted every corner. Over the decades, Jim and I changed things. We put in a pool and added a family room. When we bought this house, I was twenty-four years old and had never owned anything larger than a bike.

It didn't make financial sense to stay in an old house like this one all those years. Not in Vegas. But we had not wanted to move. Roots mattered to me. Knowing every family in the neighborhood mattered to me. And this was the home Emily had known, the only one in which she had ever lived. Jim and I never brought this up—as one of the reasons we did not sell our house and move on to something newer—but it was always there. If we left this house, then the few memories we had, the trailing decrescendo of images left to us, might be gone altogether.

I'm not a religious person. I didn't grow up with religion, and, somehow, I never found it later, but I prayed and prayed when Emily was sick. There were even some hours, right after she died, when I thought that I could pray her back to life; when it really seemed that if I prayed hard enough, God would hear me, and he would turn back time, and she would be alive again. She would be lying in that ICU crib, and her breath would be fluttery, fluttery, and then she would gasp, and breathe in. And breathe in again. And the nurse would come, and call the doctor. And the doctor would say, with a little catch in his voice, that she had turned the corner, that she was going to make it, that it had been a close call, but she was going to make it. I really believed.

I THINK ABOUT THAT MEETING Jim and Lauren and Nate and I had last December. The one where we talked about what I had seen Nate do to Lauren. Jim and I didn't learn anything that day. We hadn't wanted to learn anything; it was a relief to believe that nothing was expected of us. After all, Nate was a grown man; our parenting days were over. Jim had his new life with Darcy to think about. I had my new life without Jim. Every one of us was emotionally stretched.

But in the middle of the night, I wake up, and I wonder: *what about Lauren?*

There haven't been any phone calls, there haven't been any signs. I do watch. When I talk with Lauren, when we meet for lunch, when they come for dinner, she gives no hint that something is wrong. She seems quieter than she used to be. And older. But she is not bruised, she does not seem afraid.

And what one thinks in the middle of the night is never true anyway. I never worry about the right thing in the middle of the night.

When did I start thinking that I could prepare myself? I, who grew up with Sharlene; I, who watched Emily die.

I AM NOT A SCRAPBOOKER, not somebody who tries to organize what I will remember. After all, there are a lot of years I want to forget. Nor did I want to shape something after it happened. I didn't even like to write things in a baby book. It seemed like my interpretation of what had happened would get in the way of the actual experience. I wanted to remember things as they were, and not as I created them, by choosing certain photos, or saving certain items, or labeling certain moments.

Of course, I had that all backward. It turns out that most of what I remember are the things that accidentally did get labeled, or pulled out, or sorted. How is it possible that I can forget the dearest moments of my life? I never wanted to forget Nate's first word, the silly tune Jim sang when he changed either baby's diaper, the look of the sun glinting off the lake in Idaho. I never wanted to forget those things; I never thought I could forget those things. Turns out, forgetting is easy.

At least until I come across something that brings the memory back. A lopsided teacup from the pottery shop at the lake, an overheard melody that happens to be almost the same as Jim's jingle, a baby repeating "ball" from a nearby grocery cart. Or this house. This house, as I pack it up and decide what should be tossed, what should be given, what should be kept.

A MEMORY SLIPS IN. CHERYL and Margo and Julie and I are sitting outside on a January afternoon on the patio at Mon Ami Gabi. We are having wine and the chicken pate with the hot mustard sauce and the pickled olives. I have known these women for decades. Cheryl is telling Realtor stories, listing the things that sellers have left behind when they packed up their houses.

"The usual," she says, "rotted trash, used condoms, a dead mouse in a trap. And, of course, the forgotten. An entire shelf of china cups, minus the saucers. The winter coats lined up in a side closet. The box of bowling trophies, carefully packed."

We start to laugh. Cheryl is holding up her fingers. She has recited this list before.

"The inconvenient: The six-foot bean bag, covered in Denver Broncos logos. The one-hundred-pound weight from some gym set. The family cat."

We laugh again. Julie sighs about the cat. Cheryl continues.

"How about the tin box labeled 'Brownie's Ashes'? Or the pickled gallbladder in a bottle with the date of surgery written on it? I still remember, it was kind of translucent, like a mood ring or something. Oh, and teeth. What is it with dental detritus? Baby teeth. Molar teeth. Teeth impressions."

She pauses. I hold my wine up to the clear winter light.

"Also gym bags. With moldy socks and slimy shampoo bottles still inside. But the worst was this poor couple, buying their first house—so innocent you could squeeze their cheeks—and they come sailing into their home that first night, and into a back bedroom, and find six stuffed hummingbirds in what must have been a homemade taxidermy lab. Where was that when they toured the house? Where'd they hide *that*?"

She makes her voice indignant. We are enjoying it.

"Why would someone stuff a hummingbird?" asks Julie. "Sounds like some sick cult. I would not have stayed in that house."

"Perfect," says Cheryl. "Remind me not to sell you a house."

And we all laugh. We are good friends. Sitting there, with the whoosh of the Bellagio fountains and the honk of taxis and the faint sound of music piped from across the street, our lives are easy. We are not thinking about packing up our own pasts; we do not imagine how many times our lives will change.

THERE IS ANOTHER THING JIM and the girls don't know about me.

When Nate was four, my closest friend was a man. Young, pretty mothers, taking care of children at home, aren't supposed to have men friends. Everyone knows what is going on.

His name was Jess. I met him at the playground, watching his girlfriend's child. A little boy the same age as Nate. Luke. Nate and Luke were best friends. And for a while, so were Jess and I.

Jess was a musician and had a musician's life. His girlfriend had a job in a dentist's office. Jess played nights and could take care of Luke after preschool. It worked well that he was easygoing, that a small child's fits and temper did not unnerve him, that he could sit and strum the guitar, or let Luke strum his guitar while he sang along, hour after hour.

I had Luke over to play once. I thought Jess would drop him off, would be glad for the hours off, like most of us moms were, but Jess came in and just hung around with me. I was uncomfortable at first, but he made me laugh. He got on the floor and wrestled with the boys. He helped them turn all the cushions into the Alamo. He sang me a song he was writing as we made lunch.

I had never had a friend like Jess before. I guess I never have had since. Someone who knew immediately what Sharlene must have been like, who could guess where I had grown up, who teared up and didn't stop the first time he heard about Emily. Of course, we couldn't stay friends. But for one year, I had a friend who didn't belong to my life before or my life after, who bridged my worlds, who seemed to understand that all of it was me: the rent-by-the-week motel rooms and the big suburban house, the string of men with Sharlene and the conventional marriage with Jim, the things I did to get out of one life and the things I did to stay in another.

Jess and I kissed once. A real kiss. Knee buckling, gut wrenching, soul releasing.

I thought about that kiss for years.

Played it out in my mind. Played it forward.

Just once.

So when Jim explained about how he and Darcy had gotten closer, working together every day, when he told me that he could talk to her and that she helped him think about things, when he said that being with Darcy made him a better man, I just kept wondering: *what does that have to do with ending our marriage? Did you think you couldn't have a friend?*

THE GIRLS KEEP TALKING ABOUT dating.

"Oooh, Avis, you are on the loose again!"

"Bar dates, hot countertop sex, romance!"

Are they kidding? I don't want hot countertop sex.

What I want is for the life I lived to matter still.

I have already been young. I have lost a child. I have reared another one. I was in love. I married. I worked. I made friends. I cooked twelve thousand meals. Made eight thousand beds. Kissed a child awake and kissed a child asleep, encouraged and discouraged and recouraged, over and over. And now, am I supposed to start anew?

I don't think I'm interested.

I had my good shot at this life. I cared, and I knew it was precious, and I dove in, full all of me, straining to feel all of it, and, still, now it is gone, just like that.

I worked so hard to imagine a life I had never seen. And I made that life. I did it. The baby who arrived in Las Vegas with a couple of hitch-hikers. She made an unimaginable life come true.

IT'S NOT THAT I CAN'T see the path before me. I'm Sharlene's daughter. I know how to pick myself up and move on.

I just don't know if I am willing.

And really, after this much life, why am I looking for more?

I thought it would go on longer. I thought Jim and I were going to grow old together. I thought we would bounce our grandchildren between us. But I expected Emily to live too. And she did not.

It comes down to this: Do I want a new life? And if I don't, isn't that my choice too?

I'm sure there's something wrong with being able to think these thoughts in this matter-of-fact way, I'm sure this is why I should have asked someone to help me out today, but it just seems like one of the options.

I am fifty-three years old. I have a gun in a drawer upstairs. I no longer have a husband. I have a child who is not sentimental and who has his own life. I could simply choose not to live.

Which, of course, is not actually a suicidal thought.

I'm mad. And I want my life back. But I don't want to die. Not even a little. I want to live.

SO, DAMN, I DO HAVE to pack up this stuff. I do have to sort it all out: the precious from the unneeded from the still useful. What am I going to do with Nate's baseball uniform from the seventh grade? Or the box of cards his first-grade class made for him when he broke his elbow? Or the plastic bracelet the hospital attached to Emily's newborn wrist?

If I don't save these things, I have lost something. It's not just that objects release memories, it's also that they keep them in check. As long as I have Emily's plastic band, I know the actual diameter of her wrist, not the one I've come to imagine. Which doesn't matter, except that somehow it does. If I just have this one life—if I made all these mistakes in it, felt all this joy and all this pain—I want to know what it was. I want to know what it really meant.

THE LIGHT HAS SHIFTED NOW. It is no longer streaming into the kitchen. I pull out a box, label it "Precious," and begin again: opening cupboards, looking at walls, deciding what the box should hold.

Upstairs, the gun still gleams in the drawer, silent, unmoved, waiting for me to get to it. Me and my boxes and my choices. What is precious. What isn't needed. What is simply the next phase of this life.

What do they say—if you weren't crying, you'd laugh? Or is it, if you weren't laughing, you'd cry?

20

Bashkim

TODAY I AM HELPING Baba and Nene at a baseball tournament. Tirana is sleeping in the backseat, so one of my jobs is to listen for her. Nene is afraid that Tirana will get out of the truck by herself, and something will happen to her before she walks back to us. Since Nene has said this, I am nervous about it too. I am also trying to pay attention to the game, though we are parked behind a tree, and it is hard to see what is happening. I am going to tell Luis about the baseball games. I might not say I am on a team, since he already knows about being on soccer, but I might say that I used to play baseball. I know some of the boys on the teams, and even one girl, because it is a tournament for eight- to twelve-year-olds, and that is how old I am.

What I like about baseball uniforms is you know exactly what sport the person is playing. I would like to hold one of the bats and wear a glove, but I don't think I can. My baba, who doesn't know anything about baseball, found a baseball hat in the park last fall, and he is wearing it. It is dark blue, with an orange letter. The letter is so fancy that I am not sure if it is a *B* or a *D,* and Baba doesn't know either, so when people make comments about his hat, he is kind of careful how he answers.

Baba and Nene have been mad all morning. They have been arguing about money for two weeks, and something happened yesterday that Baba is really worried about. We have to pay the power bill, not just rent, and last month it was too high. Baba said Nene was not being careful enough. Plus Tirana got sick, and Nene took her to a clinic, and she had to pay for a medicine too, and Baba says that we can't afford that. He says Tirana would get well by herself, and that it is healthier to get well by yourself, but I know he was worried about Tirana too. She didn't even want to get out of bed when I came home from school, and usually she is jumping all over me and trying to give me baby kisses when I come home. Tirana is really happy to see me every day. Since she is so little, she doesn't know about not hugging people at school, so if she and Nene come and get me there, it is embarrassing.

Baba and Nene are trying not to argue while we are working, because they both know that people don't like to buy ice cream when they do that, but Baba is so mad, he cannot control himself. He thinks that if he speaks in Albanian, people won't know he's mad. Actually, it's worse in Albanian. Baba doesn't know about how Albanian sounds in America.

When Baba is like this, I get very nervous. I am listening for Tirana, and trying to see what the kids are doing in the game, and watching my nene too. Everything about Nene is different when Baba is mad. She keeps her elbows right next to her body, and she moves her fingers together, in and out. I hate it when she does that with her fingers. She is really quiet too, except with the customers, but her voice doesn't even sound right with them. I want to help her, but it's hard to do anything right. And the truck is crowded with three people and all the ice-cream freezers, so we keep bumping into each other. I can tell that everyone wants to be far apart.

Nene sends me out of the truck. She says she will listen for Tirana, and that she and Baba can handle it. I walk over to the baseball field and stand by the fence, a little away from where the moms and dads sit. The sun is bright, even though it is February, and it smells good here. I think

I would like playing baseball. Some of the players who are waiting for the ball to be hit to them are looking right at the sun, and they have their hats pulled down low so that they can block it.

"Okay, Ryan. One more. Right down the center. You can do it."

"Eye on the ball, Jake. Eye on the ball."

The boys who are waiting to bat are lined up inside the cage where they sit, and everyone is watching Jake try to hit the ball. On the other side, I can hear people yelling at the boy who is throwing the ball to Jake, and the coach keeps touching his hand to his arm and chest. I think that baseball might be sort of complicated, and I am not sure I should write about it to Luis. I am also thinking that I would not want to be the batter or the thrower, because everyone is staring at them. I think I would get pretty nervous.

But it looks fun to be in the cage. Boys are laughing, and they say things like "Batter uuuuup," and one kid keeps crawling partway up the fence, he is so excited. I wonder if everybody has to hit with the bat in baseball.

"Hey, Bashkim!"

It is Derek, a kid who was in my class last year. I sort of nod at him, because he is in the cage, and I feel funny watching them.

"What are you doing here? Do you play baseball?"

I shake my head no.

"Well, okay. Maybe I'll see you after the game."

I say okay, and I feel pretty good that Derek wants to see me later. Then I think about Derek seeing me in the ice-cream truck, and about Baba being mad, and I get worried, so I stop watching that game and walk over to watch a different one. There are four games at the same time, and the fields are arranged in a circle, with the food and stuff at the center. It's nicer than the soccer fields, because there you have to walk really far to see another game, and it's hard to park our truck where everyone will come by it. At baseball, everyone goes to the center, so as long as Nene gets a license to park there, we sell a lot of ice cream.

I can see Baba and Nene in the truck from here. Baba is shaking his head at a little kid, and I can see that Nene does not like it. The kid is handing his ice cream back to Baba. It doesn't look open, but Baba is shaking his head about taking it back. I can't hear what he says, but I see Nene come over and reach her hand out to take the ice cream. Baba gives her his worst look, and even though I can't see anything from this far, I know Nene is clenching her shoulders the way she does. I really don't want Derek to come to our ice-cream truck, but I don't know what I am going to do about it.

I don't feel like watching any more baseball, so I start walking away from the games and the food and the people. There are some trees at the edge of the park, and there is a dry wash over there, which sometimes even has water in it, and I think that I will hang out there for a while. Nene will get worried if I am gone too long, but I don't want to go back there right now. I don't know how I can help Nene anyway.

It is quiet and peaceful in the wash. There isn't any water today, but I see two lizards, and a chipmunk, and a whole bunch of quail. They get so nervous when I come that they run right at me. Quail are not very smart. I am not supposed to play with chipmunks, because Mrs. Jimenez says they carry a disease. I am pretty sure I couldn't catch a chipmunk, but it would be fun to have one for a pet.

I have to be careful where I walk because a lot of bushes look soft, but they have thorns. I am wearing jeans, so it will only hurt if they scratch my face or neck, but sometimes I have gotten a lot of pricklies in my jeans and scratched myself when I took them off at night. I find a big rock, and I sit down there to think for a while.

It is quiet, but I can hear things. I can hear the people cheering at the baseball game, far away, and I can hear those quails rustling around in the bushes. There is a bird making *sqwaaack* sounds too. The sun is on my face, and I close my eyes. It feels so warm.

Sometimes at night, before I go to bed, my nene and I watch TV. My nene likes *Jeopardy!*, even though she doesn't know very many answers, and I watch it with her just because she likes me to be there. When she tries to answer the questions, she gets all mixed up about the question words. She says, "Why is Abraham Lincoln?" and "How is a thermometer?" I like my nene's questions better than the right ones, and I sit on the couch next to her, not really watching, but listening to her funny question words. It feels sort of like I feel right now, all warm and peaceful. Sometimes my nene is trying to win, and she sits straight up, watching. Other times she sits back like me, and then she touches my head and my face real soft. My nene has long fingers, and she can make circles on my head and face that are softer than soft. I almost can't feel her fingers, they are so soft, but I know they are there barely touching me. I think I might be too big for her to do this now, but I really like it. I wish *Jeopardy!* would last longer when she is doing it.

I almost fall asleep there, and then I remember how worried Nene will be if I don't come back to the truck. I walk back fast. Derek's game is over, and I don't see anyone wearing his uniform, so I think I probably don't have to worry about him coming to the truck.

"Where were you?" Nene asks, kind of mad and kind of relieved.

"I was in the wash, and I forgot how long I was gone, Nene. I'm sorry."

"It's okay, Bashkim, but I couldn't see you and I couldn't leave the truck. I have been watching and watching."

I feel bad because I know how nervous Nene gets, and I am also worried that Baba is going to punish me. But Baba is really busy. One of the ice-cream freezers isn't keeping everything cold, and he is trying to figure out what the problem is. Plus, Tirana is up, and she wants someone to pay attention to her, so I don't really get in trouble because nobody has time to do it. I right away tell Tirana that I will play Mouses with her, so I know that helps Nene too.

I think we have had a pretty good afternoon at the baseball field by the time we leave, but Baba is upset about the freezer compartment. He says that fixing it will take all our profits for the day, and we still have to pay the power bill and the doctor bill. I think we are eating too much too. All of the baseball kids are pretty much gone, and we are cleaning up the truck to leave, when Baba and Nene finally start yelling. I think that they almost made it until we got home, but at least nobody I know is still here.

"Arjeta, you throw away this ice cream? You think I am such a rich man that you can throw away perfectly good ice cream?"

"It is half melted, Sadik. We can't sell melted ice cream. You know that we can lose our license for that."

"What difference does it make if we lose our license if we are already out on the street? Hmm! What difference does it make if we lose our license if I can't pay the rent this month? Foolish woman! Do you see an inspector here?"

My nene is quiet, and I know that she does not want the argument to get worse, but then, she can't stop herself. Very softly, she starts to say the worst thing.

"For love of Allah, Sadik, just kill me and my—"

Arrrgghh! Like that, my baba is shoving my nene into the side of the truck. Nene's head kind of thunks against it, and both Tirana and I scream. That makes Baba furious.

"Shut up! You children. Shut up! You have no idea what she is doing to us. Do you want to starve?"

I get quiet real fast, and even Tirana sort of gulps and stops crying. I can't believe she is big enough to figure out that she has to be quiet right now, but I guess she is getting more mature too.

Nene has moved away from the side of the truck, and she hisses at Baba.

"Stop it. Do you want someone to see us? Do you want someone to call the police? We are in a park."

This makes Baba stop, because he is afraid of police and because he knows Nene is right. He slams down the sliding panel that closes the counter on the truck, and I help Tirana get in the seat and buckle her belt. My heart is beating so loud that I am afraid Baba will hear it and get mad, so I try to take big breaths to stop it, but those are sort of loud too. I put my arm around Tirana, because it will really help if she can stay quiet. Baba and Nene get in the front seat, and we start to drive away. I notice that Baba and Nene don't buckle their seat belts, and this worries me, but it is not a good time to mention it. Nobody is saying anything in the truck, but it feels loud anyway, like someone is screaming, and I am just hoping that we can get home, and that they won't start yelling now, because I am afraid of my baba's driving when he is yelling, and I am not sure that I can keep Tirana quiet. I think about the dry wash and how peaceful it felt in there, and I feel so sad that I almost start to cry in the car. But I don't. That could set everybody off.

21

Bashkim

NOBODY TALKS ON THE ride home. Baba makes noises with his mouth, like he does when he is mad, but Nene does not react. I know she is afraid of what he will do, and I am glad that she is being really quiet, because I am afraid too. I keep one arm around Tirana, hoping she will stay quiet and figuring that nobody can see me doing this anyway. Tirana is such a baby that she starts to fall asleep right away. I wonder if she just forgot about being afraid a minute ago or if going to sleep is how a baby deals with it. I deal with it by counting my breaths: one, two, three, four. Our PE teacher has us lie on the mats and count our breaths sometimes, and now I do it on days like today. It sort of helps, except I am so nervous that I can't even count to four. I keep forgetting where I am and having to start over.

I don't recognize the sound at first. Baba curses, very loud, and Nene makes a kind of *aye* sound, and then I hear the whoop of a police siren, right behind us. I know this means Baba is supposed to stop, but he doesn't right away. He keeps driving, and I see Nene look at him, and she is about to say something, and then he swings the wheel right, very

fast, and the seat belt catches me hard at my waist as my head knocks
into the window, and Baba stops.

Nene is praying. Baba tells her to shut up. But she doesn't. She keeps
praying. I think about that a lot later. How Nene was praying. She was
praying, so where was God?

The police officer raps on Baba's window. Baba rolls it down, but it
takes him a minute, because he is shaking and the handle for the window
is kind of hard to roll down anyway, and the police officer raps a second
time, like he is already mad.

"Sir, I need your driver's license. And your registration and insurance, please."

The police officer doesn't sound mad, really, just sort of stern. Like
Mrs. Monaghan.

Baba doesn't react right.

"I'm American citizen," he says. "I'm American."

"I just need your license and your registration, sir."

"You can't stop me for nothing," Baba says. "You have to have a
reason."

The police officer steps slightly away from Baba's window. Stands up
straight. He waits a second before he speaks. I can hear Nene breathing.
I try to take a breath, because for some reason, I can't tell if I am breathing too much or not at all.

"Sir, I am going to ask you to step out of the vehicle. Your brake
light is out. And I want you to get out of the vehicle. *Now.*"

Baba starts to protest, and I am just begging him with my mind
to get out of the truck. Nene doesn't say anything, and Tirana is still
asleep, which is amazing. I notice again that Baba and Nene don't
have their seat belts on, and I wonder if they can get a ticket for this
too. Baba's back is shaking, so I think that he is afraid, because of the
prison and the police officer in Albania, but in America, the police
officer will not understand that, and I am just about to speak, to tell
the police officer to wait a minute, but he says, "Sir, you have children

in the backseat. I don't want this to get ugly. Now please get out of your vehicle."

He sounds real firm but not as mad as before, and that is enough for Baba. He fumbles with the door, and then he sort of stumbles out. The police officer tells him to face the truck, to spread his legs, and to place his palms on the door frame. Baba does, but he is still shaking, and this makes the truck shake, so that Nene and I can feel it. It is almost like having Baba's heart beat in my chest.

"Ma'am," says the police officer. "Could you please open your glove compartment and hand me your insurance and registration?"

Nene should just do this right away. Even I know that. Every kid in Mrs. Monaghan's class knows that. But Nene doesn't do it right away. Instead, she says, "We can't pay a ticket. We don't have any money. We can't get a ticket. Do you see my children? We have to feed these children."

Nene's voice is high and squeaky, and it wakes Tirana up. She starts to cry, but in a sleepy way. The police officer is getting annoyed.

"Ma'am, hand me your registration and insurance now."

I shush Tirana and make a fish face to try to get her to stop crying. Nene opens up the glove box and starts pulling out all the stuff that is in there. I think the police officer is probably getting more annoyed, but he is smart enough not to talk to Nene for a minute. Unfortunately, Baba does talk to Nene, even though he is standing against the door frame, and any kid would know he should probably be quiet right then.

"This is your fault, Arjeta. I can't pay everything. All the bills you get. Doctor. Medicine. Gas bill. I can't pay it. You are killing me."

Nene stops looking for the registration and says something to Baba in Albanian, which I don't catch, and then the police officer says, "Shut up. Stop talking. Ma'am, you have fifteen seconds."

I don't know what is going to happen in fifteen seconds. My heart is pounding, and my head is banging, and I am starting to see funny in the backseat. But Nene finds the papers. She can't hand them to the police officer through the window because Baba is standing against that door, so she gets out, and she walks them to him. Tirana holds out her arms and says, "Nene, Nene." I put my fingers in my ears and try to get Tirana to look at me. I should smile at Tirana when I do this, but I am having a hard time controlling my face. Nene walks toward the police officer with the registration.

"Stay back, ma'am."

Nene is surprised.

"Step back to the other side of the vehicle, ma'am."

That's when I see there is another police officer. He must have been in the car waiting, but now he is standing a little bit away from all of us. He is staring at Nene, and his look scares me. I don't think, I just open the door and slip out. I want to run to Nene, but I hesitate, and I stand next to the truck for a minute. Nobody seems to notice that I have gotten out. Nene walks away from the police officer, closer to me, but she still hasn't noticed that I am out of the truck.

"Sir, this registration expired three weeks ago. Do you have your new registration?"

Baba starts yelling.

"It's not my fault. I did not have the money. She takes all the money. She and these kids, and I did not have any money to pay this registration!"

Baba's voice is screechy, and his English is getting confused, and I am not even sure that the police officer knows he is speaking English because it sounds a lot like Albanian.

Then Nene starts. She is yelling at Baba and the police officer at the same time, all mixed up.

"You want that I should let our baby die of fever? What are we supposed to eat? Ice-cream cones? We cannot get a ticket. We have no money for a ticket. Would you put us in the street? What do you want me to do? Not feed our children?"

Nene's English is fine, but she is getting louder, and she is very upset. She loves me and Tirana so much, and she is afraid of Baba and afraid of the police, and even I know that she sounds crazy to these Americans.

And I want to tell them that she is not crazy, and that if they would just stop talking a minute, if they would just wait a minute, then Baba and Nene will be able to calm down. I am trying to figure out a way to tell the police officers this, and I don't know how, so I just run out and grab hold of my nene at the waist. I am crying, though I am trying not to, and the police officer says, "Stop. You cannot get out of the vehicle. Tell your son to get back in the vehicle, ma'am."

And maybe Nene is trying to push me back to the truck, and maybe I am clinging to her. I don't remember. I don't remember all of that. But I see the second police officer move his feet apart, and I see him reach for his gun. He is behind the first police officer. I don't think the first police officer even knows he is there yet, and my nene, she sees the second police officer too. She starts wailing, in Albanian. I think it was Albanian, but maybe it was just wailing. And Nene's cries make Baba start wailing. They are both so loud, and they don't know how Albanian sounds in America, and I don't know what to do. I keep staring at the second police officer because he has a gun, and he is staring at us.

I pull at Nene. I try to get her to come back to the truck with me. I can hear Tirana crying. But Nene is pushing me away. She pulls her ice-cream scoop out of her jacket, and she waves it, and says, "For the love of Allah, just kill me and my children!"

And like that, the second police officer, the one behind, I see him lift his gun, and he aims it at my nene, and I am trying to yell, but nothing comes out of my throat, and then I see his finger move, and I think, "He is going to shoot my nene!" And then his finger is done moving, and I didn't hear anything, so I think that he did not shoot her, that it is not a real gun, but then I feel Nene jerk, and sort of slump, and her breath comes out like a puff. She isn't yelling anymore.

"What the hell!" The first police officer is yelling at the second.

"What the hell are you doing? Put that weapon away. What the hell did you do?"

And the second police officer is just sort of standing there, like he doesn't know where he is, and he says, "She has a knife. She was going to kill her kid."

And the first police officer says, "What knife?"

And then Baba looks at me, and at Nene, and maybe he realizes, just then, that the gun has been fired. I didn't even hear it, but Baba looks at us, and he realizes, and he lets out this scream, and he just screams and screams.

And then the second police officer is handcuffing Baba, and the first police officer is looking at me and Nene, and I am holding on to Nene, and she has this funny look on her face, but she is standing, and I am thinking "Was she shot?" and I think that the first police officer is trying to figure this out too, and then Nene just makes this funny sound, and sort of sinks, right out of my arms, and sits on the curb, with her head down.

"Ma'am," says the police officer. "Ma'am, are you okay?"

And the second police officer yells something at Baba, and I hear Baba get banged against the truck, and then the first police officer says, "Nate, put him in the squad car. Go easy. I don't know what's happening over here."

And he comes over to me and to Nene, and he lifts Nene's face, and I see his face, and the way his cheeks suck in, and I scream, and I hold Nene, and I hear him on his radio, calling for an ambulance.

22

Avis

I CLICK ON THE television to see if the cable has been turned off or not. The instant I see the banner going across the bottom, I know. "Las Vegas police officer shoots woman at traffic stop." I sink to my knees, gripping the remote as if it could change time, as if I could turn off the TV, and with the force of the no inside me, turn time back, back an hour, back two hours—how long would we need, to start over, and for this not to be true?

There is no other information. The banner runs below a Channel 10 special about Nevada's wild horses, which was taped months ago, and even though it is almost evening, I cannot find local news on any station. I know that I should call Lauren, or Jim. I know that I should do something, confirm something, but already, I know.

I knew when Nate wrecked the car.

I knew when he was pulling Lauren's head back with her hair.

I knew when I heard him tell Jim that he and the guys had pounded shots after work in a dive off Boulder Highway.

I knew when he stepped off the plane the last time. I knew the instant I hugged him, that little course of energy through his body, that slight shiver.

THE PHONE RINGS. FINALLY STOPS. Starts again.

I don't recognize the number, and I don't answer it. Has a name already been announced?

I turn on the laptop and see that there is already a short story in the *Las Vegas Sun*. Just the minimum. No names yet. But the woman is dead. And my God, she was driving an ice-cream truck. At Pecos and Hacienda, not three miles from me. Worse, there were two children present. No more details.

The six-thirty news leads with the story. A routine traffic stop escalates to a shooting. There are preliminary reports that the woman had a knife, that she was threatening to kill her own son, that she did not speak English. The woman's husband and children were inconsolable. The father is in temporary custody, the children have been sent to Child Haven. There will be more later. Channel 8 will provide more details as they learn them.

I check the phone then. Lauren called at 5:51. Jim at 5:58.

I hesitate, not sure who I should call first, and then dial Jim's number.

"Avis, where are you? Have you seen the news?"

"Yes, I've seen the news."

"Nate was the officer who shot the woman."

"Yes, I imagined so."

"You imagined so? Really, Avis?"

I hear the anger in his voice. Should I hide that I knew? What good would that do? There's a pause, and I can't think of what to say, so I don't fill it.

"Nate's at the station. He'll probably be there awhile. His phone's not on, and Lauren's pretty upset. Darcy and I are headed over there right now."

Darcy. Did he tell me to warn me, or so that I would not come?

"I can leave now. I'll be there in twenty minutes."

"Um, sure, yeah. You should probably be there."

This will be the first time that Jim and I and Darcy have been together with the kids.

"Maybe it's better if you and Darcy go now. I can go later, or when Nate comes home. I can go tomorrow."

It is Jim's turn to be silent.

"Jim?"

"Yes."

"We knew Nate wasn't right. I knew he wasn't right. I don't know what to do."

"I can't talk about that now, Avis. You don't even know what happened. Already, you're blaming Nate. If he needs a good lawyer, we'll get him one."

If he needs a good lawyer.

"Darcy knows a lot about public relations. About how you handle this sort of thing. She can help."

Darcy. Public relations.

"Jim, call me when you know something more. If Lauren knows something. I'll be right here."

I don't wait for his answer. I know that I am close to losing control.

ABOUT EIGHT THIRTY, THERE IS a new banner on the bottom of the screen: "Witness disputes that woman had knife, and says she was 'clutching child.'"

At ten, there is a statement from the chief of police. They are investigating the events that led up to the shooting. The officers involved have been placed on administrative leave pending an investigation. The department extends its condolences to the family of the deceased, particularly her children.

The phone rings again. It's Jim.

"Nate's still not home, but he called Lauren. Apparently the woman had some sort of mental illness. She freaked out when they stopped her. Started yelling about Allah. Nate thought she was going to kill her son."

For a moment, I am hopeful. Maybe Nate hasn't done anything. Maybe it is Nate who has been saved. Maybe my son was almost killed this evening, and he was not. He is still alive.

"The partner's a problem. A witness heard him asking Nate why he took the shot. Where the knife was."

And I fold. Maybe Nate is innocent, and damn me if his own mother didn't believe him, but I have seen Nate's hand twisted cruelly in Lauren's hair, I have seen Nate rushing toward Rodney, and I know that my son is not himself. Something has happened to him, and now something has happened to someone else.

"Avis. Pull yourself together. I don't know what you've been doing all night, but we're still a family. Nate needs you, and you're going to have to get it together."

We're still a family.

"Avis, are you there? What are you doing?"

I don't know what I am doing. I never knew what I was doing. I just jumped in and tried, no manual, I tried as hard as I could, and for the second time in my son's life, I missed the important cue. The first time, a boy was paralyzed. The second time, a mother has been killed. It wasn't because I didn't care, it wasn't because I was lazy, it isn't because my son is a bad man. Nate is a good man.

"Avis? Avis?!"

I hear Jim's voice, and just as clearly, in just as ordinary a way, I hear two children crying. I hear Rodney and I, huddled in the closet, crying, while our mom's head is banged, once, twice, three times, against a wall. And I hear two other children, I can't see them, but I hear them, they are crying for their mother. They are terrified, and I hear the sound of the shot, and then I hear them crying.

Should I explain this to Jim? That my mind is playing tricks on me and that I can hear children crying while he is speaking? There was a time when he would have understood.

Instead, I tell him that I will be at Nate and Lauren's house tomorrow. I tell him that I am sorry, sorry for everything, I ask him to tell Lauren I love her, and then I hang up.

Immediately, the phone rings.

It's Rodney. Did he hear the crying too?

"Avis. It's Rodney."

His voice is thick. He's been drinking, of course. But he knows. Just like me, he knew as soon as he saw the story.

"Was it Nato?"

"Yes."

I hear Rodney's shivery, shallow breathing. He always has a hard time breathing, and when he drinks, it's worse.

"Avis?"

"Yes."

"Do you remember Mark?"

"Yes."

Again, the breathing. I am fighting to breathe too. Thinking of Rodney. He'll be sitting in the dark, just the television on, his lunch plate still on the coffee table, a bottle of Jack Daniel's within reach.

"Mark was a vet. Do you remember that?"

"Yes."

"Remember that time Mom said she wanted to go to Italy? She wanted to dance with an Italian man?"

I want Rodney to stop. I remember the time, I remember what Mark said, I remember what happened.

"Rodney, I remember. Please, I remember."

"Our Nato's not Mark, Avis. He's not Mark."

"No, he's not Mark, Rodney."

There's no sense trying to talk to Rodney. He's too drunk, and there're things he won't talk about anyway, but I wish I could talk to him. If there's anyone in the world who could understand what I feel tonight, it's Rodney.

SHARLENE SAID IT AGAIN.

"Fifty dollars. The guy gave me fifty dollars! He just peeled one off the top of the stack. Said he could take me to dinner later too."

This time Mark does not even bother to curse at her, to scream. There is just this roar of his body flying across the room, and my mother's yelp, and then the sound of both of them slamming to the floor.

Sharlene screams. Mark yells.

"You slutty, shitting bitch! You fucking bitch!"

And there are more sounds, of struggle, of body on body, of pain.

I take Rodney by the hand, he shakes violently, and without a sound, Rodney picks up his blanket, and I take two pillows, and we slip into Sharlene's closet. This is where we go when we are afraid, when Sharlene comes home too late, when something bad happens on the strip of concrete outside our apartment door. In the back of the closet, where the roof slants too low for Sharlene to stand, and where she has stashed winter clothes she rarely wears, Rodney and I keep our own stash. My old black bear. A bent postcard from Stanley, who was one of Sharlene's boyfriends, the only one that ever wrote to us. Two decks of casino cards, with a hole in the middle of each one. Rodney's plate with the picture of Elvis on it.

I curl into my usual spot, but Rodney puts the extra pillow in his and settles into my lap. We often sit like this for the worst bits, Rodney's soft blond hair against my cheek, my arm wrapped across his small body. Having Rodney changes everything. His warm body relaxes me, and I can feel his shaking start to slow, soften, almost stop. But it is harder this time, since it is not just that Mark has hit Sharlene or that they are yelling. No, they are still fighting: their bodies crashing into furniture, into the walls.

Thunk. Thunk.

Rodney wiggles out of my lap and stands up at the other end of the closet. When he comes back, he has the gun he told me about, the one in Mark's brown bag, the one he found when he was playing in the closet alone. He hands it to me, and I take it. I have never seen a gun, much less held one. It is heavy. And cold.

Thunk.

Rodney shivers in front of me, eyes on mine.

So quickly, before I can be afraid, I take the gun and go out to the living room where Sharlene and Mark are fighting. I aim the gun in the direction of Mark, not sure how to hold it. It is much too large for my hands.

"Stop!"

"What the fuck?"

"Stop hurting her."

I can feel Rodney behind me, his chin against my back.

"Give me that gun, you little shit."

Mark lunges at me. And then fast, faster that I can think, Sharlene is there, tugging the gun from my hands, throwing me and Rodney backward onto the floor, and Mark is grabbing at Sharlene, and they are struggling, struggling for the gun. But Sharlene wrenches away, aims the gun straight at Mark—it is not too big for her hands—screams at him to get out, get out, get out.

And Mark's voice is soft now—he is calling her a crazy, stupid bitch—but I can hear the uncertainty, the fear, in his voice, and he backs away toward the door, and Sharlene is screaming, "Get out! Get out!" And then Mark lunges toward her. And the gun goes off. There are two sounds, the bullet pings off something and then hits something else, but it does not hit anyone—not Mark, not me, not Rodney. Mark flees.

Sharlene stands there, a stunned look on her face. There is total silence.

Then the sound of a siren.

And Sharlene sinks to the floor, crying harder than I have ever seen her cry.

"I could have killed him. I wanted to kill him."

She is bleating like an animal and moaning, and she has not looked at me or Rodney at all. She does not know that the ping, the ricochet, did not send the bullet our way. She didn't look.

"I could have killed him."

Rodney stares at me, eyes wide. He is perfectly quiet.

When the officer walks in, hand on the grip of his gun, our door is wide open, and we are just like that: Sharlene murmuring and crying, and Rodney and I, motionless, silent, stunned.

"Ma'am. Ma'am. What happened here? What's going on here?"

And then Sharlene is trying to stand up, and she motions to the gun on the floor where she has dropped it, and she is muttering, "I almost killed him, I could have killed him."

By the time the policemen leave, there are two of them, they have taken the gun, they are telling Sharlene that they will find Mark, that she might want to think about moving to another place, getting away from this guy, that she has two kids to look out for, that next time they might have to take the kids, send us to Utah for foster care, that a gun is a really serious thing, and if someone had been shot, they wouldn't be able to do much, to protect her, to protect the kids. They say they will stop in every now and then to see how she is doing.

And Rodney? He goes to sleep. One of the police officers gives him a chocolate lollipop, and he eats it, eyes wide, watching the policemen. And when the candy is gone, when he has eaten the stick into a gluey white pulp, he falls asleep, in the middle of the upturned chair, the broken lamp, the police officers talking to our mother, one with his arm around her shoulders.

I don't take a lollipop. I don't say anything.

Not to the policeman. Not to Sharlene.

She never looked at Rodney and me. She never looked to see where the bullet went.

I REMEMBER THIS. I DO not want to remember it. I have spent my life not remembering it. But I can't stop it now, now that I have talked with Rodney, now that Rodney knew, right away, that it was Nate who shot the woman with the ice-cream truck. I remember it, I remember it all. I remember the closet, I remember the crying. I still hear two other children, crying, crying, as their mother falls to the street in front of them.

Because I need to do something, because I learned a long time ago that remembering, by itself, is a path to hell, I do what I should have done years ago—should have done when Emily was still a baby, should never have allowed in the first place.

I go upstairs, and I take that gun out of my dresser, and the bullets out of the closet. How many times have I thought nervously about that gun since I first discovered it in my drawer five months ago? How many times have I wondered if someone would find it, if someone would use it? How many times have I tamped those thoughts down, not wanting to remember, not wanting to have this very memory that I have now had?

I am not sure how to dispose of a gun. But I don't want this gun to be used ever, so I put it in the toilet, thinking that the water will rust its parts and make it useless. It looks bizarre there, a gun in a toilet, and just for a second, I laugh. I try to remind myself that this is not funny, but the laugh releases something. I wish Rodney were here to see this: a gun in a toilet, his fifty-three-year-old sister gingerly placing it there. And then it comes to me in a rush. The six-year-old girl who picked up that gun, carried it out of the closet, aimed it at a violent man, was brave. She was wildly, brilliantly brave. I've never thought of that day with anything but shame—the shame of a child whose mother did not look—but right now, staring at that gun in the toilet, something like elation comes over me.

I suppose I've always seen that day the way I saw it when I was six.

And now I see the six-year-old.

I sit there, shivering in a cold bathroom, staring at a gun in a toilet, knowing that my son's life is coming apart, and I feel, well, whole. Avis Eileen Briggs. No one in this world cared if that little girl lived or died; almost no one in this world would have known one way or the other. But look what she did. Look who she was. Look who I was.

I'M SURE BULLETS COUNT AS a hazardous waste, but I decide that I don't care. I tie them into a trash bag tightly, and then I put that bag inside a bag of kitchen waste, and then I put the kitchen waste in the middle of the largest garbage can. It's possible that they will be found, but I doubt it.

Before I leave the house, I will get the gun out of the toilet. I'll hide it the same way I hid the bullets. It won't be the worst thing to make it into a landfill.

23

Roberta

SOMETIMES BEING A CASA is scary. The weeks of training don't seem like much when I'm walking into a bombed-out shell of a house off Owens by myself. I carry Mace for the dogs, but what do you carry for the slurring, blank-eyed drug addict who doesn't want you to talk to her two-year-old child? What do you carry for the mentally ill brother, or the old man in the corner yelling about the gooks? Of course, I don't have to make those sorts of visits. A lot of CASAs don't. It's just that I know my recommendations can upend a child's whole world. I like to be sure.

I've volunteered as a Court Appointed Special Advocate for thirteen years, so I can generally choose which families I work with. As soon as I read the reports of the shooting, as soon as I heard that the children had been there, that the father was going crazy, as soon as I read the same newspaper articles everyone else did, I knew I would request the case. Those children would end up in foster care, at least for a while, and they would almost certainly be assigned a CASA, even though we were short-handed. I wanted to be that CASA. I'm as afraid of making a mistake as anyone else, but if there's one thing thirteen years have taught me, it's that I'd rather live knowing I made a mistake than wondering if I could have made a difference if I'd tried.

The way I see it, nothing in life is a rehearsal. It's not preparation for anything else. There's no getting ready for it. There's no waiting for the real part to begin. Not ever. Not even for the smallest child. This is it. And if you wait too long to figure that out, to figure out that we are the ones making the world, we are the ones to whom all the problems—and all the possibilities for grace—now fall, then you lose everything. Your only shot at this world.

I get that this one small life is all we have for whatever it is that we are going to do. And I want in.

LOU WAS FINE WITH MY request. She said she had expected it, and that even though Bernie might also want the Ahmeti children, one of his current cases was in too precarious a situation for his attention to be divided.

So that was that, and now we waited. ·It would take a while, even after the children were placed in foster care, for the CASA request to be made. I got ready. I tracked down a contact at Catholic Refugee Services, because I saw that the Ahmetis had originally been sent to Las Vegas through them. I looked up the family's address and searched the school district website for information about the elementary school that Bashkim probably attended. I even found a couple of listings for Albanian cultural organizations, just in case the Ahmetis were involved with one. And then I called my nephew, who works at LVPD.

"Ari, it's Roberta. I was wondering if we could get together, talk about that shooting, this week?"

"Hi, Roberta. I thought you might call. Have you got the case already?"

"No. It hasn't come in, but it will. Can you talk?"

"Yeah, a little. I'm headed out of town for a week, so we can talk now and meet when I get back if you want. Let me shut my door."

"So, Ari, do you know anything about this guy? What's going to happen?"

"What's going to happen? Nothing. There'll be an investigation. He'll be cleared. That'll be it from our end."

"Yeah, I suppose so."

"The thing is, the cop's a local kid. His dad's Jim Gisselberg, from MGM Resorts. That's how he got on the force so fast, though he would have made it anyway. Served three tours in Iraq."

"Iraq?"

"Yeah. Army. Special Forces."

"So is that the story? He was trigger happy? He's got anger issues? What happened?"

"Roberta, I can't tell you much about that. I mean, everybody's talking. He's a popular guy, but there are a couple of people who have had doubts. He's gotten pretty drunk off duty, and he can get wild. He's been with guys from the force, so they've stopped him from doing anything too crazy. I mean, he just barely got out of the service, and he was a cop. Right into the academy, right into a patrol. So who knows?"

"Ari, why does LVPD do this? Why so fast?"

"I told you. He's got a dad. He's a war hero. He's a local Vegas kid. He tests well. Look at it from our side: he's a great hire."

"Yeah? Do you know him yourself? What do you think?"

"I've talked to him. Our paths cross. But I've never had a drink with him. I don't work with cops on the beat anymore. So he's just a big, buff-looking guy. I talked with his wife at the Christmas party. She seemed nice. I really don't know anything more."

"Okay. Yeah. What about the dad? Sadik Ahmeti. What are they saying about him?"

"Oh, well, nobody here's going to have a kind word for that guy. He's a nut job. No trouble with the law, though. Got citizenship last spring. Hasn't paid some parking tickets. Obviously didn't pay up on his truck registration. This is the kind of stuff we know about him. He was a political prisoner in Albania. Probably made him paranoid. That's the last guy that a cop wants to meet on a bad day."

"It doesn't sound like he's going to be in any shape to take those kids. And the paper says that there are no relatives in this country."

"I read that too. You know the other cop that was there, Nate Gisselberg's partner, nobody's heard from him all week. They're both on leave, until everything gets settled, but Corey—the guy's name is Corey Stout—he didn't even come in to pick up his check. Nate's dropped in every day, wanting to talk, wanting to hear what's being said, but I got the feeling Corey is in a bad way over this. He's a really nice guy, solid, honest. And he's got three little kids. I'm guessing that he's taking it hard."

"Poor guy. Wrong partner."

"Yeah, maybe. How are you, Roberta? Still trying to save the world? Still working so hard?"

"Come on, Ari. What else is there to do? Save the world. See a movie. Go to bed."

"Yeah, and when was the last time you saw a movie? How about Marty? How's he holding up?"

"Marty? He's great. Maybe he'd like me to slow down a bit. Who knows? But he's great. Listen, Ari, have a really good time next week. You and Melissa have earned it."

"Thanks, Roberta."

AFTER THAT CALL, I START making a list with the names of everyone I might want to meet in the Ahmeti case. There would be a caseworker, of course, and if we were lucky, both kids would get the same foster family. But maybe not. The system's never been more crowded. When the economy's tough, kids come into our system like we're offering dessert. Parents bolt, or overdose, or beat the hell out of anyone that seems weaker. And the kids just pour in. So who else? The dad. His lawyer. He'll certainly have a lawyer, sooner or later. Not much money, so probably no lawyer for the children. That makes my job easier. See, if a child has a lawyer, that lawyer has to argue for what the child wants. But my job is to argue for what the child needs. And they're not always the same. So it's easier for me if there isn't a lawyer.

Who else? The principal at Bashkim's school. His teacher. Maybe a school counselor. No relatives. My friend at Catholic Refugee Services said the Ahmetis were pretty much on their own at this point but that there was one caseworker who had stayed in touch. I'd go to the apartment complex where they lived, too. See if there were any neighbors who knew the family. Also, the kids might have a pediatrician. I'd made the mistake of not tracking down a pediatrician before. And, of course, the CPS caseworker would probably order a counseling workup on both kids, so I would want to talk to that counselor too.

It's a long list, and as I meet these people, the list will get longer. That's why I wanted to be the Ahmetis' CASA, because not every CASA will be this thorough. Some of them don't know they can meet with anyone they want, whether or not the caseworker recommends it, and some of them think too many meetings just muddy the issues. Me, I want to know everything. I want to meet every person myself. And when it comes time to make a decision, I want to know that I did everything I could to make sure that the recommendations I make to the judge are the recommendations I would want a CASA to make for my own child.

24

Avis

THE DAY AFTER THE shooting, I call before coming over. Lauren sounds tired and afraid, and when I say I will be there in an hour, she says she is going to see her mom. I had forgotten that her parents were in town. I don't want to imagine what they are thinking—it is too much right now—so I say I will see her later and that she can call me, and to tell Nate I am coming.

When I arrive, I see Nate's motorcycle through the bars of the back gate. It looks as if he has been tinkering with it again. The house is very quiet, as is the street. Nobody is out, though it's going to be a beautiful day: bright, and just barely cool, with the sound of sparrows in the trees and a mockingbird somewhere down low.

I feel suddenly tired. Aware of all the ways that this moment might not have come to be. I ring the bell.

It seems like minutes before Nate answers.

"Mom," Nate says. His voice sounds strained. I wonder if it surprises him to push out the word so uncomfortably.

"Hi, Nate."

I reach up to hug him, and we embrace uncomfortably.

"Come in, Mom. I've been waiting for you to come. You could have come when Dad was here."

He walks toward the kitchen, and I follow. I can smell coffee, and that will be a good way to begin.

"Do you want a cup?"

"Yes. I'll get it. Do you want more?"

"No."

We sit down then, at the table I brought them months ago. I wonder if Nate remembers that I came the day he was on suspension. Knowing what I know, I wonder what happened after I left, after Lauren had blurted out why he was home, after Nate had looked at her that way.

I'm glad we're alone.

"How are you, Nate?"

He doesn't answer.

"It just seems like your Dad and I can do better on our own right now."

"I know, Mom."

"Will you tell me about it? What happened?"

"Why, Mom? Haven't you already made up your mind? Don't you already know that I went crazy and killed a kid's mom? Don't you already know that, Mom? You and everyone else who watches the local news?"

His voice is angry and hurt and oddly high. And for once, this emotion does not make me afraid. What else could he feel?

I wait.

"They were both crazy, Mom. The man and the woman. He was just belligerent. Corey could handle him, but she was really crazy. She was shaking and grabbing her son and holding him by the neck and talking about Allah and how she would rather be dead, and her children too. I was trying to save that kid's life, Mom. I was trying to protect my partner. That's what I was doing."

Nate believes what he is saying. Others are going to believe him too.

Because it's true. It is what Nate believed, it is what Nate was thinking. But it's not the whole truth. And as much as I want it to be, as much as I want my son to be innocent now, I know that what Nate was thinking is not quite the right measure here. What was he thinking when he had Lauren by the hair? What was he thinking when he crashed that car? What would someone else have been thinking faced with that woman and her child?

I don't speak.

"You're my mother, and you don't believe me. Dad believes me. Lauren believes me. The guys on the force believe me. My sergeant believes me. What does it say that you don't believe me, Mom?"

"I believe you, Nate."

And I do. I believe that this is what he believes and what he was thinking. How can I tell him that I don't believe that what he was thinking was rational? That I don't believe he can be trusted to think rightly? At least, not always.

"Do you, Mom? It doesn't feel like you believe me. You're sitting there, and I don't think you believe me."

"Nate. I love you. I have loved you your entire life. But I am afraid for you. I see—"

He interrupts me.

"What, Mom? You see what? What do you think you see? What do you think you know? Do you think I'm crazy? Do you think I'm some crazy-ass warrior, Mom? Some guy who can't stop fighting? What do you know about it, Mom? What do you think you know?"

"Nate. Please."

"Please what, Mom? You obviously think I'm crazy. Maybe you've always thought I was crazy. You always blamed me for Paul. You're so on your high horse about a fight I had with Lauren. Did you ever think about my side of that? Did you ever think Lauren might have been at fault? No, it's always Nate's fault. I'm your son. I'm your only child. You're supposed to be on my side."

"Nate, what are you talking about? Stop this. I am on your side. I will always be on your side. I think you need help. I think something happened to you, in Iraq, this last time. I think you need to see a doctor."

"So, it's my fault. Right. Some crazy immigrant tries to kill her son, and I stop her from doing it, and I'm the one who's wrong. That's how you see this, Mom? That's how you see it?"

He is standing now, and he is angry, and for an instant, I am afraid. But then a deep calm comes over me. If Nate is dangerous, if Nate cannot control himself, then I am the one who should be here. Better me than Lauren.

"Mom, do you know what it was like being your kid? Being the child who was born after Emily died, being the only kid you and Dad had? Do you know what that was like, Mom?"

"Nate, what are you talking about?"

"I'm talking about you, Mom. You and Dad and me. It was so intense. I could never get away from it. Being everything to both of you. Just me. There was no one else. I don't even have a cousin."

"Nate, this isn't the problem."

"Yes, it is, Mom. It was too much. It was too much for me. Too much for Dad. Why do you think Dad's with Darcy now? Don't you see, nobody can take it? How much you care? How intense you are?"

I don't know how this conversation got started. I don't know how we are talking about me, about what is my fault, instead of about what has happened. I intend to place my hand on the table, but it comes down hard. It lands with a clunk, and it rattles the cup, and that startles me, so perhaps that is why my voice is not as strong as I want it to be.

"Nate. This isn't what we are talking about. This isn't the point."

"You scared the hell out of me, Mom. You were always afraid something was going to happen to me. I was going to run in the street, or fall out of a tree, or get cancer or something."

"Nate, I didn't hold you back. I let you climb to the top of every monkey bar, ski in Utah when I knew there were avalanches and you would not stay on the trail, drive around in that truck as soon as you were sixteen. You joined the Army at eighteen, and you think I held you back? You think I was overprotective?"

"You weren't overprotective, Mom. You weren't overprotective."

His voice is so bitter. And we both sit. Silent.

Finally, I speak.

"Nate, it's true. I was always afraid for you. I tried not to let that limit you. I tried to let you be who you were. This bold, bold boy. I didn't want to hold you back. The last thing I wanted was to make you afraid."

"But I was afraid, Mom."

His voice breaks.

"I'm scared, Mom. I'm going out of my mind. It's not about you. It's not about what you did or didn't do. I always knew you loved me, you and Dad. Hell, I felt like the whole neighborhood loved me. I'd never have survived Iraq without that. Because you can't imagine, Mom. What it was like there. What we had to do."

He's crying now, fat, slow tears that drop on the table between us.

"I thought I would die every day. Every hour. Not at first. Crazy shit happened in the first tour, but I don't know, it didn't bother me like it bothered some other guys. I mean, we were at war. We did what we were told to do. People died. Kids died. Women died. But I thought we had to do it. I thought it was part of a grand plan. What my generation had to do.

"And then, I don't know, it just changed. I mean, what were we doing over there? What was the plan? Why were we there? Some hot-shit general would come to Baghdad, or some senator, and it was all the same. They didn't know what they were doing. They didn't know what they were talking about. They didn't even listen to our officers, the guys who really knew what was going on. We were fighting one war in Anbar, and they were fighting some whole other war, with a whole different set of rules, in Tikrit. So what were the rules? Was I supposed to know who should die and who shouldn't?

"And the way guys died, Mom. The way our guys died. Not when you were expecting it. Not when you were all geared up and looking for the enemy. No, guys just died going to take a piss. Picking up an old lady's scarf. Backing up to throw a football. You never knew when.

"Or how it would happen. There'd be a lid on the ground, just a standard garbage lid. And you'd think the wind had blown it off. Like if you saw it on your street at home. And some guy would be talking, telling us about how he was going to paint his house for his wife, and then he'd lean down, start to pick up the lid, and the whole thing would blow. And the guy would blow too. Just blow apart, right in front of you. You'd be throwing your arms up, trying to get away from the blast, and you'd see the guy's leg in the air next to you.

"And there were kids everywhere. They were hoping we would have chocolate. They'd want to play ball. Until one of them would light some-one up. Someone would lean over to hand the kid a piece of chocolate, and boom, the kid would go up. A bomb on his back. Did he know it? Did he know he had a bomb? Who put it there?

"You're afraid of the kids. You're afraid of the old ladies. You're scared as hell of any rock you can't see around, any building with a hole up high, where a gun might come through. You're looking for it all the time. You're seeing it even when it isn't there. And then guys are doing stuff. Stuff you can't believe. Sick stuff. Cruel stuff. Stuff you couldn't imagine in training. And the officers are looking the other way. And you're thinking that if they weren't doing that stuff, you probably would be dead already. Because maybe they're scaring the locals a little. Maybe their crazy stunts are keeping things a little in control.

"And then you get back. And you're home. And Lauren is asking me about my life there. And what am I supposed to say? You can't even imagine it. It's like a dream. Only you're still so damn jittery. And I'm still looking for that hole in the wall up high, and the rock, and the kid with the bomb. I'm looking for it all the time. I can't stop. If I hadn't been looking when I was there, I'd be dead. I wouldn't be here, Mom.

But I'm still waiting to get killed here. I can't stop feeling like something is about to happen, something bad, something I have to be ready for, I have to be quick, I have to be ready."

I don't think Nate has ever said this many words in one burst to me.

And perhaps for the first time I see that Nate is like Rodney, and like Sharlene. Something has happened to him that is more than he can bear. He wants to steel his courage, to soldier forth, but he keeps sliding back. I try to look at him, try to say something that will help, but he can't look me in the eye, and I can't think of what to say. I wait, looking at him, hoping the right words will come to me. I want to tell him that the pain will go away, that it will be possible to go back to the way life was before, but I don't know this. I have seen that this doesn't always happen, so the words won't come.

He sets his head on the table, and I lay my hand on his hair.

I tell him that I love him, that I will always love him.

He doesn't respond, doesn't move.

But I know he is listening, and I tell him over and over.

IT'S FUNNY WHAT COMES TO mind when the worst possible thing happens. After Jim left, I thought my life was over. I had tried so hard, and Jim had stopped loving me anyway. But failing isn't proof that nothing matters or that we were fools to care. We fail even though things matter very much; it's the possibility of failure that makes them matter even more.

I can hear Cheryl's voice telling me her "fraction of a mite of an atom of a life is fucking great." I can hear myself asking her why anyone would care if an ant stepped on the leg of the ant in front of it, or whether a mussel dried out after a high tide. And finally, for the first time since I wagged my middle-aged ass at Jim, who coughed, I can see clearly how crazy my thinking was. At fifty-three years old, I almost lost what I had somehow known from the time I was a small girl. I almost lost the knowledge that made my life work, the awareness that got me out of Sharlene's world, the faith that made three decades of marriage possible and everything good that happened in those years: the family we had, the friends we made, the laughs we shared, the tears, the everything of it. At fifty-three, I almost forgot what Avis Briggs always knew.

It all matters. That someone turns out the lamp, picks up the windblown wrapper, says hello to the invalid, pays at the unattended lot, listens to the repeated tale, folds the abandoned laundry, plays the game fairly, tells the story honestly, acknowledges help, gives credit, says good night, resists temptation, wipes the counter, waits at the yellow, makes the bed, tips the maid, remembers the illness, congratulates the victor, accepts the consequences, takes a stand, steps up, offers a hand, goes first, goes last, chooses the small portion, teaches the child, tends to the dying, comforts the grieving, removes the splinter, wipes the tear, directs the lost, touches the lonely, is the whole thing.

What is most beautiful is least acknowledged.

What is worth dying for is barely noticed.

I GREW UP, THE BASTARD child of a dirt-poor mother, in downtown Las Vegas. I raised my son in a town nicknamed Sin City, in a place most American families wouldn't dream of bringing their children, in a state where prostitution is legal and gambling is sacrosanct. And the little world we created, Jim and I and all those other hopeful families, was a little bit of perfect, a little bit of just what children are supposed to have, of just what families are supposed to be.

"Tell me the truth, how much time do you spend wishing you lived somewhere other than Las Vegas?"

"That's a trap. Don't waste your time thinking of that. Live this moment."

"Bullshit, Avis. I know you've thought about leaving. I would kill for a street with a bookstore and a coffee shop and something to look at. I would kill to be able to walk somewhere. To see a tree."

"Oh my God, to live in a city with a subway system. Not to even own a car."

"Where our kids could like go somewhere, without someone driving them? Where we could be outside in the summer?"

"Where there are schools with windows in the classrooms? And green grass? And some normal number of children?"

"What if our kids could all bike to a decent park? Or the store? What if the store wasn't a 7-Eleven?"

"Ahhh. Bliss."

"Yeah, but what about us? What about all of us gals? Where could we all go? We're in this together. Ella wrote in her second-grade essay that she had four moms. I mean, yeah, I wish I had some family in town, but if we all did, we wouldn't need each other. It wouldn't be like this."

"Julie, you're a sap. We love you."

"That calls for a drink. Let's open the wine. Someone order pizza before the kids start collapsing."

Julie and Cheryl and Jill and Margo and I might have had that conversation a hundred times when our children were young. Over and over. And Julie was right. Having each other was enough. What we had done was enough.

Yes, visiting some other place, some beautiful city, a beach, a forest, street life, yes, all that could make one wish for something else: for something other than asphalt and concrete and strip malls, desert dirt, stucco roofs, skinny little trees being held up by thick bands of rubber. For a day or two, one might dream of another life, a life that would make a better-looking film clip, and then get back to this one, this life that was also easy, where the money was good, the houses were cheap, the sky was always blue, and everyone was free to make a friend, to join a group, to try something new.

Boomtown.

And because it was so easy, so take-it-for-granted easy, we did take it for granted. My friends dreamed of the lives they were meant to live. As they kept on living this one. I dreamed of the childhood I didn't have. As Nate lived it.

And it seems like we were right. Living in the picture-postcard city, in the beautiful place, wouldn't have been everything we imagined. Because if we already had all that, would we have tried so hard to make it work here? Would we have worked so hard to keep our children friends, to put on musicals at the school, to insist that the city add a crossing guard on Pecos, to spend all our New Year's Eves together in one chaotic champagne and Scrabble and noisemaking heap?

Because we did.

Because that was the thing about making it all work in a boomtown.

We created a community out of nothing. And we were proud of it. And maybe we didn't look like a lot of other communities out there. We weren't much alike. One of us had turned a trick in a casino before she finished high school. Others of us had gone to college. One of us had never been inside a church. Others of us prayed daily. One of us had never known a grandparent, an uncle, or a cousin. Others had grown up in families in which nobody had ever divorced. Some of us had relatives who were drug addicts, some of us had worked nights in casinos, some of us had grown up thinking *darn* was a curse word. Some of us were military families, some of us could barely stand to recite the Pledge of Allegiance.

We weren't a community anyone would predict.

That's what we were trying to say in all those conversations about wanting to leave but not wanting to leave each other. We lived in a misunderstood city, in a place that thrives only by convincing outsiders that it is something it is not, and the magic is how free it leaves those left within. That was true for Sharlene, and it was true for me, and it was true for my friends.

And what we built did matter.

Even if it didn't last. Even if it didn't change the world. Even if lots of families were doing the very same thing in lots of other communities.

It still mattered. For a little while, a man and a woman fell in love and did the best they could for their children. For a little while, a neighborhood of families helped each other out, and loved each other's kids, and tried to make the world better. And some of those kids will do the same thing. And some of those kids will have a hard time. And some of those marriages will last. And some won't. And it still all mattered.

25

Roberta

THE AHMETI CHILDREN WERE assigned to Lacey Miller, and I had known her for years. I stopped by on Tuesday, just after the staff meeting. They would have gone over all the new cases, and Lacey would have an idea what the options were for Bashkim and Tirana. The children had been placed in separate foster homes, at opposite ends of the city, and my first priority was to find out if there was any way to fix that.

Lacey's desk was in a kind of open alcove off the stairs, and we couldn't discuss the case in a coffee shop, so we met in the director's office. Lacey didn't care for him, and even though he was out of town, her body radiated a slight unease at being in his space. We sat at a small conference table near the window. Lacey's head was silhouetted against the black lines of the window frame and the sunny panes of glass. It hurt to look directly at her, and I couldn't see her face clearly. I kept trying to avoid the painful contrast of light and dark behind her head.

"Lacey, I have the Ahmeti case. I'm worried about the children being in different homes. Is that temporary? Is there any chance of them being placed together?"

"Roberta, no. Really, not much chance. We have twenty percent more children in the system than we had last year, and ten percent fewer families to take them in. The economy cuts both ways for us. More children need help, and some of our best families are leaving town or taking in their own family members. We're left with the ones that do it mostly for the money, and they're happy to cram a few more children in corners, but that's not where we want kids."

"Yeah, I understand. But these children are small, and there's going to be a lot of media around this case . . ."

"Right, you mean they deserve special consideration? Because they don't have a drug-addicted mom? Because they haven't been in and out of the system since birth? I really don't think that means that they should get a break from us."

"Lacey. That's not what I'm saying. We've worked together for years. You know I don't think that."

"Well, I can't do anything about it. Those kids both got great foster families, and they put those families over the limit. There's no way they are going to end up together, not for a long time, and if you push for that, you just run the risk of getting them stuck together in a bad home."

"Okay, I get it. Thanks for telling me. Is there anyone else? Family anywhere? Friends?"

"Are you kidding? This family was totally cut off. The dad's a piece of work. Probably beat her. Really angry. They're Albanian, but no one in the Albanian community knows them. Catholic Refugee Services tried to set them up with some connections there, but they never followed through. I talked with Gina. She says she thinks the mom was really lonely. She wanted to go back to Albania, but, of course, they couldn't. He's a political refugee. But they were tight-knit. Mom never admitted anything that was going on. Dad's paranoid. Afraid of the system. Afraid of authority."

"What about the kids? What are they like?"

"That's the amazing part. They're really sweet. Both foster families rave about them. The little girl doesn't understand that her mom is gone. She keeps asking when she gets to go home, and if her nene knows where she is. The little boy's quiet. And smart. They like him at school. He is with Jeannette Delain. You must have worked with her before."

"Yes, I know Jeannette. Where's Tirana?"

"With a family that's only been in the system a year. They're very good, though. Mormon. Five children, teenagers and up. We place a lot of young children with them because the older kids are good with babies too. Kelly and Robin Stoddard. She's Robin."

"How's the boy? What has Jeannette said?"

"Well, I don't know. He's very sad, very serious. I got him placed with Jeannette because she lives right across from his school. Her foster kids have been going there for years. So she knows the principal, he can stay in his same classroom. I really tried hard to place them well. Even though it's crazy around here."

"Yeah. Thank you, Lacey. I'm sorry I roared in with wanting them placed together. I get it. But there's just no place for them to go outside the system? What about the dad?"

"Well, he wants them. He wants his family together. But I doubt that he knows a thing about taking care of them. And he's a mess. They checked him into Desert Care. They don't really have room for him, but he's on a suicide watch right now. As I said, he's angry. He gets violent. He's paranoid. He's going to be hard to deal with. And once he gets out of Desert Care, he's going to get these kids back. He hasn't done anything to lose them. And that's when things are really going to get bad, because he can't take care of them, and there's no support system. That's why we called you in. We really don't expect to have them long enough to need a CASA, but we're hoping that there's an option we can't see yet."

"Hmmm. Okay. I'll do what I can. I'll talk to everybody. There must be someone. Somewhere. What about family in Albania? Anything?"

"That's strange too. Nothing. They've only been here eight years, so she must have had some family. Maybe Sadik hasn't notified them. Maybe they don't even know."

"Can I get those records? From Catholic Refugee Services?"

"I doubt it. You'll just have to ask the dad."

"Okay. Thanks Lacey."

"Sure. Good luck, Roberta. Stay in touch."

I MET SADIK AHMETI THE next day. We met in his room at the mental health hospital, which was just a bedroom, with a sink and a bureau. There was, of course, nothing on the walls, nothing sitting on the bureau. They wouldn't have left anything that he could use to hurt himself, and he probably came here straight from the city jail, after the traffic stop.

"Mr. Ahmeti. My name is Roberta Weiss. I am a volunteer with CASA—Court Appointed Special Advocates. My job is to make a recommendation to the judge about the placement of your children."

"The placement of my children? What does this mean? What you mean?"

He is immediately agitated. A small man. Maybe five foot seven. Very thin. And much older than I was expecting. He's got to be in his sixties—with a round bald spot in the middle of his crown, and long, thinning hair just above his shoulders. His explosiveness is alarming. I look around, wonder if I should suggest that we meet in the common area. It will be hard to talk to him where other people can hear us, but I am uneasy.

"Mine children are mine. They place with me. I am not going to be here much longer. You cannot say where my children place."

"Mr. Ahmeti. Of course. Your children are yours. And you have parental rights to them. But they are in foster care now while you are here, and a judge has to remove them from foster care, even if it is back to your care."

"I have to go to court?" he asks.

"There is a courtroom. And a judge. It's not a trial, though. It's just part of the system. Part of making sure that your children are some-where safe."

"Where are my children? You see them?" His voice breaks here, and I realize how scared he is. I'm still nervous, but I see that this case will not be simple. This is not a man who's had a simple life.

"I haven't seen them yet. I will. I'll see both of them, several times."

"Several times? They keep me here long?"

"I don't know, Mr. Ahmeti. I don't know anything about your situ-ation."

"I don't know. I don't know what do. My children should be with me. We are family. But no mother? Children need mother."

As he says this, he swings his head to the side and hits his head against the edge of the bed frame. There is a loud crack when he hits, but he doesn't even acknowledge what has happened. He just shakes his head and keeps talking. His hands are moving all the time.

"I don't know how care for my children. But they are mine. They are mine. In Albania, someone help me. Another woman. Here, I don't know what do."

"Mr. Ahmeti, do you have family in Albania?"

"Yes. But we not speak. When I left Albania, I left forever. I tell Ar-jeta no need to keep heart open to Albania. We can never go back. We only hurt them if we stay in touch."

"Did Arjeta have family? Do they know what happened to her?"

"I tell you! I tell you already. We not speak to family in Albania. I sorry for this now. I sorry for Arjeta, so lonely. But no choice."

He seems even older when he says this. His voice catches, and he stops his agitated moving, and he looks like an old, tired man. It is hard to imagine him with a three-year-old. I wonder about the boy, about Bashkim. Is he ready to raise them both?

THE MEETINGS WITH THE FOSTER mothers go well. Lacey is right. The children are lovely. Both women report that the children are easy, even in the situation. I think that Arjeta Ahmeti must have been a good mother, and perhaps even Sadik has capacities I could not see, but I'm not sure of that.

I don't spend much time with Tirana. She's making cookies with a teenage foster sister in the kitchen, and I watch them awhile, introduce myself, but decide I will come back another day. I don't want to remind this child of what has happened to her, when she is so pleased with what she is doing. With Bashkim, it's different. He's not doing much of anything when I come to speak with Jeannette Delain, and after we've finished, I ask him if he would like to take a walk with me. He looks to Jeannette, and then says yes, he will.

We leave the house silently. I notice that he has a key and that he locks the door behind him, even though Jeannette and some of the other foster children are there. Then he places the key carefully in a side pocket on his pant leg. It has a button and a flap, so it will not come out easily.

We walk down the hill and past the tiny green space with benches in Jeannette's subdivision. I suspect that we're headed to the park, just past the school, and after I tell him who I am and why I'm meeting him, I just walk along silently. We veer off before the park and cut through a small opening in the school fence, large enough for a bike to fit through. We're on the playground, near the swing set, and I think that this is perhaps where he is headed. But, no, we pass the swing set, and the painted lines on the ground for hopscotch and four square, and we head to the school itself, to a small addition that juts out onto the asphalt.

I've never been to Orson Hulet School, and I've never seen the addition to which he is taking me. I see that the outer walls are decorated with a long tile mural, and I see the painted words "Orson Hulet Marine Lab" above the door. Oh yes. I remember when this was built. There were articles in the paper. Bashkim goes to the school with the marine lab.

"I like this mural."

This is the first thing he says to me, other than hello and yes. He looks at me, and he looks at the wall. I look too, and I notice that the mural appears to be an underwater scene, filled with fish.

"Do you want to see my favorite fish?"

"Yes."

He points to a fish that looks like a bowl of rice, complete with a Japanese character on the side, and a fish head and tail sticking out either side of it. I smile.

"I've never seen a fish like that."

He doesn't say anything, but he drags a finger along the wall, and pauses at a fish that looks like a basketball, and another that looks like a trumpet. I realize that most of the fish are fanciful and that they are wonderful in their unexpectedness.

"Who made this wall?" I ask.

"Kids. When the marine lab was built. They painted the tiles in the hallway. Everybody had to paint the same kind of background, so it would look like a sea when it was done, but each student got to paint his own fish."

"Did you paint one?"

"No. It was all done when I came."

"They're not signed."

I don't know why I say this, except that the fish are so original, and they make me wonder who painted each one. In any case, Bashkim does not respond. Perhaps he cannot think why that would interest me.

Some of the fish are quite large, over multiple tiles, and some are tiny. The mural must be a hundred feet long. It stretches around three walls.

"Do you like the marine lab?"

"Yes."

He is still looking at the wall intently and moves away from me to the far end.

I follow him, but a ways behind.

"What do you like about it? What do you do in there?"

"There are sharks," he says.

"Really?"

"Yes."

"Do you like sharks?"

"Yes."

"Are they frightening?"

"They swim. All the time. They can't stop swimming, or they can't breathe."

"Hmm. I didn't know that."

"And they can see. They can see students. Because they look at them. And when they like you, they watch you."

"Really? Is there a shark that likes you?"

"Yes."

With that, he walks away from the wall and toward the park. I follow. We have to walk the length of the playground to find another opening in the fence, but he knows exactly where he is going. The park isn't large. There's a small baseball field, a grassy area for picnics, and several swing sets at the far end.

"Do the schoolchildren use this park? Do you use it for recess?"

"Yes. Sometimes we come here for PE, and if there are enough monitors, we can play kickball here during lunch. But there has to be a monitor here, so if someone gets hurt and has to go to the office, then we can't play kickball."

"Do you like kickball?"

"It's okay."

"Bashkim. Do you know why I want to talk to you? Do you know what my job is?"

"Mrs. Delain told me that you decide where Tirana and I live."

"Well, sort of. I make a recommendation. The judge decides where you live."

"I want to live with Tirana."

"I know."

"I have to live with Tirana because she is just a baby, and she must wonder where I am. I haven't even seen her. My nene . . ."

He stops here, and I see that he is not ready to speak. We keep walking.

"I have to live with Tirana," he finally says.

I don't answer, because I know that I can't promise this. The best thing might be to keep him in foster care as long as possible, until Sadik is somehow more capable, but Lacey has made it clear that they won't be placed together. He hasn't mentioned his father, and I debate whether to bring him into the conversation.

"Can you tell me about your dad, Bashkim?"

"My baba? What? Is Baba okay?"

I notice that he sounds worried, which seems to me a good sign.

"He's fine, Bashkim. I met with him a few days ago. He misses you and Tirana."

Bashkim is quiet.

"He's very upset. That's why you and Tirana aren't with him."

"I know."

We walk a little farther, but I see that Bashkim isn't paying attention to where he is.

"My baba was in prison. That's why he's like that. He had to go to prison because he saw a policeman hurt someone."

I think that Bashkim meant to go on, but at these words, he freezes. I wait, to see what he will do, but he doesn't look at me. He starts walking, a little bit faster.

"Your father was in prison in Albania, right?"

"Yes."

"That must have been very hard."

Bashkim says nothing.

We stay on the trail in the park, and it circles around so that we're headed back toward Jeannette's house again. Bashkim's whole body has changed. I can feel his tension. Just before we turn right to cross the street into her subdivision, Bashkim asks:

"Are we going back to Baba? Tirana and me?"

I can't tell from his question whether he thinks this is a good or a bad idea.

"I don't know," I say.

He doesn't answer, and we walk the rest of the way in silence.

ON MY WAY ACROSS TOWN, I phone Marty.

"I met that kid, the one who was with his mom when she was killed. Bashkim Ahmeti."

"Yeah. How was he?"

"He's great, Marty. He looks like Jake. He acts like Jake. You wouldn't believe it."

"Come on, Roberta. Take it easy. You have to keep some distance, you know that."

"But Marty, he really looks like Jake, and he acts like him too. There was a moment, I thought, maybe I should just put him in my car. Take him home."

"Jesus, Roberta. We're not taking in a kid."

"Marty, come on. I know that. I'm just saying I felt like that. It wasn't a rational thought. It was a feeling."

"Roberta, we've gone a long way over some of your feelings. Tell me that you understand this one is not possible."

"It's not possible, Marty. You're too old. No court'd give that kid to us."

"Very funny. But you're right, Roberta. I am too old. Even for a temporary stay, even if he were Jake. I'm an old guy."

"Geez, Marty. Could you stop? I'm not taking him home."

"Okay, Roberta. I'm sorry. You know, I just, I worry about you. You can't fix everything, Roberta. You know that. You gotta be careful."

"I'm careful, Marty. I'm careful. But, you know, there's a world out here. We're in it."

"I know, Roberta. Listen, I gotta go. I got a meeting in ten minutes, and I've got to make another call. I'll see you tonight. I'll make dinner."

After Marty hangs up, I pull off the road and think awhile. I have Bashkim Ahmeti in my mind, the way he dragged the toe of his shoe in the dirt of the kickball field, the way his voice wobbled when he said "policeman," his choice of a rice bowl fish. I wasn't kidding about wanting to throw him in the car. Even with a CASA, even with a dad, even with a caseworker as good as Lacey Miller, he's in for a tough ride. And my whole body is screaming with the desire to get him off it.

JEANNETTE DELAIN TOLD ME THAT the principal of Orson Hulet school, a Dr. Moore, had taken an interest in Bashkim before this happened. She suggested that I talk to her. So I called and made an appointment to see her that week.

When I enter the school, I see that they have carried the marine lab theme throughout. There's a wall painted with a large fish dressed in school clothes and a backpack, and there are fish-themed pictures and colors everywhere I look. But there are no windows. The walls are cinder block, and the hallways dark with a strip of fluorescent light down the middle.

The school has an elaborate system for visitors. I have to show my driver's license, which is sent through a machine, so that a photo of my license appears on a computer monitor. I sign my name on the screen, and then the school secretary pushes a button that unlocks the gate leading to the office suite itself.

My meeting with Dr. Moore is surprising, because she has a surprising story to tell about Bashkim. We start with basic information, who I am, what my role is, and she tells me that Bashkim is quite talented academically. She also tells me that the school had a difficult interaction with Bashkim's parents in October, and she fills me in on what happened with the pen pal letter to Iraq. I comment that some kids just seem to be born under an unlucky star, and she says she doesn't think that's quite right in this situation.

"You see, the soldier who wrote to Bashkim wrote him again. In fact, they've been exchanging letters for a few months now."

I must look a bit uneasy, because she quickly assures me that she monitors the communication.

"The letters come to me, and I read them before I send them either way. The soldier, Specialist Rodriguez, is also in a vulnerable position. I don't want anyone hurt."

"You said that the parents were quite upset about Bashkim communicating with a soldier. Why would they allow this?"

Dr. Moore hesitates before she speaks.

"It's a big risk, I know. One that many would argue I don't have the right to take. But the parents don't know about Bashkim's letters to the soldier. I offered Bashkim the chance to tell them, I offered to speak to them for him, but I left it to him to decide: whether he would read the soldier's letters, whether he would write him, whether he would tell his parents.

"I did it, at first, because I thought it would help Bashkim to know that the soldier was sorry for what he had written. And I continued to do it because it seemed to me that the letters and the relationship were good for Bashkim. He's a shy child, and really shut down after his parents came to school that day. The letters pleased him, and they gave me a way to interact with him.

"Of course, I never imagined what would happen to Bashkim. I was trying to keep tabs on a child that might be in a risky situation at home."

I'm not sure how to respond to Dr. Moore. It's my job to find everyone in the Ahmeti children's lives, to come up with a plan for children who seem healthy but who have been suddenly left quite alone. This pen pal is a complication, and it seems like it could get Dr. Moore in a lot of trouble. I appreciate that she has told me, because it would have been easier for her to keep this quiet.

I tell her this, and she says, "I've been in administration for fourteen years, and I was a teacher for twenty before that. I could have retired three years ago. I don't do this job for my career. I don't even do it for the salary."

I nod. She has still taken a risk, but not without knowing what she was risking.

THERE ARE CASES THAT I just can't forget, that stick. Marty always wants to know why. What it is. I don't know, I think it's the ones where something small changes everything. Where the tiniest act, the smallest space of time, the most inconsequential of decisions, changes a life. A split second separates the long-lost friends who either see or miss each other at an airport. And from that, a relationship does or does not develop, perhaps a lifetime partnership, perhaps even children. Human beings who might or might not have existed. Whole lives born out of the most fragile of happenstance.

And maybe that's why our lives are beautiful; why they're tragic. One perfect child can be born of an accidental encounter, and another lost to a split-second lapse in attention. If a motorist leans over to change a radio station at the same moment that it first occurs to a four-year-old that he can let go of his mother's hand as easily as hang onto it, and that if he lets go he will be across the road first, before his mother, and that she will certainly laugh and say, "How fast you are, Johnny!" If the child does this, and the motorist does that, and if the world then changes forever and unbearably for everyone involved, then is that not life in its simplest form?

That so little matters so much, and so much matters so little.

What if Nate Gisselberg had been in some other patrol car?

What if Sadik's brake light hadn't burned out?

26

Bashkim

I RIDE TO THE Islamic Center with Mrs. Delain, and I suppose that Tirana's foster mother will be bringing her. The van seems really big with just me in it, but I sit in the far backseat anyway. When I buckle my seat belt, I think about Baba and Nene not buckling theirs, and my eyes start crying again. My eyes cry a lot, but I don't feel like I am crying. I feel like there's a big blanket over my head, and nobody seems to see it.

Mrs. Delain doesn't try to talk to me too much, but when I got in the van, she touched my back. Maybe that's why my eyes are crying. Mrs. Delain is nice. She has a lot of foster kids, but most of them are older than me, except Daniel, who goes to my school. That's why they put me in Mrs. Delain's house, so I could keep going to Orson Hulet. They couldn't put Tirana there, because I am already too many, and Mrs. Delain doesn't have little children. I would rather be with Tirana than at Orson Hulet, but Mrs. Miller said it was just temporary.

I hope that's true, because there's a teenager at Mrs. Delain's who has never gotten to live with his brothers, and he has been in foster care for years. When Jeff said that, I just left the living room and sat in the closet upstairs for a while. Mrs. Delain has a closet with pillows for sitting. She says sometimes there's not enough space to get a room by yourself, but you can always get a closet.

I have only been to the mosque once before, when Tirana was a baby, but I still remember the orange domes and the tower. The mosque is the biggest building on the road; across from it, all the houses are turned backward, and I can just see their roofs over the long block wall that stretches down the street. Nene said the mosque looked lonely, but I don't tell Mrs. Delain that. I wonder if Mrs. Delain has ever been here. I don't know what religion she is. I also don't know what I am supposed to do today. I have never been to a funeral. My eyes keep crying, even though the blanket feels heavier around me, so I squeeze my arms together and try to imagine that I am still in my bed.

Mrs. Delain takes her time getting ready to get out of the car, and I see that there are a lot of news trucks in the parking lot. There aren't very many other cars, but there are a lot of people with cameras. I wonder if they are going to try to take pictures of me, and I wonder where Baba and Tirana are, and I can't think of any way to make Mrs. Delain go back to her house. I don't think I can go in the mosque, but I won't have a choice I know.

"Bashkim, I brought you this scarf. I thought you might want to wear it when we walk in. I'm sorry that I don't have anything else."

It's a big black scarf. It sort of looks like the blanket that nobody can see around me, so I think I will wear it. I walk up to Mrs. Delain's seat—I don't have to crouch very much—and then she wraps it all around my head. Now it looks like the scarves women wear in pictures in Albania, and this makes me think of Nene, even though she never wore one, and I almost break down.

"Bashkim, this is one of the toughest days of your life. I can't fix that for you. But I am going to be right here, and you are going to be all right. I promise."

I make a sort of shuddery sound, and I nod my head.

"I'll get out first, and when I open the side door, you just get out, and we will walk straight to that door there. Do you see? We will just walk quickly and not talk to anyone, okay?"

I nod, and she gets out.

People start walking toward us fast when they see me get out of the van, but nobody yells or anything, and everybody stays a few feet away. I think Mrs. Delain is keeping them away somehow, but I don't look at her or anyone else, and we just get inside the building.

Baba is already there.

I have not seen him since the bad day, and I am so relieved to see him that I start crying for real when I get to him. He is crying too, and taking my scarf off, and I never thought holding Baba could feel so good, but it is the first time that I have felt safe since Nene.

"Bashkim, *zemer*. My son."

Baba is crying too much to talk, and I know that Tirana and I are in foster care because he has not been able to get calm, so I don't expect him to say anything. I just want to keep holding him. He is so bony, and I don't know if I got bigger or he got smaller, but I am more than half as big as him now.

"Baba," I cry. "Please, Baba, don't leave me. I want to be with you and Tirana."

Baba starts crying harder, and the lady from Catholic Refugee Services, the one who used to come to our house sometimes, puts her hand on his shoulder. Mrs. Delain has her hand on my arm, so the four of us are a big clump of people there in the mosque. Mrs. Delain is brown and small, just a little taller than me, and the Catholic lady is big and blonde, so just for a second, I think that Nene would laugh if she could see us. Thinking of Nene feels really bad, so I bury my head in Baba's stomach.

I don't see Tirana. I am sure she is coming. They wouldn't keep her away today, would they? Even though she is so little. I haven't seen Tirana either, not since the ambulance took Nene, and the fireman took us to Child Haven. They didn't put us together, and when they took me to

Mrs. Delain, I didn't know I was not coming back. I never said good-bye to Tirana, and I don't know where she is living. She's in foster care too, but Mrs. Delain doesn't know where, and I am afraid to ask Baba now.

The Catholic Refugee lady says that we should move inside, and so I take Baba's hand, and we walk to a room next to the main mosque. There are some people already there. I see Dr. Moore and Mrs. Monaghan on the side, but I don't want to talk to them, so I pretend that I don't see them. I also see the man we buy ice cream from, and I see another man who looks sort of like Baba, but I have never seen him before. The imam is there too. I met him when we came to the mosque three years ago. I think he won't remember me, but he crouches down and talks to me right away.

"Bashkim, hello. I am Imam Hadiz. I am so glad to see you."

He has nice eyes, and I don't mind that he puts his hand on my arm, but I don't have anything to say. He touches my cheek before he stands up again.

He shows my baba where we should stand, and then he shows Mrs. Delain and the other woman where they should stand. I don't want Mrs. Delain to leave me, but I know that my baba and I are supposed to stand with the men. What about Tirana?

"Baba, where's Tirana? I want to see Tirana."

The Catholic lady hears me, and she turns back to say, "She's coming, Bashkim. She will be here."

And just then, I hear her.

"Baba! Bashkim!"

Her baby voice is just the same. She sounds scared, and too loud, so I run straight to her. It feels so good to have Tirana's tiny arms around me. She is squeezing me as tight as she can, which is pretty tight, and I sort of can't breathe. Then Baba is there, and he is holding both of us, and for a second, I think it is going to be okay. I think if we can just stay in that room, on the floor squished together, and never leave, that it will be okay.

Then I hear a funny sound, and when I look, it is the casket coming in the room. There are two men in black suits that I don't know wheeling it. It is a pink casket, which doesn't even look like Nene, and there are flowers all over it. A third man is carrying a big photo of Nene, and I know that it is not going to be okay at all. It is never going to be okay. And there's nothing I can do. I can't seem to get away from this.

Tirana gets real quiet when she sees the casket. I don't know if she even knows Nene is in it. I don't know what Tirana knows. Baba picks her up, and I take his hand, and we walk to the front and stand behind the imam. I can't see Mrs. Delain or the woman from Catholic Refugee Services, but the other woman, the one that brought Tirana, comes with us. Nobody says anything to her.

Somebody with a camera comes in the side door, but right away one of the men that brought the coffin in makes him leave, and that man stays by the door so no one else can come in. The imam talks to everyone for a minute, and then he turns around, kneels on his rug, and starts to pray. I don't know any of the prayers, and I can't understand them. I see Baba chanting sometimes, but I don't think he knows the prayers either, so a lot of times it is just the imam and the one man who looks a little bit like Baba who are praying.

I look around once, but I don't see anyone there who knew my nene. I can't really think of anyone my nene knew. She talked to the lady who lived in the apartment near ours sometimes, but she is not there. And there were some moms from the baseball field that my nene talked to in the ice-cream truck, but I don't see any of them either. My nene's parents are in Albania, and they are old. Baba must have told them, but I don't even remember them, and they are not here.

Nene had brothers and a sister too. I wonder if they loved her like I love Tirana. Under Nene's bed, there is a box of photos. They're square photos, and the faces are hard to see because they're kind of green. But I can tell Nene was pretty. She had curly hair, like Tirana does, and dark eyes. Baba's eyes are blue, but Tirana and I have dark eyes like Nene.

And Nene had a big family, with lots of cousins too. Some of the pictures were at a festival, and when I asked who all the people were, she said, "They are all our family, Bashkim. Everyone in this picture is your family. We're all Lekas. You're Ahmeti, but you're Leka too." Nene always tells the truth, so this must be true, but I can't imagine my family in Albania. In America, there is nobody but us.

At the festival, people were dancing, and playing guitars, and all along the wall, there were big vats of wine, which Nene calls *raki*. Nene showed me where she was in the picture. She was seven then. She had a white dress, and flowers all through her hair. And she had a basket, with more flowers in it. She and her sister wore dresses that looked just alike, but Nene was prettier. Her sister stares at the camera like she is mad, but Nene smiles. She looks as if she is almost ready to laugh. Nene said that's because the photographer was funny, and he called her sister "walnut cheeks," which is why her sister is mad and she is about to laugh.

In Albania, there are mountains and lots of trees with fruit. Nene missed those trees. When I was little, before Tirana was born, she took me to a place that sold plants, and we bought a pear tree. We put it in the back of the ice-cream truck, and Baba was surprised when we drove up with it. "Why you buy that?" he said. "We rent only."

But Nene didn't care. She showed me how to dig a big hole, and how to put orange peels and apple cores and coffee grounds in it, and then how to make a moat around the tree, like a castle, and how to fill the moat with water every day. Then she measured me against the tree. She said that every year we would measure me and the tree, and watch us grow up together. The trunk of the tree was as big as my arm, which wasn't really very big then, but it was taller than me. Now it's way taller than me, and much fatter than my leg, but that tree didn't make Nene happy. It grows lots of pears, but they don't taste nice. They don't taste like anything. They just fall on the ground and make a bump sound outside my window some mornings.

I wonder where Nene's box of photos is. I heard the CASA lady telling Mrs. Delain that Mr. Cummings took our apartment back. When she first said that, I started to think about everything in my room, and to feel really bad, but then I remembered about Nene, and I realized that the worst thing had already happened, and my room didn't really matter. The imam is still praying, and Baba is moving his head back and forth beside me. I don't look to my right, where the coffin is, because I don't like that pink box, and I don't want to think of Nene in it. I just want to go home. And then I remember I don't have any home, and I think that I just don't want anything.

Tirana is on my prayer rug, and her shoulder touches mine. After a while, she snugs in next to me, and I put my arm over her back, and we just lie down, while everyone else prays. We lie there, as close as we can be together, and I hear some of what is happening, and I see some of it, but mostly I smell Tirana's bath smell, and taste her hair sticking into my mouth, and feel her chest moving in and out against my arm. Tirana and I just stay like that until it is over.

27

Luis

THE ATTENDANT LEFT THE manila envelope on the table next to my bed. It was part of my physical therapy to spend some time in the courtyard every day and to make it to and from my sessions on my own. Some days, that takes a while.

I recognized the logo on the envelope right away—Orson Hulet Elementary School—but Bashkim had never sent me anything this large before. And it wasn't his handwriting on the label. This label was typed.

I didn't open it right away. For one thing, I was wiped out from dragging my crippled ass to the courtyard. I set my cane next to the table and tried to get myself into the bed in a comfortable way. I'm always slouched too far down or sitting up so high that the bed bends beneath my thighs, so getting myself into the bed in a reasonable way is one of my big daily events. My room is right outside the nurse's station. It's there so they can keep an eye on me, but I really hate to have people watching me try to do this bed maneuver thing.

"How you doing in there, Luis?" someone calls.

"Fine. I'm fine."

"Fucking fine," I whisper.

"Do you need a hand?"

"No. I'm good."

Good like hell, anyway.

I'm not supposed to get a hand with anything. I've been here longer than a lot of patients, so everyone has gotten more relaxed about the rules. But I'm leaving soon, and as much as I owe everyone here, I can hardly stand to be noticed. The Army is flying me home, to my abuela's, but I wish that I could go somewhere completely alone. I've had enough of being a patient. I love my abuela, but I'm not looking forward to going to her house either. I'm a man. And I've had about all I can take of being so fucking dependent.

I keep to myself as much as I can when I'm not in therapy. It's not that I don't like the people here. I'm grateful. How hard they work. How hard they've made me work. A rehab center is an amazing place. I wonder what my mother's life would have been like if there had been a rehab hospital for her. If there had been people working with her, hour after hour, day after day, teaching her brain to work differently. Wouldn't it be possible for anyone to change? For anyone to be different?

I keep to myself because I don't want to talk about how I got here. I don't know who knows. I don't know what goes in a medical file. I don't know how much anyone gets to read. Or what they say to each other.

This floor is all brain injuries. But I figure I'm the only one that injured my own brain. I mean these guys here—some of them with other injuries, some of them blind, missing an arm or a leg, deformed—they got whacked by the enemy. They're heroes. I'm the fucking coward.

I don't want to talk about how I got here, and I don't want anyone thinking I'm a hero, either. I'm afraid someone's visiting kid will ask me what happened. I've promised myself I won't lie, but there are some things I'm never going to say.

I'm in the bed now, too damn low as usual. I fumble with the lever on the side and try to scrunch myself farther up as the back gets more vertical. I sort of succeed, but now the sheets are tangled beneath me, and I'm cocked a bit to the left, and this is how it is every damn day. I've got occupational therapy in forty minutes, so I think I will just close my eyes and try to forget about it.

As soon as my eyes are shut, I remember the envelope.

Should I open it?

I could really use a rest before another session, but I'm curious too. Maybe Bashkim sent me some of his schoolwork.

I don't want to admit it, but the letters from that kid mean a lot to me. My abuela's visits help, and Dr. Ghosh still comes by once or twice a week, but what really makes me feel good these days is that I fixed what I did to Bashkim. That might be the smallest sin against me, but one thing I'm learning from my physical therapy, every step forward counts, every step forward makes the next one easier. I hang on to that. Especially at night, when things get really bad.

I lie there with my eyes closed another couple of minutes, and then I decide to open the envelope after all. It's been a few weeks since I got a letter, and I was hoping he hadn't quit writing.

At first I'm pleased with myself. I open the little metal clasp at the back like there's nothing wrong with me at all, and though I tear off a good section of the top of the envelope trying to get the flap unsealed, I still feel pretty good about my small motor control. Inside there's a typed letter on school stationery, a couple of newspaper clippings, and several letters on lined school paper from Bashkim. I don't even look at the rest of the stuff. I go right to his letters and carefully put them in order by date. He's funny that way. He dates every letter.

He's written me seven letters. Which is more than he has ever sent. Some of the pages are wrinkled, like he wadded them up, or they got wet. I notice right away that his handwriting is different too, not as neat as usual.

February 26, 2009

Dear Luis—

    How are you? Are you out of the hospital? I am playing a lot of soccer, and my team almost always wins. My baba is really proud of me.
    I might be moving out of Las Vegas soon, so I don't think I can see you when you get here.

Thanks for writing to me,
Bashkim

February 27, 2009

Dear Luis—

    Since I won't be seeing you, I thought I would write another letter.
    Did I ever tell you that my sister Tirana sings baby songs? She sings them all day long. And she doesn't know about not kissing people at school, so when she comes to pick me up, she kisses me in front of everyone. And if I tell her not to do it, she just says that she loves me.
    She's really little is why.

Bye,
Bashkim

March 1, 2009

Dear Luis—

    If this was a leap year, today would be February 29. If a person is born on February 29, he only has a birthday every four years.
    My birthday is in April, but I don't care about birthdays anymore.

I hope your hospital is going okay.

It would be nice to see you in Las Vegas, but I am not going to live here anymore.

Bashkim

March 4, 2009

Dear Luis—

My baba has decided to stop playing soccer. I think I will quit too.

You never told me why you were in the hospital. Did you get hit by a bomb? Did someone shoot you?

You never told me about that boy you shot, either.

I am kind of thinking about those things now.

Bashkim

I read slowly, because I have some field-of-vision issues. When my hand shakes, I can't read. I can't follow the letters if the page moves at all. So I stop here because I can't keep reading, and I don't want to anyway. There are three more letters from Bashkim, but I lie back, and the wrinkled pages spill across my stomach.

It's really lonely here. Sometimes I think I'm going to make it. I have a lot of therapy, and it keeps me busy, and I have to work really hard to do certain things, and sometimes that makes all the rest of it go away. I feel like I am Luis again. And I get a bit hopeful. Maybe things will work out. Maybe I'll be able to make up for some of the stuff I've done.

But it was naïve to think I was making anything up to Bashkim. He never forgot what I wrote to him. He's still afraid of me. And he should be.

"Luis, you ready to work?"

It's Terence, one of the therapists.

I keep my eyes closed, as if I am asleep.

"Hey, Luis, what are you doing? It's time to get going."

Terence is a big, gray-headed guy with a tattoo of a gravestone on his right arm and another of a rose on his left. He wears his hair in a thin ponytail at the back of his neck. Most days, I am glad if Terence is on duty. He fought in 'Nam. He never asks me how I got here, we never talk about being soldiers at all, but I feel good around him anyway. He just gives off a sense that he knows. He knows what pain is like.

I keep my eyes closed. In rehab, this is akin to disobeying the order of a commanding officer. The whole place operates on mutual effort, and the therapists make it clear that if I don't want to work, I don't belong here. And I'm not trying to make a scene. I definitely don't want any more attention.

But Bashkim's letter, that "you never told me about the boy you shot" in his eight-year-old handwriting, is burned on my eyelids. I can't open my eyes. I can't move. I can't speak. Why didn't I die? Who bolos his own suicide?

"Luis." Terence's voice is a little bit quieter. Slower. "Luis, you okay, man? Something going on?"

I am holding myself rigid in an effort not to let Terence see anything on my face, and when I feel his hand on my shoulder, I practically elevate off the bed. I still can't trust my voice, and I can't open my eyes, so I just lie there, cocked even more to the left, almost falling off the side, and just pray he will go away.

He doesn't. But he doesn't say anything, either. And he doesn't touch me. And we sit like that, motionless, quiet, for a while.

I think I should say something or do something, but I don't want to get started. I don't want to hear what he has to say. I know what he will have to say. Dr. Ghosh has been saying it to me for months. And even my abuela, now that she knows a little about what happened. Not everything. But some of it.

Sometimes it's not that you don't want help. It's that you can't bear to be offered help that just keeps turning out not to be enough after all.

I shouldn't be in this rehab. The Army shouldn't be spending all this money fixing me. I didn't get shot at. I'm not a war hero. I shouldn't be here with these soldiers. And I shouldn't have a bed that some real soldier needs. And I've tried to explain this. I have tried to make it clear that even though I botched my own suicide, it wasn't because I wanted to live. It wasn't because I should live. It wasn't a cry for help. It was just another fuckup.

I hear Terence standing up then. He doesn't say a word. He doesn't even try. And he doesn't touch me. He takes the letters from my stomach, from the floor where some have fallen, and I hear him shuffle them together. Quick enough that he's not reading them.

He sets the letters on my table. I feel him standing there looking at me. I feel a little foolish, still not opening my eyes, but I can't. I fucking can't. He stands there a moment longer. And then he pulls the blanket over the bottom half of my body, and he shuts the door most of the way as he goes out. And I am alone. And nobody can see me from the nurse's desk. And I have my eyes open, and I'm still falling half out of the bed, and I am wondering where I go from here.

DR. GHOSH SHOWS UP ABOUT an hour later. I thought they might send him, and I don't know if I have been waiting for him or dreading the thought of seeing him.

"Hi, Luis," he says in that slight Indian accent.

"Hi, Dr. Ghosh." It's the first time I have used my voice, and it sounds fine, sounds normal.

"I got a call from Terence."

I nod my head.

"Do you want to talk about it?"

I shake my head.

He waits. Then he gestures toward the letters, still piled on the table where Terence left them.

"Something in those letters?" he asks.

I look away. I can't even trust myself to nod.

"May I read them?"

I nod, without looking at him. I hear him shuffling through the letters, then opening the manila envelope, pulling out the pages I didn't look at, shuffling through those. It takes a long time, and finally I roll my head back around and look at him.

The expression on his face surprises me. Dr. Ghosh looks shocked, or like he is ill. His mouth is very slightly agape, and he takes a sort of ragged breath.

"Did you read all these?"

I'm curious now, because this isn't what I was expecting.

"No," I say. "I just read the first couple of Bashkim's letters. I . . . I don't know. I got upset when he asked about what I had told him. I stopped reading."

Dr. Ghosh nods. Then stops. Keeps looking at the pages in front of him. I see that there are several news clippings from the Las Vegas paper, and the typed letter on school stationery, and for the first time, I wonder what that letter says. Why did Bashkim's letters come in a bunch? What was in that packet?

"So you just read these first letters from Bashkim," Dr. Ghosh says.

"Yes."

He takes a breath.

"I can see why Bashkim's comment upset you."

Something about the way he is sitting, about the measured way he says this, tells me that he is just operating out of habit, that his training is taking over, and that he is not thinking about my response to that letter at all.

Just like that, I forget about what I was thinking. About all the crazy thoughts in my head for the last hour, and I want to know what else is in that envelope—what Dr. Ghosh knows that I don't.

"Dr. Ghosh. I can see that there was something in that envelope. There was more than what I read. What happened?"

He doesn't answer me right away. I suppose he is thinking about it—thinking about how strong my reaction was to the letters I read—wondering if I am strong enough for whatever else is in there.

"Dr. Ghosh. I'm okay. I'm okay now. Please tell me what else is in that envelope."

He nods.

"Let's read Bashkim's letters together first. Here they are, in order."

I take the seven letters and skim through the first four before starting into the rest.

March 6, 2009

Dear Luis—

You don't have to tell me about that boy. And I don't want to know how you got hurt.

I don't want to think about war. I don't want to think about anything bad. I'm really tired of bad things. I'm tired of thinking.

My nene told me that some men shouldn't go to war. I don't want to go to war, and I don't want to be a soldier.

Do you know that northern Nevada looks like Afghanistan and southern Nevada looks like Iraq?

Do you know that a lot of soldiers come back and are policemen?

Bye,
Bashkim

I cringe at this letter, but I am not feeling shocked like I was before. There's something more than Bashkim's letters here, and even I can see that something is wrong with him. This is not the kind of letter he has been writing.

March 7, 2009

Dear Luis—

    I don't think soldiers should be police. Like my nene said, some men shouldn't be in war, and they shouldn't be policemen either.

    I think the president should say that soldiers can't be policemen. It would be a lot better that way.

    My baba doesn't like policemen or soldiers. He tried to tell us they were bad.

    Hope you feel better in the hospital—

Bashkim

March 10, 2009

Dear Luis—

    Tirana is only three years old, but she can speak English and Albanian. And she can make some letters too, like T and O.

    When Tirana grows up, I am going to take care of her. I am going to buy a house for her, and some red shoes too. If she has a husband, he might want to do that, but I will do it if he doesn't.

    Also, when Tirana grows up, I am not going to let her marry a mean man.

    I am still leaving Las Vegas, so you won't be able to see me—

Bashkim

Well, Bashkim sounds different, but I really don't know anything that I didn't know before. I look at Dr. Ghosh. He hands me the typed letter from the school.

March 11, 2009

Specialist Luis Rodriguez-Reyes
c/o Walter Reed Army Medical Center
6900 Georgia Ave, NW
Washington, DC 20307-5001

Dear Specialist Rodriguez:

I am writing to you because there has been a significant change in Bashkim Ahmeti's life. I have been holding his letters to you, and I have enclosed them here.

As you know, I have been sending Bashkim's letters to you since he first wrote last December. I did this without the permission of Bashkim's parents. Bashkim did not want his parents to know of your communication, for reasons that made sense to me, and yet I thought your correspondence with him was positive. I have read your letters to him before allowing him to see them, and I have read all of his letters to you. I felt this was necessary to ensure Bashkim's protection.

Last month, Bashkim's mother, Arjeta Ahmeti, was killed by a police officer during an otherwise routine traffic stop. The details of the incident are in dispute, and I enclose some newspaper stories about what happened. I know little more than what these stories indicate.

Bashkim was with his mother when she was shot. His father, who has a troubled past, has been distraught since the shooting and unable to care for Bashkim or his sister. They are each in separate foster homes. Bashkim was placed in a home nearby, so he is still attending school here, and I see him every day.

Bashkim's letters to you have not always been strictly honest in their details. I did not find this particularly unusual, given his

situation, and I did not see any harm in his minor embellish-
ments. The letters he has written since his mother's death are
somewhat different. It seems to me that he is able to express some
significant ideas to you, and that your responses might be import-
ant to him.

I don't have any advice for you in this situation. Only information.
If you would like to contact me, please do so. I would be happy to
talk with you.

Sincerely,
Dr. Martina Moore
Principal, Orson Hulet ES

I am not able to hold this letter still long enough to read all of it, so Dr.
Ghosh reads the last several paragraphs aloud. When he is done, neither
of us speaks. I hold out my hand for the newspaper clippings, skim the
headlines, read parts of the articles.

Woman Shot in Routine Traffic Stop

Las Vegas, Feb. 21—A woman was shot and killed
by a Las Vegas traffic officer around 5 pm this evening. The woman and her husband had been pulled
over for a missing brake light, but the incident es-
calated.

Las Vegas Police Department officials have yet
to release any information, but witnesses said that
the woman who was killed was standing next to her
child.

LVPD Says Officer Who Shot Woman Feared for Child's Life

Las Vegas, Feb. 22—In the first official statement from the police department on the death of a woman stopped by a Las Vegas traffic patrol, Sergeant Lee says that the officer who shot "feared for her child's life." According to LVPD, the woman was holding her son while brandishing a knife and threatening to kill him.

Witness Claims Woman Did Not Have Knife, Was Holding Son

Las Vegas, Feb. 23—A witness to the Las Vegas traffic stop that resulted in the death of Arjeta Ahmeti says that Ms. Ahmeti was holding on to her son, and that she did not have a knife, as was stated by LVPD Sergeant Lee this morning.

LVPD Officer Who Shot Woman Identified

Las Vegas, Feb. 24—The Las Vegas PD officer who shot and killed Arjeta Ahmeti has been identified as Nathan Gisselberg. Officer Gisselberg has been an officer since October 2008, and served three tours of duty in Iraq prior to joining the force. Per department policy, Officer Gisselberg, and his partner Corey Stout, are on administrative leave until an internal investigation into the shooting has been completed.

Woman Was Holding
Ice-Cream Scoop, Not Knife

Las Vegas, Feb. 25—LVPD spokesperson Sergeant Lee acknowledged that Arjeta Ahmeti, the woman killed by a Las Vegas police officer on Saturday, was not holding a knife at the time of the shooting. "It appears that Ms. Ahmeti pulled an ice-cream scoop from her pocket and brandished it as if it were a knife. LVPD officers are trained to practice restraint in tense situations, but obviously the safety of the child at the scene was of paramount importance to the officers."

Coroner's Inquest
into Las Vegas
Shooting Scheduled

Las Vegas, Mar. 3—Clark County officials announced on Monday that a coroner's inquest into the shooting of Arjeta Ahmeti will be conducted next month, on April 16.

Funeral Held for Vegas Woman Killed by Police Officer

Las Vegas, Mar. 9—The funeral for Arjeta Ahmeti, who was killed by an LVPD police officer after a routine traffic stop three weeks ago, was finally held today. Imam Omar Hadiz officiated at the small service held at the Islamic Center of Las Vegas.

The news media was not allowed inside, but photos showed Ms. Ahmeti's children and husband arriving in three separate cars. The children are under the care of Child Protective Services, presumably because the father is unable to care for them in his grief.

I'M NOT SURE IF I'M dizzy because I haven't read this much in a long time, or if I'm dizzy because of what I've read. I've spent a lot of time feeling sorry for myself here. Which really takes the cake, when you think about what I did to deserve what happened to me, and about what happened to Bashkim, who didn't do a thing.

I wonder how he's doing in foster care. My friend Kevin had to go to a foster home when we were in the fifth grade. His dad was already in prison, and then his mom did something, and she got put in jail too. They sent him to Child Haven, which was this terrifying place to me, a place that the news always reported—"The children have been taken to Child Haven"—and when I first heard that Kevin had gone there, I was petrified for him. I didn't see him for a couple of weeks, because they just made him go to school there, but when he finally got back to our school, he said Child Haven wasn't really that bad. He said the foster home was worse. His foster dad was mean.

I didn't see Kevin much after that. He didn't come back to our school the next year. I don't know if he ever got out of foster care. I don't know anything about him. This is the first time I've thought about Kevin in years, but I still remember the way he looked, kind of nervous, when he said his foster dad was mean. I wonder about Bashkim. About who his foster parents are. About how he's doing. I look at the dates on his letters, and see that they were all written after his mom was killed. Poor kid. Eight-year-old kid. He should still be sleeping on the floor next to his mom's bed.

28

Avis

IT'S BEEN A MONTH, and except for the fact that Nate still isn't working, isn't doing much but going to the gym and riding his motorcycle, things are sort of normal. I'm getting used to my new little house, and while there are bad hours when I drift into thinking about how I thought my life was going to be, there is also the task of getting a second gallon of paint for the study, or figuring out how to move the sprinkler pipe so I can extend one of the flower beds farther into the lawn. I signed up for a weekend seminar two months ago, how to start a business, and I'm still planning to go. I don't want to work in a casino again, even in the administrative offices, so I might use my alimony to buy a franchise; I want to work hard.

For now I've always liked a home project: liked planning it, liked doing it myself, liked the puttering and the fixing and the unexpected problem that has to be solved. Cheryl wants me to call her designer, and Margo has a workman who takes care of everything, but if it's up to me, I'd like to see what I can do in this house on my own. And, of course, it's all so easy now. I check YouTube whenever I get stuck. People who post videos about installing bathroom tile or fixing refrigerators with busted defrost thermometers are my new heroes. I've already made friends with the man at the corner hardware store, and yesterday the waitress at the deli next door to it asked if I wanted my usual (cabbage soup, with an onion ring), and none of these people knows my full name, can't connect me to the stories about the shooting, or to the police officer who just got back from Iraq. I am grateful for this space.

Still, there is this vague sense of children in trouble. Is it me I sense? Me and Rodney? Or the Ahmeti children? I don't know. I'm not quite able to think about that; to think about what I am feeling. Maybe it's progress just to know I have a feeling. But the shush of children's cries is always there, like the low hum of summer cicadas, vibrating me, reminding me: the way absolute powerlessness feels.

I can't go to the next thought, the one that connects my son to this pain, because that does hurt too much, that does drop me to my knees. I love my son. Being his mom is who I am. We were one body grieving his sister, and his is the body that cuddled next to mine, snug between Jim and me in the big bed that had felt so desperately empty after Emily died. There isn't any way for me to feel this: the Nate that I adore—every mother has the right to adore—and the Nate who somehow, somehow, took those children's mother away.

"Mom. Are you in the back? I've been ringing the bell."

It's Lauren. She's got coffee in one hand and my red garden shears in the other.

"Did you remember that I had these? I figured you'd be looking for them."

"Oh, no. I didn't. I haven't started cutting things yet."

We both smile, because my penchant for scalping everything on a certain kind of a spring day is a family joke.

"Come on in. I painted two walls of the study. I want you to see them."

It's nice, having a daughter-in-law. I hope that she and Nate can make it, though I will understand if she can't. I don't know what I would have done faced with something like this when I was still newly married to Jim. And I don't know if Lauren should stay with Nate. I'm not ready to think about that, either.

"How's it going? How are you?"

She looks away before she answers, just a bit. Lauren is so young. So little ever happened to her. She's easy to read.

"I'm good. We're doing fine, Mom. Nate's keeping really active, because not working is driving him crazy. And . . . and he's stopped talking about it so much. He's stopped talking about her and the boy and . . . what happened."

If I were someone different, I would put my arm around her. I would comfort her. But her words slice right through me. I can't risk touching her.

"Yes," I say. Slowly. "Do you want something to eat? I could make a salad?"

"Sure. That'd be nice. Thanks."

So I open the fridge and pull out some vegetables, and Lauren finds the cutting board and a paring knife, and we make the salad together: two women who love the same man in different ways, two women who don't know what to do about what that man has done, about who he might be, about whatever has happened to him. That's something, isn't it? That we each have someone else in the world with the same problem?

"Nate's sergeant says the coroner's inquest is no big deal. He says there's never been an inquest that found fault with a police officer. He says Nate should just take it easy, enjoy the time off, and get ready to come back to the force when it's done."

"Mmmm," I manage.

"Nate tried to call Corey, to talk to him, but Corey's wife said he didn't want to talk. She said Corey doesn't want to talk until after the inquest. Do you think that's weird?"

"I don't know." I remember what Jim said the first night. Nate's partner didn't see a knife, asked him what he had done. The cicada hum grows louder. I shake my head. Lauren is looking at me, waiting for me to reassure her.

"I don't know what Corey's thinking, Lauren. But I'm sure Nate's sergeant knows what he's talking about. I don't think the inquest is anything to be afraid of. Is there an internal investigation? Has Nate said anything about that?"

"Yeah. There is. But Nate doesn't talk about it. He says the guys have all been really nice to him. That everyone says it could have happened to anyone."

"Good. That's good. How are things with you and Nate?"

I brave the question, mostly so she'll stop talking about the shooting. She should be able to talk to me about it—who else should she talk to?—but I can't take any more right now.

She ducks her head again.

"We're good. We're fine. Nate's okay. He hasn't gotten mad, really."

I open my arms then, and she leans her head on my shoulder. Nothing terrible has ever happened to Lauren before—that I know of, anyway—and her puppy way of hiding breaks my heart.

I ALMOST WENT TO THE funeral. There wasn't much said about it, just a little note in the paper when it was over, and then I was relieved I hadn't gone. The *Sun* said it was a small service, and I couldn't bear to have been recognized. But I wanted to go. I knew what day it was, what hour. I spent that morning outside, stabbing at the hard dirt with an inadequate gardening fork, striking caliche or maybe just bits of concrete left from the formation of the back wall, and mixing in a rich, smelly loam that reeked to me of decay and fecundity at once.

I couldn't go, of course. There's nothing I can do, for that woman, for those children, for that family. I've run the options in my head over and over. Could I give money. Could I send flowers. Could I speak to those children. To their father. And, of course, I can't. Because I am Nate's mother. I'm on the other side. Whatever this is, I'm on the other side. But I don't always feel it. That mother. Those children. They don't feel like the other.

ON TUESDAY I CALL JIM and ask to meet him next week. I've been thinking about the inquest, about the way we will all be together, about the press, and whatever happens, I want Jim and me to be able to speak normally. We haven't been alone together since the shooting, and it's just better if we have been.

He says he's really busy, that he doesn't know if he can, but then he agrees to meet at the coffee shop at the Bellagio. We set the time, and then I call Cheryl, because I'm going to need a drink with the girls after. Also, I know they're worried about me, and they've stumbled around, trying to talk about Nate, and, at least today, it seems clear to me that I should get all of this settled before the inquest.

"Avis, how's it going? How's the manor?"

"Cheryl, you would hate it. But I like it. It's fine. And it's nice to be busy."

"Yeah. Good for you. How's Nate?"

"He's fine, according to Lauren. He's still off work, and his sergeant says he should think of it like a vacation."

Cheryl knows I hate this.

"Avis, you can't do this to yourself. This isn't your fault. And this town isn't your fault. I know it's killing you, but the best thing that could happen now is just to have a plain old Las Vegas inquest, where nobody gets charged, and everyone goes home, and somebody tries to make those kids' lives work again. It sucks, but that's what you want, Avis. It is what you want."

"I don't know what I want."

"I know. But this is what's going to happen. And this is best for you. And best for Nate. It's a bad deal, Avis, it's as bad as bad can be. But now we've just got to go forward."

"Cheryl, please. I don't want to talk about it. I can't talk about it. I want to see everyone. I want to do something else, have some fun, do something ridiculous on the Strip. Can we go see Kenny Kerr or something?"

"Kenny Kerr? Hel-*lo,* Avis. I think his show closed, like, two decades ago."

"Well, okay, maybe not Kenny Kerr. Something really bad like that, something really Vegas."

"But that's the thing, he wasn't bad. He was great. It should have been bad, but he was so damned good."

"Okay, fine, okay, Kenny Kerr. You're right. I don't want to go to something terrible. I want to go to something great that the tourists have never heard of. I want to go to a lounge act where the singer makes me cry. I want to drink scotch, and watch Julie flirt with some younger guy, and take bets on whether Margo's husband will show up to see what we are doing. And I don't want to be at the Bellagio. I don't want to be anywhere Jim might be. God, I absolutely do not want to see Darcy."

"Oh, Darcy. How is the home wrecker?"

"I don't know. I don't care. I just don't want to see her."

"All right. Let me work on it. I'll set something up, get tickets if we need them, get everyone out. We're here for you, Avis. But really, Kenny Kerr? You are going to have to step up your act."

I laugh. Cheryl has no idea how really hopeless I am. She thinks that because I grew up in Las Vegas, I have some sort of kinship to it. She doesn't know a thing about the Vegas I grew up in.

29

Bashkim

TODAY IS DANIEL'S BIRTHDAY. He's seven. Mrs. Delain made him a cake. She asked me to put the candles on it, and I put them in a row, right across the middle. My stomach started to hurt when I put them in; I put pink candles on Tirana's cake on her birthday. She liked them so much. She cried when I made her blow them out, so Nene said we would light them again and wait until they burned out. Of course, Tirana didn't want to wait that long, so she just blew them out again right away. She really wasn't doing it to get two turns, and, besides, she let me blow out one the second time. Which is pretty generous when you only have three candles. Anyway, my stomach didn't feel that good, so I just put the rest of Daniel's candles in quick and told Mrs. Delain I wanted to go upstairs for a while.

The older kids are still sleeping. They have to get up earlier than me and Daniel for school, but on the weekend, they just keep sleeping. Daniel is up, but he is watching cartoons. His birthday party is at two o'clock. He invited all of the kids in his first-grade class. Mrs. Delain thinks that parties need everybody. I helped write the children's names on the invitations, because Mrs. Delain says I write just as well as she does. Daniel helped too, even though he writes like a first grader, but I guess the kids in his class are used to that. Daniel's teacher is Mrs. Wilkes. He goes to my school, and I have seen him on the playground, but I never knew he was in Mrs. Delain's foster home. I didn't even know what a foster home was. Daniel has blond hair and thick glasses, and Mrs. Delain is as old as a grandma, but Daniel calls her Mom, and he has been living here a long time. He doesn't even remember where he used to live.

I never asked him about his mom, because I don't want to talk about family things. I don't ask anybody why they are at Mrs. Delain's, and nobody has asked me. Mrs. Delain doesn't talk too much either, about that sort of stuff, anyway. She says things like "Do you want to help me make the salad?" or "Can you help Daniel with his sheets?" but she doesn't say things about Nene or Tirana. Also, Mrs. Delain is really busy, and there is a lot to do when I am here. After school, we have chores and homework, and some nights after dinner, we have family project.

The big kids take turns choosing the projects. My favorite was Keyshah's. She got all of Mrs. Delain's old sheets, and we tied them together, and we made the whole family room into a fort. Jeff is tall, so he tied the sheets to the highest parts of the windows, and then we moved the furniture so that we could all sit in the fort together. Keyshah wanted to tell ghost stories, but Mrs. Delain said no, so she and Jeff and Ricky made up rap songs for Daniel and me. There was one about me: "Your name is Bashkim / You think you are mysterious / But you are a funny man / Even if you're serious." Usually family project is not like that, but that was a really good night, and Mrs. Delain let Keyshah leave the fort up until Sunday.

Ricky is the only person here who scares me. He got so mad at Keyshah when she wore his sweatshirt that he broke one of Mrs. Delain's doorknobs. She said he has to pay to fix it, and he also is grounded, which means that he is always home after school. I don't like Ricky. Keyshah's the only one who does like him, I think. She laughed when he got really mad at her. I don't even think she was afraid. But I think he could have hurt her. Daniel says that Ricky is not that bad, not like some other kids that have lived here.

I wonder how long I have to live in foster care. I wonder if Baba is getting better. I miss Baba, but thinking about going home with him makes me worry. At Nene's funeral, he kept pinching my shoulder, and when he hugged me, his tears made my neck all wet. Baba does not even know how to cook, and he is too sad without Nene. How can Tirana be home with Baba all day while I am at school?

I miss Nene so much that I wish I were dead sometimes. I am not going to tell anyone this, because I don't know what they do with boys who think that, but I just don't want to live without Nene. The thing is, I have to live without her, because I have to take care of Tirana. I have only seen Tirana one time since the bad day. And she cried so hard when her foster mom took her in a different car than me that I don't know if they'll let us see each other again. Nobody tells me.

I tried to tell that lady—the lady who tells the judge what to do with us—that I have to be with Tirana, but she didn't say I would be. Sometimes now I know why Baba was so mad at the mayor. Why does someone else get to decide where Tirana and I live? How come I am not with her, when she is just a little baby still? Nene would be really mad if she knew we were not together. She would not want Tirana to be in a foster home without me. I don't even know where Tirana is. I don't even know how to see her.

Mrs. Delain wants me to come downstairs now, because she and Daniel are decorating the table for the birthday. Mrs. Delain let Daniel choose all kinds of party stuff with horses. He got napkins with horses, and party hats with horses, and cups with horses. Keyshah and Jeff are going to blow up balloons when they come downstairs, but I try to blow up a green one first. I blow really hard, but the air just doesn't go in, so I quit trying. Mrs. Delain has plastic forks and knives from another party she had, so I put those around the table. The cake is already sitting in the middle, and my candles look pretty good on it.

When it's almost two o'clock, Mrs. Delain says we can start eating the pizza, and we can also start playing games. I think it's sort of funny that we are not waiting for any of the children to get here. The doorbell keeps ringing, but it is always some of Mrs. Delain's friends, or some of Jeff's friends, but not any first graders. I sneak out the back door quick and walk around toward the park, to see if any kids and moms are coming, but I don't see anyone.

When I went to Alyssa's birthday, all the girls wore dresses, because it was a diva party. The boys didn't wear anything special, but Mrs. Button gave us crowns when we came in. I start to worry that Mrs. Delain should have gotten something for Daniel's friends to wear. At Alyssa's party, Mrs. Button also gave us presents when we left, even though it wasn't our birthdays. We all got a bag that had colored diamond squares on it, and inside there was so much candy. Nene put it in the cupboard, and Tirana and I got one piece each after dinner. It lasted a long time that way.

We didn't make anything for the kids to take home today, but I don't think that's why they are not here, because how would they know that before they came? I haven't been to too many birthday parties, and I never had one, but I am starting to get really worried about Daniel's party. Where are the first graders?

I go back inside, and I don't feel like eating any pizza or anything. It's funny, though. Everyone is having fun at Mrs. Delain's. Daniel is the only little kid, but some of the grown-ups are playing Pin the Tail on the Donkey, and Ricky says that he is going to blast the piñata all the way to Pluto. Which isn't really a planet, you know. But I don't tell Ricky, because he probably wouldn't care, and I suppose he could still blast something to whatever Pluto is anyway.

I think maybe I will have some pizza, because I really like pizza, especially pepperoni. After I eat my pizza, I drink some watermelon-colored punch, which doesn't taste like watermelon but is still pretty good. Then I go and stand by the people who are playing Pin the Tail on the Donkey, because I have never played that game before. A really fat man, who is Mrs. Delain's friend, says I can have his turn. He has done it lots of times. It's kind of scary when he wraps the blindfold around my eyes, and then he turns me around, which I don't like at all, and I am just about to pull the blindfold off my eyes when I bump into the wall, and I feel the paper that has the donkey on it. I run my fingers along the edge of the paper and try to remember just where the donkey was. I'm pretty sure that I tape my tail right where it is supposed to go, and sure enough, as soon as I put it there, everyone cries out, "Bashkim, can you see? You got it!" And when I take my blindfold off, I see that my tail is too high but still close, and I am happy about that. This is a pretty good birthday party.

Now it is time for Daniel to open his presents. There is a big stack on the side table, and I see my note, looking a little bit crumpled, near the bottom. It took me a while to figure out what I could give Daniel. I don't have any money, and I don't think we are allowed to ask Mrs. Delain for money. Also, I don't know how to go to the store.

So I made Daniel something that I made for my baba last year. It is an aircraft carrier with airplanes on it. I cut a box and taped it back together to look like a ship with a flat top, and Mrs. Delain let me use some paints that she had. There wasn't any gray paint, or white, so I mixed up a whole bunch of colors. It doesn't really look like gray, more like brown, but it still looks pretty good. I folded the planes out of white paper, and I didn't paint them at all. I like them just white. My baba and nene showed me lots of different ways to fold planes, and I made three different kinds for Daniel's aircraft carrier. Then I glued them down, which might have been a mistake for Daniel. It was a good idea when I did it for Baba, because he just wanted to look at my aircraft carrier, but Daniel probably would want to fly the planes. I glued them before I thought of that, and then I couldn't really figure out what to do, so I just left them glued.

There isn't any way to wrap an aircraft carrier, so Keyshah said I should hide it and give Daniel a note telling him where to find it. That's what I did. I put the present on a shelf with the towels, and I wrote a note that says: "Happy Birthday Daniel. Your present is on the towel shelf." And then I drew some pictures on the note, so it would look better. Keyshah said I should make a lot of notes and make it like a scavenger hunt, but I didn't want to do that. Sometimes you just want to get your present.

I'VE BEEN BACK AT SCHOOL for two weeks. I don't like going, even though I know that I'm at Mrs. Delain's because everyone wants me to be at Orson Hulet. I don't know why they think that's a good idea, because being here isn't the same at all. For a while, everyone was looking at me. Some of the teachers tried to talk to me and say they were sorry, and I hate that. I can't even be at school if I think about Nene. I don't want someone to talk to me about her.

Mrs. Monaghan is nice. She doesn't say anything about Nene—or not anymore, not since the first day when she gave me a picture of a quoll. That's an animal in Australia that has a pocket like a kangaroo. She said I should keep it in my pack, and if anything was making me feel bad, I could just set the picture of the quoll on top of the desk, and she would know. I could go in the closet or to Dr. Moore's office, or do whatever I wanted. Mrs. Monaghan is like that.

I have used the quoll two times, once when Levi asked me how it felt to have my mom die, and once when the fifth graders made bread in the marine lab, and it sort of smelled like *buke*. Both times I went to the office and laid down in the nurse's room, but I took a long time walking, because I have my own way to get there. I walk all the way down to where the kindergarten rooms are, and then I walk back to the art room, and then I get a drink at the fountain, and then I walk real slow to the office. Mrs. Monaghan gives me a pass when I go out, and I hold it in my hand so nobody ever asks me what I am doing. The nurse doesn't ask me either, because I think Dr. Moore told her not to.

Nothing feels the same now. In science class, Mrs. Jimenez asked if I wanted to help her clean the tidepool tank on Tuesdays, but I don't want to. In music class, we are making a play about buccaneers, and normally I would really like buccaneers, but now I don't. I don't like anything. I just try to be quiet, and not think about Nene, and do whatever the teacher asks. I know that Mrs. Monaghan is watching me, even though she doesn't bring it up, and I know Dr. Moore is sometimes looking at me when she comes to class and says it is her day to observe the teacher. Dr. Moore only observes the teachers one or two times a year, and she keeps observing Mrs. Monaghan. I would be worried about that, but I can tell they like each other.

Today is a little bit better, because Daniel asked me to help him with the Lego set he got for his birthday, and I still do like Legos. Daniel got a backhoe, which is the biggest box of Legos I've ever seen, but it says you're supposed to be eight years old to do it, and Daniel's only seven. I think it's real nice of Daniel to share his birthday present with me. Daniel doesn't feel sad about living with Mrs. Delain. So I'm going to help him, but I won't do any of the really good parts, because he doesn't even know about having his own mom.

We are going to build the backhoe right after we get home and do our homework. Jeff said he won't mind if we leave the pieces out in our bedroom for a long time. He says he might even help us if we get stuck. Which we won't. I don't know why I want to build those Legos when I don't even want to clean the tidepool tank.

AFTER SCHOOL, DANIEL AND I meet by the swings, and then we walk toward Mrs. Delain's house. I don't get to cross the street with Mr. Ernie anymore, but I can see him from where Daniel and I are waiting to cross, and I keep looking at him, hoping he will see me so I can wave. I haven't talked to him since I came back to school, and I don't know what he thinks about why I don't cross with him anymore. I know he saw me last week, because he held both his arms out to me, but Keyshah had come to walk Daniel and me home, and she was going fast. When Mr. Ernie held his arms up like that, I almost started to cry. Maybe he knows about Nene, because lots of people in the neighborhood do, and I hear them stop talking when I go by.

Mr. Ernie doesn't see me, and Daniel's crossing guard says, "Pay attention" when I don't step off the curb quick, so I stop looking at Mr. Ernie and Daniel, and I hurry up the hill toward Mrs. Delain's. When we get home, she is talking to someone in the living room, probably someone from Child Services, because people like that come here all the time. Daniel rushes right in to her. He's still kind of a baby, and he always hugs Mrs. Delain when he comes home. I hear Mrs. Delain ask him how school went and then she says, "Hi, Bashkim. There's something to eat in the kitchen."

I walk to the kitchen instead of going in the living room, and put my backpack under the bench where it belongs. Then I take some of the toast Mrs. Delain has left for us on the table. When Daniel comes in, he races right by the toast because he is so excited about the Legos. He throws his backpack on the floor and races up the stairs to get the backhoe. We haven't done our homework yet, but Mrs. Delain is busy, so Daniel might just open the box right now. I go up the stairs quick just in case.

30

Luis

I LEAVE WALTER REED on Friday morning, March 20, five months after I arrived. I still don't remember anything about my last days in Iraq, or the week I spent at Landstuhl, or even the first days in DC. Dr. Ghosh says I probably won't remember. I still know that I shot myself, but not like I knew it when I first realized it. Then it felt like a memory, even if one without any details, but now it just feels like a piece of information. It could be about anyone—but it happens to be about me.

I'm not going back to the Army, though. I've been given a general discharge, and at least for now, there's no investigation into anything I did. Not what I wrote in my letter, and not what happened to Sam. I suppose there's nothing to investigate with Sam, and I'm guessing that there's no reason for the Army to open a can of worms over a note that a suicidal soldier sent. Nothing corroborates what I wrote, nobody has protested. It's a bit like a loaded gun there in my file. I guess it could be found and turned into an investigation, perhaps a court martial, at any time. This should bother me, but it doesn't. See, I'm not trying to get away with anything.

I'm glad to be getting out of rehab, I've been ready to leave for a while now, but the actual leaving is still emotional. People keep dropping in to say good-bye, at the end of whatever is their last shift before I leave. Alison gave me a book. It's called *Soldier's Heart: Coming Home from Iraq.* The print is pretty small, so she said she hoped it would motivate me to keep working. I don't need motivation. I will read and write again. Terence came by at eleven last night. I hadn't seen him since Monday, when I wouldn't open my eyes, and when he first came in, I felt awkward. But he acted like nothing happened, and he gave me a big hug, and told me that I'm going to have a good life and that I deserve it, at least as much as anyone else, and to please remember that for him.

It's Dr. Ghosh that I'm dreading saying good-bye to. I don't need to talk to Dr. Ghosh the same way that I did. In fact, I'm ready *not* to be talking to him like that, but, still, he's the closest thing I ever had to a dad—which he doesn't know—and I wish there were some way that he wasn't a doctor, and I wasn't his patient, and that we could just be friends or something.

He comes in very early, about five in the morning. I've been lying awake, thinking about what is to happen today.

"Good morning, Luis." His slightly clipped accent is so much a part of my days here, a part of everything that has happened. I suppose that every Indian I ever meet will now remind me of him.

"Hi, Dr. Ghosh."

He sits in his usual chair and stares out the window past my bed for a while.

"You're going to be all right, Luis. You're a good man."

I don't say anything, and he watches out the window awhile more.

"I've been talking to Bashkim's principal, Dr. Moore. You could meet her if you like. She's quite an unusual woman."

I think about that. Meeting Bashkim's principal. I can't quite imagine it. Imagine why. Would I meet Bashkim too? I've been wondering if I'll meet Bashkim when I get home, or if the letters now are just at an end. His situation is terrible. It doesn't seem like meeting me would fit in.

"I believe that coincidences can be powerful, Luis. I don't think they're entirely random, nor do I think that they must be acted on. I believe the strangest coincidences are opportunities. I wanted you to know that. There is something unusual about you having written that letter to Bashkim and about what has happened to Bashkim now. You have a great heart, and there is a child whose heart has been broken. Perhaps this is not only a coincidence."

Dr. Ghosh has never said anything like this to me before. Our conversations are about how I think, and I see now that I don't know very much about how he thinks. And I don't know what I think about what he has just said.

Making something up to Bashkim, for what I did to him, changed a lot for me. There were a lot of dark days here, right to the end, but the days that weren't dark began after I started writing to him. I haven't really taken in what happened to Bashkim; what we learned from Dr. Moore on Monday. I don't know what to do with it. I keep thinking about how the officer who shot his mother was in Iraq. I wonder which unit. I wonder where he was. I wonder who he lost. I wonder what he saw.

Dr. Ghosh is still sitting there, not looking at me, not looking out the window. I realize that we have become friends—whatever that means in our situation. But it means something. I trust him, and he trusts me. I can feel it.

"Dr. Ghosh. I don't know how to say good-bye to you. I don't know how to thank you."

He turns to me then, listening.

"You are the first face I saw. I wanted to die. I wanted to die so many times here."

That is all I say. That's all I get out. Nothing that I want to say. Nothing about what he means. I've been practicing in my mind, trying to find some words, but they've all been taken, all used for ordinary considerations that mean nothing in comparison to what he has meant.

We say "Thank you very much" and "I so appreciate what you have done" to people who fill our grocery bags, to people who offer us a ride across town. What are the words to say to someone who gave you back your life, who believed that you still had a soul, who acknowledged how bad it was possible to feel? Shouldn't there be another language for this? Different words altogether? And if I use the same old words, did I change what I was trying to say? Did I make it a same old thing?

I should not risk words. But some come out.

"I wish you were my father."

The faintest surprise scrims his face. A pause.

"I would be proud to have you as a son."

MY ABUELA COMES AT ABOUT ten. She has flown out to bring me home. She surprises me by saying that she's just been in Dr. Ghosh's office. I wonder what they discussed, and who set up their meeting.

I suppose that Abuela knows everything now. She knows about Sam, and if she knows about Bashkim, then she would have to know about the other boy. Without the one, there would be no reason to know the other. And why am I so certain that Dr. Ghosh has told her about Bashkim?

I know that she and Dr. Ghosh have been speaking to each other for a while. They don't talk about it, but they don't not talk about it either. Abuela might mention something about Dr. Ghosh, or vice versa, and I never know if these are slips, or if they're trying to find a way to tell me that they're in conversation—that I might as well include Abuela in my thinking about Sam and Bashkim and the boy in the market. Perhaps, but I've been careful to ignore these hints. I'm not ready to talk with Abuela about these things. I can't bear to look at Abuela and admit what I did.

Dr. Ghosh says that secrets aren't healthy, and it's because of him that I won't lie about anything that has happened. Not lying is not the same, however, as telling, and I'm not ready to tell. It's partly being a patient. I have so little control of what is private, so little opportunity to be unobserved. If I told Abuela something while I'm here, or Terence, who is someone I could imagine telling certain things, then I could do nothing about the response. I couldn't get away from it, from whatever the reaction might be. Being able to close your eyes just isn't fucking enough.

THE FLIGHT HOME IS A lot harder than I expect it to be. The airport is exhausting, and there's too much to look at. By the time I board, my head is pounding, and the six hours of sitting straight depletes me. I can't make it up the gangway without a wheelchair, and my final return home from Iraq is punctuated by my abuela's ragged breaths as she pushes me into the terminal.

Home. For a Las Vegas kid, the lights and sounds of a hundred slot machines are more natural than rain, and a public space backgrounded in the bells and chimes and gravel rolls of bored travelers standing at kaleidoscopic games is as commonplace as sky in Montana or snow in Vermont. Even so, I'm overwhelmed by McCarran Airport on a Friday evening. The crack of a suitcase dropped on its side makes me jump, and the clanging of coins sliding into a metal tray brings out beads of sweat on my brow. I don't know how I will make it to the baggage claim, and I wonder if Abuela plans to hail a cab. I've seen the long lines of people waiting for taxis, the cabs rolling in twenty at a time to pick them up, the traffic guards and the exhaust and the airport security yelling at people to hurry along or slow down or wait a minute.

Six months ago, I was the guy who ran down ninety-one IEDs in Iraq, and now I'm the guy who can't get through an hour in the Las Vegas airport.

I DON'T KNOW WHETHER MY abuela has kept my homecoming a secret or just told everyone we know that I'm not to be disturbed the first night, but the house is dark and quiet when we arrive, and we have the evening to ourselves.

My room is more or less as I left it four years ago. Which hits me hard, since I'm not here on leave, and since the progress that seemed exceptional at Walter Reed now seems like a lot more disability than I was thinking I had. What am I going to do? What happens next? What about what I've already done? I'm trying not to go down, down, down that road, but I'm thinking about Sam, and about the market, and about Dr. Ghosh, and about the end of being a soldier, and about my mother, and I don't know what to do with this much pain and this much failure. I'm twenty-two years old, and there's nothing left to hope for.

I have a trick I use when I'm feeling this way. I think about that little girl I heard in the hall in the hospital, the one who liked her dress. It's fucking loco, but if I imagine her voice—I just try to hear that little-kid voice in my head—I feel better. I don't know how long this trick will work, but Dr. Ghosh told me that using whatever works is a good idea. He calls this the postwar version of survival skills.

THE VISITORS START THE NEXT day. My aunt Rosa brings tamales and her three dogs. I have some bad memories of dogs in Iraq, but one of the dogs, who has a thin brown nose and a black coat, sits next to my chair and lays his snout on my thigh. He doesn't move for the entire visit. It feels just like someone's hand resting there, reminding me to stay calm, like one of my therapists encouraging me to see if I can push just a little longer and just a little harder, and though I'm afraid to move, or pet the dog more than the slightest bit, in case it should decide to move away as mysteriously as it decided to stay near, I feel better. I sit there while my cousins and my uncles and my abuela's friends talk and laugh around me, and I think about how nice that dog's head feels on my knee. Maybe the point is just to get through one hour, and then another, and not think farther ahead than that.

That evening, the clouds streak neon peach against a turquoise sky, and I slip out the door, and sit on the large rock where Abuela used to take pictures of me for our Feliz Navidad cards. The sky is crazy colorful, and I think how long it's been since I've seen the world like this. Out my hospital window, the sky was often gray, and even when it was blue, it wasn't turquoise, the clouds didn't heap on top of each other so improbably, the sun didn't turn everything into a screaming, Strip-muffling blaze.

Iraq's a desert, and sometimes it even felt like Vegas. It was comforting, when I was scared out of my mind, to see the sky go on and on, to see the ridged angles of flat brown bluffs against the blue of a desert firmament. There was a guy from Nebraska in our unit, and one night he told us that the first time he ever went west, in a car with a friend from high school, he had to lay down with a towel over his head when they drove through the Rockies. The sight of all those mountains made him sick, made him feel like he was about to slide off the world. This is a guy who was the first one to volunteer to take a new position in the middle of a firefight. I mean, he was crazy-ass courageous, and he had to lie down and hide when he drove on an American interstate through the mountains.

But that's the thing, how you feel about the place that's home. About its sky, its air, its smell, the color of the light, the way the rain falls (or doesn't), whether it's hot or cold. For a lot of guys, Iraq might as well have been the moon. They had to get over that, past it, the way the land felt so strange, the sky so vast, the heat so overwhelming. At least I didn't have to deal with that. It was almost the opposite—for guys like me. I mean the heat was hell, it's really brutal there, hotter than Vegas, but the idea of heat wasn't scary, it wasn't strange, it didn't ever feel like a place humans weren't supposed to be.

I get up from the rock. It's hard for me to sit without something behind me still, and I walk down the block, past all the lookalike houses—this one with a red door, that one with an overgrown olive tree—the details that keep you oriented in Vegas, so you know where you are, know which house is yours, and I watch that sky. I watch it go from brilliant to bright, from neon to glow, I watch it slowly fade, turn gray, then darker, somber, black. And when the street is dark, when not a single car passes me for minutes on end, I turn and I walk my crooked uncoordinated brain-fucked-up walk back to the house I grew up in—the one with the big rock in the front. Back to my abuela, back to whatever life I am about to lead.

31

Roberta

THERE'S NO CHANCE THAT Nate Gisselberg won't be exonerated at the coroner's inquest. There's no possibility that Arjeta Ahmeti's death will be declared needless. This is just what Vegas is.

For all the national reporters writing breathlessly that the era of diamond belts, alligator shoes, and bad toupees is over, for all the financial shows intoning the rise and fall of Wynn Resorts stock, for all the revisionist architectural tomes declaring the Strip a new Americascape, Vegas is still a town where everyone knows who was living here in 1960; where nobody forgets whose father worked for whose uncle; where the only ones who really understand why this casino makes money, why this charity is funded, why this hopeful is anointed, are the same ones who also remember that Mormon bishops ran the gaming commission, that the Las Vegas mayor was Tony "The Ant" Spilotro's lawyer, that a gangster funded Sunrise Hospital, that all of these entities—the Mormon Church, the Eastern mobs, the gamblers, the bar brawlers, the hustlers, the dreamers, the cathouse owners, the losers, the crooners, the onetime murderers—they built this town. Nothing in nature disappears. Helium becomes carbon becomes diamonds become rings. Bodies become bones become dust becomes earth. And in Vegas, murderers become patriarchs, card sharks become benefactors, the unredeemed become the redeemers.

And cops are not convicted of excessive force.

It's true: it's not a small town anymore. For decades, people have been streaming in from all over the world, from every country on the planet: stateless people, desperate people, eager people, ambitious people. They come for easy work, for the ability to pay someone off, for the chance to start over. They come because they are rich, they come because they are poor, and some day, maybe even some day soon, all these hundreds of thousands, millions, of newcomers may even wipe clean the slate drawn by Vegas's earliest dreamers. But not yet. Not yet.

Arjeta Ahmeti has no chance of vindication in that coroner's inquest. Not in this town. Not at this time.

AND SO I TRY TO figure out what will happen to Arjeta's children. To a little boy she must have cherished, to a little girl who will not remember her. Of course, the system doesn't need me. Children whose mothers die go to their fathers if their fathers are alive, if their fathers haven't done anything wrong. Wrestling those children from such a father would take years. Things would have to go very badly, over and over, for Bashkim and Tirana, before their father would lose his right to them.

So what am I doing?

Why am I part of this story?

Why did I ask to be their CASA?

Marty says I've bitten off more than I can chew, and that there just isn't anything that can be done about these children, no matter how badly I feel. The first time he said it, I got mad. It felt like he was saying my work didn't matter. But that's not what he meant. Marty knows the system as well as I do, after all this time. And the bottom line is that Sadik Ahmeti has the right to his children.

But I'm not ready to give up. I'm just not giving up on the Ahmeti kids yet.

I MET WITH SADIK AHMETI again last week. He's not at Desert Care anymore. He's staying in the Budget Suites, and the Albanian Society is paying his weekly rent until he can get set up with a Section 8 apartment.

I know that Budget Suites well. I've been there many times. A lot of kids that end up with a CASA start out in the Budget Suites. Furnished apartments. Weekly rent. No down payment. Filthy kitchens where you might be able to save a little money doing your own cooking. The Budget Suites at the south end of the Strip are one of the stops in the trek that down-and-out families make through this town. Some of them start there, when they drive in on I-15 with all their possessions crammed into a twenty-year-old minivan, hoping to start over. Some of them end up there, after they lose their home or are evicted from their apartment, before they end up in one of the homeless shelters or in a makeshift tent at the edge of Sunset Park.

Yeah, I know the Budget Suites.

Mr. Ahmeti has one of the small units facing Las Vegas Boulevard on the second floor. It's just one room, with a microwave and a fridge along the back wall, and a bathroom with a shower tucked in the corner. There's a big dip in the middle of the bed, with a dirty white cover dragging on the floor. When I arrive, Sadik is curled up on the one chair in the room. He's got his head in his hands, and although he called to me to open the door, he doesn't respond when I say hello.

"Mr. Ahmeti, it's Roberta Weiss. I'm the court-appointed advocate for your children."

He doesn't move.

"Mr. Ahmeti, I was hoping we could talk about your children. I've been to see them several times. I know you're going to see Bashkim soon."

Nothing.

"I'd really like to talk. I'd be happy to take you to lunch. We can go anywhere you like."

Still, he doesn't move.

I'm not sure what to do, but I sit down on the edge of the bed—there's nowhere else—and wait. I'm a little irritated that he's ignoring me, but he's just so damn pathetic, the place is so damn pathetic, and I'm starting to feel overwhelmed by his situation. He should probably still be at Desert Care, he clearly needs help, but it was amazing that Lacey was able to get him a stay as long as he had. There just isn't anywhere for someone like Sadik Ahmeti to go.

"I heard that the Albanian Society is helping you out. Has someone been to see you? Do you have someone who comes by here?"

This is his only hope. The Albanian Society. How big could that be?

"I don't want to see no one. I told them. I'm American."

This is a guy who knows how to make friends.

"I'd like to talk about Bashkim and Tirana. Could I take you to lunch?"

"I ate."

"Is there something else you need? I have a car. I could help you with an errand?"

At that, he looks up. Incredulous.

Part of me wants to take this guy and shake him. There's something about his weakness, his fury, that makes me angry, and at the same time, it makes me want to cry. I start wracking my brain, trying to think of services that he might qualify for, somewhere he could go, get some help. And I'm panicking too, thinking of Bashkim and Tirana. I had hoped he would be better and that we could talk about where they would live, how he would manage with two small children.

There's just no way.

He's not going to be able to do it.

But the court is going to give him those kids, and it won't take them away until something terrible happens. Until a lot of terrible things happen. I can't stand this.

"Mr. Ahmeti, I understand you're waiting for an apartment. How do you feel about that?"

He looks at the floor and then he makes the effort to raise his head, to look straight at me. But he doesn't speak.

"You'll be able to bring Bashkim and Tirana home when you have an apartment. Have you thought about that?"

He makes a low sound, half roar, half cry.

"They're mine children. Mine children should be with me. They should be with their nene. I'm American."

He starts to stand as he says this last, his voice rising, and as thin and sad as he is, he's still frightening. But then he sits back down, his hands over his face, and after a moment, I realize he's crying. I know he's an angry guy, I know he must have hurt Arjeta, but right now, what I see is someone pitiful and powerless and poor, someone who's never gotten a break.

Sadik Ahmeti's not going to give up those kids. But he sure as hell can't take care of them.

MARTY'S OUT OF TOWN, SO when I finally get home, I take last night's spaghetti out of the fridge and pour myself a glass of wine. It's a perfect March evening, windless and purpling and clear, and I sit outside, drink in hand, plate untouched, and try to let the day slide off me.

Visiting Sadik has shaken me up. I think of myself as one of the good guys. I'm proud of who I am, of what I do. Truth told, I'm pretty damn sure of myself. The beauty of being a CASA is that I'm almost always on the right side, defender of children. Plus, as a CASA, I'm a volunteer. Which means I don't have a boss. I don't have a client. I can't do anything I want, but I volunteer as a CASA because it gives me a lot of room, I can operate on my own, I can do what I think is right.

But what is right?

Should I try to find some way, some legal way, that I can take Sadik Ahmeti's children from him? A guy who spent two decades in a police state prison for trying to do the right thing? A guy whose wife was killed by a traffic cop?

Should I accept that there's no legal way to take those children from him? Should I accept that he's a guy who's never going to let anyone help him, even if I found someone, someone in the Albanian Society, who was willing to step in? For sure he'd mess it up.

Am I supposed to look away while an eight-year-old boy and a three-year-old girl are sent to his care?

Poor Arjeta. She had no way out.

I see a lot of desperate people. I see what happens when people get desperate. And right now, I let myself think about Arjeta Ahmeti. I imagine her as someone sailing out into the world, all alone on the little boat that is her one life. I imagine her running crouched out from the shore, then hopping in the vessel, putting a paddle to the rough sea, setting sail, losing the wind, stopping to rest, continuing on, all alone, a boat no bigger than an almond, a sea larger than the sun. When I have all that in my mind, when I think of Arjeta, alone in America, two children who needed her, a husband so wrecked, then my heart fills, and cracks, and fills again.

How can I quit, knowing what Arjeta lived?

32

Luis

SOME THINGS YOU DON'T think about when you sign up for the Army. Like how the system's going to work when you get out. Which in Vegas means it isn't. There's a veteran's hospital at the base, or half a hospital. The Air Force has the other half. Though, of course, if you've got anything really wrong with you, they send you to California. I guess that's why they left me in DC so long. But I don't need a hospital. I just need a lot of therapy. And in Vegas, there are twenty-two different places for a vet to go for medical help. And apparently there isn't anyone who's really sure where I should go.

Vera, who answers the phone after twenty minutes of soft-rock covers, tells me she thinks that the clinic on Desert Inn would work, but they might send me out to the clinic on Shadow Lane, or I might have to go to the base first and get an order from *there* for Shadow Lane, and then Shadow Lane sends some of its people to a care center on Torrey Pines. My head sort of spins. I can't drive—not now, any-way—and there isn't any set of buses that is going to take me on that route; not in a day, anyway. Which means Abuela will have to drive me. Which means I'm not a hell of a lot more independent than I was back at Walter Reed. Fuck.

Talking to Vera wears me out—it doesn't take much lately—and I start thinking about Bashkim. He's out there somewhere, right here in Vegas, which is weird, because it was easier to think about him when he was far away, when there was no chance that I'd see him somehow. Not that I'd know him if I did, but his school's not that far from our house, he lives in the same part of town.

Of course, who knows where he lives? He's in foster care.

It starts bugging me, wondering just where he is, just where he used to live, and I get on Google Maps and try to figure a couple of things out. Pretty soon I'm reading whatever I can find about what happened, which isn't that much. Bashkim's principal already sent me most of the articles I find. Except when I look those articles up on the Internet, I can see these online comments that readers have posted. And man, they're fucked. It's all immigrants and Muslims and terrorists. I mean, the lady sold ice cream to kids. But "Vega$Truth" thinks she was taking down the Constitution. And "BeenHereDoneThat" says that people who don't speak English should be driven to the border and told to run before they get shot. Somebody named "MoonStar" says LVPD's been out of control for years, so some other posters forget about Bashkim's mom and call MoonStar names. Shit.

There's a coroner's inquest coming up, and I wonder what that means. What happens? Will Bashkim be there? I think about Googling the cop, Nathan Gisselberg, to see where he was in Iraq, what he did, but I don't know, that could be bad. I might not want to think about that.

I've still got the envelope that Dr. Moore sent me. I pull it out and look through Bashkim's letters again. I see how hard he tried to tell me without telling me: *Do you know that a lot of soldiers come back and are policemen? I'm really tired of bad things. My baba doesn't like policemen or soldiers.*

I try to imagine Bashkim. I don't know anything about Albanians, whether they're dark or fair, but I picture a little boy, something like my-self when I was eight, and something like the boy in the market, whose face I will never forget. That face makes me think about his mother, about the way she sounded, the way she fell right on top of him, and I feel myself starting to slide, starting to get overwhelmed. That boy, his mother's keening, Sam's face—they're at the back of my mind all the time. They come forward at night, and leave me twisting and terrified and never sure if I am awake or asleep.

That boy. Bashkim's mother.

When I was a kid, I used to want a mom. I used to imagine Maricela picking me up at school instead of Abuela. Pretty weak stuff compared to Bashkim, compared to a kid whose mom was killed right in front of him. A kid whose dad can't even get it together enough to keep him out of foster care. Nobody came to his mom's funeral. That detail sticks in my head from the stuff Dr. Moore sent. No wonder he kept writing me letters. How is it that I'm the guy they picked for your pen pal, Bashkim? How the hell did that happen?

LATER THAT DAY, I START thinking about Mike Rodriguez again. Uncle Mike. I'm not mad at Abuela anymore. I mean, I got no business judging her, and I wonder if there's some way to bring this up. I want to know more. I want to know everything.

So at dinner, I just ask her.

"Abuela, a guy came to visit me when I was at the hospital."

"Sí?"

"Yeah. He said he was my uncle. Miguel Rodriguez. He said I looked like my dad."

I want my voice to be neutral here, I'm not mad, and I hope I've done it, because there's some things Abuela doesn't like, and if she thinks I'm trying to slip in some sort of criticism, underhanded, not up front, she'll get mad.

She's quiet. She doesn't say anything. She just keeps stirring the pot on the stove, which I'm pretty sure is done cooking, since I've already got some of it on my plate.

I don't say anything either. Me and Abuela, we give each other time. Finally, she does speak.

"Miguel. Yes, I know Miguel."

She knows Miguel? I wait.

"He's a lot older. A lot older than your dad. He wasn't living with him when your dad—when Maricela and your dad—were going out."

She hesitates with that last bit. My mom got pregnant in high school, and for my abuela, that isn't going out. That's something she doesn't really have a word for.

"Yeah, he came around. After. You were already crawling. Maricela had never met him. She didn't know who he was when he knocked on the door. She told him to leave."

Abuela gives up on the pot now, and she sits down. Not right at the table with me but on the bench under the window, where she likes to watch the birds. She looks out the window now. I can see the side of her face, but not her eyes.

"He came back, though. When I was home. Maricela was out. She was already gone a lot then, Luis, she was already going, already lost, but I didn't know it. I was trying to keep her. Keep her with us.

"And I guess that's why I didn't let Miguel in either. Maricela was so mad about him, so scared, and I didn't want her getting mad at me, I didn't want to do anything that would make her leave. I thought she'd take you. I never thought she was going to leave you. So I didn't know what would happen if I talked with Miguel. I didn't want to do anything that might make things worse."

She doesn't look at me. I keep quiet.

"He wanted to see you. I could tell he was a nice man. Real broken up about Marco. Trying to figure out what happened. I don't know where he'd been, I don't know why he hadn't been around.

"And I felt terrible, not letting him in, not giving him a chance. So

I told him that I'd bring you out to him—that if he'd just stay in the yard, where we could watch for Maricela coming back—that I'd bring you out to him.

"And he agreed. He said it was okay, he understood. So I went in and got you. You were just waking up. You were hot, so your hair was kind of matted on your forehead, and your cheeks were red, but you were a happy little guy. You used to shriek when I came in, you were so happy.

"And you went right to your uncle. He held out his arms, and you just bobbed right out of mine and into his."

Abuela stops now. I hear her take a deep breath. I think I see a tear on her cheek, but I'm not sure. She's not looking at me, and I'm not saying anything. I can hardly breathe.

"He held you, and he talked to you. He talked in Spanish, about your papi, about your abuelos. He kept saying he was sorry."

Her voice is ragged now. I can't believe she's telling me this. I can't believe this happened. Isn't this the kind of thing she should've told me? Why don't I know this?

She doesn't talk for a while, and when she does, her voice is calm and steady.

"He was pretty upset when he gave you back to me. He was a nice man, Luis."

So finally I say something. I want to say a lot of things, but I focus, in case I never get a chance to hear about this again. I ask the important question.

"Was that it? Was that the only time you ever heard from him?"

She shudders, so I know the answer before she speaks.

"No. He came by another time. When you were about three. And he sent letters. Not too many. But some."

He sent letters.

He sent me fucking letters.

Where are they? Did she read them?

The anger's coming over me like a wave now. I've never felt this way about Abuela, I mean never. Not like this. And it scares me. It scares the hell out of me.

I start trying to picture Dr. Ghosh, trying to think about the little girl in her dress, trying to remember what Terence would say. I'm breathing heavy, which is actually some of what they told me to do in the hospital; some of how they told me to cope. And Dr. Ghosh would say to feel it, to let the feelings come. Not the anger. The other feelings. He'd say, "Luis, what is the feeling? What are you feeling?"

So I try.

And what I'm feeling is so fucking lonely, I don't know what I'm going to do.

THREE DAYS LATER, ABUELA AND I get a visitor. It's a woman named Roberta Weiss, and she works for something called CASA. She's a sort of caseworker for Bashkim Ahmeti, and Dr. Moore has told her about me.

I'm shocked.

I haven't discussed Bashkim even with Abuela, and I haven't written him or tried to get in touch with him since Dr. Ghosh and I got the news about his mother.

Abuela's not shocked. Abuela has already talked to Roberta Weiss, and she's talked with Dr. Moore too. She knows everything about Bashkim and about our letters, so I was right that she must know everything about me.

She and I haven't done much talking in the last few days. That conversation about Uncle Mike threw me hard. I went to my room and stayed there awhile. Abuela didn't push it. She brought me food, she tried to talk a little. She said she was sorry, that she meant for me to know, for Mike to be able to see me.

I shook my head, though, and didn't let her talk. I got to take things slow. That's one of the things Dr. Ghosh taught me. To control how much I'm taking in. How much stimulus is coming at me.

Abuela knows this too.

So we haven't talked much, real superficial, and then this Roberta lady shows up. Talking about Bashkim. And me. And Abuela's been talking to her.

I thought that when I got out of the hospital, I'd have more control. But when this Roberta comes in, I feel as if I'm a child. When I was a soldier, I was a man. Nobody looked after me but me. I had a private life. When I shot myself, I gave that up. Being a man. The right to privacy. I was a patient, in a public place, for so long. I want my life to be my own again.

Abuela is telling Roberta Weiss to sit down. Telling her she has some coffee ready. I guess I'm curious, and maybe I even think I can take a little stimulus, because I go in the extra bedroom and get on the computer. I can hear them talking from in there.

They act like they know each other. They must have talked on that phone quite a while. I hear Roberta's voice, deep for a woman.

"It looks like they'll be in foster care for another month at least. Their father could take them at any time, he's out of the mental health ward, but he's not in good shape. And he's staying at a Budget Suites, so I don't think the judge will release the children there. Catholic Refugee Services is trying to get him a Section 8 apartment. He hadn't paid rent for a couple of months, so the minute the landlord heard the news, he evicted the family. The CPS caseworker went crazy over that, so at least he hasn't yet disposed of their stuff. It's sitting in a garage where they used to live. Can you imagine if the landlord had thrown out all of those children's things? All of their mother's things?"

Abuela murmurs, asks questions. I wonder if she's taking notes. There are these pauses as they speak. I'm trying to figure out what is going on. Why this woman is in our house. How my letters to a third-grade kid could somehow have put my abuela in the middle of his life. My mind drifts to some of the things Bashkim wrote me—about his soccer team, about his baba. I wonder how much of what he wrote was true. I wonder if his baba was his coach.

"Child Protective Services is open to options on this family. Their ability to do anything for these children will be over as soon as the father takes them back. But everyone knows that's going to be a disaster. He was probably violent with their mother, he's paranoid, he's very Old World. Nobody can imagine him taking care of a three-year-old. I've spoken with him. I don't think he can imagine it. If he had family, if they had any connections here, it would be one thing. But they were really isolated.

"And the thing is, by all reports, the kids are fine. They're nice kids. Everyone wants to do something before it's too late. Before they're the worst part of this tragedy."

Roberta and Abuela talk on and on. I stop listening, even though I'm interested. I can't really walk out of the room without saying something to them, so I plug my headset into the computer and listen to some music.

After a while, I see Roberta Weiss walk past my door. Abuela is right behind her. I try not to let Abuela see me looking. I shut my eyes, like I'm listening to the music.

THAT NIGHT, I'M UPSET ABOUT the visit from the woman from CASA, and about Abuela somehow being interested in Bashkim. I tell myself that I'm going to talk to Abuela about this, that I have to talk to her, but I get myself so worked up that I don't even go to the kitchen for dinner. I take a walk outside, too far, until everything hurts, and then I go to my room, and shut my door. Abuela does not come up.

It goes on like that for another day and night, and I'm thinking that it's crazy for me to be living here with my abuela, who lied about my dad's family and who has somehow inserted herself into my letters to Bashkim, and, man, I got a lot of other stuff to worry about without this shit.

Still, Abuela doesn't say much.

She makes food, she offers to call Vera and see if she can figure out where I should go first, but she doesn't say much else. It's weird. It's uncomfortable. And finally, I just break down and blurt it out.

"I don't want you to be talking about Bashkim, Abuela. Some things are private. Why was that woman here? Why was she talking to you?"

My abuela takes her time. She can hear how freaked out I am, even though I was trying to hide it. I can't control my body, and I can't control my voice. I'm a fucking cripple.

"Luis."

I wait. I feel pretty worked up. I wish Dr. Ghosh were here.

"Luis, I know about the letter you wrote to Bashkim. I know about the boy in Iraq. I know about Sam. I've been waiting and waiting for you to tell me about them . . ."

She looks at me then. I look down.

" . . . but I know why it's hard for you."

My heart is pounding like a Marine Corps drum. I wonder if she can hear it. I can feel my lungs getting tight. I want to take a deep breath in, to relax, but it's like that part of my body doesn't belong to me anymore.

"Luis. There's nothing you could ever do that would make me stop loving you. There's nothing your mother could ever do that would make me stop loving her. Nothing. I've lived a long time. I've seen a lot of things. And I know what is important to me."

She says this, and her voice doesn't even shake, but I'm still trying to breathe. My heart is still banging away. I speak anyway.

"Why was that woman here?'

Abuela nods slowly. She's thinking about what she will say.

"Bashkim's in a really tough spot. His father's not right. Roberta's trying to find a way to make sure Bashkim and his little sister will be okay. She learned about your letters from the principal at Bashkim's school, and she's a thorough kind of person. She called me. We've talked quite a few times. She even talked with Dr. Ghosh."

Will I ever be a man again?

Will I always be the crippled fuck? The last person to know what's going on?

"Roberta wanted to make a recommendation about whether or not you should be allowed to see Bashkim. You mentioned playing soccer with him some time. It's her job to know everyone who's around him. At least for now. At least until he goes back to his father."

Baba.

For some reason, I'm breathing a little better now. I think of Bashkim in foster care and of Kevin saying his foster dad scared him. I mean, I get so caught up in myself. And here's this poor little kid. What the fuck difference does it make if Roberta Weiss wants to talk to my abuela? Why the fuck am I upset about it? I mean, damn, if any kid ever needed someone to look out for him, it's Bashkim. And if his caseworker wants to talk to my abuela, then why not? Why would I do anything that might make it worse for that kid?

"I'm sorry, Abuela. I'm having a really hard time . . . and sometimes I just can't think straight. I'm sorry. You can talk to anyone you want."

My voice is kind of weak, but I get that out, and I feel sort of proud of myself. But Abuela isn't quite done. She has something more to say.

"Luis. I've never talked to you too much about Maricela. She was fourteen, you know, when your abuelo died. And she was sixteen when you were born. It was a really hard time for me. I didn't do the right things for her. I didn't take care of my own daughter. I was hurting so much. And I was scared."

It's true. Abuela never has told me much about what happened to my mother. I mean, I know my mother, I've seen her now and then all my life. I pretty much figured out for myself what went down.

"Raising you, Luis, is how I loved your mother. It's the only thing she would let me do for her, the only way I've ever been able to show her I love her."

She looks down now. It's Abuela's turn to have difficulty speaking. Abuela's turn to have trouble breathing.

"I know I should have told you about your Uncle Mike. I pushed him away at first because I was afraid of losing Maricela. And then once she was gone, once I knew she wasn't going to come back, not really, not ever, I don't know. I'd lost so much. First my Hector and then Maricela. I couldn't bear to think that you had another family, that they might want you."

My face must show my dismay. The way this makes me feel like I've been stomped.

"I was always waiting for someone to come and claim you, to claim their share of you."

She's shaking now. I've never seen Abuela like this. I've never seen her weak.

"But Abuela"—I'm stammering—"Abuela, how could you not tell me? How could you keep me from meeting my father's brother?"

"I'm sorry, Luis. I'm ashamed. I didn't mean for it to last so long. I was waiting until you were twelve, and then when you were twelve, I sent a letter, but it came back. The address was no good. I didn't try after that. I just thought he would be in touch, and when he was, I would make it right."

"And he never tried again?"

Abuela is silent. A long silence.

"Please tell me."

"He tried. When you were fifteen, he finally called again."

"And?"

"And I was afraid then. Because I had caught you drinking with Jorge and Austin. And I didn't know what sort of life Miguel had. So I told him. I told him that you were challenging me, that I was worried about you. I mean, I wasn't sure. And he backed off right away. He said he understood, he asked me to stay in touch."

"Did you?"

"Yes. A little. I wrote him when you graduated. And when you enlisted. He knew where you were. That must've been how he found you."

"And he never asked to see me? He didn't try?"

My abuela waits a bit.

"No."

I sit on this a minute. It's a blow. I wish I hadn't asked.

"But *Nietecito,* he thought you knew about him. I didn't tell him you did, but he thought you knew. I had just let it go so long, and then you were going to Iraq, and I was waiting, I guess, for the right time."

I say nothing. This hurts.

"Luis, I made a lot of mistakes. I did a lot of things wrong. I should have told you about your uncle. He didn't want to hurt you. I didn't want to hurt you."

I don't say anything. I sort of nod my head, and I listen, but I don't have anything to say right now.

"I'll help you find Miguel. You're a good man, Luis. Maybe you don't know this right now, but I do.

"Luis, I didn't help Maricela when she needed it.

"And nothing I do helps her now. Every day, I hope that there's someone, somewhere, who can help her, who will help her. Someone who has enough love. Someone who gives that love to her."

Abuela stops then. She looks smaller than I've ever remembered her being, and when I see her, small, crushed, I'm ashamed.

Who am I to criticize her?

Have I already forgotten what I did?

And it drains away then, the anger and the hurt and the bitterness that was beginning to form deep inside me. Abuela's human, she's not perfect, and if she made a mistake, if she took something important from me, she also gave me everything I am, everything I ever had. She didn't kill a boy carrying burned charcoal in a bag.

I open my arms, and just as if I were a man, just as if I had the ability to protect her, Abuela leans into my body. And we stand there, lopsided grandson and tiny grandmother, doing the best we can. I feel Abuela's body shake in my arms, I hear how she muffles her tears, how she tries to hold them back, and I know how much she has hurt, and I feel how my knowing this soothes her.

33

Bashkim

TWO PEOPLE COME TO visit me before Tirana and I go to the judge. The first is Baba. He comes with the caseworker, Mrs. Miller, on a Saturday afternoon. Mrs. Delain told me he would be coming two weeks ago, because he was supposed to come last week, but then he got sick—that's what Mrs. Delain said—and so when the doorbell rings, and I hear Mrs. Miller talking to Mrs. Delain, I'm a little surprised.

I wait until Baba gets to the living room, and then I run to him.

"Baba! Baba!"

I am crying like a baby Tirana's age, but I can't stop myself. I didn't even know how much I was waiting for him. All of a sudden, I know what I want. I want to live with Baba. I want to live with my own family. I don't want to be here anymore.

"Baba, have you come to get me? Can I go home with you?"

I am yelling this right in front of Mrs. Delain, and I don't even care what she is thinking. Because now I know, I know what I want. I want Baba. I look at the caseworker, Mrs. Miller, because I know she's important—Daniel has explained it to me. She gets to decide everything, and I look right at her, so she will know I am not making a mistake, I am not kidding, and I say:

"I want to live with my baba. Tirana and I want to live with Baba."

She looks at me. She's tall—taller than Mrs. Delain, taller than Baba—and she looks way down at me, and she says, "Bashkim, I'm so happy to see you again. Mrs. Delain tells me that you've been doing really well. We're all so proud of you."

I don't understand why she says this, so I look at Mrs. Delain, and I look at Baba, who is holding me but not really looking at me, and I can't figure out what's going on. They don't look right. They don't look like they've been listening.

"I want," I say much softer. Now I'm not sure if I'm supposed to say this. I thought this was why they were coming, to see if I wanted to go with Baba or not, and I didn't know what I wanted, but now I do. "I want to live with Baba." My voice comes out quiet this time.

Baba suddenly squeezes me. He makes a loud sound, like he made at the truck, when the policeman shot Nene, and he squeezes me. He squeezes me so hard, I can't breathe, and I try to get out, to push his arms back, but he squeezes harder and harder, he's smashing me, so I wiggle. It makes him tip, and he loses his balance, and we both fall against the couch and then slip down, crushed together, on Mrs. Delain's floor.

"Oh!" Mrs. Delain rushes to help us. She tries to pull Baba's arms away from me, to lift his head. I am still trying to breathe, Baba has not stopped squeezing me, and I squeak, "Baba, you're hurting me." I am trying to take a big breath, trying to get some air, and Baba hears me, and he lets go. We lie there on the floor, panting, me because I couldn't breathe and Baba because we fell, I guess, and when I look at him, when I look at his face, I see that there are tears all over it—that Baba is crying, and still he does not really look at me.

"Bashkim," Mrs. Delain says so gently, like she is waking me in the middle of the night. She strokes my hair, still sitting on the floor next to me, and she puts her other hand on Baba's shoulder.

"Lacey," she says. "Help me get him up."

And then Mrs. Miller and Mrs. Delain help my baba stand up, and they bring him some water, and he sits down in the red chair with the foot part that comes up. He sits there, and he doesn't talk, and he doesn't look at me, not for a long time, and finally, I just sit down on the couch. I just sit down and wait.

Then Mrs. Miller speaks.

"Bashkim, it's been too long since you and your baba have seen each other. That's my fault. I'm sorry. I'm very sorry."

I don't look at her. Does she know I haven't seen Tirana either?

I haven't seen Baba or Tirana since the mosque. Does she know that? Does she know I'm eight years old, and I've been at Mrs. Delain's, where I didn't even know anyone before I came here, all by myself? Does she know that?

"Bashkim's been so brave, Mrs. Miller." Mrs. Delain is speaking. She has such a nice voice, it always makes me feel better, and for a second, I'm sorry I yelled that about wanting to live with Baba. Except I do.

"I met with his teacher last week, and she says that he's one of the best students in her class. And he's been so good for Daniel. Bashkim helps Daniel with his homework every afternoon."

Mrs. Miller smiles at me, and maybe she says something, but I am looking at Baba. I can't tell if he's listening or not. He doesn't look at us.

"Baba?" I say. "Baba!"

He looks at me.

"Baba, I missed you. I miss Tirana. And I miss you."

Baba looks at me, and he opens his arm, and I fly over to the red chair and crawl in his lap. I never sat in Baba's lap much, only in Nene's, but it feels good there. Baba looks at me. "*Të dua, shpirt*," he says. "*Të dua.*"

"I love you too, Baba. I love you."

And then Baba and I just sit there for a while, and Mrs. Delain and Mrs. Miller talk. And when Baba feels well enough, Mrs. Delain suggests I show him around the house, so I do. I show him where Daniel and Jeff and I sleep, and where I do my homework, and how we each have a green basket for our own laundry. Baba looks at everything—he looks like he's never seen a washing machine or a bed before—but he doesn't talk too much. I hold his hand, and once in a while, he squeezes my fingers tight. It doesn't hurt, like when he hugged me. It feels good.

After that, we eat tuna fish sandwiches in the kitchen with Mrs. Miller, and Baba and I go outside and walk a ways down the block, but we don't really do anything, because Baba seems tired. I think about Baba when we had to sell ice cream all day at the soccer tournament. Now it doesn't seem like he could even stand up all day. Can being sad make your legs weak?

When we get back, Mrs. Miller says that she and Baba have to go. She says that I probably won't see Baba until the court date, but that I can call him on the phone any time. He has a phone now, and she gave the number to Mrs. Delain.

Baba and I hug each other before he goes, and it's not like at first, when I was yelling and when he was crying. It's just a hug. It's a good hug, and Baba tells me to be good, like an Albanian boy, not American, and I say, "Yes, I am good, Baba." And when they drive away, I see Baba waving at me through the window, and I wave until the car turns left and I cannot see it.

ON THURSDAY, WHEN I GET home from school, the second visitor is there. She comes with Mrs. Weiss, who is supposed to tell the judge where Tirana and I should live. They are waiting in the living room. I try to go past the doorway quick and get to the kitchen, but Mrs. Delain says, "Bashkim, can you come in here?"

I go in.

All three ladies look at me. I notice that Mrs. Weiss has red glasses, which I don't think she had when she came before. Red glasses are nice, like red shoes.

"Bashkim, you remember Mrs. Weiss, and this is Mrs. Reyes."

Both ladies smile at me, and I say hello, and I hold out my hand, because Mrs. Delain expects boys to shake hands and open doors. Mrs. Delain motions to me, and pats the couch next to her, so I sit down there, and she puts her hand on mine.

The lady named Mrs. Reyes asks me how my day at school was.

"Fine," I say. And I don't really want to say anything else, but I feel Mrs. Delain's fingers on mine, so I say, "We had art today. I'm making a bowl out of clay." I didn't really mean to say this, since I was thinking about giving the bowl to Mrs. Delain if it turns out, but maybe she'll forget about it before then anyway.

"I like to make things too," Mrs. Reyes says.

"What do you make?" I ask her.

"I sew. I make lots of clothes, and sometimes I make quilts or pillows. I took a pottery class once, and I made some pots that are on my porch. I grow herbs in them."

Mrs. Reyes has a soft voice. She sounds a little bit like the librarian at school, so she probably speaks Spanish, but I'm not sure about that. Her voice is pretty American too.

"Do you like art?" Mrs. Weiss asks me.

"Yes," I say. "I like science better, but I like art too."

"Because of the marine lab?" Mrs. Weiss says, and I remember that we walked by the lab when she came the other time.

"Yes," I say. I look at Mrs. Delain then, because thinking about things makes me worried, and she guesses right away what is wrong.

"Did you want to get something to eat, Bashkim? There are apples on the counter. I am going to talk to Mrs. Weiss for a bit, so you can run and find Daniel if you like. Or start your homework."

I say good-bye to the ladies, just the way Mrs. Delain likes, and I go upstairs. I don't look for Daniel, though. Instead, I go to the closet, the one with the pillows where we can be alone, and I sit there for a while.

Some days, I forget to think about Nene. Today was so busy at school, I don't think I thought of her once, but now Mrs. Weiss is here, and I just want my nene. I've been trying not to think about Baba's visit, about what happened when he hugged me, because my chest hurts again, just like it did then, and I don't know what to do about that.

I hold the biggest pillow in my arms and put my face in it, so nobody can hear me. I'm tired of living here. Everyone is nice to me, but nobody is Nene, and I just want my own house with my own bed next to Tirana's. I want the kitchen to smell right, like it does when Nene cooks, and I want Baba to fall asleep in the big chair and make his snore sound, and I want Tirana to wave her arms and say she is a flutterby. I don't want to be by myself anymore. I don't want to see Mrs. Weiss. I don't want to meet ladies that come to Mrs. Delain's house. I don't want to talk to Keyshah or Jeff or Ricky. I don't want to be around teenagers at all.

For a while, I just hold the pillow as tight as I can, and feel bad. I feel so bad it seems like I will burst. I start to think about nights when Nene felt bad, when I would hear her crying after Tirana and I said good night, or when she would sit on the patio and look at the sky, and not talk to any of us. I wonder if Nene was thinking of her nene then. I wonder if she missed her.

Sometimes Nene would tell me about growing up in Albania. Sitting in the closet, holding the pillow, I think about Nene telling me her stories. I concentrate until I can almost hear her voice. Nene said she could walk up a hill from her house and sit on a wall where her mother had sat, and her grandmother, and her mother, and hers. The stones would be warm, even in October, and she could see down to the red roofs of the next village, and to their gray olive trees. She could see green fields, and the indigo line of a stream, and because she was so high, she could see blue sky below her as well as above her.

The wall that she sat on was built a thousand years before she was born. Nene said it was built to circle a castle, and when she sat on the wall, she would pretend she was a princess. She would eat a fat, warm fig, and dream about marrying a prince. Her nene and gjyshe would have to cook for weeks to prepare for her wedding, and her baba would have to borrow mules to carry in all the vats of walnut raki. There would be dancing, and singing, and the wedding would last three days.

Sometimes my Nene would laugh when she told this story. Sometimes she would tell it sad, but lots of times, she would laugh. A wedding for three days! What would Americans say about that?

I can't help it. When I think of my nene's laugh, I smile. I feel better. I don't think I'm supposed to feel better, because Nene died, and I need her, but I just do. I guess that's how Mrs. Delain's pillow closet works. You go in there sad, and you come out one of her strong kids. That's what she says, anyway, that this is a closet for getting strong in.

34

Avis

Coroner's Inquest Rules Killing of Las Vegas Woman Justified

Las Vegas, Apr. 17—Las Vegas Police Department officer Nathan Gisselberg was exonerated of all charges in the killing of Arjeta Ahmeti last month.

The Clark County Coroner's Inquest ruled that the shooting was justified. The inquest met for six hours. The district attorney called seven witnesses to testify, and read a number of questions requested by the Ahmeti family's lawyer. Attorneys for LVPD waved off questions after the proceedings.

Jeremy Price, president of the Las Vegas chapter of the ACLU, and Fatmire Bardici, of the Albanian Society of Clark County, expressed dismay at the ruling.

Since the inception of the coroner's inquest system in

1976, only one shooting has ever been ruled unjustified,
and in that case, it was the number of bullets released in
a residential neighborhood that elicited the ruling, not
the death of the victim.

I'VE HANDLED THE CLIPPING SO many times that the paper has slight,
sweaty finger marks. I was there, of course, at the inquest. With Lauren
and Jim and Rodney and Corey Stout's wife. Darcy didn't come. That was
good. And, of course, there were the photographers and the reporters, the
cameramen, and the head of the ACLU, someone from Catholic Refugee
Services, a few Albanians, a local imam, a steel-haired woman whom I
later saw identified as the principal of Bashkim Ahmeti's school.

Nate and Mr. Ahmeti sat at separate tables, each with an attorney.
Several people, lawyers I suppose, sat at the district attorney's table, just
in front of the judge. Nate had a lawyer, but the DA was as good as his
lawyer. Mr. Ahmeti was older than I expected him to be, old to have
such young children. His hair was gray; it wound into long curls at his
neck. He wore, even for this formal process, a shapeless old sweater, and
wool pants with a pale herringbone texture, and shoes that looked like
he had owned them his entire adult life.

I could barely stand to see him sitting there. Old and odd and poor.
Like someone who would go to all the city council meetings and speak.
He kept glancing behind him nervously. When the door swung shut, he
jerked, and his chair scraped loudly across the wooden floor. Nate sat perfectly still. He never looked around. His back was massive by comparison.

I wondered what the old man was thinking. There was no chance
that the shooting would be ruled anything but justified. Certainly not a
decorated Iraqi vet, a local kid, with a father that lots of people knew. If
the inquest ruled the shooting a criminal act, the DA could, and would,
choose not to prosecute. Everybody knew that. We all knew that. Maybe
Sadik Ahmeti didn't know that.

Nate testified. Corey testified. The officers who were called in and who had pulled up just as the shooting happened testified. They each described a woman who was irate and out of control. At one point, she had her son by the neck. She was yelling that it would be better if she and her children were dead. She called for Allah. She reached in her pocket and pulled out a long silver object. Nate was thinking of the boy. He knew it would take less than an instant to slit the boy's throat, if the object had been a knife, if the woman were as crazy as she seemed. She was calling to Allah, saying she and her children would be better off dead.

One witness—who looked terrified through the whole thing—said that she didn't see the ice-cream scoop or the knife. She said the mother sounded frightened. That the mother looked like she was protecting her son from the police. That the officer took out his gun, and the mother was afraid.

Sadik Ahmeti and his attorney kept consulting. They submitted questions on yellow cards, furiously writing them as each witness spoke. The DA read each question to himself, and then set card after card on the table, without saying what was on the card, without asking any question. He did read one. He asked the frightened bystander, "Why did you think she was protecting her son?" The bystander said, "Because she is a mother. That's what mothers do." She seemed not to realize that this answer had no impact, that it did nothing to suggest that Arjeta Ahmeti was acting rationally. She seemed pleased to have said something on the victim's behalf.

There was a tense moment. Another bystander, a man, much more confident, said that he heard Corey Stout asking Nate, "Why did you do that?" and "What knife?" It was damning, the way he put this information out there. He wasn't nervous, that witness, and he didn't try too hard to be convincing. He simply said what he heard, loudly and clearly. I saw Nate scribble something on a yellow card, give it to his attorney. But his attorney did not give it to the DA.

There was a rustle in the room; Mr. Ahmeti's lawyer handed the

DA two yellow cards. The DA read them but did not ask the witness whatever questions were written there. Mr. Ahmeti's attorney scribbled wildly, trying to get another card to the DA, but before he was finished, the DA had accepted the man's testimony and motioned for him to sit back down.

Corey Stout was called back to the stand. The affair had had the opposite impact on him. Whereas Nate had gotten larger and stronger over the last month, Corey looked thin. And sad. His sadness was the most palpable thing about him. I don't even remember what he said, how he explained what the witness had overheard, because the sadness that emanated from him dampened everything in the room: the anger, the self-righteousness, the desperation, the fear. Every other emotion there paled by comparison to Corey Stout's sadness.

I had the thought that he would not be a policeman next year.

When it was over, when the jury had deliberated less than an hour and had given its verdict to the judge, when the judge had read the verdict, when the news reporters and the cameramen had started to make the room hum with their questions and their talking and their requests for information, Lauren and Jim and Rodney and I left. We waited in an atrium downstairs until finally Nate arrived, waving away reporters with his hand. The first thing he did was lean over and hug Rodney. They held each other a long time: the burly blond soldier and the shrunken uncle in his wheelchair. I had loved each of them from the moment they were born.

When Nate stood up, I hugged him and felt the flutter of his heart, beating rapidly, beneath his broad chest. I thought of the little boy with the football, running on bare tiptoes into his father's arms.

ALONE THAT NIGHT, I RAN the hearing over and over again in my mind. I couldn't stop seeing the trembling back of Sadik Ahmeti, the way his lawyer kept scribbling questions, faster and faster, the way the DA seemed to ignore one question after the other.

I did not want my son to go to jail. I did not want my son to be convicted of murder. But if LVPD had a case, if LVPD believed that Nate was justified, then why did today feel like a charade?

THE PHONE RANG JUST AFTER nine at night. The phone in my new house didn't ring often. Most people called my cell. I am not even sure why I hooked up the landline.

I hit my hip on the corner of a desk as I raced to get the call. I wasn't used to where things were. It was the first time I had lived in a new place in almost thirty years. It took me a while to remember that bump when I saw the blackish mark turning green a few days later. "How'd I do that?" I thought. "Where did that come from?" For a second, I thought Nate had somehow done it.

"Hello?"

"Mom?" It was Lauren. I could hear the strain. My heart started to race, very quick, a bit ragged. Just like that.

"Hi, Lauren." I made my voice cautious. I was afraid.

"Mom, can you come over here? I need some help."

There was a huge bang in the background, as if someone had pushed over a bookcase or slammed a door. "Lauren! Who are you talking to? Who's on the phone?" I heard my son's voice, though it was not a voice I knew from anytime before this year.

"Nate? Nate, I'm calling your mom."

"My mom? My mom?" His voice roared in the background.

"Mom, I have to hang up. I'm sorry."

And *click,* the phone was dead.

I SHOULD HAVE CALLED 911, of course. I knew that. But I hadn't yet decided. I was still fingering the clipping, trying to get my mind around the relief that Nate would not be tried for an unjustified shooting and around the fear that he had been allowed to get away with it.

Instead, I found my sandals, grabbed my purse, and flew out the door. Nate lived in Southern Highlands, at least a twenty-minute drive away. I took Warm Springs and then the Beltway. I thought it would be the fastest, but I had forgotten about the construction at the interchange, about the lanes closing down at nine each evening. I saw the snaking line of traffic as soon as I came up the ramp. Semis trying to get to LA, and a motorcyclist speeding fearlessly between the creeping rows of cars. There was no way back and no way forward. It took an extra fifteen minutes.

There weren't many streetlights leading to Nate's house. Huge tracts of land, partially developed, master planned but abandoned when the real estate market crashed and everyone in construction lost their jobs. Lots of Las Vegas looked like this now. Short streets of carefully designed houses, small playgrounds with swing sets but no swings, roads paved in disconnected bits, construction equipment parked, for months, on the empty lots that were supposed to be your neighbors' homes.

There was just one light on at Nate's, and the house was silent.

I didn't stop to think about why. I was parked and out of my car and ringing the doorbell before the engine gave its last dieseling cough.

Nate answered.

"Mom, we don't want you here. It's almost ten o'clock. We're going to bed."

He stood in the doorway, and I thought again how big he had become. Every time I saw him, he was larger.

He was still my son, and I was not afraid of him.

"I want to talk to Lauren. Let me come in."

I thought he might resist, but he stepped aside, and I walked in. I still find that surprising, given what had happened.

Lauren wasn't in the living room. I called her name.

Nate neither helped me nor stopped me. There was silence.

I walked to the kitchen, called Lauren's name again. By this time, my heart had started to beat faster.

"Lauren?"

They must have fought in the family room. Nate had not even tried to hide it. The coffee table was pushed on its side, and the overstuffed armchairs had been shoved askew. The rug was pushed up into a wave of fabric against one of them, which made a lamp wobble and then teeter precariously when I stepped on the far edge of the rug.

"Lauren?"

I know my voice sounded frightened. Had my son killed a second woman? Pray God, I had this thought.

There was the squeak of her voice from the hall bathroom. I asked her if I could come in. And then I opened the door, gently.

I don't know where Nate was. He had not followed me.

She was there, sitting on the closed toilet lid with a bag of frozen peas in her hand. Her nose had been bleeding, her left eye was swelling shut, there was a distinct cut at the left corner of her lip. She had been crying, so that her right eye was almost as swollen as the left. When she stood up, I saw the red marks of five fingers on her bare right shoulder. Had he held her with one hand as he punched her with the other?

Lauren was slight. Taller than me, but at least twenty pounds lighter, with fair, translucent skin. That she could take one of Nate's punches, and stand, was surprising.

My head was reeling, and my stomach was sick, but I opened my arms, and she fell into them. I held her, stroked her hair, made a humming sort of sound in my throat. But I was just going through the motions, because my heart was beating, and in my head, everything was flashing by. Nate at seven months, Nate at seven, Nate in high school, Nate when he joined the Army, Nate when he stood in the doorway tonight, huge, and then when he let me in. How could this be happening?

"I think we should take you to an emergency room."

"No!" Her no was so fast, so adamant, she pulled slightly away from me.

I pulled her gently back in, so I wouldn't have to look at her while we had this conversation.

"You could have a broken bone. Or a concussion. You need to see a doctor."

"No. Please, Mom, please. I am not ready to see a doctor. Please, just stay here with me."

And I protested awhile, but in the end, that is what I did. Nate had disappeared by the time we left the bathroom. Maybe he left the minute I came in. But he was not there. I did not have a chance to confront him, to attack him, to question him, to apologize to him, to . . . to what? He was not there, and he did not come back that night.

So I stayed with Lauren.

I made her tea, and a muffin with raspberry jam. I held the frozen peas on her eye, and she lay on the sofa while I did this, and we watched a Lifetime movie with the sound off. Eventually she fell asleep, and when she let me, I persuaded her to stumble into bed, and I stood there and stroked her hair until she was deeply asleep again, and then I sat on the sofa and watched television with the sound off all night long.

In the morning, Lauren told me that she was going to go to a friend's house for a few days, that she would tell her friend something, maybe the truth, but please, let her handle it, let her decide. I stayed while she packed a case, and we left together about ten. Nate had not returned.

THAT NIGHT, THE PHONE RANG again. Lauren had texted me in the afternoon. Said she was fine. Said she had spoken with Nate. I had replied that she could come to my house, she could stay with me. She did not respond to that text.

So the phone rang again. Even later. I was already asleep. This time, nobody spoke. I heard breathing, and something slight in the background, but nothing else.

"Lauren?"

Nothing.

"Lauren, is that you?"

The phone clicked off.

I lay awake, wondering if it was Lauren. If it was Nate. If Lauren had gone back to Nate.

I thought of Sadik Ahmeti berating his wife, and I thought of him raising two small children. I thought about an eight-year-old boy and a three-year-old girl without their mother. I thought of my son's part in that. I thought of Emily. I thought of Rodney and me when we were kids. I thought of Nate.

WHEN NATE WAS SIX, HE found a stray dog at the park. He carried it over to me—its legs sticking out absurdly, his arms around its belly—where I sat on a bench.

"He's lost, Mom. He can't find his family."

"Have you set him down? Maybe he knows right where to go."

"No, Mom, look. He's thirsty and he's scared. And there's branches and things in his fur."

He was right. The dog did look the worse for wear, probably was lost.

"We can't keep him, Nate. We can take him to the pound. They might know where he lives. His owners might be looking for him."

"No, Mom, no. Not the pound. They'll kill him. Luke says the pound kills dogs. Please, Mom, please don't take him to the pound."

"Nate, we can't have a dog. I don't even know if he's well. He looks pretty dirty, and he might be sick."

"Please, Mom."

"Nate, we're not taking that dog home."

"Mom, I want to be a good man. I want to help the dog."

I want to be a good man. I still remember. Such a funny phrase from a little boy.

And we kept the dog. Years later, we buried him in the backyard. I wonder who will dig up his bones some day, who will buy our house, who will decide to plant a new tree and strike bone with her shovel. Will she be shocked when a skull appears in the dirt? Will she know that we loved the dog, that we cried when he died, that we couldn't bear to throw him in the garbage or allow the vet to do it? Will she imagine that the dog slept on my son's bed until he joined the Army? Will she know that he whimpered at the door for months after Nate left, that he barked when he heard Nate's voice on the speaker, all the way from Baghdad? And will she intuit that the dog waited to die until my son was home on leave, that he dragged himself around, blind and crippled and covered with pink growths, and did not die until Nate came home and spent one last night with him, curled together on the floor because the dog was too old to jump on the bed? Will her shovel strike that skull, and will all those images waft up and into her imagination?

Nate wants to be a good man. Remember. He wanted to be a good man.

ON MONDAY I CALL LVPD and leave a message for the chief of police that I need to meet with him, today if possible. He's not available Monday, but his secretary makes an appointment for one thirty on Tuesday. I spend the day going through some of the boxes I moved from my house. I call Lauren, but she doesn't answer, and I leave her a message letting her know that I'm worried. She doesn't call back, but she sends a text and says that she's feeling better. I don't know what this means. So I call Nate, and he doesn't answer, either. I leave a message asking him to call me, asking him to come over, telling him that I need to talk to him tonight. I don't call Jim. I want to tell Jim what I'm going to do as well, but I can't trust him not to stop me.

Nate doesn't call, and he doesn't come over. I leave one more message. I give him one more chance. Then I go to bed.

On Tuesday I wear a brown linen suit and a cream silk blouse. I tell the chief of police that my son has a problem and that he needs help—that he should not be using a weapon now. I tell him everything I know about his relationship with Lauren. I tell him that he hasn't been the same since he came home from Iraq, and that there might be services available to him as a veteran. And finally, I tell him that if anything more happens, I will tell the media about our meeting.

Then I leave the chief of police's office, and I call my son again, so that I can tell him what I have done. He's my son, and something enormous has happened to him. But we will find a way through it. Whatever happened to Nate, however this has changed all of our lives, *is*. Now we go forward. We figure it out. We act with courage. We eye the felt, we size up the stickman, we call our bet, we roll our dice. Nate and I, Lauren, Jim, Rodney, Darcy, we're still in the game. We play.

35

Bashkim

I GO TO THE hearing with Mrs. Delain. She says that children don't always come to these, that she's only gone once before, but that Mrs. Miller wants Tirana and me to be there.

We drive in Mrs. Delain's van all the way to the middle of Las Vegas, where I have never been. We park inside a building, under the ground, and I do not like how heavy it feels in there. There is a sign at the elevator that says we are on the orange level. The sign says to remember this, so I do. We get in the elevator, and Mrs. Delain straightens my sweater and looks at me to see if I am clean and everything. I guess I am, because she doesn't do anything else to me.

The elevator lets us off in a big room, the biggest room I have ever been in. It echoes, and there are so many people walking back and forth, wearing shoes that click, that I think I am inside a drum. Mrs. Delain looks at a big sign that says the names of all the courtrooms and the judges, and then she says that we will have to wait in the line at the far end of the room.

We walk over there. *Tap, tap, tap.* People's voices are echoing too, so I hear people speaking who are not near me. I can't tell what they're saying, but I listen just in case. It is so surprising to hear voices in that way.

When we get to the front of the line, there are policemen. One says I will have to take off my sweater, and a different one opens up Mrs. Delain's purse. My stomach starts to hurt. I take my sweater off quick, because I don't want the policeman to talk to me again. But he just waves his arm, and Mrs. Delain and I walk through the machine, one by one. When the man behind me goes through, the machine lights up and makes a terrible sound. Mrs. Delain and I both jump. Mrs. Delain explains that it is a metal detector, and that you can't have any metal in your pockets or it will go off. They're looking for guns. Thinking of that makes my heart go thump thump, and I take Mrs. Delain's hand. Today the judge will decide where I am going to live, and Tirana. I've been trying not to think about this, because I can't think of anything that will be good without Nene, but nothing could be worse than what has already happened anyway.

We take another elevator, which has carpet and mirrors, and a lot of people are in it, and we get off on the eighth floor. Mrs. Delain says hello to someone in the elevator, and she says, "Hello, you must be Bashkim" to me, but I am feeling sick, and I don't say anything back. I want to leave. I wish Mrs. Delain would just take me back downstairs. I would like to be in the alone closet at her house now. I try to pretend that I am in a movie and that this is happening to another kid, not me, but it doesn't really work this time.

The courtroom is big. There are lots of rows for people to sit in, and there's a place for the judge at the front, which is above everyone else. I think Mrs. Delain and I are early, because there is only one other person in the room when we sit down. It's Mrs. Weiss, who writes the letter to the judge. She smiles and waves hello from her seat on the other side of the room, but seeing her makes me feel really bad, and I don't smile back. I am worried that I am going to throw up, and I can't breathe right, and my eyes are seeing funny too. I slide closer to Mrs. Delain, and I put my head against her arm, just for a minute, because we have already talked about how it is important for me to be brave today, and I don't want her to think I forgot. I just really need to smell her smell right then.

Mrs. Delain puts her arm around me and squeezes me just a little bit.

"You're okay, Bashkim. You've been through worse than this. Everybody here wants to help you."

Mrs. Delain always makes me feel better. She knows all about how kids have to do hard things, and she tells us that there aren't any tougher kids in the world than her foster children. Mrs. Delain believes that people like me and Keyshah and Daniel are going to make the world better some day. She says that nothing makes a heart bigger like experience.

I see Mrs. Miller, our caseworker, come in. She doesn't look at me or Mrs. Delain, though. Then Baba comes. He is with that big blonde woman from the Catholic place. He's a lot smaller than she is, and when I see him, my heart gets fluttery and I need to breathe more. Baba looks sick, and small, and scared. I try not to think about him hugging me in the living room.

He comes right over to me and Mrs. Delain. I stand up, and he holds me for a long time.

"Bashkim, Bashkim," he says. "My son, Bashkim."

I hug him back as hard as I can. When we are done hugging, he and the lady sit next to us.

Now I am waiting for Tirana. I wonder what she will think about this big room. I wonder if she knows what is going to happen today. Baba's lawyer comes over to us then. He asks Baba to come and sit at the table with him, and Baba looks a little nervous.

"That table? By the judge?"

I know that Baba went to prison, and I wonder if he also went to a judge. He has never told me that, but I know Baba, and he doesn't want to sit at the lawyer's table. I look over and see that there is a security guard standing at the front of the room too. Baba doesn't like security guards either.

"Yes. The judge will want to direct some questions to you, and it is better if you are sitting with me."

Baba nods. Looks at the security guard.

"It's okay, Baba," I say, and pat his arm a little bit. He looks at me with his wet eyes—they are always wet—and he says okay, he will go to the table.

So now it is me and Mrs. Delain and the woman with yellow hair. She says hi to me, and she says that she met me when I was only a year old, when we first came from Albania.

Finally, Tirana comes in. I almost don't recognize her because she has on a fancy white dress and socks with lace at the ankles and pretty shoes. Her hair is longer, and it has a blue ribbon at the back. She looks taller, and different. She doesn't look like a baby. She looks like a little girl. She is holding her foster mother's hand, and she says something to her, and suddenly I really want Nene. I can't stand that Tirana is holding that woman's hand, and I think how bad Nene would feel, to see me and Tirana with different mothers.

Why did Nene say that?

That she and her children would be better off dead?

Why did Nene say things like that?

She didn't mean them. Nobody ever understood about my nene and how she needed to say things like that sometimes.

Tirana seems so strange that I am a little afraid to call to her. But she looks over and sees me, and instantly she lets go of the lady's hand and runs to me.

"Bashkim!"

She jumps right into me, in her dress and everything, and kisses me in front of everyone. Then she sees Baba, and wiggles out of my arms to go to him. I am afraid that Baba will not act right, but of course he holds his arms out, and Tirana kisses Baba too. We all watch her. She is so pretty. Then Tirana comes back to where I am sitting. She wraps her arms around my neck and buries her head in my sweater, and now she won't look up, even when Mrs. Delain says hello and when her foster mother comes over and sits down. So that is how we sit. Mrs. Delain, then me, then Tirana half in my lap, then the Catholic lady, then Tirana's foster mom.

Some other people come in the courtroom too. The woman who came to Mrs. Delain's house that afternoon, the one who liked to make things, and a man walk over and sit near Mrs. Weiss. The caseworker stops and talks to them before she sits down at the table across from Baba and his lawyer. Then the judge comes in. The security guard says, "Please stand for the honorable judge Robert Kohler," and we all stand, and the judge enters and sits down very quickly, and looks at the papers in front of him.

He's not a scary judge, but I am feeling scared anyway.

"Mr. Ahmeti?" he says. And Baba stands up.

"I am sorry for the circumstances that bring us here. The court acknowledges your great loss."

Baba stands a minute, nodding his head over and over.

"I know this day is hard for you. You had a very difficult decision to make, and I thank you for making that decision in time for our meeting today. Your decision shows courage. I know it took courage."

Baba has a strange look on his face, but he sits down.

"Bashkim Ahmeti?"

Mrs. Delain motions for me to stand, and when I move Tirana over a bit, she stands up too.

"Tirana Ahmeti?"

We look at the judge, and he looks at us.

"Thank you for coming to this hearing, Bashkim, Tirana. Everyone tells me that you are very special children, and I am going to try hard to take care of you."

Tirana turns and buries her face in my side, but I look at the judge. I think I should say something, but I don't know what to say. I am thinking about how much I wish my nene were here, and how nothing the judge does can really help, but then I think about whether or not Tirana and I are going to live together, and whether we are going home with Baba, and how I don't know if that is a good thing or not. I just look at him and then look down. I don't know what I want.

"Mrs. Delain? Mrs. Stoddard?"

Our foster mothers stand up.

"Thank you for taking in these children, and for the thoughtfully written reports that you each submitted. They were very helpful to me. We are lucky to have people like you as foster mothers."

Mrs. Delain and Mrs. Stoddard sit down. I see Mrs. Delain look at Tirana's foster mother and smile, just a little, the way she does.

"Ms. Miller. You surprised me with your recommendation."

The caseworker explains to the judge that she spent a lot of time thinking about it, and that she is confident it is the best option under the circumstances.

"Ms. Weiss."

The lady from CASA stands up.

"Roberta, the court and the city of Las Vegas owe you and your fellow CASA volunteers a great debt. Thank you for the extraordinary commitment you made to this case, and the number of hours you put in. This is a system that could not protect children as well as it does without volunteers like you. I thank you profoundly."

"Graciela Reyes?"

The woman who came to Mrs. Delain's stands up.

"Luis Rodriguez-Reyes?"

I almost yell out, *Specialist Rodriguez? My soldier? Why is he here?*

I look, and a man, not much older than Ricky or Jeff, stands up. It takes him a while, because he has a cane, and there is not quite enough room for it in front of his seat. He looks over at me, he looks right in my eyes, but I can't tell what he is thinking. My heart goes thump thump.

I wrote him some lies.

And I told him that I wanted the president to say soldiers could not be policemen.

And he shot a boy.

Does the judge know he shot a boy?

I can't sit still, and my heel thunks against the seat. Mrs. Delain puts her hand on my knee.

I look at Baba. Does he know who Specialist Rodriguez is? Is he going to yell at him? Are they going to fight?

I don't hear what the judge says to the woman or my soldier. I see them sit down, and then I can't stop thinking about them. I want to look at Luis, but I am afraid. I keep watching Baba, waiting for him to remember who Specialist Rodriguez is. I don't know what he'll do. I remember him in Dr. Moore's office. That was such a long time ago. Nene was there too. Dr. Moore wanted Nene to talk to her without Baba. Nene could not do that.

I remember Baba and Nene fighting that night. It was the worst fighting ever. Even Tirana couldn't stop crying. If Baba figures out who Specialist Rodriguez is, something really bad could happen. I see that the security guard is wearing a gun, and I can't stand it anymore. I stand up, and I think that I am going to run out of the room. I can't be brave anymore. I don't want to be. I want my nene. I want my own house. I don't know any of these people. I don't want any of them to help me. I have to leave.

Mrs. Delain reaches out to pull me back in, but I jerk away. I don't care. I don't care how mad they get. I can't do what they want anymore. I have to get away.

Just then, Tirana calls my name. I look over and she is sitting there on the bench, right next to where I was, and I can see that I've scared her, and that she's starting to cry. Her foster mother trades places with the blonde woman, tries to get Tirana to look at her, but Tirana is looking at me. Her face is filled with fear. I can see that she knows I'm running away, that I'm leaving her there, and that it is the worst feeling she has ever had.

She feels like I felt when Nene slumped to the curb.

I stop. I look at Baba. He has turned around, to see what I am doing, and his face looks like Tirana's. He looks just as scared as Tirana.

I look at them both.

I am so tired.

I want my nene so much.

And I step back in, past Mrs. Delain, and sit next to Tirana. She grabs hold of me even more tightly than before with her skinny little baby arms. I can't leave. I can't leave Tirana. And I can't leave Baba. I am just going to have to stay here, even if I feel like I am going to burst.

"Bashkim."

It is the judge. I look at him. His face is kind. He doesn't look mad that I've interrupted him.

"Bashkim, this is a hard day. You have been very brave. We are proud of you. And your mother would be proud of you."

I look at him, and I feel a little better. I don't think he's going to hurt me, me or Tirana or Baba. Mrs. Delain reaches over and puts her arm around me and Tirana both. She is not going to let anyone hurt me either. I breathe in, and I sit back against Mrs. Delain's arm.

"I've been a judge for many years. In family court, and in criminal court. Before that, I was a lawyer. And I'm not a young man. So, like all of us, I've seen my share of tragic circumstances. I've seen the smallest error lead to the most painful outcome: the harried mother who forgets her baby in a hot car, the exuberant teenager who leaps into a too-shallow lake, the young driver who doesn't see the child chasing a ball. And I've seen my share of cruelty, of violence, of criminal acts that sicken the heart.

"There are times when all this pain, all these misunderstandings, all this hatred, has made me wonder if we deserve this beautiful world; if we human beings should really be left in charge of it.

"But if, sometimes, an unspeakable horror arises from the smallest error, I choose to believe that it's possible for an equally unimaginable grandeur to grow from the tiniest gesture of love. I choose to believe that it works both ways. That great terror is the result of a thousand small but evil choices, and great good is the outcome of another thousand tiny acts of care."

Judge Kohler looks around when he is talking. I can tell that he has practiced saying this. He doesn't really look at the papers in front of him, and his voice is kind of like a speech. I wonder if this is what he always says.

"Every single person in this room has chosen to act against the horror, has chosen to act in care. The death of Arjeta Ahmeti, and her loss to her children and her husband, whatever the circumstances were, created a hole in their lives. She may have been a lonely and frightened woman, but she loved her children, she cared deeply for her family, and they needed her. Without her, they are at risk.

"But against that loss, all sorts of people offered a gesture of love. Each of you offered one. And all these gestures are the reason why there's hope for these children. That's what I see when I look at this case, at this report. And so, I am granting the recommendation of the caseworker, Lacey Miller, and the CASA, Roberta Weiss. I accept the offer of Graciela Reyes, and the voluntary renouncement of rights of Sadik Ahmeti. It's an unusual arrangement. But here in Nevada, where we are short of funds and services, where many people are without family, where we are accustomed to working creatively, I think it's a far better plan than we might have thought possible.

"I remand Bashkim and Tirana Ahmeti to the care of Graciela Reyes, and grant her full physical custody, with the following conditions.

"Sadik Ahmeti and Graciela Reyes will share legal custody of the minor children.

"Sadik Ahmeti will have the right to full and unconditional visitation with his children.

"Sadik Ahmeti will move into the Sierra Nevada Apartments, near Mrs. Reyes's home.

"Bashkim Ahmeti will stay at Orson Hulet Elementary School, at least until the end of this school year, and through fifth grade if he so chooses."

WHAT? TIRANA AND I ARE going to live with Luis? With his mother? How did this happen? Does the judge know who he is? I can't stop myself. I jump up.

"No! He killed a boy!"

Luis stood up as soon as I did, but he moves more slowly than me, so when I turn to look at him, he is still trying to get his balance, his hand gripped on his cane. He looks right at me, and the expression on his face stops me cold. He looks as if I have struck him and also as if he will cry.

I stop, because I hadn't meant to hurt him. I remember how nice his letters were. I remember that I wrote him over and over right after Nene died. So we just stare at each other. And I don't know what I think. I don't want to live with someone I don't know. I am afraid to live with Baba. I think I should stay with Mrs. Delain and Daniel and Keyshah, but what about Tirana? I have to live with Tirana. If Tirana lives with someone else, she will be part of their family. Like when she walked in holding her foster mother's hand. She already seemed part of a different family.

I start to sit back down, and then I notice that the caseworker and the judge are talking, and that the CASA is approaching the judge too. Mrs. Delain holds my hand, but she doesn't say anything to me; her face doesn't tell me what she is thinking.

Luis is still standing where he was before, looking stunned and so sad. The woman who came to Mrs. Delain's house is looking at me, and then she stands up and motions for me to come toward her. Tirana sees this and grabs my hand, so that I won't leave. The woman notices Tirana, and she walks slowly toward us instead.

"Bashkim, I'm Graciela Reyes. We met before. I would like to be your foster mother. Yours and Tirana's. I am Luis's grandmother. I raised him when he lost his mother."

I look at her, not knowing what to say. Am I supposed to say yes to someone I don't know?

"Your situation is very special, Bashkim. Your father has the right to raise you. He doesn't want to give you up, and he understands that he needs help. Everyone has tried to come up with a solution. I can offer you and Tirana a home together, and Catholic Refugee Services has found an apartment for your father down the block. If the arrangement does not work out, Ms. Miller and Ms. Weiss will still be involved. They'll be in touch with you often. You will have someone that you can trust."

I like Mrs. Reyes's voice. It is very calm and gentle. Even Tirana has noticed. Mrs. Reyes offered her hand while she was talking, and Tirana took it. They are holding hands right now.

I look at Mrs. Delain, who is watching me closely. I think about how she told me to be brave today and how she says that her foster children are going to make the world better. She is looking at me with eyes that say I am tough enough, that this is not my worst day, that I have already been through worse.

I look at my baba, who doesn't look at me. He is sitting at the table, still seeming too small to be him, with his face in his hands. Even from here, I see his back trembling. I think of the truck, of the bad day, and of how Baba shook like that when the police officer came.

I think of my nene. I think about her picking me up at school, with Tirana. How Tirana would kiss me. How Nene would touch my hair. How I didn't care that she didn't talk to the other moms, didn't know the teachers' names. I think she was pretty. How I used to check quick, when I saw her coming, if it was a good day or a bad day. If her fingers were moving together, over and over. If she was talking with Tirana or just holding her face very still. How I would feel so light if she was talking, if she was just holding Tirana's hand.

Nene would want me to stay with Tirana. She would not want Tirana to be a different family from me.

I think about how Baba will live near us; how we will visit him. I think that Baba knew Nene's family, Baba lived in Albania with Nene, Baba knew Nene.

I think about how it is me that wrote the letters to Luis. That told Dr. Moore she could send my letters, that told Dr. Moore not to tell Baba or Nene. The judge was talking about me. I let Luis say he was sorry, because I knew about Baba and the prison and how a man might not be meant for a war. I let Luis say he was sorry, and that made Luis write to me, and that made Luis's grandma care about us. The judge isn't trying to hurt us. Because I let Luis say he was sorry, Luis's grandma can help Tirana and me. That's what the judge means.

And just then, just when I haven't felt this feeling in such a long time, I think I feel Nene's fingers on my head, soft, soft, like when we watched *Jeopardy!* And I think that I did something good, that I made it possible for Tirana and me to be together, for Baba to be nearby. I am the one who did the small good thing first. And I think that Nene is smiling at me. And that she has her hand very soft very soft on my head. And that maybe we are going to be all right.

Author's Note

This is a work of my imagination, but the explosive event at the center of this novel was inspired by someone else's explosive event.

In writing my novel, I didn't know any more about the real event than I had read in the newspaper. I didn't know the details of how the event actually unfolded. I didn't know what led the real people involved—the mother, her children, her husband, the police officer—to that catastrophic minute; I don't know how they have fared since. I didn't write about them.

Instead I used certain elements of that incident—that they were Albanian immigrants, that the father had been imprisoned there, that they had an ice-cream truck, that the police officer was a veteran—as the catalyst for a fictional story with fictional characters. The immigrant family scarred by one set of political events, the young veteran scarred perhaps by another: for me, those ideas perfectly capture an essential quality of the boomtown I call home.

I am often caught by the way in which a disaster can be rooted in the trivial: by the terrible weight of an incongruous cause. One could spend a life thinking about the single step from a curb in front of an unseen bus; about the tossed cigarette that traps two children in a burning closet; about the toes gripping the edge of a bridge, the arms reflexively balancing, the mind racing, the millisecond before it is too late.

The one thing that almost kept me from writing my story was that it was so unbearably sad. It seemed to me that the world was sad enough, that some people have enough to bear, and that using my bit of a life to throw in another such story wasn't a very good use of my time. So the challenge I set myself was this: could I write a story that accepted the full unbearableness, and still left one wanting to wake up in the morning? Could I do it without being trite, without relying on mere wishfulness? Is it possible to live past the unthinkable with beauty? Can a coffee spoon counter calamity?

Now that the book is done, now that someone has decided to publish it, now that it will go out in the world of sadness, I am left thinking about the event that first inspired me. I met the real mother once. She sold me an ice-cream treat while my son played baseball. It was a cool, dark October night; she had almost no customers. She told me she had to keep working because she needed the money. She told me she had a son about my son's age.

I'd like to say to the real people involved in the real story: I remember. I remember the worst moment of your life. I remember its utter unacceptability, its utter finality, its utter inaneness. I remember it. I honor it. I wish you peace.

Acknowledgments

To that serendipitous someone who chose me for a Yaddo residency, I tip my hat. To Stephanie Cabot, who cheerfully sold the novel as if it were no more than eating a piece of pie, two tips of the hat. And to Trish Todd, whose light touch and savvy skippering made all the difference, the hat itself. Wear it in joy.

Simon & Schuster: you're like a first boyfriend. I'll remember every moment. In particular, thank you to Jonathan Karp, Richard Rhorer, Jessica Leeke, Lance Fitzgerald, Jessica Lawrence, Andrea DeWerd, Wendy Sheanin, Marysue Rucci, Cary Goldstein, Loretta Denner, and Philip Bashe. I am grateful as well for the generosity of my fellow writers: Eleanor Brown, Sarah Blake, Sugi Ganeshananthan, Carol Anshaw, Kathleen Grissom, Vaddey Ratner, Rebecca Wait, and Charles Bock.

With brimful heart, I acknowledge Deb Newman's enthusiasm, Jamie Jadid's encouragement, Jodi McBride's insight, Dan McBride's generosity, and the early support of Tracy McBride, Joan McBride, Vicki McBride, Catherine Angel, Rachel Beach, Sandra Bird, and Anna Worrall. Also, to the Corporation of Yaddo (lovely Yaddo) and the College of Southern Nevada. Finally, I am ever thankful for Barbara and Don McBride. To all the others, friends and family so dear, yes, you too. Yes, always.

About the Author

Laura McBride is a writer and community college teacher in Las Vegas, Nevada. She once thought of herself as an adventurer, having traveled far from home on little more than a whim and a grin, but now laughs at the conventional trappings of her ordinary suburban life. She's been married for twenty-five years to an expat she met in Paris and has two lovely children. A long time ago, she went to Yale. *We Are Called to Rise* is her first novel.